SPELLBOUND

SPELLBOUND

GEORGIA LEIGHTON

bantam

TRANSWORLD PUBLISHERS
Penguin Random House, One Embassy Gardens,
8 Viaduct Gardens, London sw11 7bw
www.penguin.co.uk

Transworld is part of the Penguin Random House group of companies
whose addresses can be found at global.penguinrandomhouse.com

Penguin
Random House
UK

First published in Great Britain in 2025 by Bantam
an imprint of Transworld Publishers

A CIP catalogue record for this book
is available from the British Library.

isbns 9780857505910 (cased)
9780857505927 (tpb)

Typeset in 12.5/16pt Granjon LT Std by Jouve (UK), Milton Keynes
Printed and bound in Great Britain by Clays Ltd, Elcograf S.p.A.

The authorized representative in the EEA is Penguin Random House Ireland,
Morrison Chambers, 32 Nassau Street, Dublin D02 YH68.

Penguin Random House is committed to a sustainable
future for our business, our readers and our planet. This book is
made from Forest Stewardship Council® certified paper.

MIX
Paper | Supporting
responsible forestry
FSC® C018179

For Aurelia,
my golden ray of sunshine

'Some day you will be old enough to start reading fairy tales again.'
C. S. Lewis

[map – to come]

[map to come]

PART ONE

PART ONE

THE CASTLE WALLS hummed with magic. The King's hounds ran whimpering to their kennels and the milk in the kitchens soured. The gulls nesting in the turrets soared and dived through the sky in sudden eddies; the flowers in the gardens wilted and drooped. The magic stretched to the very edges of the small island where waves rolled and sucked at the rocks, and even the sea drew back from the pulse that rang through the air.

The servants of the castle cast quick glances at their foreign guests. They prayed that it would be over soon – for the Queen's sake, of course, but mostly for their own. It was late summer and the King should have moved to his hunting lodge in the north, but he had delayed the royal household's departure so that his child could be born at Mont Isle. At first, the servants had thought it an honour to welcome the long-awaited firstborn, but they had not anticipated the Queen's strange guests, travelling from her home-land to bless the child.

They had not known there would be so much magic.

The fishermen, who lived in the stone cottages that clung to the cliffs of the mainland, tutted over such customs. All this pomp and ceremony was not the Bavaughian way. The King's mother – may she rest with the Great Creator – had been caught unawares by the early birth of her son. He had been delivered without fuss by a maid in the Queen's chambers at Mont Isle. The next day, trumpets had

3

sounded from the battlements and the proud King had paraded the tiny Prince through the streets of the small fishing town of Guil. That was that.

It would not be so bad if the whole thing were not taking so long. The Queen had been confined to her chambers for almost three days and her guests had started arriving the moment she yelped and clutched her stomach with the first contraction. Her homeland was at least a whole moon's travel away, and no one wanted to ask how the guests had managed to arrive so punctually. Before news that the baby was coming had even reached the mainland, cloaked figures had appeared in Guil. They slipped through the cobbled streets, then passed across the causeway to the tidal island, the air ringing behind them.

In his chambers, the King paced back and forth. He had been locked in these rooms for almost three days, only emerging when forced and eating sparingly. The Kingdom of Bavaugh had waited many years for an heir and he longed to announce the arrival of his firstborn. Surely it would be a son. Sometimes he thought he heard a scream echoing through the stone walls of the castle, but when he held his breath and listened, he could hear only the crackling of the logs on the fire. With teeth clenched, the King continued to pace, praying and waiting.

On the other side of the castle, in the Queen's bedchamber, the fire burnt low and the milky light of dawn seeped through the windows unnoticed. All eyes were focused on the writhing figure in the four-poster bed. Sheets wet with sweat were twisted around her legs and her dark hair stuck in slick coils to her cheeks. She gasped and groaned as the birthing maids and Ladies-in-Waiting urged her to push. They had stood vigilantly by her side these past three days, tense and fussing, but finally it was clear that the baby was coming and their relief was palpable.

'Almost there, Your Majesty,' they promised. 'Almost there.'

The Queen tried to shake her head. She was exhausted and burning with agony, but there was something else. She longed to call for one of her guests and ask if they could feel it too. But she had heard her Ladies-in-Waiting whispering about the strange, cloaked figures in the castle and she knew such a request would upset them. Besides, she did not have the energy to speak as pain ripped through her body. All she could do was push with everything she had left, praying that her worries were for nothing.

'The head is crowning,' gasped one of the birthing maids. 'Just a few more pushes, Your Majesty.'

The Queen clenched her fingers into fists and screamed. A moment later, there was a coo of awe from her attendants, then a sharp cry split the air.

'A girl, Your Majesty,' said the Chief Lady-in-Waiting. 'A Princess.'

Fresh towels and linens were brought in, the baby was bathed and the gowns for the Blessing were readied.

'Tell the King!' someone called and there was the sound of scampering feet, the slosh of warm water on the royal infant and the excited murmurings of a relieved room.

'We are to begin the Blessing right away, Your Majesty,' said the Chief Lady-in-Waiting. 'Just as you ordered it.'

The Queen lay panting, her body trembling with the ordeal. Somehow she managed to nod. Exhausted though she was, she would not allow herself to rest. Her long-awaited child had been born and now she suspected they were all in great danger.

Sel

Guil, West Bavaugh

SEL STOOD ON the shore of the mainland, looking at the island surrounded by sea. Pale light peeked over the distant horizon, trimming the waves and rocky edges of Mont Isle in gold. A castle rose from the island's centre, twisting turrets of tanned stone and criss-crossing battlements soaring higher and higher towards the watery sky.

Sel pushed her hood back from her face and cursed under her breath. She was late. The royal baby would be born any moment, then the Blessing would begin. She needed to be on that island. If she missed the Blessing, the whole journey would have been for nothing.

She scanned the shoreline, looking for something or someone who might be able to help, and further down the coast she spotted a wooden jetty stretching out into the sea. Breaking into an ungainly sprint, she hurried towards it, her black boots scattering pebbles and the waves roaring in her ears. As she drew closer, she saw three men climbing into fishing boats. One of them caught sight of her and he must have said something because they all turned to watch her approach, their weathered faces pulled into scowls.

'Excuse me,' she panted in Bavaughian, the words feeling round and unfamiliar in her mouth. 'Can I pay for passage to the island?'

She stepped on to the jetty and the men flinched. One of them said, 'When the tide goes out again you can cross the causeway.'

'But I need to be there now.'

Silence.

'Are you about to go out to sea?' she persisted. 'I can pay you handsomely.'

She was desperate and she could see that she had tempted one of them enough to step out of his boat.

'How much?' he asked.

'Two flecks of gold.'

By the expression on his face, this was more than he had expected. She wished she had offered one.

'Get in,' he said, and the men behind him shook their heads.

Sel clambered into the rowing boat, pulling her cloak tightly around her; the faint drizzle that hung in the air had turned the thick material soft and heavy, so that the clasp almost choked her throat. Taking two flecks of gold from the pouch tied at her waist, she handed them to the fisherman. He watched her with an expression that was half suspicious, half curious as he took up the oars.

The little boat lurched into motion and Sel fixed her eyes on the island ahead. Magic radiated from it in tendrils that curled through the wind and chafed her cheeks. It had been a while since Sel had felt so much gathered power and her fingers itched to take it and shape it, but she knew she must wait. As much as she would have liked to mutter a charm to dry her wet cloak and clean her grimy

8

clothes, she needed to save everything for the Blessing. She had not travelled all this way to fail now. A whole moon of bumpy cart rides, stomach-churning sea travel and bland food, trudging down muddy roads and remaining ever watchful for thieves and predators lay behind her. It was in stark contrast to how she had spent the seasons of her adult life, poring over dusty books in dark, warm rooms.

It will be worth it, she told herself. *It has to be worth it.*

She slipped her hand beneath her cloak and touched the worn edge of folded parchment tucked into the lining, a gesture she had repeated on the road, reassuring herself of the journey's purpose. It was an invitation for her late Master, Florentina Samara the Wise. It called Florentina to pay respects to the firstborn child of the former Princess Violanna, fourth daughter of King Lepon of the Diaspass Kingdom, now Queen of Bavaugh. The invitation was written on thick, creamy parchment and the royal seal of Bavaugh was stamped in red wax at its corner. At the bottom, scrawled in the Queen's own, nervous hand was a message: *Please, Florentina, I beg, you must come.*

'There's steps over there.'

The fisherman's mutter made Sel jump and she turned to see the island's stone pier looming beside them.

'Oh, good. Thank you . . . for your service,' she replied.

When it became clear that the fisherman was not going to offer her a hand, Sel wobbled to her feet then leapt at the nearby steps, heaving herself on to the pier. Before she had even straightened her cloak, the fisherman was rowing away. With a sigh, Sel smoothed back her dark, wet hair and hurried towards the gatehouse.

Liveried guards watched her approach and Sel stopped before the nearest one, pulling out her invitation.

'"Florentina Samara the Wise",' read the castle guard, his eyes flicking from the invitation in his hands to the young woman in front of him.

'That's me.'

The guard frowned and Sel forced a smile.

'You're younger than the others,' he grunted, peering under the hood of her cloak.

'I'm older than I look.'

His frown deepened. 'You're late.'

'And I think I might be later if I wait here much longer.'

When there was no reply, she added with as much haughtiness as she could manage, 'I'm the Queen's royal guest and I must pass through now.'

'All right, all right.' He thrust her invitation back at her and signalled to the other guards on duty.

Ignoring their glares, Sel held her head high and passed through the gatehouse. Behind the castle walls, the courtyards and corridors were deserted and all was wrapped in the expectant hush before a momentous occasion. There were no guards or attendants to direct her, so Sel hurried blindly through archways and up flights of stairs, hoping the ceremony had not started. She could feel magic emanating from inside the stone walls above, like the beckoning warmth of a fire, and she hastened towards it, crossing quads and rushing down passages. Finally, at the end of one corridor, she spotted a cluster of jittery servants. They were waiting before a set of thick, carved doors and they drew back against the walls as she approached.

'It's about to begin!' cried a sentry. 'You're very late.'

Behind the doors, Sel could hear the hum of many low, babbling voices. Excitement and nerves simmered through her stomach as she handed over her invitation and stood back to let the guards haul open the doors.

'Florentina Samara the Wise,' called out the Sergeant-at-Arms.

Sel took a deep breath and raised her chin, mimicking the posture of her old Master. Then she pulled back her shoulders and walked into the Great Hall.

Meredyth

The Queen's Chambers, Mont Isle

MEREDYTH DABBED POWDER across the Queen's slick brow. She tried to appear calm and untroubled, but she felt neither. Something was wrong. After the birth of the Princess, the Queen had refused even a quick bath, insisting that they must all get ready for the Blessing – that strange, magical custom from her homeland – without delay. But standing in the dressing room, the Queen listed from side to side, her face waxen and strained, her eyes sunken and her gaze distracted. The edges of her petticoat quivered as if at any moment she might crumple.

The maids pulled the Queen's damp, oily hair into decorative plaits and strapped her still-swollen waist into the royal gown, exchanging glances. The little Princess had been taken to an adjoining room with her wet nurse for a feed before her public debut, and every few moments the Queen's gaze would flit to the open doorway. Meredyth could almost attribute such behaviour to the apprehension of a new mother, but there was an unsettling look in the Queen's eyes that she did not understand.

'I can manage the rest,' said Meredyth sharply, catching one of the maids blanching at the sight of dried blood crusted on the Queen's elbow. 'Out now.'

The maids gladly ceased their fussing and scurried from the room, chattering about squeezing into the servants' gallery of the Great Hall to watch the ceremony.

Meredyth shut the door of the chamber behind them and rubbed her brow with the back of her hand. She had been at the Queen's side throughout the birth, catching only snatches of sleep, and she felt faint and weary. Her nose was still clogged with the scent of sweat and blood and her gown was creased from hours of fretful attending.

'Your Majesty,' she said, 'can I not encourage you to take a moment? Let me send for some tea and a meal to revive you.'

The Queen shook her head, her brown eyes downcast, her chest heavy with laboured breaths. 'No,' she managed. 'Not now.'

Meredyth stepped behind her and straightened a pearl droplet at the Queen's neck. 'Please, Your Majesty,' she tried again after a pause. She thought she noticed the Queen's expression soften. 'You do not seem well.'

'I am only a little tired.'

Meredyth knew this was not true.

'You have suffered a difficult birth, Your Majesty,' she whispered. 'No one would begrudge you some rest.'

'I do not need it.'

Pursing her lips, Meredyth turned away and dipped a cloth in a water basin. She was not used to the Queen ignoring her counsel. She had been Chief Lady-in-Waiting since the Queen had arrived in Bavaugh: a shy, lonely bride, a long time ago. The two women had always been close, but they had grown closer still throughout the Queen's seasons of barrenness.

'Perhaps you would like a moment alone with your little one before the ceremony, Your Majesty?' Meredyth suggested, trying a different approach. She wrung out the cloth and dabbed away the bloodstain on the Queen's elbow. 'I know I craved some time alone with each of my newborns—'

'No.'

Meredyth wiped her hands on her rumpled skirts, not caring that it left a faint stain. There were blotches of lilac underneath the Queen's eyes and a pale crust of white skin over her lips.

'Your Majesty,' she began, stepping closer to her friend. 'Please listen to me—'

Meredyth gasped in surprise as the Queen grabbed hold of her wrist and pinched it tightly.

'You must stay by our side until the end of the ceremony,' she hissed, locking her dark gaze on Meredyth. 'You must stay with me and the Princess.'

'Your Majesty, is . . . is something troubling you?'

'Promise!'

'Of course, I promise.'

The Queen abruptly turned away, releasing her, and peered once again into the adjoining chamber at the wet nurse and the Princess. 'We are ready and must delay no longer,' she said.

'But—'

'I said we must delay no longer!'

Meredyth nodded and curtsied, chastened. Turning, she called to the guards to escort them to the Great Hall and instructed the nursemaid to bring forth the Princess.

A warm bundle of lace was pressed into Meredyth's arms and she smiled. She adored newborns and had given birth to six of her own, though only four had survived. There was nothing quite like the milky, sweet scent of an infant; she knew this precious time would pass all too quickly. She looked up at the hunched figure of the Queen in front of her and her chest tightened. She just hoped that the Blessing would be over soon, then she could rush the Queen and the Princess back to bed.

Their party left the Queen's quarters and made slow, limping progress to the Great Hall. As they shuffled down a passageway, a door at the opposite end opened. A flock of guards poured out, followed by the King. Meredyth had expected to see King Felipe sooner, but she had heard from an attendant that he was toasting the arrival of his first child with his advisors. She had wished she was surprised.

'Ah, my Queen!' cried the King, striding towards them. The rubies studding the crown on his dark-blond head flickered in the lamplight, and the royal sceptre, encrusted with jewels, glinted in the crook of his elbow. 'Everyone is ready and waiting for the ceremony to begin . . .' He trailed off as he approached and saw his wife's uneven gait and pallor.

The Queen attempted a shaky curtsey, whispering, 'Greetings, my King.'

'Is all well?' he asked. The lines around his blue-grey eyes were creased and a red rim of wine stained his lips.

'It is time for the Blessing,' the Queen replied. 'Let us be on our way.'

The King glanced at Meredyth. Then his gaze fell on the infant and he smiled. 'Is that the Princess? Is she . . . healthy?'

When the Queen did not reply, Meredyth nodded with a curtsey.

'Long live King Felipe of Bavaugh,' she said. 'Your Majesty, the Queen has delivered a perfect little girl.'

'I heard. It is not a Prince, but it is good news.' The King cupped his hand around the Queen's cheek and kissed her forehead, not noticing her wince of pain. 'We have waited so long and the Great Creator has blessed us.'

Still the Queen did not respond, so Meredyth added, 'I believe she has your eyes, Your Majesty.'

'Really? Maybe she takes after my mother.'

'She looks as though she may also be fair like Queen Aruelle,' said Meredyth. 'Perhaps Your Majesty would like to hold the Princess—'

'No,' said the Queen. 'We must not delay the ceremony.'

'But—'

'*No*.'

Meredyth cleared her throat. 'Maybe after the Blessing, you would like to retire to the Queen's chambers with your new family, Your Majesty?' she said, filling the silence. 'You should all rest after such an ordeal.'

The King nodded, though his brow remained creased. 'That seems wise. Thank you, Lady Lansin.' He offered the Queen his arm. 'Let us go to the Blessing, then.'

The Queen took his elbow and continued her shuffling gait.

As they made their way slowly down the corridor, Meredyth could see King Felipe muttering to his wife and patting her hand, but the Queen did not respond. Instead, she stared straight ahead, beads of sweat rolling down her neck like raindrops.

Sel

The Great Hall, Mont Isle

SEL LEANT TO one side and craned her neck to peer down the line of black-cloaked figures ahead of her. Most of the Diaspass Masterhood were in attendance, despite this kingdom's distance from their homeland, and the queue stretched from the front of the dais to the end of the Great Hall, a dark ripple cutting through the grand, bright room. Sel was last in the line, which was a relief. She had not yet attended a royal Diaspass Blessing and she wanted to watch the other Masters give their gifts to see how it was done.

Trumpets sounded and, at the head of the Great Hall, the royal party appeared on the dais. The noblemen and women around the edges of the room clapped and the servants in the gallery above cheered as the King and Queen took their seats on their thrones, decked in finery. Between them stood an ornate cradle decorated with gold filigree and strung with ribbons and rosettes. An important-looking brown-haired woman carrying a wriggling

bundle stepped forward and lowered the newborn Princess cere-
moniously into her bed, which produced a coo of delight from the
crowd.

While everyone else watched the cradle rock gently from side to
side, Sel squinted curiously at the Queen – the fourth Princess of
the Diaspass Kingdom, who had become the Queen of another
kingdom, albeit a rather small and bleak one. The Queen seemed
fidgety and nervous, pulling at her blue-black hair and scratching
at her neck.

A horn sounded and the King rose to his feet. He stepped forward and cleared his throat. 'We welcome you, our . . . esteemed
guests, to Bavaugh and thank you for travelling the long journey to
bless our firstborn.' His booming voice bounced across the Great
Hall, but his gaze skittered reluctantly down the line of black-
cloaked figures. 'It is an honour to have you in our midst and we
humbly thank you for your gifts . . .'

While the King continued his halting speech, Sel peered around,
noticing with a suppressed smile the voluminous-skirted gowns the
noblewomen wore, which even she knew were seasons behind the
latest fashions in her homeland. This kingdom really was at the very
edge of the realm. Attached to the Wildlands in its south-eastern
corner and otherwise surrounded by the Dark Sea, Bavaugh's nearest
neighbouring kingdoms were the Fringe Islands – Tolbi, Wescove,
the Karkels and more. They were all small and insignificant in the
eyes of the Central Realm.

'. . . and now, the Queen and I would again like to thank you in
advance for the great honour you bestow on us with these gifts,' the
King carried on, casting a questioning glance at his wife. 'We . . .
welcome you to approach the Princess.'

He returned to his throne and as he sat, a black-cloaked figure walked to the dais.

The Master threw back their hood and Sel recognized Lalious Grele the Mighty, a middle-aged, grey-haired woman with angular features.

Anticipation thickened the air as the Bavaughians watched this strange foreigner bow to the King and Queen then turn to the cradle.

'I am Lalious Grele the Mighty and I come from the Diaspass Kingdom as a guest of the Queen of Bavaugh to bestow my gift on the newborn Princess,' said Lalious, in a high, clear voice. 'And my gift to her is grace. May the Princess move with infinite elegance, full of poise and charm.'

Lalious raised her thin hands and muttered the language of magic. For a moment, the air fizzed and sparked, pleating itself around the edges of the cradle, then all was still. Lalious stepped back, bowed again and pulled her hood over her head.

The Great Hall was silent and the Bavaughians all exchanged glances. Someone clapped, then dropped their hands to their sides when no one else joined in.

'Thank you,' said the King hurriedly. 'What an honour.' He looked over at his wife, but the Queen was sitting tense and rigid, her eyes staring off into the distance as if she had not heard a word. 'We both thank you,' he added.

Sel watched with a thrill as Lalious turned away and walked down the line of cloaked figures to the back of the Great Hall. The Master brushed past her, sending a waft of magic that made Sel's teeth ache and her fingers tingle.

When the Blessing is over, I will go to her first, thought Sel. *I'll ask her – no, beg her – to take me as her apprentice.*

Lalious was one of the High Masters and forever travelling the realm. Sel would likely never get an opportunity like this again to talk to her directly. Which was exactly why she had come.

At the front of the Great Hall, the next cloaked figure approached the dais and announced themselves as Rossure Coltheseus the Cunning. He was a small, stout man who bequeathed the Princess the gift of exceptional beauty – eyes as blue as the summer sky, lips like a red rose in full bloom and hair as bright as the dawn light.

Sel resisted the urge to roll her eyes and watched as the air around the cradle folded and snapped with the gush of the spell. Florentina had once told her that royal Blessing gifts were like this – dainty, frilly trinket glamours meant to charm and delight – but she still thought it rather silly. She had a more useful gift planned.

The King thanked Rossure, who bowed in return then walked to the back of the hall.

The next Master stepped up to the dais, then the next and the next, each bestowing their magical gifts on the Princess: a voice as sweet as birdsong, a gentle manner, a laugh like the peal of silver bells, a kinship with animals, a spirit as wild as the wind, a clear sense of justice – so it went on, Master after Master approaching the dais and the line of black-cloaked figures shuffling forwards. The air growing heavier with each one.

Sel was getting closer to the front and beginning to feel a little nervous. She had practised her gift during the long journey to Bavaugh, but she had never conjured in front of an audience before and she needed to make a good impression. She was glad, at least, that the several fires in the hall and the many bodies packed inside it had dried out her cloak and clothes so that she did not look as dishevelled as she felt. When she finally reached the front, she took

a deep breath and pushed her hood away from her face. She wondered if the Masters at the back of the Great Hall were looking at
her dark hair in confusion, expecting to see Florentina's long white
locks.

The King dragged his gaze to Sel. He was pale and rubbing at his
forehead, his expression a grimace.

It must be the magic, Sel thought.

Around the Great Hall, she had noticed the brows of the watching Bavaughians start to pucker, plagued by headaches from the
rising pressure. The weight of magic in the room was making her
own ears ring, so she could only imagine how much it was affecting
these people who shunned even simple charms and spells.

Everyone on the dais – noblemen and guards alike – looked nauseous, but no one more so than the Queen. Sel almost gasped at the
sight of her up close: eyes flickering, body shivering and sweat seeping through her gown, leaving dark, grey patches. The rest of the
royal household seemed too wrapped up in the fog of their own
sickness to notice.

Sel bowed. 'I am . . . here on behalf of Florentina Samara the
Wise,' she called, her voice quivering slightly.

She saw the Queen raise her head.

'I come from the Diaspass Kingdom as a guest of the Queen of
Bavaugh,' Sel continued. She could feel the Queen's frowning gaze
on her, clearly wondering who she was, but Sel pushed on. 'I am
here to bestow my gift on the newborn Princess.'

This is it, she thought, her heart thudding in her chest and her
hands twitching by her sides.

'My gift to her is—'

But before she could finish, the Great Hall was filled with an
almighty roar that split the air.

21

Sel spun around in bewilderment as the fires were extinguished with a snap and the stained-glass windows shattered.

The Masters were knocked to the edges of the room and a biting wind rushed through the hall, pushing Sel to the floor.

'No!' howled the Queen, but her cry was lost in the screaming of the crowd.

Meredyth

The Great Hall, Mont Isle

MEREDYTH TRIED TO pull herself up, but her arms would not move. She lay slumped against the wall of the Great Hall where she had fallen. Her scrambled mind attempted to piece together what had just happened: a roar of noise that had sent spikes of pain through her temples followed by a great gust of wind that had knocked her off her feet, then unsettling silence.

Guards and noblemen lay prone on the ground near by. From the contorted, bewildered expressions on their faces, Meredyth guessed that they too were trying to move, but had found that their limbs were frozen. Ignoring her throbbing head, she peered through the sudden darkness that had filled the room, confusion and fear churning together in her stomach. Despite the shattered windows, the Great Hall was gloomy, as if all the morning light had been sucked away. As Meredyth's eyes adjusted to the shadows, she could see the Queen, slumped in her throne, enlarged stomach heaving.

Then a voice cut through the silence. 'Hello, Violanna.'

A woman was standing in the middle of the Great Hall, where the air crackled and spat. She had black hair and dark eyes, and she was wrapped in a cloak like the Masters.

A wave of alarm rushed through Meredyth.

'It has been a long time, Violanna,' said the woman. Her voice was not loud, yet somehow it resounded. 'But I do not think you have forgotten me.'

Unlike everyone else, the woman moved freely. She took a few steps forward, glass crunching under her booted feet.

'I see all the great Masters are here,' she added, looking over her shoulder at the black-cloaked figures pinned to the back wall, who were thrashing their limbs as if fighting invisible bonds. 'I always knew that I would one day be more powerful than them. And you knew it too, Violanna. That is why you did what you did.'

The Queen stared back, her gaze fixed.

'I suppose I should address you as *Your Majesty*,' continued the woman. 'You are a Queen now. Although I am surprised you have banished yourself to this far-flung kingdom. It almost seems like you have been trying to hide.' The woman's eyes flicked to the King, who was sitting stiff and frozen in his throne. 'Your husband?' she said. When there was no reply, she stepped forward and the air around her swirled with dark, terrible shadows.

Panic seized Meredyth's chest. She wanted to run to the cradle and snatch the Princess away. She tried to move her arms, but they stayed hanging limply at her sides. She tried to scream at the guards to attack, but her lips remained still.

No one could stop the uninvited guest as she peered into the cradle. 'Hello, Princess,' said the woman. 'I have come to bestow a special Blessing gift on you too. Something far richer and much more interesting.'

Meredyth felt her panic turn to dread. She did not know who this woman was, but it was clear that the Princess was in great danger.

'As these Masters have declared, you will be graceful, beautiful and noble,' continued the woman. 'The loveliest creature this kingdom has ever seen . . .'

The woman's words began to echo and vibrate around the Great Hall.

A sharp wind pulled at Meredyth's skirts and the air thickened with heat. She tried again to move, but she was pinned in place, unable to do anything but watch.

'You will be the fairest of the realm,' continued the woman. 'In fact, yours will be a great and terrible beauty.' She raised her hands, arcing them through the air in strange shapes. 'And before seventeen winters have passed, I will return for you. On that day, the spell will end . . .' The woman paused and looked at the Queen before turning back to the cradle. 'And you will die.'

The dark gloom in the Great Hall clotted the air and the woman stood tall. She opened her mouth and low, guttural sounds gushed from her lips. Writhing shadows erupted from the ground, hunched and contorted. They wound through the air, then leapt at the cradle, settling upon the Princess.

The woman smiled. 'Violanna, I also have a gift just for you,' she said. 'You must never leave this island. If you do, the spell will end at once, and your daughter will die. Instead, you must stay in this remote, bleak place, dreading my return.'

She spread out her hands and flexed her fingers. More shadows cascaded through the air and swarmed around the Queen.

'Violanna, you will never forget me,' she added, tilting her head to one side. 'You should never have tried.'

Then she was gone.

All at once, Meredyth felt her arms and legs release. She gasped in shock and heard others around her panting and whimpering in surprise.

Then the screaming started from all sides of the Great Hall as the crowds scrambled to their feet, panicked. Meredyth peered around her with smarting eyes; the darkness was everywhere, like smoke.

'Your Majesty?' she cried. 'Queen Violanna?'

She wrenched herself to her feet, tripping over her skirts, and stumbled through the gloom. Someone tore past her yelling and almost knocked her to the floor again, but she staggered on until she nearly fell into the Queen's throne.

'Your Majesty!' she said, pulling at the Queen's limp arm. 'Get up!'

All around them were shouts and shrieks as Bavaughians ran into and trampled each other in their haste to escape the Great Hall.

The Queen's eyelids quivered and she clutched at her stomach, her face creasing with pain. 'The Princess . . .' she moaned. 'My baby.'

Meredyth nodded. 'I will get her.'

While the Queen tried to rouse herself, Meredyth scrambled through the dark, her hands stretched out in front of her. The cradle loomed in the blackness and she clutched at it, realizing with a start that there was already someone standing there. She was ready to fight them away with all the strength she could muster when she saw that it was a Master.

'You!' she cried, snatching a handful of black cloak. 'We need to get the Queen and the Princess to safety. You must help me!'

The Master – was she called Something-the-Wise? Meredyth could not remember – turned with startled, wide eyes.

'I – I—'

'You must help me!' Meredyth repeated, her grip tightening. 'Now.'

Sel

The Chapel, Mont Isle

'I'M NOT A real Master!' cried Sel, wringing her hands. 'My name is Selhah. Florentina is – *was* – my Master. I'm not a proper Master . . .'

She had helped the Bavaughian noblewoman escape the Great Hall through a concealed door at the back of the dais. Together they had dragged the semi-conscious Queen with the newborn Princess down a long corridor, away from the chaos. Now they were standing in a small, dim chapel, cool and hushed.

'I came in Florentina's place,' Sel continued. 'I'm her apprentice, you see. It was not deception . . . exactly. I'm almost a Master. Very close.'

She was speaking to the back of the noblewoman, who was leaning over the Queen. Though she continued to babble on, Sel suspected no one was listening, but now that she had started, it was almost impossible to stop.

'Florentina died a few moons ago. It was unexpected and terrible and it left me Masterless. She had not properly passed her robes on to me. But she was about to. Then the invitation arrived and I thought I'd come and try to find a new Master to finish my apprenticeship. I'm so close to finishing . . . it seemed like a good idea.'

The noblewoman turned abruptly and pressed a lacy bundle into Sel's arms. 'Hold the Princess,' she said. 'I need to attend to the Queen.'

Sel looked down at the tiny, pinkish creature now propped against her chest. She did not know what had made her run to the cradle when the sorceress disappeared from the Great Hall. After the binding spell pinning her in place had lifted, she had instinctively fought her way through the darkness to the dais, dodging shouting guards, their swords drawn, and screaming civilians, running in terror. She supposed she felt partly responsible; she had been closest to the Princess when the sorceress appeared and she should have done something. Or tried to. But she knew in her heart that even Florentina would not have been able to stand up to such powerful, dark magic.

'You're safe,' she whispered to the angelic, serene face resting in the crook of her elbow. The Princess had slept through the whole ordeal – dozy with the weight of the magic cast over her – and outwardly appeared unharmed, although Sel shuddered to think of the spell and what lay in the girl's future. Sel knew the tales of the sorceress, of course, but no one had heard anything for so long. It had almost become a Diaspass myth. Sel had thought it unusual that so many Masters had travelled so far for this royal Blessing – and High Masters, at that – but perhaps they had suspected something. She remembered again the handwritten note scrawled at the bottom of the invitation to the Queen's old, favoured schooling Master: *Please, Florentina, I beg, you must come.*

Sel did not have much experience of babies and the Princess felt a little awkward in her arms. As much as Sel wanted the Princess to be safe, she also wanted to pass her back, and she looked hopefully to the noblewoman, who was crouched beside the Queen on the stone floor of the chapel.

'Perhaps you could take . . .' began Sel, but then trailed off when she caught sight of the Queen; collapsed against a pew, clawing at her stomach.

'What is it? What is wrong, Your Majesty?' whispered the noblewoman, grabbing hold of the Queen's shoulders.

'I need to push. I need to push.'

'To push?' said the noblewoman with a frown.

The Queen did not respond and instead she convulsed, her face squeezed with pain.

'Is this magic?' snapped the noblewoman, turning to Sel.

Sel shook her head.

Grey morning light filtered through the stained-glass windows of the chapel, casting shattered bursts of colour through the air.

'Your Majesty, is something hurting you?' said the noblewoman.

The Queen moaned and the sound echoed around the stone walls and bounced off the high ceiling.

The noblewoman pulled back the Queen's skirts. Then she gasped.

'What is it?' asked Sel after a pause, leaning closer. 'What's wrong?'

'I think . . . I think she is about to birth another baby.'

Violanna

The Chapel, Mont Isle

PAIN SWELLED, BUILDING to a surge that crashed through her body, violent and unbearable. She thought she might die from it. Her jaw ached from gritting her teeth and bile stung the back of her throat. The surge lulled for a moment and she gulped a mouthful of air. Her eyes fluttered open and she saw the painted, vaulted ceiling of the chapel above and two women close by: Meredyth and someone else – a young woman who said she had come in the place of Florentina Samara the Wise. In the young woman's arms was a froth of lace. The Princess. Her daughter. Her poor child. If Violanna had not been in such agony, she would have wept in despair.

'Your Majesty?' said Meredyth, her voice loud and clear. 'Are you giving birth?'

Yes, she wanted to reply, but suddenly another contraction took hold and she was lost in a haze of agony. She was tired. She wanted to stop. But another baby was coming. She had long suspected that there were two lives inside her, fluttering and spinning together in the tight, rounded bloom of her stomach. After her many seasons of barrenness, no one else had guessed. But another baby was coming. A second child.

As soon as one surge left, another hit like hot, burning bands tightening inside her. Unspeakable pain barrelled through Violanna's body and she thought that she might tear in two. Her mother had died in childbirth, as had three of her aunts and countless other women whom she had once known. She was aware that to give birth was to teeter at the very edge of death, ready to tumble into the hands of the Great Creator. Even so, she had spent many winters longing for a child with a deep, visceral urge that she could not explain. Not just to fulfil her Queenly duty, but for herself. Despite the danger, she had wanted to trade the bloody agony of birth for tiny fingernails and mewling cries.

When she had first felt stirrings inside her and her moon blood was late, Violanna had been both euphoric and frightened. Frightened because she might lose the baby like she had lost others. Frightened because she might die herself. Frightened because she knew it could attract the attention of someone who wished to hurt her – someone surely lying in wait. And she had been right to be fearful, because the worst had happened. It was all her fault.

Violanna was lost in her agony and sorrow, at the mercy of her body which stretched and pushed of its own accord. Pain seared through her and she felt another wave rising and rising until it burst on top of her, blasting its way down her body and between her legs. Everything became raw, white-hot and shattered. It felt like eternity and it felt like an instant.

Then, suddenly, the baby arrived. Violanna reached down and grasped it – *her* – as the baby was expelled. She held the slippery, wet life. A second daughter. White, blue and bloody, with miniature, clawing hands.

Fluid gushed from between Violanna's legs, but she did not notice. She stared at her perfect second daughter. She looked at the sticky, uncurling limbs and the squashed, pure face, and she was filled with a wild, dangerous love. She raised her head and through dizzy, bleary eyes, she saw her other daughter in the arms of the woman standing opposite. Two Princesses.

Something stirred inside her. An idea. Her gaze fell back to the baby in her hands and she felt the idea taking shape.

Perhaps there was a way to protect her daughters – a way to save them both.

Sel

The Chapel, Mont Isle

SEL STAGGERED TO a pew and sat, bent over with her head between her legs, trying not to be sick. She laid the Princess – the *first* Princess – on an embroidered kneeler at her feet. She did not trust herself to hold the newborn any longer; her hands were shaking, and she thought she might pass out. Of course, she had always been vaguely aware of how babies were born, but she had not realized it was so . . . messy.

Taking slow, deep breaths, she tried to forget the sight and smell of blood and imagined herself at home instead; in the dark, dusty back room of Florentina's townhouse with a stack of books beside her and a page of Novtook symbols waiting to be translated on the desk. She could almost hear the creak and whirl of carriages passing by the front of the house on their way to market, could almost smell the musty old furniture that cluttered Florentina's house, its surfaces peppered with magic that had settled like dust. It was the place she had called home since her girlhood and it felt very far away.

A high-pitched cry broke through Sel's thoughts. She opened her eyes and turned her head to see the Queen propped against a pew, the voluptuous skirt of her ceremonial gown pillowed around her, stained and sticky. The Bavaughian noblewoman Sel had heard the Queen call Meredyth crouched at her side, and wrapped in a torn petticoat in the Queen's arms was a baby. A second baby.

'Is everything . . . well?' Sel asked, realizing the absurdity of the question. Obviously everything was not well.

'The baby is alive, but we need a birthing maid or a physician,' replied Meredyth. 'The Queen has lost a lot of blood.'

'I can find someone,' said Sel quickly, clambering to her feet, glad of an excuse to leave. 'Just tell me where to go.'

But the Queen shook her head. Taking a deep, shuddering breath, she said, 'You are not the Master I invited. Where is Florentina?'

Sel chewed at her lip. Finally, she replied, 'Florentina is . . . gone.'

'Gone?'

'Dead.'

The Queen winced and the baby in her arms squawked.

'It was a terrible sickness,' began Sel, all the helplessness and sorrow of the last few moons bubbling up inside her. 'There was nothing I could do—'

'Then it must be you,' said the Queen.

Sel glanced at Meredyth, who was frowning, a rusty streak of blood swiped across the noblewoman's cheek and the skirts of her dress damp and ripped to wrap around the new baby.

'Me?' she replied faintly.

'I needed Florentina because, of all the Masters, I thought she would know best how to protect us should something like this happen. If you are her apprentice, then it is your duty to aid us in her place.'

Sel shook her head. 'Florentina is – was – a great Master, but even she could not have stood against that magic.' Sel shivered, remembering lying pinned to the floor of the Great Hall, feeling the wild heat and energy of the curse whipping through the charged air, so much darker and stronger than anything she had felt before. 'None of the High Masters back there were able to stop it,' she added. 'It was too deep and complicated. Too powerful.'

'I know that now!' snapped the Queen. Then she added quietly, '*She* has grown stronger than any of us could have guessed. She has lost herself to darkness.'

'Who?' interrupted Meredyth. 'Who was that woman, Your Majesty?'

There was a pause. Sel and the Queen glanced at one another.

'It was a sorceress,' replied the Queen, her gaze sliding away. 'A lone wielder of magic. A dark and dangerous being.' The Queen turned back to Sel and said, 'It is your duty to take Florentina's place. You must protect us.' Her voice was quiet, but there was a steeliness to it that made Sel nervous.

'But what can I do? I can't—'

'You must take the Princess away.'

Sel stared at the Queen. She wondered if her language charm was wearing off and she had misheard, but when she opened her mouth to reply, she could feel the magic forcing her lips into the unfamiliar shapes of Bavaughian.

'I don't understand,' she said.

'You must take the Princess and hide until the time of the curse has passed. There is a second Princess now, a double. A baby that no one but us knows about – that *she* does not know about.'

36

'But surely—'

'The sorceress will return to finish her spell and it will be the wrong Princess – do you not see?'

Logically, Sel did understand that a spell initially bound to one individual would not transfer to another, but panic and hysteria were rising through her chest, closing her throat. She could feel herself shaking her head again, but the Queen had already turned back to Meredyth.

'You must help me get this baby ready before we are found. No one can know what has happened.'

'But we need a birthing maid to cut the cord and deliver the afterbirth, Your Majesty.'

'You must do it.'

'Your Majesty! How could I? You have lost too much blood and when the physician examines you, he will be able to tell what has happened.'

'We will say it is the magic and he will believe it.' Then she added, 'Please, Meredyth. Trust me.'

Meredyth hesitated, as though she wanted to protest. Finally, she nodded and climbed to her feet. She pushed past Sel and picked up the sleeping Princess. Briskly, she untied the newborn's gown and switched it with the torn rags from the wailing second baby.

'I will find something to cut the cord,' she said.

'First, she must go,' said the Queen, gesturing at Sel. 'She must leave now, while the castle is still in disarray.'

Meredyth scooped up the Princess, bundled in rags, and pressed her into Sel's unwilling arms.

'Remove her cloak,' instructed the Queen.

Meredyth unfastened the clasp at Sel's throat, which roused Sel from her daze.

'You cannot take Florentina's cloak!' Sel cried as it was tugged off her shoulders. 'You must not take a Master's cloak!'

'You can have it back when you return with the Princess.'

'But . . . but . . .'

'Do you think I *want* to give you my daughter?' the Queen hissed. 'You heard the principles of the spell – I cannot leave this island. This is what we must do until we find a way to break the curse, or until seventeen winters have passed – whichever occurs first. If you do not take my baby, she will surely die. I am entrusting her to you in Florentina's place.'

'I am just not sure . . .' Sel began.

Then there was the sound of voices from outside the chapel. All three women turned their heads.

'You must go now!'

Sel found her arms curling around the creature at her chest despite the fact that she was still shaking her head. 'This is impossible,' she said. 'Where are we supposed to go? I have nothing.'

'That will make you safer,' said the Queen. 'You must hide in the kingdom, but never leave it. Raise her like an ordinary girl in Bavaugh. I will stay on Mont Isle with the other Princess and no one will suspect anything. When the time comes to return, you will be rewarded handsomely for what you have done.'

Sel stopped shaking her head. She was Masterless, destitute and alone in the realm. She had pinned all her hopes on securing a new apprenticeship today. Now she had nothing. Surely the protector of the firstborn heir to the Bavaughian throne would be handsomely rewarded indeed – though that reward would not be for many winters yet.

'Your Majesty,' said Meredyth. 'Please, there must be another way. What you are suggesting is unthinkable.'

The Queen ignored her. 'You must raise the Princess in obscurity so that the sorceress will suspect nothing. You must keep my daughter safe until the danger is over. And there must be no magic. No trace.'

'No magic?' Sel squeaked. 'But—'

'Please!' cried the Queen. 'You are our only hope.'

Somewhere in the chapel, a door creaked then voices yelled, 'Your Majesty?'

Sel looked down at the infant in her arms and made up her mind.

Meredyth

The Queen's Chambers, Mont Isle

MEREDYTH STOOD AT the Queen's bedside, swaying on her aching feet. Hunger gnawed at her stomach and her dry throat burnt. She was still dressed in the dirty, ripped gown she had been wearing earlier, and she longed to retire to the guest chambers and change, but she could not bring herself to leave.

'Your Majesty,' she whispered yet again. 'Please rest.'

The Queen sat in bed with tears slipping down her cheeks, dampening the collar of her fresh white nightgown. She was staring straight ahead across the room to where the nursemaid was sitting by the fire, feeding and soothing the Princess. Despite constant questions from the Royal Guards, the physician and the King, the Queen had remained silent since they had left the chapel. A bowl of honeyed porridge congealed on a tray beside her, next to a pot of cold tea, and no amount of cajoling could encourage her to eat or drink either.

'Your Majesty,' Meredyth said again, touching the Queen's clenched hand. 'You need to sleep.'

On the other side of the canopied bed, King Felipe smacked the wall in frustration. 'I cannot understand why she refuses to speak!'

'She is in shock, Your Majesty.'

'Are not we all?' muttered the King's Chief Advisor, Lord Rosford, from the doorway.

'We must understand what has happened,' said the King. His other hand rested on the hilt of his sword and had done since he had entered the room, as if in anticipation of the sorceress appearing again. 'We have been *attacked*.'

'What has happened is magic,' said Lord Rosford. 'It is evil.'

'Violanna, you must speak!' said King Felipe. He glanced at the nursemaid then leant closer to the Queen, lowering his voice. 'Did you know this was going to happen?' he hissed. 'Is this something you planned?'

Relations between the King and Queen had been so much better since the announcement of the Queen's pregnancy. Meredyth had not heard raised voices from the royal chambers in the evenings, and the King's bastard son had disappeared from court. She did not want to see it all unravel again.

'Violanna—' began King Felipe, when there was no response.

'She had no knowledge of what would happen!' said Meredyth. 'You saw how fearful she was in the Great Hall, Your Majesty. I was with her in the chapel before the guards found us and she was terrified. Now she is in shock.' From the corner of her eye, Meredyth could see Lord Rosford watching her. 'She is just a mother worried about her baby,' she added.

The King's shoulders slouched, and he turned his head to look at the infant. 'Yes,' he replied faintly. 'The Princess.'

'Do not fear, Your Majesty,' said Meredyth. 'Despite everything, the Princess is healthy and well.'

'You said before that she has my eyes?'

'She does, Your Majesty.'

'You would know,' whispered Lord Rosford from the doorway.

Meredyth glanced quickly around the room, but no one else seemed to have heard.

'The curse,' said King Felipe, and his fatherly expression of joyful pride melted away. 'That creature, that . . . *thing* cursed her. What can we do?'

Meredyth thought of the blood on the chapel floor, the second baby and the bundle of rags carried away in that young Master's arms. She shivered.

'I do not know,' she replied.

'We do not have "Blessings" in Bavaugh,' said Lord Rosford. 'It is strange that the Queen wanted this ceremony and stranger that this should have happened.'

'What do you mean by that, Lord Rosford?' snapped Meredyth, but Lord Rosford was looking at the King.

'The Blessing is a royal Diaspass custom and it is natural that Violanna should have wanted one for the Princess,' replied King Felipe, but he did not sound wholly convinced. 'It was supposed to be a celebration,' he added. 'I have waited so long.'

'Of course,' said Lord Rosfrod. 'No one would think there was anything amiss. It is just . . . odd.'

His words lingered.

'I need some air,' said the King, walking to the open window. 'Gather the Royal Council together, Rosford,' he called over his shoulder. 'We must discuss what can be done.'

Lord Rosford hesitated, then bowed and finally disappeared.

When he was gone, Meredyth joined the King at the window, welcoming the cooling salty breeze on her damp skin. The magic had left a dull ache at her temples that still throbbed with pressure, and she desperately wanted to lie down and close her eyes. She wanted to forget everything that had happened.

'The Queen has had a difficult birth, Your Majesty,' she said. 'She was exhausted even before what happened in the Great Hall. She needs to rest.'

The King did not respond, but after a moment he said, 'They are leaving.'

Meredyth followed his gaze out of the window to where the sea was drawing back from the island below, leaving a twisting, paved path of dark, gritty stones. In the distance, black-cloaked figures were fleeing to the mainland, one behind the other. Servants and courtiers followed them, tripping in their haste to get away. They must have been waiting for the tide to turn.

'Soon the whole kingdom will know what has happened,' hissed the King. 'Then the rest of the Fringe Islands. It is the sign of weakness the Tolbiens have been waiting for.'

Meredyth tried to think of something soothing to say, but the King was already striding across the room to the door.

He turned back abruptly and glared at the Queen. 'Violanna, you will rest now,' he said. 'And I will return once I have spoken to the Royal Council.'

He had almost disappeared out of the room when the Queen suddenly said, '*Talia*.'

Meredyth jumped and the King stopped short.

'Your Majesty?' said Meredyth, hurrying over to her bedside.

'The Princess will be called Talia,' said the Queen, her voice thin and wavering. 'It means "dawn" in Diaspass.'

The King frowned. 'The Princess is called Aruelle Constanti-nella, after my mother,' he said. 'It is the Bavaughian custom—'

'Her name is Talia.'

The nursemaid averted her eyes, and Meredyth put a warning hand on the Queen's arm.

'Her name is Talia,' repeated the Queen. 'She was born into the morning light.'

There was a pause and Meredyth looked at the King. His expression had become hard and dark.

'Name your cursed daughter as you please,' he spat. 'It is of no consequence to me.'

PART TWO

PART TWO

SOME OF THE Guil townsfolk say they saw the magic bursting from the castle that day. On the mainland, they watched as it swelled out of doorways, windows and chimneys, leaking from Mont Isle like black ink pooling in the sky.

Servants from the castle, terrified of what they had witnessed in the Great Hall, fled across the causeway to the mainland as soon as the tide turned and ran to the stores and taverns to tell breathlessly of the day's events. 'A sorceress has cursed the Princess!' they cried. They did not know why or how, but it was some kind of magic. It was not long until everyone in the fishing town had heard of what had happened.

As the days passed, the rest of the magic that had clotted around Mont Isle slowly dispersed. The hounds stopped howling endlessly through the night, the bread in the kitchens began to rise again, and the roses in the Queen's Garden restored themselves for a final burst of colour before the onset of autumn. But though the magic was gone, the damage remained.

On the King's orders, a party of Royal Guards rode out to capture and question the Masters. They searched every nook and cranny of Guil, then the surrounding towns and villages, but found no sign of the black-cloaked figures. The foreign guests had vanished as quickly as they had appeared, taking any hope of understanding or reversing the curse with them.

'Good riddance,' the people of Bavaugh said.

And when they heard next that the Queen had gone mad, they shrugged. She had invited the magic into their kingdom with her foreign ways and now she was reaping the consequences. No one had wanted the Blessing – it was widely put about after the event that the King *certainly* had not wanted to hold the ceremony – so this was what had come of it: a deathly curse on the Princess. Well, at least she was not a Prince. But what was to become of a kingdom with a cursed heir? Mutterings and whisperings ran rife.

As the land throughout Bavaugh turned amber and crisp, the royal household departed from Mont Isle – all except the Queen and the cursed Princess. It was alleged in all the towns and villages that the Queen had locked them both in her bedchamber and refused to leave. 'We always knew she was strange,' said the people of Bavaugh, forgetting the day of the Royal Wedding, when they had danced and celebrated the union.

Instead of travelling to his hunting lodge in the north, as was his custom, the King returned to the capital, Lustore. There he paraded through the streets, sitting astride his blood bay stallion with a forced smile, waving at his subjects. From Lustore, he set out on a tour around Bavaugh, riding through every town and village he could, flanked by royal banners that snapped and lashed in the biting wind. And despite the saddle sores and freezing, numb fingers, King Felipe addressed merchant and peasant alike with a cheery greeting.

'Damage control,' whispered his courtiers, with raised eyebrows.

But many Bavaughians had not seen their King since the tour following his wedding all that time ago, and so they received him excitedly, their anxieties about the day of the Blessing soothed. He responded to his subjects' queries about his daughter with a quick nod of his head and a reassurance that all was well. 'The Princess is healthy and beautiful,' he repeated to crowds gathered in town squares, on hillsides and by docks. 'You may have heard of a curse, but there is no need to worry. We do not tolerate dark magic in the Kingdom of Bavaugh.'

It was a gruelling winter tour, trudging through snow and hail in the south, which gradually turned to sludge and mud as they moved north. When the first signs of spring swept through the country, King Felipe returned to the palace at Lustore, aching and exhausted. The maids said they could hear his racking cough from the servants' quarters, and the courtiers remarked that he looked old and tired. He had travelled the length and breadth of his kingdom, as his advisors had instructed, and now he wanted to settle at his palace.

King Felipe called the Royal Council to a meeting that lasted all that day and late into the night. Raised voices were heard from the corridors outside and at one point Lord Rosford was seen marching from the room, his face mottled with rage. The next morning, the King sent a messenger riding south-west to Mont Isle, calling for the Queen to return. In the meantime, the Royal Court began the spring season with aggressive enthusiasm: feasts were planned, balls were arranged and tourneys were set. The King waited for news of his wife's arrival, but still none came.

The sticky buds in the trees bloomed and the days turned bright and warm. The King sent another messenger to the west coast. 'Do not return until you have confirmation of her departure,' he instructed. He waited as the evenings grew long and balmy and the rising heat made the Lustore streets fetid and rank, but the messenger did not return.

As the end of summer loomed and rumours of the Queen's madness raged through the kingdom, the King went to the Royal Council chambers and announced he was setting out for Mont Isle the next day. 'If the Queen will not return at my request,' he said, 'I will go and bring her back myself.'

Sel

Dawvin, East Bavaugh

FLOUR CAKED THE lilac veins at Sel's wrists. She pushed the heel of her hand into the dough, feeling its warm, spongy form stretch as she dragged it across the wooden tabletop. It shrank when she released it, its edges drawing back like a tide. She folded it over and repeated the action. Then again. And again.

She clenched her teeth as she worked, and tried to knead from her shoulders, as the woman at the bakery had taught her. Her elbows and wrists burnt, but the action – which had once felt so odd – was gradually becoming familiar and she hoped her body would soon adjust itself to this new daily task.

There was a lot she was having to adjust to right now, Sel thought grimly as she worked the dough. Too much. She had to be careful not to let her mind wander these days, because her thoughts would soon spiral to dark places and she had spent too many evenings staring blank-eyed into the dying embers of the fire, wishing her life had not come to this.

The baby at her feet gurgled and Sel looked down into a pair of large blue eyes framed by long black lashes. She was with Briar every moment of every day and still she was often left breathless by the child's impossible beauty.

'Sit tight; we have another batch to go yet,' she said.

Briar smiled and grabbed a knotted rag from the floor, gnawing at it. For all her other-worldly splendour, she was still a baby.

'*Sit tight; we have another batch to go yet,*' Sel repeated to herself as she kneaded, trying out different inflections. Learning Bavaughian was proving more difficult than she had anticipated. Sel prided herself on her ability to study hard, but her winters as an apprentice, learning to sign magic, whisper charms, weave enchantments and read Novtook symbols, had not also included looking after a baby and ensuring they had food in their bellies and a safe place to lay their heads. She had fooled no one when she had first arrived in this small fishing town on the east coast of Bavaugh two seasons ago. With Briar bundled into a sling on her back, she had walked into the first tavern she saw and enquired if there were any small lodgings going in Dawvin. The barmaid had paused, squinted at her and said, 'Where are you from, then? The south? Don't recognize that accent.'

Sel had quickly replied that she was indeed from the south – the south-east, on the border of the Wildlands. She had discovered that mention of the Wildlands halted further questioning and seemed to account for any oddness on her part.

True to form, the barmaid had nodded, then told her that there was a small room for rent down the street. It was not much to look at, with a mud-packed floor and a cobwebbed ceiling, but it was cheap. Sel had gratefully moved in, keen to be off the roads during the height of winter. She did not want to be sleeping in hay barns and sheltering in ditches with a baby when the cold came.

At least life in Dawvin was an improvement on the many days she had spent on the road. During her travels across Bavaugh, farmers' wives had often taken pity on Sel, spotting her in the crowd of labourers who had spent a long day working the land. 'First baby?' they would ask, glancing at her ears for a matrimony band. When Sel nodded wearily, they would press a crust of bread into her palm, offer up their wisdom and sometimes disappear into their houses to return with an old blanket 'for the little one'.

The first time this had happened, the woman had asked, 'What's her name?'

Sel had blinked. After a sleepless night spent in nearby woodland and a day of sweeping and cleaning in return for a hot meal, she could barely stay conscious.

'Don't you have a name for her?' asked the woman.

Since leaving Mont Isle, Sel had thought of the baby only as 'the Princess' but, of course, that would not do.

'Yes, she has a name,' Sel said, wracking her exhausted brain for something appropriate.

'And that is . . . ?'

Sel looked past the woman to the hedgerow on the lane, where a tangle of thorns and grass grew. 'Briar,' she said. 'Her name is Briar.'

The woman raised her eyebrows. 'Well, she's a mighty sweet thing. I don't think I've ever seen such a pretty complexion on a little one.'

Sel gave a weak smile. 'She takes after her father.'

Since then, the name had stuck. It was simple, nondescript, and Sel did not have the energy to think up anything else.

As a general rule, she tried to ensure Briar went undetected on their travels. She knew logically that no one would suspect the dirty bundle strapped to her back to be the firstborn Princess of Bavaugh, but she would rather not draw attention to her all the same. However, despite her best efforts, there was something about Briar's enchanted loveliness that people could not resist.

'I haven't heard that bairn cry once,' a peasant woman had remarked one morning a few days after Sel had left Mont Isle. The woman had worked alongside Sel the day before, milking cows, then slept the night in the stables on a hay bale near their own. 'Ain't heard nothing but sweet gurgles.'

'Hmm,' replied Sel, trying to translate the woman's heavily accented Bavaughian; her language charm had started to wear off.

'Seems to me like you've got a good one there,' added the woman, craning her neck to peer at the baby cradled in Sel's arms.

'Thank you.'

It was true that Briar never cried or fussed. Sel did not have much experience of babies, but she was vaguely aware that they were meant to whine, grumble and scream. Occasionally Briar would emit a melodious wail if she was hungry, but that was all. The local wet nurses Sel paid to feed Briar in the early days always commented on her tranquil nature.

'Shall I hold the bairn while you get ready?' asked the woman.

'No.'

'Just for a moment. It'll surely help you.'

'No, we must go,' said Sel, the words tumbling awkwardly out of her mouth.

Before the woman could reply, Sel had snatched up her things and fled.

She did not have a strong sense of where she was going as she travelled through the kingdom, except that it must be away from Mont Isle. She could have headed north but, as she began her journey, she had found herself veering south, roughly following the opposite coastline. Sometimes she wondered if this had been an error – it was warmer in the north and perhaps she could have gone to the capital and blended into the crowds – but she had not had time to stop and think the day she set out, and it felt too late to turn back now.

Sel had fled from the chapel on Mont Isle after the Blessing into screaming, frantic chaos. Courtiers were running to their chambers and bolting the doors, servants were wailing and cowering in groups, and the Royal Guards were charging down corridors, swords drawn, yelling for the Masters. At first, Sel had stood frozen to the spot, her breath catching in her chest, but when a guard shoved past her, knocking her back against a stone wall, she remembered that she was no longer wearing her black cloak. She was no longer a Master's apprentice.

Without stopping to dwell on this painful realization, Sel had followed a pair of howling Ladies-in-Waiting across a courtyard and down flights of stairs, out of the castle. In all the turmoil, no one had noticed her hurrying away, clutching a pile of dirty rags. As she'd raced to the castle walls, Sel had had the sense to lift a few useful items on the way, the survival skills of her childhood returning to her. She had grabbed a grey woollen cloak left slung over a chair and a pouch of flecks someone had abandoned in a jacket pocket hanging in a hallway. In hindsight, she wished she had taken more, but at the time she had felt the pressing need to escape, so she had joined the trembling, sobbing crowd of Bavaughians fleeing across the causeway to the mainland, blending into their babbling midst. Reaching Guil, she had not stopped and, using some of her new flecks, she had purchased a seat on the first wagon she could find heading out of the fishing town towards the south-east.

She had carried on in this direction since, mucking out stables, scrubbing floors and sweeping yards to get by. It had been a relief to finally allow herself to stop in Dawvin for the winter and take up odd jobs for a local baker in the fishing town. It was demanding work, but it could at least be completed inside with Briar playing at her feet. Sel had told herself that in the spring she would move on, but it was almost summer now and she still had not left. She had some notion that she should be continually moving with Briar, avoiding detection, but their lodgings were simple and cosy and it was hard to contemplate returning to nights in woodlands and ditches again.

As Sel kneaded the dough, she found herself becoming more and more convinced that she should settle in Dawvin for longer. She reasoned that she had have travelled far enough away from Mont Isle to be safe – surely this was the perfect place to hide. The Queen had said that they must stay concealed until the spell was broken or seventeen winters had passed – whichever came first. Sel desperately hoped it would be the former, and that at this very moment the Masters of the Diaspass Kingdom were working together on a solution. Then, when the danger was gone, Sel could return the Princess to the Queen, receive the handsome reward for her troubles and use it to resume her studies. Simple.

It'll all end soon, Sel told herself, but something inside her ached. She missed the *feel* of magic. She missed the tangle of energy in her grip; the wild, precarious power of it. Sometimes she would catch herself about to mutter a charm and she would stop with a wince. The Queen had said there must be no magic. No trace. It was almost too much to bear. Sel could never stand to dwell on it long – all those days spent slaving over texts, the many sleepless nights reciting symbols and her battle to convince Florentina to take her as an apprentice in the first place. It could not all be for nothing.

'It is said that magic is most potent in the Central Realm, where it originated,' Sel muttered to herself in her own language, picking speckled globs of dough off her forearms. 'That is the leading theory of the Fourth Age, although recent sages have discovered what they believe to be origins on the western islands of the Known Realm . . .'

Sel patted the dough into an oval shape and covered it with a cloth to prove, before turning her attention to the next batch. Wiping a floury hand across her forehead, she pressed on with her work, continuing to recite the introduction of her favourite academic text and promising herself that no matter how many seasons passed, she would not forget it.

Violanna

The Chapel, Mont Isle

VIOLANNA WAITED. SHE stood in the nave of the chapel, her hands clasped and head bent, her eyes focused on the milky marble floor threaded with green. From her bedchamber windows she had seen the royal party crossing the causeway and, just moments ago, she had heard the clatter of hooves in the nearest courtyard. Violanna told herself that she was not fearful – after all, the worst that could happen had already occurred – but her knees still trembled. She closed her eyes and prayed harder. She had heard the whispers of the servants: *the Queen is mad*. But they were wrong; she had not lost her mind yet. On the contrary, she had a plan – she just did not know whether it would work.

Behind her, the doors of the chapel burst open. Violanna did not stir. It was not until Felipe stood in front of her, panting for breath, that she looked up.

'What exactly do you think you are doing?' he spat.

Violanna quickly dropped into a low curtsey, her knee banging the cold, hard floor. 'Long live King Felipe of Bavaugh.' Rising, she saw that this had had the desired effect, and the purple tinge of rage was fading from her husband's face. 'How was your journey, Your Majesty?' she asked.

'The journey was fine.'

'I am glad to hear it. Have you visited the nursery yet? Our daughter has already grown so much—'

'Violanna, what are you still doing here?'

Violanna arranged her face into an expression of naive confusion. 'Your Majesty?'

'I sent for you. I sent for you over and over again, and you ignored me.'

The purple tinge began returning to Felipe's cheeks and Violanna felt her carefully laid plans slipping away. She longed to turn and flee from her husband, lock herself in her bedchamber again and refuse all entry. But she knew that would not work. Not this time. Felipe would send guards to break down the door and drag her off to Lustore, curse or no curse. If she was going to get her way, she would have to be careful.

'I am afraid I have been unwell, Your Majesty,' Violanna replied, hunching her shoulders. 'I did not mean—'

'You disobeyed me!' bellowed Felipe and his shout echoed around the chapel. 'You did not heed the orders of the Crown.'

'I could not come; the curse means that if I leave—'

'You have made me look foolish!'

'Forgive me, Your Majesty!' cried Violanna, dropping to both knees and clasping his boots. 'I was too ill!'

She could tell by his pause that Felipe was startled, and she could feel his eyes on the back of her head.

'All right. Get up.'

'Your Majesty?'

'All right, I said. Now get up.'

He did not offer her his arm and Violanna scrambled to her feet, tripping on the hem of her gown. Felipe seemed calmer, but she sensed she had not won yet. 'Thank you, Your Majesty,' she whispered. 'Thank you—'

'Stop it. Stop that. Go and pack your things; we are leaving tonight. I cannot stand to be in this place a moment longer.'

Violanna hesitated.

'I said go.'

She took a deep breath. 'I cannot go, Your Majesty,' she said.

Felipe stared at her and Violanna noticed his fingers squeezing into fists, his tendons bulging. He had never struck her, but she had seen a few of his favoured ladies about court with violet blotches on their cheeks. The tremble returned to her knees, but she told herself that she would not give in. The lives of her daughters depended on it.

'What did you say?' Felipe hissed.

'Please, Your Majesty, it is not by choice that I disobey you,' she replied in her most even voice. 'I cannot go. It is the curse.'

'We have a great deal to discuss on that matter.'

Violanna kept her expression neutral. 'I believe I know as much about it as you.'

'The Masters, the sorceress. They are your people,' he said with a sneer of disgust. 'You must know more. Everybody is saying so.'

'I promise, I do not.' Violanna took a deep breath and added as earnestly as she could, 'The Blessing is a custom from my homeland and I wanted my first child – our daughter – to be properly recognized by the Diaspass Kingdom, as we had discussed. That is all.'

'And can nothing really be done about it? The curse?'

'I have written to the Masters of the Diaspass Kingdom . . . I am sure I will receive a response soon.' Violanna did not add that she had written to her father too, but all appeals had been met with silence. More tears streamed down her cheeks.

'Control yourself, Violanna. We will discuss this properly later. Now go and pack your things; you are leaving this island with me today.'

'If I leave, Talia will die! That is part of the curse.'

'She is as good as dead already – that is the view of the Council.'

Violanna flinched. She had suspected this would be her husband's opinion, but it did not make hearing it any easier. She thought of the gummy, smiling baby in the castle's nursery, whom she visited often but always watched from a distance, never allowing herself to get close. Talia reminded her too keenly of the *other* baby; the secret, missing child far, far away, whom she longed for. It was not Talia who would perish if Violanna left Mont Isle, but Felipe did not know that, and he was willing to trade his daughter's life for the favour of political advisors. A bitter lump of loathing bubbled up Violanna's throat, and she had to force herself to swallow it down.

'You have shown you can carry a child, so you will have another,' continued Felipe. 'A boy. You are not so old yet. That is what the Council have agreed. So leave the baby here and come to Lustore with me.'

'I will not.'

The chapel became so silent that Violanna could hear the scratching of seagulls on the roof.

This was the difficult part. She knew what she was about to say next would enrage her husband further.

She licked her dry lips and continued, 'I will not let Talia – our daughter – die.' She forced herself to look at the King directly. 'And I will not have another child.'

Felipe lunged forward and grabbed her. 'That is not your decision to make!'

She gasped and resisted the urge to shove him away. She knew she must appear weak. 'There is a chance that Talia will live,' she gulped. 'I cannot abandon her. Please.'

Felipe's grip loosened slightly, but he did not let go. 'Everyone warned me I should not have married you. Are you shocked to hear me say so? Are you ashamed?'

Violanna had also been advised not to marry the King of a backwards kingdom tucked away at the edge of the realm. 'It would be better to wed a Diaspass Earl or even a wealthy merchant,' one of her sisters had said. And Violanna agreed – if she had been like her sisters, that is exactly what she would have done. But she was not like them.

'I am sorry I have disappointed you, Your Majesty,' she replied as sincerely as she could manage.

'It is not just me; it is the people, the kingdom.' Felipe released her arm and rubbed his pale, lined face.

When Violanna had accepted his proposal as a young Princess, she had hardly bothered with the portrait sent for her approval, and so she had been pleasantly surprised, on the day of her wedding, to see that her betrothed was handsome in a clean, neat sort of way. Felipe had mostly kept his looks throughout the winters, though they had seasoned with age, but now he appeared old and drawn.

Violanna suspected he was aware of this, and she knew it would only add to his frustration.

'You are clearly not in your right mind,' added the King. 'Enough of this. Go and pack your things.'

'I cannot, Your Majesty.'

This time Felipe grabbed her shoulders with both his hands and shook her. 'Do you realize what that curse has done?' he roared as her head snapped back and forth. 'Do you realize how delicate the situation is? The Tolbiens have been waiting for an opportunity like this. The Council are in a panic and the kingdom is still unstable. Everyone – the people of Bavaugh, the Tolbiens, the whole Western Realm – needs to forget this ever happened. *I* want to forget it ever happened.'

Violanna waited until he released her and staggered back, fighting to keep her composure. There was blood in her mouth from where she had bitten her tongue and her head throbbed. She did not care about Tolbi or the rest of the Fringe Islands or the Royal Council or the people of Bavaugh. She only cared about her daughters.

'We need an heir,' added Felipe, rounding back on her with a snarl. 'The kingdom needs a Prince. And I do not care what you say; I will take you by force if I must.'

Violanna pressed her palms against her bodice, trying to stop herself from shaking. She did not doubt that what he said was true. There had been times during their many seasons of childlessness when he had been rough with her. Their marriage and their love-making had always been fraught and loveless.

'I understand you,' she said, and she was surprised by how clear and level her voice sounded. This had not played out in the way she had hoped, but there was still one last chance. 'I have another idea.' She took a deep breath and said, 'You will take a new wife.'

Felipe stared back at her. His eyebrows rose and a muscle in his cheek twitched. She knew she had piqued his interest. She had won.

'You will take a new wife,' she repeated, her voice becoming louder. 'And Bavaugh will have a new Queen and a new heir.'

Sel

Dawvin, East Bavaugh

SEL SAW THE palinkie before she heard the Diaspass accent and she stopped short, the excitement of familiarity overriding all other thoughts. The palinkie was perched inside a cage on the edge of the dockside, its talons curled around iron bars and its magenta wings pinned back with ties. There was a man standing next to it smoking a pipe and the Diaspass accent belonged to him.

'Get a move on!' he bellowed at the sailors lugging crates on to a nearby ship. 'We were supposed to set off at dawn.'

'Is the palinkie yours?' asked Sel in Diaspass, before she could stop herself.

The man paused and looked her up and down. 'It's for sale if you want it?' he replied.

To speak and hear the language of her homeland was both wonderful and strange, and Sel felt almost giddy. She stared at the palinkie, which glared back with its pink, reptilian eyes.

'I've nowhere to keep it,' she said. 'I just haven't seen one in a long time.'

The man raised his eyebrows. 'From Fakcil, are you?' His own sing-song accent suggested he was native to the rural south of the Diaspass Kingdom. 'What're you doing *here*?'

Sel remembered herself and stepped back. 'I did grow up in Fakcil, as a matter of fact.' She quickly glanced around the Dawvin dockside and was relieved not to see anyone she knew. 'But I married a sailor and moved here.'

'A little place like this would be quite a change from the Diaspass Kingdom's capital. You must've been in love.'

'Ha! Yes.'

'But I can see you have your hands full,' he added, nodding to Briar, who straddled Sel's hip, staring at him with her huge blue eyes. 'My, that's a pretty little'un.'

'She takes after her father.'

Sel's native language tumbled so smoothly and effortlessly from her mouth that she found herself lingering despite knowing she should move on.

'You've owned a palinkie before?'

Sel shook her head. 'There was a flock of them in my quarter in Fakcil growing up.'

Looking at the creature, she could hear again the high-pitched screeches and clicking that used to wake her every morning.

'I've heard there's a wild flock that lives in the slums of Fakcil, but you don't sound like you're from there.'

'No . . . I mean, I was. It was just when I was little.'

The mist that had shrouded Sel's journey to the bakery to drop off fresh loaves that morning was burning away and there were the beginnings of a fine summer's day in the clear blue sky. Sel knew she was saying too much to this man. She knew she should leave now, but she could not seem to get herself to walk away.

'You're about the only one that's taken an interest in this fella,' said the man, gesturing at the palinkie. 'I thought a merchant or lady might want an exotic pet, but I didn't realize these Bavaughian folk were so against enchanted beasts. Everywhere I went with it, they ran in the opposite direction. You'd think I was turning up with the yellow death. We heard mutterings about some kind of curse that's sent all of them suspicious. Something to do with the Queen? My Bavaughian is basic and I didn't catch most of it, but what did they expect?'

'I don't think most Bavaughians know the particulars of the Queen's past,' said Sel carefully. 'Not even the Bavaughian King.'

The man sighed. 'I'm headed to one of the Fringe Islands next – Tolbi. Perhaps those folks might take more kindly to a palinkie.'

Sel did not think it likely – she had heard that most of the kingdoms in the Western Realm shunned formal magic – but she decided it was best to keep that to herself. Instead, she asked, 'Do you know what the Diaspass Kingdom makes of what happened to Queen Violanna? What's everyone saying?'

Sel had heard no news from her homeland since she had left and sometimes she missed it so much it made her feel sick – the honey-coloured afternoon light, the froth of wild bougainvillea tumbling over stone walls, and the hazy warmth of a summer's evening. It hurt to remember and mostly she tried not to think of it at all.

'I'd heard nothing of a curse till I arrived,' replied the man with a shrug.

Sel tried not to show her alarm. If the Diaspass Masters were dismantling the sorceress's curse, the events of the disastrous Blessing ceremony should be common knowledge in her homeland. But perhaps it was all being kept quiet. Sel tried to soothe herself with the thought that she would likely receive word from the Queen soon that the curse had been broken and Briar could be returned. The other possibility – that Sel would be trapped in Bavaugh for seventeen winters, hiding until the end of the spell – was too daunting.

'Our King is still preoccupied with Journier,' continued the man airily. 'No time to concern himself with this little kingdom.'

The Diaspass Kingdom's historically, fractious relationship with its bordering country, Journier, was similar to Bavaugh's volatile past with the neighbouring Fringe Island, Tolbi. Sel had not lived in Bavaugh long before encountering sneers of disgust towards the Tolbiens from Bavaughians both young and old, as well as references to bloody battles and political clashes of times gone by.

'And what's the latest on Journier?' asked Sel, trying to push thoughts of the curse from her mind. She longed for more news – very little Central Realm politics seemed to reach this far west.

'We've aligned ourselves with the Journier rebel forces and the fighting continues,' replied the man. 'No further progress made, as far as I hear.'

He banged his pipe against the cage and the palinkie shivered its wings and snapped its beak. Briar giggled in surprise and the sound was soft and sweet like the ring of a tiny bell.

'It looks to me like you might be a little homesick?' The man waggled his eyebrows and tugged on his shirt. 'Could you be tempted to hop aboard and go back?'

Sel swallowed and forced out a chuckle.

'I'm only half joking,' said the man. 'I could cut you a deal for passage on my ship. I'll let the little'un ride free.'

Sel felt herself involuntarily leaning forward, as though she might suddenly sprint on board and finally see the back of this cold, bleak kingdom. She knew she could not let herself entertain the thought for even a moment or else she would be gone. Sel had never imagined a child in her future, yet now she could swiftly change a nappy and bath a slippery little body with ease. This was not the life she had hoped for – not the life she had worked hard for – and in the dark, hard moments her disappointment was crushing. But two tiny hands clung to her cloak, and she knew that she could not leave. Not yet. Queen Violanna had told her to stay in Bavaugh, and the Central Realm with its enhanced magical scholarship was a dangerous place to hide a spellbound child. Briar would surely be identified and then the attempt to misdirect and confuse the spell would all have been for nothing. Sel told herself that she had a promise to keep and a reward to earn.

'I can't,' she replied.

The man grinned. 'Off you go now, girlie, and enjoy your beautiful baby.'

Sel nodded. She took one last look at the palinkie, crouched in its cage, its coat a shocking blaze of colour against the pale, watery Bavaughian backdrop. Then she forced herself to walk away.

Meredyth

The Palace, Lustore

MEREDYTH HURRIED OUT of the ballroom to the steps at the back of the palace. Torches flickered across the grounds below, lining gravel paths that criss-crossed between the gardens, and illuminating benches where couples huddled together, whispering and giggling. Music and merriment swelled from behind her as Meredyth raked her gaze across the scene, checking the shadows. A green mask hung limply from her left hand and, in her right, she clutched a goblet of half-drunk wine.

Lord Lansin had said she was worrying over nothing, but the problem with her husband was that he *did* worry about nothing. He glided through life, responding to triumph and tragedy with a simple, benign smile. Meredyth had just left him in one of the lounges adjoining the ballroom, chortling amid a huddle of men, with no thought of their youngest child, their daughter, whom he was supposed to have been watching.

'I am sure she is having fun,' he had said, patting at Meredyth's hand. 'You fret too much. It is her first season at court and she is getting up to mischief, just as the boys did.'

Without replying, Meredyth had turned and hurried back through the ballroom to the gardens. If any mischief was being made, it was bound to be out there. She might have let her three older sons roam around unchaperoned, but she was not about to allow Jenolie such freedoms. Daughters were different.

A familiar squeal of delight sounded below, and Meredyth caught sight of Jenolie sauntering arm in arm with a figure she couldn't quite make out.

'Jenolie!' she hissed. 'What are you doing out here?'

Her daughter stopped short beside one of the fountains where candles bobbed on the surface of the water. She looked up in surprise, the flickering light turning her auburn hair crimson and catching the beaded mask strung from a ribbon around her neck.

'Mother? Mother, I am just walking.'

'Come up here this instant!'

Even in the faint light, Meredyth could see Jenolie's scowl. Her daughter turned to the figure beside her, muttering something, then the two of them strolled up the stone steps.

'Oh, Hana!' said Meredyth, recognizing the girl hanging from her daughter's arm with surprise and relief. 'I did not see you there.'

'Who did you think it was?' snapped Jenolie.

'No one. Nothing,' replied Meredyth quickly. 'You disappeared and I did not know where you were.'

She did not add that she had last seen Jenolie dancing with the son of Sir Engles, a young man who already had three bastard children to his name.

'We wanted to see the light display in the rose garden,' said Hana.

'I am sorry; it was my idea, Your Ladyship. We did not mean to alarm you.'

'Hana, may I speak to my daughter alone, please?'

'Of course, Your Ladyship.'

Hana curtsied to Meredyth, then said to Jenolie, 'I will fetch us drinks,' before turning away.

'I will meet you inside!' Jenolie called as the dainty figure disappeared into the candlelit ballroom.

'Will you indeed?' hissed Meredyth when they were alone. 'I am of a mind to take you home. What made you go off like that without telling me?'

Jenolie rolled her eyes and tossed her curls over her shoulder with a head-flick. 'Hana wanted to speak to me.'

'This is the first time I have seen you two together. I did not realize you were close.'

'We have chatted a few times this summer, since we are both skilled Tats players. But tonight Hana wanted to speak to me about something *very important*.'

'I see . . .'

Meredyth waited while Jenolie smirked at her. She was not opposed to the connection – far from it. Hana, daughter of Lord Dakson, was thought to be the greatest beauty of the season and would make the most advantageous match. Jenolie was pretty enough, but to be seen with Hana would surely improve her prospects.

Finally, with a sigh, Meredyth added, 'What did Hana want to speak to you about?'

Jenolie looked left and right, before leaning closer. 'If I tell you, Mother, you must promise not to share it.'

'Jenolie—'

'Promise!'

'All right, I promise.'

Jenolie leant in and Meredyth could smell the rosewater she had dabbed on her daughter's neck earlier that evening as they had readied themselves for the masquerade together. It had been a bittersweet moment. When Jenolie was wed and gone, there would be no more children in the Lansin nursery.

'Hana wanted to know what happened when the King went to Mont Isle a moon ago.'

Meredyth frowned. 'What do you mean?'

'The King went to Mont Isle to bring the Queen back, but she did not return. Something happened.'

'Everyone knows that the Queen is unwell. She is staying on Mont Isle until she recovers,' replied Meredyth, parroting the line put about by the Royal Council as to the Queen's whereabouts. But Meredyth also thought of the many unanswered letters she had sent Queen Violanna since leaving Mont Isle with the rest of the court last autumn. As Chief Lady-in-Waiting, Meredyth had thought it her duty to stay with the Queen, but King Felipe had ordered that everyone must leave and she had not dared disobey. 'Why is Hana asking—' Meredyth began.

'She is going to wed the King! She is going to be the new Queen of Bavaugh!'

The goblet fell from Meredyth's hand, hitting the stone steps with a clang, wine splattering across the floor.

'Careful!' Jenolie squealed, inspecting the specks of red seeping into her blue skirts. 'Mother! Look what you have done.'

Meredyth pulled her daughter away from the wine pooling on the floor and into the shadows further along the steps.

'Ouch,' whined Jenolie. 'I should not have told you, Mother! You never tell me anything. You are the Queen's closest confidante and you have not mentioned any of this.'

'I had no idea!' Meredyth hissed. 'But it cannot be true. Hana must be confused. The King will have chosen her to be . . . to be his . . . close companion.'

'She is going to be the Queen, not his whore!'

'Jenolie!'

'I am not a fool, Mother. And neither is Hana. The King has chosen her as his wife. He saw her at the last tourney – do you not remember how fair she looked? She had her hair all braided up with pink ribbons. She said that night Lord Rosford spoke to her father on behalf of the King. Apparently the Royal Council will announce it all soon.'

Meredyth blinked rapidly, her breath catching in her throat. 'But the Queen?' she managed.

Jenolie shrugged.

A playful shriek was heard from somewhere in the grounds below, followed by a deep chuckle of laughter.

'Hana thought she saw Wiloia behind the light display in the rose garden with Lord Engles,' giggled Jenolie. 'She said they were *kissing* and he had his hand—'

'What else did Hana say about the Queen?'

Jenolie sighed. 'She said the Queen has agreed to the whole thing. Hana was sure you would already know about it. That is why she spoke to me.'

Meredyth's gaze dropped to the stone floor, possibilities rushing through her mind. She wanted to discount what her daughter was saying but something about it rang horribly true.

After a pause, Jenolie added, 'I am missing all the dancing. Shall we go back inside?'

'Wait, I must think what to do.'

Jenolie shook her head, auburn curls bouncing. 'Mother, there is nothing you can do. Hana says it has all been decided.'

'I must go to the Queen.'

'Soon she will no longer be the Queen. And perhaps it would be wise to distance ourselves. We must follow the wishes of the King.'

Jenolie was right, of course. Meredyth had taught her daughter the shrewd ways of courtly life, but she wanted to protest that this was different. This was Queen Violanna, her old, dear friend. 'What about the Princess Talia?' she asked.

'Hana said she is as good as dead with that curse. The King has made a big show of denying it to everyone, but privately he says that there is nothing to be done and Bavaugh needs an heir.'

Meredyth thought of the baby she had seen born on the floor of the chapel – tiny and defenceless. And then of the other baby. The true firstborn heir of Bavaugh, who must be hiding somewhere in the kingdom with that young Master. The next moon would mark the first anniversary of the fateful Blessing ceremony.

'This is terrible for the Queen and the Princess,' said Meredyth, but something told her that this development was not unfolding against Queen Violanna's wishes. She longed to ask her old friend what she was planning. This was a dangerous game.

Before her daughter could respond, Meredyth drew herself up tall and added, 'Jenolie, go back inside to Hana and tell her I scolded you for walking unchaperoned in the grounds. Do not tell her what we have discussed.'

'Yes, Mother.'

Jenolie grinned, relieved to be returning to the merriment. She turned in the direction of the ballroom, pulling her mask back on to her face. At the doors she paused and looked back. She called softly over her shoulder, 'Mother, do not be too worried about the Queen. Hana says that she is mad.'

Meredyth nodded and watched her daughter disappear inside.

Violanna

The Queen's Garden, Mont Isle

OVER THE HIGH whistle of the wind, Violanna could hear the returning boom of the tide. It was not bright outside, but she found herself squinting, her eyes stinging from a whole day spent in the gloom of her bedchamber with the shutters fastened.

As she entered the walled rose garden, Violanna caught sight of a figure. She had thought that the maid who had come running into her bedchamber moments ago must have been mistaken, but, even from this distance, Violanna could see that it was a woman. Violanna had assumed that this surprise visitor would be a messenger from Felipe and she had been ready to dismiss them – her husband had agreed to have no more contact; it had been part of their deal – but Felipe would not have sent a woman.

Violanna passed blooming rosebushes of soft pinks and deep corals, tucking scraggly locks of hair behind her ears. The maid had hurriedly pinned it before Violanna left her bedchamber, but the clawing fingers of the wind were already pulling it loose.

At the sound of her footsteps, the unknown visitor turned.

'Fayia?' gasped Violanna and she stopped still.

The woman's gaze took in Violanna's wrinkled gown and bare face. 'Hello, Violanna,' she said in Diaspass.

In her shock, Violanna grabbed hold of a branch to steady herself. The thorns sank into her palm; she pulled her hand away, grimacing from the sting.

'What are you doing here?'

Violanna had not spoken Diaspass in so long that the timbre and inflections of her homeland language felt stilted and odd.

'I have come to see you,' Fayia replied, stepping forward to close the gap between them.

Her hazel eyes were as clear and bright as they had always been, and her dark hair was still long and thick. No lines creased her forehead and her features were sharp and defined. It was just charms – the work of magic. Violanna had used them herself in her youth to plump her lips and fill out her chest. She did not usually care much for her appearance these days, but she felt a prickle of embarrassment that though she was younger than Fayia, she looked much older. The gifts from her own Blessing ceremony had worn off long ago, along with any charms she had used in her youth. Now there were dark spots on her cheeks and slack skin at her elbows.

'Who sent you?' she snapped. 'Was it Father?'

'No, I came because I wanted to.'

Violanna tried to swallow down her disappointment. Over the last few moons she had sent more pleading letters to the Diaspass Kingdom, but all had gone unanswered. 'Who knows you are here?' she asked.

'My husband and my household. When I heard what happened, I had to come.'

'How did you hear of it?'

Violanna knew she was being rude, but she could not stop herself. It was too bewildering to see her sister like this after so many winters had passed.

'When the Masters returned to the Diaspass Kingdom, they spoke privately to the Assembly,' replied Fayia. 'My husband is a member, as you know, and he told me—'

'What did Father say?'

There was a pause. Fayia's expression was set in concentration as she chose her words carefully. 'The King was saddened to hear of what happened.'

'That is it?'

'Violanna—'

'I do not know why I thought he would care. He was always a harsh, cruel man.'

Fayia reached forward and grasped Violanna's shoulders. 'There are problems in the Central Realm, sister,' she said. 'The Assembly is consumed with the warring over Journier. It looks like the rebel forces could triumph in the next few winters and, with our backing, they can finally establish independence. Though greatly indebted to the Diaspass Kingdom, which is what we want, of course—'

'My kingdom and my father have abandoned me!' interrupted Violanna. 'I have written to the King and he has ignored me. I have appealed to the Masters and they have ignored me too.'

She did not add that she suspected she knew why – she imagined them all receiving her begging messages and turning their noses up in disgust. *You brought this on yourself*, they would mutter. *This is what you deserve.*

'Father might not be here, but I am,' said Fayia. 'I had to wait until my household could spare me, but I set off as soon as I could and we docked at a town down the coast yesterday. I am sore and weary from the journey and I have upset my husband and my children by coming, but I am still here, sister.'

Fayia let her hands slide off Violanna's shoulder. Her fingernails were clipped and neat, and the gold bands of the Royal Olier on her forefinger and thumb caught the fading light, the fine chain strung between them winking.

Instinctively, Violanna touched her own Olier on her right hand, the jewellery symbolizing her Diaspass royal birthright. She sighed, knowing her eldest sister was right. 'Tell me, how is your family?' she asked, trying to sound more welcoming. Her enunciation of 'family' did not hit right; she had been speaking Bavaughian for too long.

Fayia smiled, showing white, even teeth. 'My family are well. You have four nephews and two nieces. My second daughter, Sophenia, was born last spring.'

Violanna's chest burnt with bitterness. 'How nice for you,' she hissed before she could stop herself. 'I suppose there were no unexpected visitors at her Blessing?'

Fayia's expression faltered. 'No, it was a lovely ceremony,' she said softly. 'But I am thrilled at the thought of meeting my own new niece, the Princess of Bavaugh. I know how long you have waited for a child.'

Violanna flinched.

'I can only stay for a few nights,' Fayia carried on. 'But I should like to spend some time with you both. How is the little Princess faring?'

'Fine.'

'Is she feeding well?'

'Yes.'

'Sleeping well?'

'Yes.'

'That is good.'

Violanna shuffled her feet. Truth be told, she did not know whether Talia fed or slept well. She spent most of her days shut in her bedchamber. When she did see her daughter, Violanna could not bring herself to touch the baby. She did not think she deserved the love of her child. It was impossible to look at Talia without seeing her twin, the missing baby whom she, Violanna, had sent away.

'I understand the King of Bavaugh is not here?' said Fayia. 'Inside the castle it was . . . quiet.'

Violanna did not want to tell her sister about the state of her marriage or the new Queen of Bavaugh.

'The King is in the capital,' she replied. 'I must stay here; it is part of the spell.'

Fayia nodded. 'A fierce, dark magic,' she muttered, her gaze wandering over the looming shapes of the castle around them, set against the peach sky. 'I felt it the moment I saw the island. I have never known anything like it.'

Violanna clamped her teeth together and looked away.

'Do not worry, sister. While I am here, we can discuss what might be done.'

'We are not Masters!' snapped Violanna. 'And even if we were, could anyone unpick a spell bound half so tightly? You said yourself that the magic is dark and strong. When the curse was cast, no one could stop it, not even the High Masters. Perhaps . . . perhaps there is nothing to be done.'

Over the last few moons, as her letters to her homeland had gone unanswered and time had trickled by, Violanna had started to doubt that the curse could be broken at all. She had begun to wonder if the Diaspass Masters' silence signified defeat. The guilt she felt at sending away her first daughter in Selhah's arms never ceased, but perhaps it really had been the only way to save her first child.

'I am here all the same, sister,' replied Fayia, patting at Violanna's shoulder again. 'And I will try to rally the Diaspass Masters to the task when I return home.'

Violanna doubted Fayia had much sway in such matters, but she nodded. Glancing up, she saw that the last of the light was fading from the sky. 'We should go inside. I am sure you will need to rest after such a long journey.'

'Thank you, sister.'

As they walked out of the walled garden and made their way back to the main castle, Violanna sensed there was something else Fayia wanted to say. Her sister was fiddling with a leather belt looped around her torso and silently moving her lips. By the time they reached the threshold to the hallway, Violanna could bear it no longer. She rounded on Fayia and said, 'What? What is it?'

Fayia straightened up and blurted, 'What was *she* like?'

Violanna clenched her fingers until she felt the wound on her palm from the rosebush begin to sting again. 'She was the same but also different. Like a stranger.'

'How did she seem?'

'Angry. And powerful. The magic has corrupted her – a lone wielder of magic is a dangerous thing; you know that. It is what I always feared would happen.'

Fayia took a deep breath and said, 'Do you think she might come after . . . me?'

Violanna sighed. Was this why her eldest sister had really come – to assess the danger to herself? 'No,' she replied, then added, 'Maybe. I no longer pretend to know what she will do.'

Sel

Dawvin, East Bavaugh

SEL STOPPED SUDDENLY, the mugs of cider in her hands sloshing on to her wrists. What she had just heard did not make sense. She turned her head in the direction of a group of men hunched around a table beside the fire and tried to drown out the buzz of chatter and guffaws of laughter from the rest of the tavern. Then, pretending to peer at a local map on the wall, she edged closer to the men, until she could more easily make out what they were saying.

'. . . something had to be bloody done,' said one with a black beard. 'I ain't surprised.'

'But the Queen's not dead,' protested another.

'She's lost it, though,' said a ruddy-faced man, tapping the side of his head. 'We can't have a mad Queen and a cursed Princess.'

'And can you blame the King for wanting a nice young thing?' said the bearded man. 'If I was King, I'd have myself two wives as well.'

'Why stop at two?' chuckled another.

'And we'll get a day off for the wedding,' pointed out the one with the ruddy face. 'And a free drink.'

'Now there's the real reason he's all for it!'

They all laughed.

Then a young man with dark eyes turned to Sel and said, 'Want to join us, or are you just going to stand there?'

Sel had been so busy listening to them that she had unknowingly drifted closer. She felt herself flushing red and quickly gestured to the map on the wall, saying, 'I was just looking at this.'

'Seemed to me like you were listening.'

'No, not at all,' squeaked Sel, backing away. She could feel the gazes of the men around the table looking her up and down. 'I had better get these drinks to my friend,' she added, lifting the mugs of cider in her hands.

She turned and hurried away, weaving across the raucous tavern without looking back. As she squeezed past villagers swaying together in drunken song and skirted around prostitutes taking bookings from table to table, her mind raced through what she had overheard. She was so preoccupied she almost charged straight into Sandi, who was standing by the window, waiting for her.

'Watch out!' cried Sandi, jumping back as cider splattered on to the floor.

'Sorry, sorry. It's so dark in here. I tripped.'

'It's almost half empty! Have you been taking sips from this on your way back from the bar, Jessamin?'

As always, it took Sel a beat to realize Sandi was speaking to her. *She* was Jessamin. 'Ha!' she replied, trying to ignore the burn of guilt that always hit when she had to lie.

Sandi winked to show she was joking and took a gulp of cider.

She tucked a strand of her short brown hair behind her ear and gave Sel a searching look. 'I saw you talking to that lot over by the fire. What did they say?'

'Nothing. It was a mistake. They thought I was listening to them.'

Sandi rolled her eyes. 'They're no good. Ignore them.'

'Actually . . . I was sort of listening. They were talking about the King taking a new wife.'

'As in, the Queen?'

'No, a *new* wife. Not the Queen.'

'I don't understand.'

'They were saying the King is going to marry someone else.'

Sandi paused, then shrugged. 'Strange.'

'You think it's true?'

'Doesn't seem that unlikely. We need an heir, don't we? And the youngest of that group, Pyke, he often works in the big town northwards so he gets all the fresh news.'

Sel glanced across the tavern to the fireside, her eyes falling on the young man with small, dark eyes who was staring right back at her.

'Is that Pyke?' she asked, turning away. 'The one looking at us now?'

Sandi glanced over her shoulder then nodded grimly. 'Yes. I'd stay away from him. What made you so interested you went and listened in?'

'I'm just surprised and I . . . feel sorry for her – the Queen – to be treated so. And the Princess.'

Sandi took another swig of cider and batted such notions away with her free hand. 'The Queen can go back to where she came from and take her cursed daughter with her,' she said. 'I don't feel no pity.'

'Yes, you're right,' replied Sel, though she knew that such a thing would never happen. The King of Bavaugh would not dare to send the Diaspass Kingdom back their Princess in disgrace. Though what he planned to do when news reached Diaspass that he was taking a new wife, Sel could not imagine. She had a sudden yearning to discuss the matter with Florentina. She could envisage them both in the parlour of their townhouse, the warm scent of coffee in the air and letters from other Masters, sharing news, spread on the table before them.

'That Pyke's still looking over at you,' said Sandi with a frown. 'Come on, let me introduce you to some proper lads. Hopefully he'll drink himself silly and forget about you.' Sandi grabbed the sleeve of Sel's homespun gown and tugged her towards a nearby table where a group of men and women were playing Tats. 'Jessamin, on your first night out without your baby, we want to make sure you have a good time!' she added.

Sel smiled at each of the Tats players Sandi introduced her to, but instantly forgot all of their names. She had been enjoying herself before she had heard about the King's new wife. Now she could barely think of anything else. A kindly-looking carpenter tried chatting to her, but she could not come up with anything interesting to say in return and, after a while, he moved on.

Sandi kept catching her eye and smiling encouragingly, and Sel made sure to nod reassuringly back. Sandi worked behind the counter at the bakery and she had been badgering Sel to spend an evening at one of Dawvin's taverns for some time. Sel had eventually run out of excuses not to, and so, while Sandi's mother was watching Briar, Sel had succumbed to the excitement of an evening out. This was the first time she had been parted from Briar since the Blessing and it had been strange at first. She had only just started enjoying herself when she overheard the men by the fire. Now she felt unsettled again. She wanted to be back at her lodgings, Briar safely tucked up on their bed in the corner of the room, with time to think about what this discovery meant and whether it changed anything.

'Hey, Jessamin, it's my round,' Sandi called across the table, holding up her empty mug. 'Another for you too?'

Sel shook her head.

'Huh? Not leaving, are you?' said Sandi, squeezing her way around the table to get closer.

'I should go home and relieve your mother.'

'She'll be fine. Stay.'

Sandi's eyes were slightly glazed, and she swayed on her feet. Sel had noticed her sneaking sips from the tankard of the kindly-looking carpenter, who pretended not to notice.

'Thank you for tonight, but I really should get back,' said Sel. 'I've a batch of rolls to make or you'll have none to sell tomorrow.'

Sandi sighed and went to put down her mug.

'No, don't leave on my account. You stay and enjoy your admirer.' Sel looked pointedly over at the carpenter, who was shuffling around the table to them.

'No idea what you're talking about,' Sandi replied, but there was a coy smile playing on her lips.

Sel tugged her woollen cloak off the back of a chair and fought her way through the now very unruly crowd to the door. Sandi waved her off enthusiastically and called, 'See you tomorrow, Jessamin!' before turning back to her carpenter.

Sel stepped out of the tavern into the chilled, early autumn evening, and the roar of voices from inside faded, leaving a hazy buzz in her head. She shivered and took in a deep breath, glad of the quiet.

Wrapping her cloak tightly around her, she set off down the cobbled street in the direction of her lodgings. Her breath trailed behind her in ragged wisps as she considered what she had overheard this evening. It was shocking, scandalous news, but worse had been done to secure an heir to a throne. And if the King took a new wife and had more children, that would likely mean Queen Violanna's daughter – or *daughters* – was to be usurped. It did not change the curse, but perhaps it changed something.

Sel was so lost in thought that she had not noticed a shadow following her out of the tavern, and she did not see it now, slipping into step behind her. Turning down an alleyway off the main street, she suddenly felt something snatch at her hand, yanking her backwards.

She stumbled and fell against a wall, the breath knocked out of her. Before she could gather herself together to run, two hands gripped her shoulders and pinned her in place.

'Good evening, girlie.'

The alleyway was dark, but Sel's eyes quickly adjusted and she saw a rough, stubbled face leering at her.

'Pyke.'

'You know my name. And I heard yours too, Jessamin.'

A cold sense of dread seeped through Sel's body, numbing her limbs. She felt useless and heavy.

'I have flecks,' she said, her voice sounding eerily calm. 'Two gold ones. You can take them.'

Pyke chuckled, puffing gusts of beer-soaked breath into her face. 'That's kind of you,' he said and he leant forward, pressing his whole body against her. 'But I've got all the flecks I need.'

Sel had known as soon as she saw Pyke's face in the darkness that he did not want her flecks. She had not spent her childhood in the slums of Fakcil for nothing. But she had hoped desperately that she was wrong.

'I've always had a thing for dark-haired ladies,' hissed Pyke, sliding his hand behind her head and grabbing hold of her braid. 'And tonight you caught my eye.' He jerked her head back, wrapping her braid around his fist like a rope.

Sel felt her legs begin to give way beneath her. 'Please . . .' she heard herself whispering. 'I have a child.'

She thought of Briar, wrapped in a blanket, sleeping soundly. That perfect little face, all the more beautiful in slumber, with a knotted rag clasped in one of her hands.

'Please—'

'Stay quiet or I'll shut you up,' spat Pyke, pulling her hair harder. His free hand groped clumsily beneath her cloak, forcing open her dress.

A whimper escaped Sel's lips as he grabbed hold of her left breast and gripped it.

Not again, she thought, *I said never again.*

Pyke released her then clawed his hand down, shoving it between her legs with a groan. Sel winced, her whole body contracting and folding in on itself.

This had happened before. One night in Fakcil, a band of drunken men had stumbled across the makeshift shack she shared on the riverbank. The other street children had scattered, but Sel had not been fast enough. Afterwards, as her bruises faded and her cuts scabbed, she had promised herself that it would never happen again. She had vowed to be more careful, more alert, faster. But many winters as a Master's apprentice had softened her and now here she was.

'Don't move,' grunted Pyke, tugging her cloak apart. 'Or I'll kill you.'

Sel closed her eyes. As she heard the jangle of a belt unbuckling, her mind drifted away to the safety of Florentina's parlour, where she had often sat in one of the sagging armchairs, parchment resting on her knees, and a pen in hand. Florentina paced the room in front of her, dictating, her black cloak trailing as she turned back and forth, and her long white hair loose and rippling with her movement. 'Magic is power,' Florentina was saying, and she paused and caught Sel's gaze. 'When you can harness magic, you can protect yourself.'

Sel's eyes snapped open and her whole body shivered.

'You'd better—' Pyke began, but he never finished.

Sel flicked her wrist and whispered two words – a spell she had never dared utter before. A spell reserved for Masters.

The air shuddered and snapped. A blast of raw heat barrelled down the alleyway and the ground jolted.

Sel's terror, combined with her magical abstinence, had unleashed something. Her fingertips crackled and burnt with the heat of it and her pulse thumped through her head. It was so strong, stronger than anything she had managed before. Exhilaration rushed over her and Sel's first thought was, *I have missed this*.

Pyke was thrown away from her, and for one moment he was suspended in the air, his face in the darkness a mixture of shock and horror. Then he fell to the floor.

Sel's second thought was, *What have I done?*

PART THREE

PART THREE

THE NEXT MORNING, there were no fresh rolls at the bakery in Dawvin. Customers tutted and frowned in disappointment before reluctantly choosing a loaf or a seeded bun instead. They returned home sulkily rubbing at their brows, complaining of a headache. There was an unusual heaviness in the town air that lingered that day, like the soupy thickness before a summer storm. It made the dogs in the street whine and the horses pulling the carts shiver and sidestep.

At the first opportunity, Sandi was dispatched from the bakery to chase up Jessamin's delivery. Suspecting her friend was unaccustomed to the strength of cider at their local tavern and had overslept, Sandi knocked softly at the door of Jessamin's lodgings. When there was no response, she knocked louder until, finally, she realized no one was there.

Jessamin and her daughter were gone. Vanished. A folded scrap of cloth containing the owed rent waited on the stripped pallet inside. Otherwise, the lodgings were bare and deserted. No one knew where Jessamin was headed or why she had left so suddenly. Over the next moon, Sandi was often asked what had happened to her friend – the quiet one with the pretty baby. But Sandi did not know. She repeatedly asked her own mother whether Jessamin had said anything when she returned from the tavern that night, but Sandi's mother did not remember anything amiss. It had been late and Jessamin had thanked her for watching Briar, that was all. No indication that she had been about to disappear.

For a while, the whole affair left a sour taste in Sandi's mouth. Something was not quite right and it niggled at her. When she really considered it, she realized she knew very little about Jessamin and Briar, despite having thought them friends. And when she asked around, it was clear no one else had known them any better. No family ties to follow up with, no previous or forwarding addresses. They had come and gone, distant and unknown, like the ships that sailed in and out of the Dawvin harbour.

A while later, when Sandi overheard a speaker in the town square proclaiming that the King was to marry a new wife, she thought of her friend. She remembered Jessamin's concern for the Queen with a wry smile, which faded when she also remembered that her friend was still missing without a trace. Sandi half hoped to receive a message from Jessamin, apologizing for leaving so suddenly and giving a reason for having disappeared without saying goodbye. A good one.

But gradually, as time slipped by, Sandi stopped thinking about her friend. A new family moved into Jessamin's old lodgings and a young girl from a nearby hamlet began making rolls for the bakery instead. The kindly carpenter asked Sandi's mother for her hand in marriage and life was full of other things: engagement celebrations, wedding preparations and making house. She was reminded of Jessamin just once more, when word got around that Pyke was missing and hadn't been seen in Dawvin or the surrounding villages for some time, suspected dead.

'Good riddance,' Sandi muttered to herself, and she recalled how Jessamin had caught his eye that night at the tavern. But it was a vague, distant thought that occurred to her during a shift at the bakery, and it was gone as soon as the next customer asked for three sugared buns.

Talia

The Castle, Mont Isle

THE TIDES AROUND Mont Isle could kill. That was what everyone said. They were sudden, strong and unpredictable. The sea did not gush back in one neat, straight line; instead, it crept up, returning in stealthy pools that flooded the sandy ground. The townsfolk of Guil claimed that you could be standing on a sandbar one moment, then turn around to find the sea appearing behind you, cutting you off from the shore. There were many tales of beachcombers and children who had perished this way, straying too far. Talia had heard all the warnings, but it did not stop her wandering across the damp sand at low tide.

There was a particular stack she liked and she called it The Mountain. She could see it from the window in her bedchamber: a smattering of distant rocks surrounded by choppy, white-peaked waves that became a jagged tower when the tide drew out. It was a tricky, vertical climb that Talia had only attempted a handful of times, and far more exciting than the rocky patches around the edges of the castle wall, which she had scaled so often she could hop from rock to rock with her eyes closed.

'It's a good day for climbing,' she called over her shoulder to Iver one morning, as they scampered down Mont Isle's steep, cobbled streets. 'Follow me!'

They headed to the outer walls of the castle, their bare feet skipping across the blackened molars of cobblestones. The tide was out and the servants were busy unloading a delivery of food and supplies that had come from the mainland. With everyone distracted, Talia and Iver were able to approach the gates unnoticed, scuttling along the lengths of the walls. There, they hung back in the shadows, waiting until the guards and servants were leaning over crates of carrots and potatoes, before slipping past into the spring sunshine.

'I don't like carrots,' muttered Iver as they jumped down from the gates into the squelchy, dark sand.

'Wait while I sort out my dress,' replied Talia.

She looked left and right to make sure they were alone then scooped up her skirts and tucked them into her drawers. Her skirts were getting more voluminous lately and it was harder to fit them in.

'You look funny,' Iver giggled.

Talia grinned and strutted back and forth, swaying her bulging midriff.

There was a shout from above and their laughter vanished. They both crouched down, knees hitting the watery ground with a slap. Looking up, they saw that it was only one of the guards on the battlement, shouting across the wall to someone else.

'I thought they'd seen us,' whispered Talia.

Iver lifted his cap and scratched at his head. 'Like when those kids spotted us on the beach?' he said. 'They pointed at you and laughed.'

'Did they?' said Talia, turning away.

'We were trying to fly that kite you made and some kids from Guil were walking by the boats. They saw us and they said you were a bastard and—'

'Follow me, Iver.'

Talia knew the incident Iver was referring to, but remembering it always gave her a peculiar feeling inside. It was the only time she had ventured close to the mainland – that hulk of forbidden beach spread on the horizon. When she had seen the children in the distance, she had thought they might want to make friends, but as she drew close, they began throwing pebbles at her and shouting things she did not understand.

'Today we'll go to The Mountain,' announced Talia as they scurried around the island, keeping within the shadow cast by the castle walls.

She felt Iver hesitate, his short, stocky frame falling behind her.

'I don't like The Mountain,' he said.

'Come on, it'll be fun.'

Iver said something under his breath, but he kept following her.

Once they reached the back of the island, they broke free from the shadow of the outer walls. The guards – the few that there were – kept to the front of the castle and there was little chance of being spotted now. Talia began running and Iver dashed after her. They sprinted until Talia's chest burnt with the salty air and the soles of her feet stung with the nip and scratch of shells and stones.

'Iver, attackers are coming,' cried Talia, cupping her hands into a telescope and looking out to the horizon. 'We've got to hurry.'

'Who's invading?' puffed Iver, jogging behind her.

'The Tolbiens. They've raised an army to fight us again. We need to beat them so the King gives us shields like the ones on the wall in the dining room.'

'And you'll actually get to meet him.'

Talia did not reply. She had asked Mother again recently when her father would finally visit, but there had been no reply. She leapt on to the first rock of The Mountain instead, gripping its toothed edge with her toes. She beckoned for Iver to follow her and the two of them began bouncing from rock to rock, their arms spread wide to keep their balance.

'Argh!' yelped Talia, slipping on a straggly knot of seaweed and banging her knee. She quickly pulled herself back up and paused to assess the damage. Her skin was grazed and stinging, and her drawers were badly torn. She would get a scolding later from Dottie for that. The sandy stains would annoy her chambermaid enough, let alone a rip. Unlike most of the maids at Mont Isle, Dottie was friendly and she listened to Talia's many thoughts and constant observations. The other servants were distant and whispery; a few even looked at her fearfully, although she did not understand why. But Dottie, with her lumpy, stooped figure and brown blotches on her hands like tea stains, had always been kind, if a little grumpy.

'Are we stopping?' called Iver from below.

'No!' replied Talia, brushing the grit from her knee. 'Keep going.'

The spring sunshine beat down upon them as they climbed. It turned the wet rocks shiny and made Talia's neck prickle with heat. She was just wondering whether they should pause to check the progress of the enemy and get their breath back, when Iver began shouting below.

'Talia! Talia, the tide!'

She frowned. Looking down, she saw that a shallow river had appeared on the ground below, the gushing water dissolving their footprints.

A hot, sick feeling rushed over her. Then she noticed a breeze plucking at her fair, braided hair. Turning, she saw a glistening white line of water on the horizon behind them, welling around the island. She had been so absorbed in the game that she had not noticed the time passing, and now the tide was drawing in. With a flash of panic, she realized that even if they turned back, by the time they had climbed down The Mountain, the water would be too high to return to the castle.

'What're we going to do?' wailed Iver.

'Don't worry,' she called back, ignoring the tight, choking feeling in her chest. 'We just need to get to the top of The Mountain. It's never covered by sea.'

Iver nodded, but his little face was waxy and pinched.

Talia began climbing again, trying to quicken her pace, but this was the hardest section to scale, and her progress was maddeningly slow. She glanced over her shoulder once and saw that the water had engulfed the foot of The Mountain and when she turned to look again a moment later, it was even higher.

'Keep going!' she called to Iver, her feet slipping and scrambling.

The wind was stronger now, snatching at her clothes and pulling her skirts loose from her drawers so that they dragged behind her and tripped up her feet. There must be a storm coming. She could hear the crash and rumble of the waves getting closer and, beside her, she could see Iver puffing and panting to keep up.

'We're almost there!' she cried. 'We must be.'

But the rocks continued to rise and Talia could not see the peak. Suddenly, she felt a cold spray over her feet and, looking down, she saw that the sea was reaching for her heels. Panic seized her, and she clung to the rock face, unable to carry on.

'Help!' she screamed, knowing no one would hear. 'Help me!'

Waves hit the rocks around her, splashing white foam on to her legs like splattered milk. The gush and roar of the sea thundered in her ears and she wondered how long it would take for a wave to sweep her away, dragging her under the water. She thought of Mother, sitting down soon for lunch and tutting at Talia's empty seat. Only then would they realize that she was gone, her study books left open on the floor in her bedchamber. They would check the kitchens, the gardens, the battlements, and last of all – with a sinking dread in their stomachs – they would think of the sea. But it would be too late.

'Help!' she screeched, pressing her cheek against the rough, solid rock face.

There was no point trying to swim. As soon as she let go of the rock, she knew the tide would snatch her away. She could feel it now, pulling on her skirts as the waves crashed against her, turning them sodden and heavy. She squeezed her eyes shut and wished she had never tried to climb The Mountain, today or ever.

'Hello? Hello!'

Talia opened her eyes, wondering if she had really heard a voice. 'Hello there!'

She turned her head and saw a wooden fishing boat bobbing on the choppy grey waves. Leaning over the bow was an old man, frantically gesturing to her. Behind him was a younger man, holding an oar and a coil of rope.

'We can't get closer, girlie,' yelled the old man over the slurp and boom of the waves. 'You need to swim for the rope!' He turned and called behind him, 'It's a child! Quickly, throw her the end.'

Talia had taught herself to splash and float in the sea, but she had never ventured into deep waters.

'Be careful of the rocks!' shouted the old man.

She saw the end of the rope fly through the air towards her like a swooping gull and hit the water with a smack.

'Hurry!'

Talia took a deep breath and pushed herself into the sea, prising her fingers off the rock face. She felt the tide grab her instantly, pulling her away.

'Swim! Swim harder!'

A wave crashed over her head and salty water choked her throat. She was thrown sideways and her left leg smacked against a rock, something sharp scraping the skin. She kicked and punched blindly through the icy, dark waters and gasped as a current tossed her to the surface.

'The rope! Grab the rope!'

Talia forced her eyes open – stinging with salt – and saw the knotted end of the rope beside her. She reached for it, seizing the end and holding on tight just as another wave pulled her under again. The pointy edge of a rock smacked her shoulder and she felt a surge of pain. Then the rope was towing her, and she was being dragged along and up to the surface. She felt cold air on her cheeks and she coughed and spluttered, gasping for breath.

'Pull her in! Get her into the boat!'

'I can't!' snapped another voice. 'I'm trying to get us away from the rocks!'

Talia's head smacked against something hard and she yelped.

Spinning on to her front, she saw the wooden hull of the fishing boat.

The old man reached over the side and grabbed her arm, wrenching her up. She fell, sodden and cold, into the bottom of the boat.

'Grab the other oars and help me!'

The old man slapped Talia on the back until she was coughing and retching up seawater, then he ran to the oars.

Relief flooded through Talia, even as she spluttered and gagged, while her body throbbed with pain. She had her palms pressed against the reassuring, solid bottom of the boat, staring down at the scratches and whorls in the wood. But the euphoria coursing through her was quickly followed by dread, knowing the scolding that lay in store back at the castle. Even her mother would be upset.

'That's it!' cried the old man. 'We're pulling away!'

Talia looked up to see both men rowing frantically in unison, heaving the boat away from the rocks. Then, suddenly, she remembered.

'Iver!' she cried, scrambling on to her knees and peering over the side of the boat.

'Is there someone else?' called the old man.

Talia scanned the waves, but there was no sign of her friend. She looked back at the peak of The Mountain – now just a thin mound of craggy rocks rising from the sea – but he was not there.

'I can't see a soul,' said the other man. 'Was there someone else?'

Talia took one last look at the churning grey waves then shook her head. The problem with Iver was no one else could see him.

'Wait a moment, I think . . . I think that's *her*,' she heard the young man whisper.

Talia's teeth started chattering and she slumped back down into the boat, hugging her knees to her chest. She could feel both men's eyes on her and she hung her head to hide the tears sliding over her cheeks.

'Yes, you're right.'

'Whatever would make her venture out here?'

There was a pause, then the old man said, 'Loneliness.'

Talia sniffed and covered her ears with her hands so that she would not hear any more.

Sel

Turow, South-west Bavaugh

SEL STEPPED INSIDE the village chapel and glanced around. When she was satisfied that it was empty, she pushed the hood of her cloak back from her face and wiped her boots on the mat.

Beside her, Briar tugged on her hand and said, 'Can I look at the pictures?'

Sel nodded. 'But stay—'

'Where you can see me,' Briar finished. 'I will.'

Sel released Briar's hand and watched as the little girl scampered over to the stained-glass windows, her rag doll tucked under her arm. Briar stopped beneath a depiction of the realm seas in bright greens and blues and stood on tiptoes to trace the leaded joins within her reach. As usual, she began babbling under her breath and Sel smiled. She had once asked Briar what she was doing and Briar had replied indignantly, 'Telling Dolly Emly stories. She's heard them all before, but she still asks every time.'

Sel's boots tapped on the flagstones as she walked down the aisle of the chapel to the altar. In her hands she carried a single snowdrop, picked by Briar from the hedgerow outside. She placed the snowdrop in the holder beside the charred remains of the other remembrance blooms and struck one of the matches. The flame caught the tip of a white petal, and the flower began to burn.

'Florentina,' Sel whispered, and she closed her eyes and thought of her old Master. She pushed away memories of Florentina in her last days: bony frame, vacant expression and trembling hands. Instead, she remembered her as she had been in her prime: wavy white hair squirrelling down her back, dark eyes flashing and a wry smile on her lips. 'Florentina,' she repeated. 'Thank you.'

A door to the side of the chapel creaked open and Sel jumped. She was ready to leave, but she stopped when she recognized the rounded, smiling face coming towards her.

'Good morning, Arla,' said Paleen, bobbing her head in greeting. 'And good morning, Briar,' she called to the back of the chapel.

Briar looked over her shoulder and waved.

'It's good to catch you,' added Paleen, drawing nearer. 'I often see the remembrance blooms here, but I always seem to miss you. How're things at the schoolhouse?'

Her eyes twinkled up at Sel beneath thick locks of pale hair. Paleen's small, plump stature and unruly, wiry mane always reminded Sel of the miniature Diaspass mountain ponies that fine ladies in her homeland sometimes kept as pets.

'This season we have the most students we've ever had at the schoolhouse,' replied Sel. 'Many of them are girls.'

Paleen beamed. 'That's tremendous! I knew you would flourish in that role. I'm sure those children learn twice as fast under your teaching.'

'Lady Houstal is the headmistress—'

'Oh, please, Arla! Lady Houstal generously gives her time to the schoolhouse, but everyone knows you're the reason it is so successful of late.'

Sel blushed and scuffed her boots against one another.

'I knew I was blessed from the moment I saw you,' Paleen continued. 'When would it have been? I make it almost five winters gone. You were standing right over there, weren't you?' Paleen pointed to the entrance of the chapel. 'It was a wet, cold day and you were dripping all over the floor, but I thought to myself, *Is that there an angel?*' Her eyes drifted to the shining, golden head of Briar, standing beneath the stained-glass windows, bathed in shattered, coloured light. 'An angel,' she repeated softly under her breath.

Sel also remembered that dark winter evening, running into the chapel, dragging Briar behind her, desperate for somewhere to shelter from the rain. She had even thought they might stay and sleep on the pews that night – it would have been a great improvement on curling up under bushes. She had been wringing out her dark hair while Briar toddled back and forth over the flagstones when Paleen had appeared from the study, just as she had now.

'You've always been very kind to us—'

'Nonsense! None of that,' cried Paleen, waving away Sel's words. 'You've brought nothing but goodness to Turow.'

Sel's eyes fell on the battered book in Paleen's arms. 'Is that the volume of collected poems from the Central Realm?'

'Yes, it is. You've caught me reading it again, Arla.'

'You have good taste.'

'As my husband says, I like to fill my head with pretty nonsense. But it's his book and if he really objected to me reading it, then he shouldn't have it in his collection.'

'I'm sure he doesn't mind,' replied Sel, thinking of the silvery-haired, quiet minister, who spent most of his time letting his wife speak for him.

Paleen shrugged. 'While I'm here, would you like to borrow from his collection too? It's been so long since you did. Do you remember when you were staying with us and we would read aloud to each other in the evenings?'

Sel nodded. Before moving into the schoolhouse, she and Briar had stayed at the minister's house under the generous hospitality of Paleen and her husband. Those evenings in Paleen's company – sitting in the parlour while Paleen spun at her wheel – had been a precious balm to Sel at a time when she had felt broken and weary with life.

'I'm sure you're busy with your teaching,' Paleen continued. 'But it might be nice to have something to read for pleasure again.'

'Thank you, I'd like that.'

'Wonderful! I'll leave the study unlocked and when you've finished your remembrance, you can choose something.' Paleen glanced at the charred remains of the snowdrop. 'You're so attentive in honouring your late sister.'

Sel scratched her wrist and looked at the floor.

'You must have loved her very much.'

When Sel did not reply, Paleen clasped her hands and added, 'I'll go and chat to your lovely niece while you finish. I'm almost done making Dolly Emly a new dress and I need to ask her if she wants a lace collar or a beaded trim.'

'You're so kind.'

'Please, I enjoy it. There is nothing more beautiful in the Great Creator's realm than little girls. Especially Briar.'

Sel smiled and waited until Paleen had bustled past her. When

Paleen and Briar were deep in conversation about Dolly Emly's petticoat lengths, Sel turned back to the remembrance bloom. She closed her eyes and repeated in a low whisper, 'Florentina. Florentina, am I doing the right thing?'

Five winters ago, after killing a man, Sel had found herself standing, silent and panicking, in the alleyway in Dawvin. With her heart thundering in her chest and her body trembling, she had looked down at Pyke's lifeless, contorted body and realized she had just used magic when she had promised the Queen she would not. Would the sorceress be able to sense powerful magic so close to her own spell? Or perhaps someone else in Bavaugh would detect it. Maybe Sel had revealed everything. She had put Briar and herself in danger and she knew they would have to disappear. Quickly.

In a haze of terror, Sel had hauled Pyke's crumpled body to the dockside and dumped it into the waters before fleeing Dawvin that night. She had spent the next few seasons with Briar on the road. Making their way inland at first, Sel had worked as a fruit picker, washermaid and general dogsbody to get by – anything that kept them fed and moving. By the time autumn came around again, Sel had managed to convince herself that no one was after them and veered south-west, back towards Bavaugh's coast. Those nights on the road, when she often slept rough with her arms wrapped around Briar and her cloak pulled over their heads, exhausted and fearful, she remembered her Master. Before then, she had thought often of her old life – the books, the copious amounts of coffee, the warm townhouse, the study of magic – but she had not allowed herself to think of Florentina. It was too painful. Her Master, who had plucked her from the streets of Fakcil and taught her the power of magic, was gone. Struck by a sickness that was sudden and uncurable. Sel had turned their library upside down trying to find a healing spell, but nothing had worked. Florentina would say that she had returned to the hands of the Great Creator.

In front of Sel, the snowdrop had burnt to nothing, tendrils of smoke curling from the ashes. She wished she could ask her old Master for advice. She had found her way to some kind of life in Turow, teaching and living simply at the schoolhouse, but it was not the future either of them had imagined for her and she did not know when it would end – there had been no contact from the Queen and there were still ten winters left until the end of the curse. Sel should have been travelling the Central Realm, gathering further magical studies and conferring with other Masters, not living buried in a tiny seaside town in some small, backward kingdom.

Sometimes Sel wondered if she should leave. Just turn and walk away without looking back. Catch a ship bound for her homeland. But even in her darkest moments, she could not do it. Sel was perpetually lonely but never alone – Briar was always there, like a golden shadow, needing and wanting her endlessly. Sel could not leave her.

Sometimes, late at night, Sel wondered if there was a way *she* could reverse the principles of the magic, or a counter-enchantment to break the curse. She searched her memory for old lessons on spell formation and tried to remember if she had ever read of a similar study, but even if she were a proper Master, Sel was not sure she would be able to manage such a thing. The more time she spent with Briar, close to the core of the spell, the more she worried that even the Diaspass Masters would not be able to unwind the intricacies of the magic. Briar's curse was dark and complex, full of energy and thickly tangled. To disturb it could endanger their lives, not to mention draw attention to their whereabouts from the very person they were trying to avoid.

'Auntie! Auntie, look!'

The cry jolted Sel from her thoughts and she turned to see Briar scampering over, her perfect pink lips curved in a smile.

'Paleen gave me this!' Briar held aloft a red velvet ribbon.

'That's very generous, but we can't—'

'No, please,' said Paleen. 'I chose it especially.' Then she added quietly, 'I always wished for a little girl to spoil with pretty things.'

'It's mine, Auntie,' said Briar, tightening her grasp on the ribbon. 'I don't have any nice things.'

It was true, and Sel felt a sting of guilt as she nodded.

'Come over here,' Paleen called. 'I'll tie it in your hair now.'

With a squeal of delight, Briar hurried off and she and Paleen headed to the pews at the side of the chapel.

Sel turned back to the remembrance bloom, but all that was left were feathery grey ashes. She sighed. Looking up at the velvet drapes strung across the apse, she wondered if perhaps her old Master was watching her right now and Sel was not as lost and alone as she felt.

'Florentina . . .' she murmured, imagining her Master's long white hair and dark eyes. 'Florentina, what will become of us?'

Meredyth

The Castle, Mont Isle

MEREDYTH WAS TOLD upon arrival at Mont Isle that the Queen was in the chapel. She nodded her thanks to the attendant who delivered the message and asked him to send word that she would be waiting for the Queen in the gardens. She still had nightmares about blood on a stone floor, black smoke clogging her lungs and a pair of piercing eyes glaring through the darkness. She did not want to go to the chapel.

But the man dithered, biting at a thumbnail before replying, 'She'll be in there all morning, Your Ladyship. She always is.'

'Then I will wait in the gardens until she is ready,' replied Meredyth, grimacing at an ache in her hips. The pain had started the night she set out on the road and had only grown sharper throughout her journey. 'Just tell her I am here.'

'But—'

'Enough. I will go to my rooms to change. Have a maid sent to aid me.'

Meredyth turned and limped away before the man could protest again.

Inside the castle, she waited to be met by a serving maid, but no one appeared. With her brow furrowing, she made her own way to the guest chambers, peering down dark corridors and into empty rooms. Trails of dust collected at the edges of her skirts and in one passageway she stepped over a dead rat lying stiff in the middle of the floor.

When she reached the musty guest chambers, a maid came scurrying in, clearly little more than a kitchen girl. Meredyth swallowed her sigh of exasperation and tried to bark clear, simple orders. Even so, she practically dressed herself, since the maid's fingers fumbled with the ties and knotted the laces. Finally changed into fresh, clean clothes, Meredyth dismissed the grateful kitchen girl and left the chambers.

As soon as she stepped outside, she saw that the gardens were in a sorrier state than the castle. Hedges sprawled across the paths and weeds filled the flower beds. Meredyth was standing beside a dry fountain crusted with moss, kicking at a thistle that had attached itself to her skirts, when she heard someone clear their throat.

She turned and stopped short in surprise to see the Queen. Once they had spent every day together and now it had been many winters since they had last spoken. The Queen was thinner and greyer, but she was still as familiar a figure as Meredyth's own kin. Meredyth would have cried out in joy to see her, but the Queen was bent low in a mocking curtsey.

'You summoned me, Your Ladyship.'

'Long live Queen Violanna of Bavaugh,' Meredyth said quickly.

Her arms fluttered at her sides, longing to embrace her friend. 'I did not mean an impertinence, Your Majesty—'

'There is no need for that address. I am no longer a Queen.'

Meredyth hid her surprise by dropping into a low curtsey of her own. 'You are still my Queen,' she replied. 'And I will address you accordingly.'

The Queen's collar was frayed and there were trailing threads on her bodice. Meredyth almost felt a little embarrassed in her own lace-trimmed burgundy dress, cut in the latest shape and made especially for this visit.

'Your Majesty—'

'I said do not call me that!'

Meredyth stepped forward and laid a hand on the Queen's shoulder. 'I do not wish to quarrel,' she said. 'I asked to meet you out here because that chapel . . . I still have nightmares about it.'

'So do I.'

'Then why go there—'

'It is the only place I feel at peace.'

Meredyth's fingers squeezed the Queen's gaunt shoulder. She could see that her friend was hurting. 'I cannot imagine what these seasons have been like for you,' she said. 'I wish I could have come sooner, but it was difficult after the announcement of . . . the King's new wife. It would not have benefitted either of us if I had visited then. Later, I wanted to come, but I was struck by my own tragedy.'

The Queen's face softened. 'I was greatly saddened to hear about Jenolie. I wanted to send a tribute but . . .' She gestured around them. 'I have no means of my own.'

'It cheered me to receive a letter from you. Finally.'

'How do you fare now?' asked the Queen.

Tears prickled Meredyth's eyes. 'It is a blow for a mother to lose a child, whatever their age. Jenolie rests now with her baby in the hands of the Great Creator,' said Meredyth, fighting to keep her voice steady. 'Though it happened almost two winters ago, I have not yet recovered and I do not know if I ever will. I was there at the birth, trying to help, but the labour was long and Jenolie had grown too weak . . .'

They fell quiet.

'And Lord Lansin?' asked the Queen. 'How is your husband?'

Meredyth shrugged, tears escaping across her cheeks that she briskly swept aside. 'He never concerned himself much with the children. We have three grown sons and ten grandchildren, so he cannot understand why I am not content with that.'

'I understand.'

Meredyth sniffed. 'I have missed you, Your Majesty. You have never been far from my thoughts. Do you remember when you first arrived in this kingdom and you could barely speak a word of Bavaughian? We used to mime things to each other.'

'I remember.'

'When did we get so old?' sighed Meredyth.

'You have always been old.'

Meredyth pretended to slap the Queen's hand and they both laughed.

'Let us walk and talk,' said Meredyth. 'My old, crusty joints are getting stiff standing still like this.'

She hooked her arm through the Queen's and they began walking side by side down the gravel path, long grasses and bracken brushing their skirts. It was this rekindled friendship that Meredyth had imagined on her journey to Mont Isle. It was for this reason that she had come.

'What news from court?' asked the Queen.

Meredyth glanced sideways, but her friend's expression was blank. Having finally caught a glimpse of the Queen Violanna that she knew and loved, she did not want to spoil it, but she supposed that news would reach Mont Isle eventually.

'Hana has lost another child.'

'What a shame,' said the Queen lightly. 'You would think two sons would be enough for Felipe to leave the poor girl alone.' Before Meredyth could reply, she added, 'I heard Prince Dionathy's Appointment ceremony was quite the spectacle. Four days of celebration in Lustore. I suppose you attended?'

'As a courtier, it was my duty.'

'How lovely for Felipe. The sons he always wanted.'

Meredyth cleared her throat. 'I could not help wondering where it now leaves you and the Princess, Your Majesty?'

Meredyth had watched little Prince Dionathy crowned heir to the Bavaughian throne, and she had thought of Queen Violanna – her true Queen – willingly exiled to this small, bleak island. As far as the Royal Court was concerned, Queen Violanna and her cursed daughter were as good as dead. Out of sight and out of mind.

'It leaves us forgotten and safe – for now,' replied the Queen.

'But the curse, Your Majesty? What is to be done about it?'

Queen Violanna was a few steps ahead on the garden path and Meredyth noticed her shoulders stiffen.

'Have you appealed to your homeland, Your Majesty?'

'Of course I have! Again and again. There has been no response.'

'But your other daughter—'

'Meredyth, I do not wish to speak of this!' snapped Queen Violanna, quickening her pace, almost as if to escape. 'I have tried everything I can think of and . . . I do not know what else I can do.'

'What have you told Princess Talia?'

'Nothing! I have told her none of it.'

Meredyth bit back a yelp of alarm. 'You mean . . . the Princess does not know about anything? Even the curse?'

The Queen slowed to a walk and then stopped still. 'How could I tell her?' she whispered.

Meredyth wanted to retort, *How could you not?* But she stopped herself. 'Perhaps there is something I can do while I am here?' she replied instead.

Queen Violanna shook her head. 'You do not know what you are talking about, Meredyth!'

'But—'

'I said I do not wish to speak of any of this! Please. It is like torture.'

Reluctantly Meredyth fell quiet.

They carried on walking, listening to the screech of gulls whirling above them and the steady rumble of the returning sea on the other side of the walls.

'Anyway, *I* am looking forward to seeing Princess Talia,' said Meredyth. 'How is her schooling? Does she show musical promise?'

The Queen's eyes dropped to the ground. 'I am not sure.'

'Oh? What does her governess say?'

'She . . . has no governess.'

Meredyth tried not to betray her surprise. 'So you teach her yourself, Your Majesty?'

'No. I am not in her company often, except at mealtimes. It is difficult for me to . . . I mean, I find it difficult not to think of . . .' The Queen trailed off, wringing her hands.

She was beginning to look sullen and distant again, and Meredyth did not want them to bicker.

'Has Princess Talia started any lessons?' Meredyth asked carefully. 'Perhaps you would allow me to engage a governess for her?'

'I have no means with which to keep one!' cried the Queen, rounding on her. 'Look at this place – look at me!' She grabbed at the faded skirts of her dress, holding them up. 'I am no longer a Queen. I am a . . . well, there is not a word for what I am now.'

'This cannot continue,' said Meredyth. 'Would you allow me to appeal on your behalf?'

At first Meredyth thought the Queen was going to protest, but then she threw up her hands and said, 'So be it!'

Meredyth smiled. 'It is decided, then. After my stay, I will return to the capital and appeal to the King.' She paused before adding, 'But now, if you would allow it, Your Majesty, I would like to see the Princess.'

Talia

The Parlour, Mont Isle

TALIA STUDIED THE elegant woman standing on the opposite side of the room. She had never seen someone so well dressed and neat before, and she could not help but stare. The woman was wearing a cherry-coloured gown that fell in an exaggerated dome shape from her hips, with sparkling beads studding the hemline and white lace frothing from the wrists. Her dark hair, streaked with silver, was gathered up into an intricate pile on top of her head, and a large diamond matrimony band winked from her ear. She looked as though she had stepped from one of the portraits in the Great Hall.

'It is a pleasure to meet you again, Princess,' said the woman, dropping into a low curtsey. 'You will not remember me; you were a baby when I last visited. A sweet little thing and not a big girl of six winters.'

Talia's mouth fell open. She glanced uncertainly at her mother, who was seated beside the open window, but her mother's expression was as unreadable to her as ever.

'My name is Lady Lansin, but I would be honoured if you would call me Meredyth, Princess,' said the woman. 'The Queen is an old, dear friend of mine.'

'The Queen?' said Talia, her brow puckering.

'That is right.'

'My mother is not the Queen.'

Mother flinched and Talia felt annoyed. To be in the presence of her mother was like playing a game without knowing the rules. You were always bound to do something wrong, and it was easier just to say nothing. But Talia knew that she was right; she had recently overheard some of the kitchen girls say that the real Queen lived in the royal palace at Lustore and her mother was just a 'cast-off'.

'And I'm not a Princess,' she added, her frustration growing. 'I'm a . . . a bastard.'

Meredyth's eyes bulged slightly, but she merely smiled.

'A *bastard*,' Talia repeated, waiting for the reprimand she was sure would follow such an outburst. Dottie had threatened to box her ears when she said that word the other day and Talia did not doubt that the old maid would go through with it. 'That's what I am,' Talia added. 'A *bastard*.' She folded her arms.

There was a pause.

'Whoever told you that is sorely mistaken, Princess,' replied Meredyth. 'You are the firstborn daughter of the King of Bavaugh and your mother is a Princess of the Diaspass Kingdom, formerly the Queen of Bavaugh. There are those – like myself – who would say she still is the true Queen, but regardless, your parenthood makes you a Princess.'

Talia regarded Meredyth with mingled awe and suspicion.

'Now, I have ordered some tea and I would like it if you would sit with us,' said Meredyth. 'It is the custom of the ladies of the court to take tea mid-morning and I would like you to get into the habit of it also.'

It was difficult to defy Meredyth's clear, commanding tone and Talia found herself drifting towards a faded brocade chair. 'But Mother's in the chapel every day until noon,' she said.

Meredyth and Mother glanced at each other, then Mother said, 'Fine. We will take tea mid-morning and I will attend chapel afterwards.'

Talia had never heard her mother speak like that to anyone before – so offhand and intimate. Mother mostly muttered commands at the servants, or otherwise stayed silent, staring into the distance, looking sad. Talia had once asked Mother why she was upset, but it had only made Mother purse her lips and look sadder, so Talia had decided it was better to say nothing.

'The Queen tells me that you study your books in the mornings, Princess?' said Meredyth. 'I would love to hear what you are learning.'

Talia sat on her hands and kicked her legs back and forth, her slippers scuffing on the dusty rug. 'Umm ... I've been reading about tree cycles and insect anatomy.'

'The library here is not exactly well stocked,' said Mother.

'That sounds like ... a good start to me,' replied Meredyth brightly. 'Any languages?'

Talia blinked.

'Mathematics? Have you been practising drawing? Needlework?'

Talia shook her head. She saw Meredyth's eyes flick down to her kicking legs and she stilled.

'No matter, Princess. A blank slate is a good start.'

The door opened and Dottie bustled into the room, carrying a tray set with tea, the cups and saucers rattling. Talia jumped up to help guide the old woman to the table and together they set the tray down. She only noticed Meredyth's stunned expression after Dottie had stooped into a creaky curtsey and left the room.

'Princess, you are not to help the servants!'

'But Dottie's leg hurts her and—'

'In that case, perhaps we ought to engage some new staff.'

'No!' snapped Talia with a flash of panic. Dottie had been her attendant ever since she could remember, tucking her into bed each night and regaling her with ballads of maidens, dragons and ghosts. Most of the other servants kept their distance. 'If I *am* a Princess, then you have to do what I say, and I say no.'

Meredyth paused, then slowly smiled. 'So you can act like a Princess when you want to,' she replied. 'This is good.'

Talia reached for the teapot, but Meredyth waved her hand away.

'No, Princess, it is my job to serve you when we are in company.'

Talia rolled her eyes and slumped back in her chair. She suspected that this was also not befitting a Princess, so she sank even lower, waiting to be reprimanded, while Meredyth poured out their tea.

'What else occupies your time, Princess?' asked Meredyth, handing her a cup and saucer, and ignoring her sagging posture. 'What do you do each day?'

Talia suspected that telling Meredyth she often hung around the servants' quarters would not go down well. But she liked being in the deep roots of the castle, stealing a spoon of honey from the kitchens, watching Dottie fold laundry and sneaking pats of chilled butter from the larder that melted in her mouth and dribbled down her chin. If she was not in the lower quarters of the castle, then she was tearing across the battlements, the wind whipping at her hair, or hiding in the old dovecote at the top of the east turret, despite the fact that no one was trying to find her.

'Do you go outside?' persisted Meredyth. 'Is there anyone that you play with?'

Talia thought of Iver, who had not returned since they had tried to climb The Mountain last summer. She missed her friend.

'I'm not allowed out of the castle walls,' she said.

'Oh?'

'There was an incident,' said Mother and then reluctantly continued after a pause. 'Talia was caught by the tides and pulled out to sea. She was rescued by a fishing boat.'

Meredyth blanched and Talia thought she looked genuinely concerned. 'That is most distressing to hear,' she said. 'Princess, do you walk on the beach or visit the mainland?'

Talia shook her head.

'She must stay at the castle,' said Mother.

'Then perhaps we could schedule some walks around the gardens instead?' said Meredyth. 'It is my belief that everyone – children and adults alike – benefits from fresh air.'

Talia glared at her. 'How long are you going to be here?' she asked.

'Talia!' hissed Mother, in a rare burst of chiding. Normally Mother did not notice when Talia was being naughty, even if Talia was doing it on purpose. Last summer, when Talia had returned to the castle on the fishing boat, soaked and shivering, her mother had only said, 'You must be more careful,' before disappearing off to the chapel for the rest of the day. It was Dottie who had given Talia a proper scolding, hugging her in relief and shouting at her in fury all at once.

'I was planning to stay for a moon or so,' said Meredyth. 'If that would be acceptable to Your Majesty?'

'You can stay as long as you please, Meredyth,' said Mother.

'Then you'll leave?' asked Talia.

'Talia!'

'Yes, then I will need to return to court,' replied Meredyth, unruffled.

'To court?' echoed Talia, sitting up straight. 'You go to court?'

'Yes—'

'Do you know the King?'

'I do,' replied Meredyth slowly.

'What's he like? Do you think I look like him?'

Talia had asked all the servants at Mont Isle many times over the seasons to tell her what they knew about the King – those who would talk to her, anyway. But they all mostly said the same things: it had been a long time since they had served the King, and when they had, it had only been for a short time while he summered on the island. Everyone agreed that he was a handsome man – tall, fair-haired and a talented sportsman.

'Have you met my brothers?' Talia continued, the questions tumbling out of her hungrily. 'Do they look like me? I want to write to them, but Dottie says no.'

'Well, I—'

'Do you know why I've got to live in this castle?' continued Talia, leaning forward. 'Do you know why my father's never visited me?'

Mother stood up abruptly, knocking the edge of the table with her skirts and making the teapot rattle. 'I do not feel well,' she said. 'I will retire to my rooms until luncheon.'

Talia watched as Mother hurried from the room, hands clasped tightly in front of her. She had upset Mother *again*. She should not have said all of that about her father and her brothers, but she could not help it. She did not understand why her mother was a 'cast-off' Queen or why they did not live in the Lustore palace with the rest of the royal family. The little Talia did know, she had wheedled out of Dottie over time, but it was not enough.

When they were alone, Meredyth said, 'Princess, while I am here, I will be implementing some changes to ensure you are raised as you should be. With that in mind, I do have a few more questions.'

Talia dragged her eyes away from the empty doorway and sighed.

'Princess, can you ride?'

'Sort of. The stable boys say I'll get better if I practise.'

'It is "I will" not "I'll", Princess. Clearly you have spent too long in the company of the servants.'

Talia narrowed her eyes. 'When did you say you're leaving again?' she asked.

Meredyth snorted into her cup of tea, before quickly regaining her composure. 'You know, in some ways you do remind me of your father,' she replied.

Sel

Turow, South-west Bavaugh

SEL STOOD IN the doorway of the schoolhouse, watching the children file out into the afternoon sunshine. She could feel patches of dampness under her arms and beads of sweat trickling down the small of her back. It was proving to be an unusually hot Bavaughian summer, almost like the summers of Sel's childhood in Fakcil, and her uniform of high-necked, long-sleeved dresses in dark colours – passed on to her by Paleen – was not suited to such weather. She was already looking forward to the evening when she could escape to the beach and paddle in the sea.

'Thank you, Mam Arla!' the children cried as they scampered past her. They kicked up the brown dust with their bare feet and pushed and pulled one another with giggles and yelps of joy.

Sel waited until the last child had dashed off down the path in the direction of Turow's town, before turning back inside. She walked down the hallway, reaching behind her head to unpin her hair from the tight coil at the nape of her neck. Then she trudged into her classroom and began wiping down the blackboard. She was just about to collect the slates when she heard a tread from the narrow staircase at the end of the room.

'Can I come down?' called Briar.

'Yes, I'd like some help with the tidying.'

Sel heard faint grumbling noises, but Briar appeared moments later with a broom, her sweet, angelic face smiling. She started at the far side of the room beside the window and the buttery, hot light shone on her head so that her braided hair glowed like gold.

'You don't need to sweep over there,' said Sel. 'It's dustier over here.'

'But this bit is dirty.'

'Come away from the window,' said Sel before she could stop herself.

Briar instantly stopped mid-sweep. The air around her rippled for a moment and she turned away abruptly, a look of frustration and confusion on her face. Magic wafted like smoke through the room.

'Thank you, Briar,' gushed Sel, hoping to distract the child. 'You're so good.'

Briar's lip quivered as if she might cry in bewilderment, but then she gulped and began sweeping again.

Sel pretended to busy herself with wiping down the desks, but she watched Briar from the corner of her eye. The little girl seemed calm, all thoughts of the last moment forgotten. When Briar started to hum, Sel breathed a sigh of relief. She had not slipped up like that in a while; it was because she was hot and tired. She must be more careful.

Briar was spellbound to obey commands whether she wanted to

or not, although Sel doubted that was what Gnoxhall Weathernull the Dignified had had in mind when he had bestowed the gift of obedience at the Blessing. Royal Blessing gifts were meant to be only gentle enhancements – deeper dimples, a sweeter voice, greater discernment – that lasted a few winters before fading away, but Briar's curse had magnified everything. The twisted, evil intent of the sorceress's spell was aggravating and inflating the Blessing gifts. Or that was what Sel suspected. She wished she could remember all the Masters' gifts, but the day of the Blessing was now a blurred, panic-stricken memory. Every so often, another talent would suddenly make itself known, such as when Briar had said she liked speaking to house mice because they told good jokes, or when Paleen had taught Briar her favourite hymn and then gaped in awe at the pure, melodious sound the child emitted. Since then, Sel had encouraged Briar to keep her animal observations to herself, and to hum instead of singing.

'Did you finish the sums I set you?' asked Sel, putting the last chair straight.

'Yes.'

'What about the writing exercises?'

Briar threw back her head and moaned. 'It's too hot in the attic for thinking!'

At times like this, Sel wished she had been able to bestow her own gift of wisdom on Briar at the Blessing. The girl was not exactly the most capable or diligent student.

'I want to be in the classroom with the other children.'

'You know that's not possible—'

'*Because I'm learning different things*,' Briar mimicked.

Sel had told Briar that she was tackling more advanced studies and needed to stay away from the other students, but the girl would surely not swallow such excuses for ever. Sel did not know what would happen then.

'Auntie, I have an idea,' added Briar. 'I could do the same lessons as everyone else *and* my other work.'

'No, Briar.'

'Then I could study my extra lessons in the evenings like you do.'

Sel could not perform magic so she had started studying it instead, spending her evenings reading magical books. She had started before they arrived in Turow, while she and Briar – still a toddling baby then – had been travelling through the Bavaughian country-side, living hand-to-mouth. They had been walking through a village market, picking up food for breakfast, when Sel had seen a pile of dusty books on a stall. She could not resist wandering over to look through them while the seller explained they were from a house clearance. At the bottom of the pile was a dictionary of Nov-took symbols – outdated and in poor condition, but Sel did not care. Her hands had fallen on it hungrily, her lips breaking into a grin of delight. She had purchased it immediately for half a silver fleck and pored over its contents for days after, not caring about the cost, or the extra weight it added to her pack.

From then on, she had continued to look for more magical books, gathering a small collection. They were mostly battered and old, but Sel did not mind. She studied in the evenings after her day of teaching was done, slowly rebuilding the knowledge from her apprenticeship. Her studies were not on a par with Masterhood training, but it was better than nothing. Florentina had always chided her for being too focused on practical application and not taking the time to learn translation, theory and principles, so Sel reassured herself that she was redressing that balance. Her old Master would be pleased.

In all her reading, Sel hunted for the principles of longer spells and anything resembling the curse wound around Briar. Though she could not quite remember all the gifts bestowed at the Blessing, Sel had no trouble recalling the sorceress's curse:

Before seventeen winters have passed, I will return for you. On that day, the spell will end and you will die.

Sel had some half-dream that she would stumble upon that unique type of spell in her reading, but she knew such a thing was unlikely. The magic bound to the girl was too dark and complex and only becoming more so as time passed. Even if Sel did discover passages alluding to similar spells, she could not attempt to disturb or unpick the curse alone; it would be too dangerous. But she kept hoping that she might uncover something. If she read and studied hard enough, perhaps she could find a way to stop the curse – or at least lessen it.

'Auntie, we're all done tidying now,' said Briar, after a pause. She carried the broom back to the cupboard. 'Can we go down to the beach?'

'Later. You should complete your writing exercises first.'

'But that'll take ages!'

Sel bent and kissed the top of Briar's warm head. 'Let's go upstairs and I'll help you. We can go to the beach when—'

'When it's getting dark and no one else is there,' finished Briar, rolling her eyes.

With a prickle of guilt, Sel ushered the girl to the stairs. She did not like keeping Briar shut away, but she did not know what else to do. It was not just her strange, enchanted abilities and remarkable beauty that marked Briar as different; magic clung to the girl's very being, seeming to increase with each winter as the gifts bestowed on her at the Blessing ripened. It had not been like that when she was a baby. There had been a certain other-worldliness to Briar in infancy, but, as the girl matured, it was developing into something distinctly magical. Often Sel found it almost unbearable, to have all that crackling power forever present that she must ignore. It was like an itch that begged to be scratched.

And Sel knew that if she could feel it, then surely others could, too.

Briar

Turow, South-west Bavaugh

THE EVENING SKY was a chalky pink haze that seeped into the horizon until it met the shimmering blue line of the sea. Though the sun was setting, it was still warm, and the air was ripe with the smell of seaweed baked on hot sand. It made Briar's nose wrinkle and her throat burn as she raced towards the shore, skidding and sliding across the beach. She was desperate to cool her ankles in the waters and splash in the waves.

'Be careful!' Auntie called from behind her, but Briar was barely listening. She had spent a sweltering day in the attic of the school-house, battling through sums and daydreaming of this moment.

She screeched in joy as her bare feet pattered across the drenched sand and rushed into the shallow waters. It was instantly cooling, and she lifted her dress higher to stride deeper until the sea sloshed around her knees.

'If you go any further, you'll get your dress all wet and salt-stained,' warned Auntie, catching up with her.

But when Briar looked over her shoulder, Auntie was inching deeper into the sea too, her face softening with relief. She had unpinned her hair, as she always did at the end of the day, and it floated in a black sheet down her back, a breeze gently plucking at the ends so that they twirled around her elbows. Briar loved Auntie's dark hair, which was so different from her own. She liked to put their heads together in the evenings, while Auntie was reading one of her beloved books, and braid their locks together to create a two-tone plait.

'It feels so nice!' Briar cried, marching back and forth, kicking the water into big splashes. The hem of her dress was already soaked, and she knew she would have to help Auntie scrub it later, but she was too happy to care.

She carried on like that for some time, splashing and playing until the pink was fading from the sky and the daylight was disappearing.

'Auntie,' she called, wading back to shore. 'I need to choose a shell.'

Auntie opened one eye. She was standing with her face turned towards the horizon, eyes closed, breathing deeply. 'All right,' she said. 'Just one.'

Briar had a growing collection of shells in the attic of the schoolhouse that she often catalogued and rearranged when she was supposed to be studying.

'I need a big swirly one,' said Briar.

Auntie made a *hmm* noise. She called this her 'resting time' and Briar tried hard not to disturb her in such moments. With teaching all day and studying late into the evenings, Auntie always seemed to be yawning or rubbing her head.

Briar scampered along the shoreline, her eyes fixed on the ground, scanning the sand. Every so often she crouched down to inspect a potential shell, before ultimately discarding it with a shake of her head. Only the very best shells made it into her collection.

She was so intent on her task that she did not see the horses or the boy until they were quite close. She heard a whinny and looked up in surprise as a piebald mare trotted towards her, its lead rope trailing behind it in the water.

'Hey! Wait!' cried the boy.

Briar held out her hands and the horse splashed to a halt before her, then pushed its face into her waiting palms. She grinned, rubbing its nose as it snorted warm breath at her.

'Grab it!' the boy shouted, running towards them while dragging the other horse behind him. 'Grab the rope!'

Briar's hands grasped hold of the lead rope of their own accord. The air around her turned hot and there was a popping sound that made her teeth ache. Then all was still.

'Thanks,' panted the boy, slowing to a walk as he drew nearer.

He was only a few paces away when the other horse – a bay gelding – suddenly shot forward, whipping its lead rope out of his other hand. With a bark of surprise, the boy went tumbling face-first into the shallow waters, while the gelding pranced over to Briar and rubbed its head against her chest.

'Are you all right?' asked Briar, stifling a giggle.

The boy stumbled upright, spitting out seawater. The front of his baggy breeches and worn shirt were soaked and dripping, and there was a finger of seaweed stuck to his black hair. 'Foolish animals!' he snapped, kicking one of his bare feet at the water.

'It's not their fault,' said Briar. 'All horses like me. Once, in town, a whole wagon turned around because the shire horse pulling it wanted me to scratch behind his ears.'

The boy blinked salty water droplets out of his eyes. 'So it's *your* fault, then,' he said with an accent that was fast and sharp, like those of the children Auntie taught who came to the schoolhouse from the surrounding farms.

'Suppose so,' she said, watching him curiously. He had a slight, wiry frame, a crescent of dirt under each fingernail and wide brown eyes.

'What're you staring at?'

'Don't think I've seen you before.' Briar tilted her head to one side. 'Do you come to the schoolhouse for lessons?'

'No.'

The piebald mare and bay gelding were standing beside Briar, nudging her shoulders and mouthing at her hair.

'They want carrot peelings,' she said.

'That's what I give them before bed,' replied the boy gruffly, trying to hide his surprise. 'How do you know they want that?'

Briar shrugged.

'Suppose you really are good with horses, then, huh?'

Briar nodded. 'And dogs,' she added. 'And cats. All animals.'

'You work for a horse dealer too?' he asked, wringing out the front of his shirt.

Briar laughed and the boy stared at her. 'No, I live at the schoolhouse with my aunt,' she said.

'Your laugh is funny.'

'Is it?'

'Yes. But funny in a nice way.'

Briar was relieved but she tried not to show it. She had never spoken to the children who attended the schoolhouse, though she often longed to. Sometimes she would creep down from the attic and sit on the staircase, just out of view, listening to their lessons, wondering which of them she would choose to be her best friend.

'We come here in the summer when it gets dark,' she said. 'But I haven't seen you before.'

'I came down to exercise the horses. We can't go to the other beach today cause it's all busy with people and that field up there belongs to my Mister.' The boy nodded to the far cliff beside them. Then he added, 'You really are good with horses, you know. Maple normally doesn't like no one but me. He gets the grump and it makes him hard to sell.'

Briar reached up and stroked the bay gelding's arched neck. 'What happens if the horses don't sell?' she asked.

'They get . . . sent away.'

'Where?'

Before he could reply, someone started shouting.

'Briar! Briar! What're you doing?'

Briar turned to see Auntie some distance away, hurriedly wading back to shore, shielding her eyes from the last rays of the setting sun. Briar had wandered further than she had realized looking for shells, and she could hear the panic in Auntie's voice.

'That's my aunt,' said Briar, waving to show that all was well. 'She doesn't like me talking to strangers.'

'Why?'

'She says we're private people,' replied Briar, feeling a sting of annoyance.

'I'd better go anyway,' said the boy. 'Give us the horses.'

The air around Briar quivered and before she knew what she was doing, her arm shot out and handed over the lead ropes. She blinked rapidly and shrugged her shoulders as if shaking something off.

'I told the horses to go back with you,' she said.

The boy raised his eyebrows. 'You *told* them?'

'Yes.'

'But you didn't say anything.'

'Well, they don't understand words,' said Briar, laughing again.

The boy stared at her in silence for a moment then said, 'Are you lying?'

'No!'

'What're they saying now?'

Briar glanced at the horses, who were sniffing at the salty tang of the breeze and shifting their hooves on the soft sand. 'They're just thinking about animal things.'

He watched her closely. 'Could you teach me to understand them? That would prove you weren't lying.'

Briar grinned. 'I could try,' she said. Then she had an idea and she quickly added, 'If you come here again tomorrow evening, I can show you.'

'Will your aunt let you?'

'Yes,' replied Briar, although she had already decided to say nothing to Auntie about it. Tomorrow she would finish all her sums and writing exercises perfectly and her reward would be another evening trip to the beach.

'All right, then. Deal.'

Behind her, Briar could hear Auntie still calling.

'I'm Briar,' she said. 'What's your name?'

'I'm Jacken.'

'I'll see you tomorrow, then, Jacken?'

He nodded and began pulling the horses away.

'See you!'

Briar turned and walked back towards Auntie. She could see that her aunt's face was creased with worry, but she was too excited by her encounter to feel guilty. She had just spoken to someone who was not Auntie or Paleen or the minister. Maybe if tomorrow went well, then Jacken might play a game with her – something like tag or hopscotch. That was what the girls from the school-house played during their morning break-time. She smiled to herself. Tomorrow she would return to the beach and see Jacken again. Her first friend.

Meredyth

The Palace, Lustore

MEREDYTH SMOOTHED OUT her gown and tried to ignore the
curious gazes of the Royal Guards on either side of her. She told
herself that this was nothing to be afraid of, but she could hear her
pulse thumping loudly in her ears and when she lifted her hands,
she saw that her palms had left a damp imprint on her embroidered
skirts.

The door to the Council Chamber in front of her opened and a
male servant appeared, ushering her inside.

Meredyth pulled her shoulders back and glided into the room.
Ahead of her, she could see the King, sitting on a throne upon a
marble dais hung with bright silks. Around him were red velvet
chairs arranged in a semicircle. She sank into as low a curtsey as her
hips would allow. The journey back from Mont Isle had aggravated
the weakened joints and no amount of hot lavender baths seemed to
ease the pain.

'Long live King Felipe of Bavaugh,' she said.

'You may rise, Lady Lansin.'

Meredyth gratefully pulled herself upright and raised her head to see the King looking at her with vague boredom. *Good*, she thought. She had tried to time her request for an audience with him following one of the long Royal Council meetings for the very reason that he would likely be drained and longing to retire to his rooms for an afternoon nap.

'I am greatly honoured that you granted me an audience with you, Your Majesty.'

Someone cleared their throat and Meredyth started in surprise. Lounging on a chair to her left was Lord Rosford.

'Are you here to apply for the position of Lord Treasurer, Lady Lansin?' he asked quietly. 'I am sure you would do a better job of it than your husband.' Then he lowered his voice further and added, 'Or perhaps you're hoping for another fumble on the throne?'

At first, Meredyth did not know if she had heard him correctly. But she saw the slight sneer in the corner of his mouth and her cheeks reddened. Of course the King had told Lord Rosford about their lovemaking in the Council Chamber. She should not be surprised. Growing up, he had told Lord Rosford everything – his childhood playmate turned loyal confidant. She had always suspected that the King had dropped her on Lord Rosford's advice. She was the daughter of a nobleman and her mother had been Chief Lady-in-Waiting to the last Queen; she had been a perfectly suitable match. But after a season of intense, dizzying love, King Felipe had left her without explanation. She had waited night after night in her bedchamber for a knock at the door that never came, then she had heard the rumours about Lady Sobelle. Then Lady Chrisytina. And, finally, there had been talk of the King turning his attention abroad and looking towards the Central Realm for an eligible Princess. Meredyth had never broached the subject, but she suspected Queen Violanna knew of the past liaison. Besides, there were not many women Meredyth's age at court – and younger – who the King had not bedded in his youth. It was all so long ago and Meredyth knew she should not care, yet it still stung.

'What are you saying, Rosford?' barked the King, rubbing his head. 'Do not snicker like a kitchen girl.'

'I was just enquiring after Lady Lansin's husband, Your Majesty,' replied Lord Rosford. 'Poor Lord Lansin.'

Meredyth fought back the memories that crowded her mind of her foolish, youthful broken heart and hoped she was wearing enough powder to disguise her flushed face.

'Yes, how is Lansin?' asked the King.

'He is doing better, Your Majesty,' lied Meredyth. 'Much better.'

On her way to the capital, she had stopped in at the Lansin country estate to visit a frail, trembling old man. Her husband had been struck with a fierce, relentless ailment that had turned his eyes cloudy and made him forget his own name.

'It was a great kindness to relieve him of his Council duties,' she continued. 'He needs to rest.'

'That is one way of putting it,' snorted Lord Rosford.

'What is this all about, Lady Lansin?' asked the King, pinching the bridge of his nose. 'Why are you here?' He was leaning against the right arm of the throne, resting his elbow on the velvet pads studded with emeralds. Meredyth had a sudden memory of perching there herself, her legs curled into his lap, pressing hot kisses into his neck. She gulped.

'I have just returned from Mont Isle, Your Majesty,' she said. 'I have a request from the Qu— from Violanna.' It felt wrong to use the Queen's first name, but Meredyth did not know how else to refer to her. The Royal Council had never announced a substitute title. 'Both Violanna and your daughter are well,' Meredyth pushed on. 'Talia is a little lady now. And she looks so much like you; she has your colouring and your eyes, Your Majesty. Even as a baby she had your eyes, do you remember?'

As she spoke, King Felipe's expression grew tense, the lines of his face deepening. 'Talia,' he said softly, almost to himself.

'While I was there, I could not help noticing that her circumstances at Mont Isle are not exactly befitting her . . . position.'

'What do you mean?'

'A governess has not yet been arranged for the Princess, and she does not have any appropriate clothes. It looks most odd.'

'Why is this trivial matter being brought before the King?' barked Lord Rosford. 'You are wasting time.'

'My understanding is that the *means* to do anything about this are not available, Your Majesty,' said Meredyth. She paused and took a deep breath. 'I fear that the Qu— Violanna is not living in a manner that reflects her position as a Princess of the Diapass Kingdom. If she were ever to . . . appeal to her home country, I wonder how it would appear.'

'Is that a threat?' hissed Lord Rosford.

'Of course not,' said Meredyth hurriedly. 'I am merely pointing out that the Diaspass Kingdom seem to be unaware of her . . . marital situation.'

Lord Rosford turned to King Felipe, his dark eyes bright with outrage, but the King did not appear to be listening. Instead, he was gazing across the room at a portrait of his mother and father hung on the opposite wall.

'All right, Lady Lansin,' he said. 'You may have what you need.'

'Thank you, Your Majesty,' Meredyth gushed, feeling almost faint as a wave of relief washed over her. She dropped into a low curtsey, her joints creaking. 'Thank you.'

'But, Your Majesty—'

'I did not ask for your opinion, Rosford.'

'But we have just sat in this very room and agreed to cut expenditure! We have no need to fear the Diaspass Kingdom; it is too wrapped up in the long, drawn-out warring over Journier to concern itself with an old Princess.'

Meredyth knew this was true – Queen Violanna had said as much herself. But the King wore a stubborn expression she recognized and it usually meant he was not going to change his mind.

'Lady Lansin will not spend much, I am sure,' he said, heaving himself up from his throne with a wince.

'But it is the Tolbiens we need be worried about, not the Diaspass Kingdom!' said Lord Rosford. 'This new Tolbien King is young and bold, and that nation still holds a grudge about the Battle of Karkel; they feel they have a score to settle. We need to pull back all the flecks we can now. Wars are expensive.'

Then the court rumours are true, thought Meredyth, but she demurely lowered her gaze.

'Enough, Rosford!' said the King, tugging at the neck-ties of his cape. 'Leave it be.'

Meredyth started hastily backing out of the room, planning to write straight away to a governess she knew.

'Wait, Lady Lansin,' called King Felipe.

She paused.

'The Princess . . .' he added, his eyes straying to the portrait of his parents once more. 'What is she like?'

Meredyth tried to hide her surprise behind a cough. 'The

Princess?' she echoed, thinking of the slightly odd, lonely little girl on Mont Isle. 'The Princess is bright, thoughtful and happy, Your Majesty.'

'And the curse?'

'To my knowledge, it is unchanged, Your Majesty.'

The King nodded. 'That is all,' he said, turning away.

Violanna

The Chapel, Mont Isle

VIOLANNA SAW HER daughter – her first, unnamed daughter – skipping along the roadside of an unknown town in Bavaugh. She imagined the girl much like Talia but fairer, the details of her features blurred and undefined. She was a golden haze of a child, all laughs and smiles. Violanna saw her daughter step into the road without looking, running for a flower she had seen on the opposite verge, then, suddenly, a carriage came roaring past. The child was hit, her little body flying through the air and crumpling on the rutted ground.

Violanna's fingers clenched around the pew in front of her and she clamped her teeth together, but then another vision came.

She saw her unnamed daughter walking beside a river, carrying a rag doll. A sudden gust of wind whipped it from the girl's hands and it landed in the water. Crying out in alarm, the girl rushed into the river to retrieve it. As she waded deeper, stretching out her little hand to grasp the doll, her foot slipped and the current took her. She was pulled beneath the surface, dragged downstream by the rushing waters, her thrashing limbs becoming limp.

Violanna's insides twisted with pain and she gasped, squeezing her eyes shut tight. As much as she wanted this to stop, another part of her did not think that she deserved peace. Her self-torment must continue.

Another vision appeared.

She saw her unnamed daughter crouched in a back street of Lustore at night. She was thin and grimy, dirt caked around her feet and her hair dull and clumped with filth. She was trying to sleep, hunched in a shadow, but someone had spotted her. They crept up quietly, knowing no one would ever miss a street child. The little girl stirred, but hands were already grabbing her, fingers pinching into her skin, and before she could cry out, a blow to the head knocked her out cold.

Violanna forced her eyes open, her chest heaving with choked breaths. Sweat trickled between her shoulder blades. The chapel around her was cold, dim and silent except for the rhythmic crash of waves against the rocks outside.

She pulled herself to her feet, legs trembling beneath her. As always, her eyes were drawn to the pew near the front of the chapel on the left-hand side. There she had given birth to Talia and looked upon her first daughter for the last time. Her perfect child who she had not even had a chance to name. Through a haze of pain and fear, she could remember the sweet little face poking out of a bundle of torn skirts, held in the arms of the apprentice Master, Selhah. Then the shouts of guards had sounded from somewhere nearby and Selhah had hurried away, black boots tapping on the marble floor, taking the first Princess out of the castle and away.

Violanna thought of the moment often. Sometimes it seemed that she never stopped thinking about it – she woke with an ache already lodged in her chest and pushed herself through the daily motions, forever plagued by imagined fears.

A door to the side of the chapel opened and a tall man in a blue robe appeared. 'Oh!' he said, stopping short. 'My apologies, Your Majesty.'

Violanna knew she must look alarming in her overcoat with her nightclothes showing beneath and her hair undone. The servants called her 'half mad' and sometimes she felt it.

When she did not reply, the minister added, 'I was just going to clear the Remembrance, Your Majesty.'

'Very good. I should like to use it in a moment.'

The minister bowed and hurried to the altar. He was a kindly, gentle man who had attempted to help Violanna over the seasons with words of wisdom and prayer, but he did not understand that there was only one thing that could end her torment.

Violanna bent and picked up a white winter rose from an embroidered kneeler at her feet. She had taken it from the Queen's Garden, which was now an overgrown tangle of wilderness. Meredyth had appointed a gardener for Mont Isle, but his days were consumed with the vast vegetable patch. There was enough work for three gardeners there, growing food for the whole household, and he had no time for fripperies. But Violanna liked the roughness of the Queen's Garden and she often wandered through it at night when she could not sleep, ducking beneath boughs and stepping over nettles with the creamy moon high above her.

There were still plenty of flowers in the garden if you knew where to look, and Violanna enjoyed choosing the right bloom each day. This rose had been a particularly joyful find when the garden was mostly brown and bare for the oncoming winter. Its soft, fluttery petals swirled from a tight, curled core, and it was so full and voluptuous that its head hung heavily from the stem, nodding as Violanna held it. She had forgotten to take a knife with her and so she had bitten it off, sap oozing on to her tongue and the corner of her mouth snagging on a thorn, drawing a bead of blood. She had chuckled to herself, knowing what the servants would have thought if they had seen her then: *Half mad*.

'I will not be a moment, Your Majesty,' panted the minister.

'I do not mind waiting.'

Violanna watched the back of his head as he swept away yesterday's ash from the Remembrance and polished the holders.

'Perhaps it would help to share what is on your mind, Your Majesty?' he said, finishing up.

'The same thing that is always on my mind.'

The minister nodded. 'To lose young souls is painful.'

He thought her remembrance bloom was for her lost babies, the ones who had left her belly too soon.

'I should like to be alone,' she said.

'Of course, Your Majesty. Please know that I am always here to help you.'

Violanna waited until he had disappeared and the door of the vestry creaked shut, then she approached the altar.

Moonlight filtered through the stained-glass windows and faint, coloured light pooled on the marble floor.

It is the same moon watching over her, Violanna thought. *Wherever she is.*

There had still been no contact from Violanna's homeland. No offer of aid or support from the Royal Assembly of the Diaspass Kingdom in response to her pleas. No acknowledgement from her father. Winters ago, when her sister Fayia had visited, she had promised to speak to the Masters on Violanna's behalf. But then Fayia had had another child, then another, and her correspondence had dwindled to nothing. Violanna had all but given up hope of finding a way to break the curse. Ten winters remained until the spell's end and there was nothing she could do alone. This was exactly what the sorceress had intended: to leave Violanna anxious and watchful, dreading her return. Powerless and weak.

Placing the white rose in one of the holders, Violanna struck the match. She thought again of her first daughter – the tiny infant she could remember, and the little child she would be now – and prayed to the Great Creator. She prayed that this agony would not be for nothing and she prayed that she might one day see her unnamed daughter again.

Violanna pressed the lit match against the flower and watched as the flame took hold, singeing the petals. This was not the true purpose of a remembrance bloom, but for all she knew, her daughter could be dead. Perhaps Selhah had abandoned the baby and run off back to the Central Realm. Perhaps they had both perished in an accident. Violanna begged the Great Creator that it was not so, but she could not ignore the possibility.

She watched as the rose burnt, the white petals turning to ash and the smell of smoke catching at the back of her throat. Outside she could hear gulls beginning to squawk, and the light seeping through the stained-glass windows glowed brighter.

The night had gone and another torturous day was beginning.

Briar

Turow, South-west Bavaugh

BRIAR POSITIONED HER boot over a frozen pool in the sand and stamped down. The ice shattered like glass with a satisfying crunch, and she grinned.

'Just got a good one!' she yelled over her shoulder.

Jacken was walking a few paces behind her, leading a dapple-grey pony called Pigeon down the beach. He gave Briar a nod in return but did not reply.

Briar tugged her scarf over her mouth against the biting wind. Then she carried on walking, her eyes scanning the ground. She came across another frozen pool in a dip, which was bigger than the last.

'Got another one here!' she called, pointing. When Jacken and the pony had caught up, she added, 'I'll let you stamp on this one.'

Jacken shook his head.

'It feels really good. You'll like it.'

'Nah.'

Jacken hunched his shoulders against the chill, pulling his thin jacket tightly around himself, and leant against Pigeon's flank. Briar had already given him her gloves, but it was not enough.

'Are you cold?'

Jacken shrugged.

She tried to give him her scarf, but he would not take it.

'Maybe you'd feel better if you told me what happened to Maple?'

There was an uncomfortable silence and Briar wished she had not mentioned the bay gelding. Jacken had turned up this evening at their usual time without Maple, his eyes dark. Now he looked like he was going to cry.

'I hope somebody kind bought him . . .'

Jacken winced.

Pigeon huffed clouds of warm breath into the air that were whipped away by the wind and Jacken huddled closer into the pony's side.

Briar wanted to ask Jacken more questions about Maple, but she was starting to become afraid of the answers. Instead, she said, 'Pigeon says she wants to go for a jog.'

This was partly true. The pony was looking around at the wide, open beach, eager for a canter across the sand, but she was not so keen on the strong, whistling wind.

'You should ride her, then,' grunted Jacken, wiping his nose on his sleeve. 'I don't feel like it today.'

'But she wants you.'

'No.'

Briar looped Pigeon's lead rope over the mare's neck and gestured for Jacken to give her a leg-up. She could not vault on to a horse's back like Jacken, no matter how many times he had showed her how to do it. She wriggled into the right position and hugged the pony's sides with her knees.

You can go now, she said in the strange way she knew how.

Pigeon pricked her ears and broke into a trot over the sand, which soon quickened into a canter. The wind tore at Briar's hair and lashed grains of sand against her face. She grinned, bending forward out of the gale and burying her hands in Pigeon's pale mane. She loved to ride and usually she and Jacken would race each other across the beach, the loser always screaming for a rematch.

Pigeon's hooves smacked and splashed in the shallow waters at the shore, leaving plate-like imprints in the dark sand. Briar let the pony have her head for a while, lolloping across the beach, then nudged with her knees and asked Pigeon to loop around and turn back.

'Pigeon was scared of the wind, but now she likes it!' Briar shouted to Jacken as she and the pony trotted towards him.

Jacken stood with his gloved hands tucked under his armpits, staring at the ground.

'You can tell she likes it because she has the look,' Briar continued. 'Can you see?'

Briar had been trying to teach Jacken how to talk to horses since they had struck their bargain in the summer, but with little success. Jacken said he was good with horses 'for a normal person' and there was something strange about the way that Briar could understand animals. 'Strange but good' was what he had said. When Briar had asked Auntie about this, her aunt had got one of those shifty looks on her face and said there was nothing wrong with her at all. She had added that she was not sure Briar should be going to the beach every evening now winter was coming, but Briar had begged. Jacken was her only friend – the only friend she had ever had except Paleen, and grown-ups didn't count – and so Auntie had relented.

She just about tolerated Briar's friendship with Jacken although she never seemed very happy about it.

'Can you see the look Pigeon has?' Briar persisted.

'No.'

'It's the way her eyes are light and—'

'Don't you need to go now? Won't your aunt be mad?'

Briar bit her lip, stung. 'Auntie doesn't like me to be out too long in the cold, but we only just got here.'

'It's freezing.'

'We could go back to the schoolhouse?' said Briar, sliding off Pigeon's back. 'There'll be a warm fire and Auntie said she'd make stew for dinner with fresh rolls. She makes the best rolls; she was a baker once.'

Jacken shook his head. He always refused Briar's invitations to come to the schoolhouse, but she still asked anyway. Often she brought him some bread or cheese, pretending it was a snack for both of them, but making sure she only ate the tiniest amount. She had never met the man Jacken called 'Mister', but she could tell that he was not very nice. Jacken always seemed to be hungry, his clothes were too small and he slept in the straw with the horses. Sometimes he turned up with a black eye or a cut lip, but if Briar tried to ask him about it, he went silent.

'How about you ride Pigeon now?' said Briar, desperate not to cut their evening short. She had battled her way through one of Auntie's writing exercises today so that she could come to the beach.

'No. I should go now in case Mister wonders where I am.'

'But he's always in town at the taverns in the evenings.'

'Not always.'

'You've never left because of him before,' muttered Briar, crossing her arms. 'Anyway, Pigeon says she wants to stay.'

'I don't care. She's only a pony.'

Jacken turned and began walking across the sand, dragging the dapple-grey mare behind him.

'Wait!' cried Briar. 'I could come with you! I've always wanted to see where you live.'

'No.'

'I'd love to see all the horses. I could meet the ones you don't bring to the beach. I'd really like that.'

'I said no.'

'But—'

'Just go home!'

Jacken looked regretful as soon as the words were out of his mouth, but Briar barely had time to notice. The air around her trembled and suddenly she was turning and walking away. Her legs moved of their own accord, carrying her down the beach to the trail through the dunes, and she could do nothing to stop them. Frustrated tears slipped from her eyes, and she felt sick and strange.

'I'm sorry, Briar!' came a yell from behind her over the roaring wind. 'Can I see you here tomorrow?'

But Briar could not turn back to reply even if she wanted to.

Talia

The Castle, Mont Isle

IN HER CHAMBERS on Mont Isle, Talia shivered. She heard a gust of wind rattle at the window and she shuffled closer to the fire, dragging her lap desk with her.

'Princess, what are you doing?' asked Mistress Rashel, looking up from her book. They were sitting opposite one another in a pair of tattered brocade armchairs.

'Trying to get warm.'

'You should have said and we could have called one of the servants to move the chair for you.'

'But I can do it myself.'

'That is not the point.'

Talia sighed. 'Yes, Mistress.'

They both turned back to their books.

Talia quite liked her lessons with Mistress Rashel. She was good at basic sums and she could remember dates and facts pretty well.

She had overheard Mistress Rashel tell her mother that she was a 'surprisingly gifted student for a child of seven winters', which pleased her. But what she was less good at was all the acting – what Mistress Rashel called 'conduct lessons'. She was always opening doors for herself and pouring her own tea. Mistress Rashel said she would eventually get used to doing things properly, but sometimes she was not so sure.

'Have you finished reading that section?' asked Mistress Rashel, putting her book down and smoothing back her curly brown hair.

Talia nodded. She had actually finished a while ago, but she was waiting for the fire to warm her chilled fingers. The castle was always freezing in the winter – all the servants moaned about it, especially the new ones. If they were not grumbling about the cold, then they were complaining about the isolation or the screeching gulls or the peculiar *feel* of the castle. Talia had overheard a new kitchen girl say that the air on Mont Isle 'tasted wrong'. There had always been a high turnover of staff at the castle, and it was only the faithful few, like Dottie, who stuck it out for the long run.

'Tell me what you have learnt, Princess.'

'I was reading about Journier in the Central Realm.'

'What about it?'

'It is a small land mass bordered by four kingdoms,' recited Talia without looking at her book. 'All of the kingdoms believe it to be part of their territory and it has switched between them so often that the Journierian language is a mixture of all four.'

'Correct. In fact, the Central Realm are warring over Journier right now,' said Mistress Rashel. 'Have you heard of it?'

Talia shook her head.

'A rebel group in Journier is fighting for independence and the Diaspass Kingdom are supporting them. All assumed it would be a swift battle, easily won, but the warring has continued over many winters now and it does not look as though it will end soon.'

Talia sat up straighter. 'The Diaspass Kingdom? Where my mother is from?'

'Yes.'

'So my grandfather has done that?'

'Yes, I suppose so.'

Talia had noticed that Mistress Rashel enjoyed telling her things but did not like questions and seemed to find her interruptions irritating. But Talia could not help it; there were so many things she wanted to know.

'I wonder why my grandfather did that,' said Talia. 'Do you think I could ask my mother?'

Mistress Rashel hesitated. 'I would imagine it has been a long time since your mother was in contact with her family. She might not welcome the question.'

Talia thought it was fairly obvious that her mother welcomed no questions and as little interaction as possible. All Mother seemed to want to do was sit in the glacial, dark chapel or else stare forlornly at the wall, looking miserable. Whenever Talia tried asking her questions, Mother would become twitchy and distant before disappearing with some excuse about a headache.

'I think my grandfather has aligned with the rebels because the best invasion route is from the west, through the Diaspass Kingdom,' replied Talia, thinking of the yellowed, mildewed map in the castle's library. 'There are mountains along the other borders of Journier, which make it difficult to attack – and dragons! Have you ever seen a dragon?'

'No—'

'Anyway, the Diaspass Kingdom is in the best position to control

Journier even if the Journierians are granted independence,' said Talia, drumming her fingers on her lap desk. 'All their trade will go through the Diaspass Kingdom, so it is almost as though they are still part of the Diaspass territory, except they will have to pay taxes as well!' Talia clapped her hands and sat back in her chair. 'I think I have cracked it. That is very cunning of my grandfather.'

'Now, Princess—'

'But do you think I am right?'

Mistress Rashel frowned and sucked in her lips. Dottie called that her 'fish face' and often did impressions of the governess in the evenings when she helped Talia get ready for bed. Dottie said that Mistress Rashel was a 'stuck-up pain in the arse', but Talia thought her governess was just awkward. She was grateful to Mistress Rashel for their lessons and keen to make sure she did not leave. The servants said that life on Mont Isle was not easy for the staff, and Talia did not want to lose her studies when she was learning so much.

'It is of little consequence to us what happens in the Central Realm,' said Mistress Rashel. 'We have our own alliances to focus on.'

'You mean the problems with the Tolbiens?'

Mistress Rashel did the 'fish face' again. 'Where did you hear about that?' she asked.

There was a pause, then Talia said with a sigh, 'From the guards.'

'You know you should not be speaking to—'

'I was not *speaking* to them, I was *listening*.'

'You must do neither, Princess. These are the instructions I was given by Lady Lansin.'

Talia resisted the urge to roll her eyes. Lady Lansin was both her hero and her enemy. Lady Lansin had brought study, books and order into Talia's life, but she had brought rules, decorum and uncomfortable dresses, too – with so many buttons and fastenings that Talia always felt as though she were being tethered in place. Every moon, Talia had to write to Lady Lansin, explaining what she was learning and reading. At the same time, she would always ask for news of her father and half-brothers, though Lady Lansin never gave her many details. But Talia had not had a letter in return since Lord Lansin died at the beginning of autumn. She had asked Mother if they should be concerned, but, as usual, her mother had not seemed to take much notice.

'Fine, Mistress,' said Talia. 'But you did mean the problems with the Tolbiens, did you not?'

'Yes, that is what I meant.'

Mistress Rashel squeezed her mouth so tight that her lips almost disappeared. Talia had seen her governess make this expression once before when pressed with Talia's questions about why she had been banished to Mont Isle. Mistress Rashel had snapped that if Talia was not going to concentrate on her studies, they had better finish up the lesson. Then her governess had swiftly left the room. Talia enjoyed her lessons too much to make that mistake again and so she had not ventured to ask more questions about Mont Isle, though they still lingered in her mind.

'Do you think we should be worried about the Tolbiens, Mistress?' Talia carefully pressed now. 'The guards did not seem worried.'

Mistress Rashel fiddled with a tie on the cuff of her dress. She always wore long-sleeved, heavy dresses in various shades of grey. 'Perhaps, Princess.'

'Would we ever use magical warfare like they do in the Central Realm?' asked Talia, and when Mistress Rashel gave her a sharp look, she added, 'I read about it in a book.'

'I highly doubt it, Princess.'

'Because the Western Realm does not formally handle magic? I read in another of the history books that they even banished it for a while many winters ago and captured and killed magic-wielders.'

'Quite,' said Mistress Rashel, looking like she wished she had never allowed the conversation to stray so far. 'We leave the magic to the rest of the realm.'

'Because magic is dangerous,' said Talia.

Mistress Rashel gave Talia a strange look she did not understand. Then her governess nodded and said, 'Yes, that is right. Magic is dangerous.'

Sel

Turow, South-west Bavaugh

SEL PULLED HER cloak tighter around her and set off along the road into town. She had banked the fire before she left the school-house, wishing she could stay by its warmth, but she had decided to make an effort for Midwinter Eve and she needed supplies. She wanted to see the look on Briar's face when the little girl returned later to smell fish cooking with potatoes and white sauce. It was a fuss to get all the ingredients – not to mention the expense, since prices had just risen steeply. The townsfolk of Turow were mutter-ing that the King was building up his army in anticipation of an attack from the Tolbiens and everyone was feeling the pinch. But fish and white sauce was Briar's favourite meal and Sel thought it would be worth the cost for a special treat.

'Happy Midwinter Eve!' called the haberdasher as Sel passed the open door of her shop.

'Yes, Happy Midwinter Eve.'

Sel turned the corner into the town square, surprised to see it filled with chattering, smiling clusters of people readying themselves for the holiday. She did not usually venture into the heart of Turow except in the early mornings and she was taken aback by the crowds. There were many faces she did not recognize and the atmosphere was warm and jolly despite the cold snap in the air. A band of ringers were performing ballads with clapper bells outside the bakery, and the large tavern on the west side of the square was thick with the sound of laughing and shouting.

Having forfeited an evening studying the latest addition to her small library – a tatty book on herbology – in order to complete this task, Sel found herself enjoying the seasonal cheer. She called 'Happy Midwinter Eve,' to everyone she passed and paused for the length of a song to listen to the band of ringers chiming their bells.

'Arla? Arla!' cried a voice.

Sel turned in surprise to see Paleen bustling through the crowds, baskets laden with goods looped over each arm.

'Happy Midwinter Eve,' grinned Sel as Paleen drew closer. 'Let me hold one of those for you.'

Paleen gratefully handed over a basket and straightened her crooked bonnet. Her cheeks were flushed despite the cold, and she fanned herself with one hand. 'This holiday is always such a joyful rush,' she panted.

'I suppose it must be when you're so good-hearted that you cook a Midwinter feast for every waif and stray in town.'

Paleen shook her head and waved away Sel's words. 'You're still coming tomorrow with Briar, yes?'

'Of course, we never miss it. Briar says you have the best pickled cabbage.'

'Oh, that sweet child! Now, can I tempt you to take some spiced tea with me this evening?'

Sel sadly shook her head. 'I'm planning a special meal to surprise Briar when she gets back from the beach. She's been trying so hard with her sums recently, I wanted to treat her.'

'She's at the beach? In this chill?'

'She says she likes to run around after a day of lessons,' replied Sel with a shrug, trying not to show her own unease. 'And she has a friend she plays with.'

'A friend? Well, that is wonderful. I am so pleased to hear it.'

Sel nodded. Paleen often made gentle comments about Briar's secluded lifestyle, although what Paleen would think of a stable-boy as a playmate, Sel was not sure. She had reluctantly allowed the friendship with Jacken after much wheedling from Briar, reasoning that if the girl was going to be friends with anyone, better it be a scrappy orphan, who was not likely to cause them trouble.

'I've been meaning to ask you,' Paleen continued, her voice dropping lower. 'Would you mind if I taught Briar how to spin? I thought it might be something that she'd enjoy.'

Sel bit her lip, trying to remember if any of the Masters' gifts at the Blessing had mentioned spinning. Recently she had given Briar a handkerchief to embroider, and in the blink of an eye the child had stitched an elaborate rose with a bewildered expression on her face and the scent of magic thick in the air. Sel had had to quickly remove the embroidery and distract Briar with idle chatter until the moment passed.

'Perhaps you wanted to teach her yourself?' added Paleen. 'I didn't mean to intrude.'

'Not at all,' replied Sel quickly. 'I can't spin and I'm sure she would like to learn from you.'

Paleen beamed. 'That's settled, then. Anyway, I won't delay you a moment longer.'

'Yes, we'll see you tomorrow,' replied Sel, thinking that she would try to purchase her supplies quickly now and then be on her way.

She was about to turn away when a hand shot out from the crowd, grabbing her arm. Sel jumped in shock as fingers curled around her wrist, squeezing it tight.

'My word!' cried a voice as a figure emerged from the throng. 'The Great Creator hold me! It *is* you.'

Sel stared into a round, smiling face.

'Jessamin, I thought I'd never see you again!' gasped Sandi. 'You remember me, don't you?'

Sel blinked.

'It was a long time ago, for sure, but I've not changed that much – though I'm a little different at the moment, I'll grant you.' She rubbed her swollen, pregnant belly.

Sel opened her mouth to reply but found she could not speak.

'Jessamin, say something,' laughed Sandi. She looked from Sel to Paleen. 'I'm sorry I crept up on you like that, but I saw you across the square and I had to come over.'

A hot rush of dread hit Sel's stomach.

'I'm married now,' added Sandi, turning her head to display the matrimony band in her ear. 'I got asked not long after you disappeared and I've two babies – boys – and another on the way.' She gestured to her stomach. 'I think this one is a girl. We've journeyed to visit my husband's sister for Midwinter before this new addition puts a stop to such things. She went and married a sailor who brought her south-west and she claims the living here is better than in the east. We wanted to see for ourselves.'

Sel swallowed, her throat dry and tight. 'Congratulations,' she managed. It had never occurred to her that she might ever bump into Sandi again.

'My goodness, it's so lovely to see you, Jessamin!' Sandi cried, shaking Sel's arm once more. 'After you left Dawvin like that, I didn't know what to think! I assumed you'd write and tell me what happened, but we heard nothing. It was like you just vanished. And now here you are.'

'I'm sorry . . .'

'And where's your daughter?' Sandi persisted, looking around. 'Such a gorgeous baby,' she added, addressing Paleen. 'She must be over seven winters old now. I bet she's a real pretty little girl. What a blessing to have such a beautiful daughter.'

Sel flinched. She could not bear to look at Paleen. 'I'm sorry, Sandi,' she said faintly. 'But I must go now.'

Sandi frowned. 'What? But I've only just found you; you can't disappear on me again.'

'I can't stay.' Sel began backing away, her boots stumbling on the cobblestones.

'Wait a moment!' cried Sandi. 'Jessamin? Jessamin, wait!'

Sel turned and fled into the crowd.

Talia

The Queen's Chambers, Mont Isle

THE ROOM STANK with a cloying, sickly sweetness. Talia almost choked on it as she stepped inside and had it not been for Dottie's hand on her back, propelling her forward, she would have turned and run.

'Give your mother some company,' murmured Dottie in her ear. 'Go and sit with her a while, Princess.'

'But—'

'I'll be back in a bit to call you for tea.'

Dottie disappeared, shutting the door behind her, leaving Talia alone. Alone except for the twitching, damp-looking figure in the bed.

'Hello, Mother,' she whispered.

The figure in the bed did not reply.

As her eyes adjusted to the dimness, Talia could see her mother's chest rising and falling heavily, the sheets twisted around her limbs.

The castle was chilled and draughty, but her mother was sweating with her hair lying flat and wet against her head.

'Dottie told me you are sick,' Talia added, forcing herself further into the room. 'You have the winter fever. The kitchen girl and one of the maids have it too. The kitchen girl has it bad.'

The fire in the corner crackled and that sticky smell hung in the air. Talia wished she could pull the shutters back from the windows and suck in the sea breeze. Pinpricks of sweat were beading on her brow.

'I hope you get better soon, Mother,' she said, edging towards the bedside. 'Dottie made you her special medicine.'

One of her mother's arms was flung over her head with her hand dangling off the mattress, pale and damp. Talia had been warned not to get too close to avoid catching the fever herself, but she could not help it. She reached out and touched her mother's fingers, brushing them lightly with her own. They were cold and clammy. She gasped a little, then took hold of her mother's hand. She could not remember the last time they had touched.

Mother's eyelids flickered.

'Do not worry, it is just me,' hissed Talia. 'You have been in bed ill for many days now. You must be bored . . . Dottie said I should come and see you.'

Her mother's fingers folded over her own and Talia gulped with surprise and delight.

'The fountain in the garden has frozen over again,' she said. 'And the chimney in the dining room is blocked . . . Oh, and I overheard the maids saying that a woman from the village drowned in the sea. She was beachcombing and the tide caught her and . . .'

Talia trailed off, remembering her own brush with the dangerous, fickle tides around Mont Isle.

'Anyway, I think that is all the news there is,' she finished.

Mother moaned and puckered her dry, cracked lips.

'Would you like a drink?'

There was no reply. Talia reluctantly let go of her mother's hand and poured a cup of water from the pitcher beside the bed.

'When I was sick last winter with a pox, Dottie sang me songs to make me feel better,' she said, gently tipping the water on to her mother's lips. 'But I know you do not like singing. You never join in with the hymns at service.'

Talia put the cup down and took up her mother's hand once more, squeezing it a little too tight. Her mother's fingers were thin, and the skin around the bitten-down nails was chapped and flaking. She wore two gold bands on her forefinger and thumb with a fine chain strung between them. It had always fascinated Talia and she could not stop herself from touching it now. She traced the slim gold bands and looped her own finger around the chain, feeling its delicate links. Her mother said it was a Diaspass Kingdom custom and all her sisters wore one; it marked them out as royal.

'Oops!' whispered Talia, knotting her little finger in the chain and trying to shake it free.

Mother's eyes opened and she snatched her hand back.

Talia's little finger was still caught in the chain and, as her mother pulled away, it scraped her skin. 'Ouch!'

Mother pushed out a wheezy, shuddering breath and her gaze wandered across Talia's face, almost as though she did not know her. 'Are you still alive?' she croaked.

'What . . . what do you mean?'

'My child, you are well.'

Mother's cracked lips stretched into a smile, while her eyelids flickered.

Talia frowned and took a step back. 'I think I should get Dottie now—'

'I did what I had to do, please understand,' gasped Mother, sweat trickling across her forehead. 'I did it for you, my daughter.'

Talia started backing away towards the door, almost tripping on the dusty rug.

'I did it for you. Because of . . .'

Talia stopped, curious and unsure.

'The curse,' Mother said, raking a hand across her face, leaving raw, red lines on her cheeks.

'A curse?' Talia whispered.

She knew little of magic, but she had read about spells in one of the old, yellowing books in the castle library. She knew a curse was a bad, dark thing.

'Yes.'

'A curse . . . on *me*?'

'I tried to stop it, but I could not. I am sorry, my daughter.' Mother shook her head from side to side, slowly at first, then faster and faster, until she was thrashing back and forth, her eyes rolling.

Talia turned and fled the room. Stumbling through the sudden brightness of the corridor, she almost knocked into Dottie, who was walking towards her, carrying a fresh set of bed linen.

'You're leaving already?' said the maid.

Talia raced past her, ignoring her shout of alarm.

Talia kept running, rushing through passages and down flights of stairs, panting and shaking. She reached a set of heavy double doors and threw herself against them until they creaked open. Then she dashed inside the Great Hall – no one would find her in here.

It was cold and dark in the cavernous room and Talia hugged her arms to her chest. Long, fuzzy tails of dust collected at the edge of her skirts as she paced back and forth, and when she ventured close to one corner, a splinter of glass crunched under her foot. She paused and looked up at the huge window high in the wall above her, little chinks of light seeping through its boarding. A few summers ago, she had spent several days scouring the Great Hall for little shards of coloured glass, amassing a small collection that she kept in a trinket box in her room. Now her time was spent in lessons and study, and she did not have the inclination for such things.

Talia padded across the cold tiles to the huge portrait hung at the back of the Great Hall. Portraits and paintings lined the walls of the room, but this was the biggest and it was her favourite.

'Hello, Father,' she said, gazing up at the handsome, haughty face.

She had spent many long afternoons studying the portrait, looking for parts of herself. She thought she probably had the same eyes – dark blue, almost grey – and maybe a similar dimple in her chin. Lady Lansin had said that there was something in Talia's facial expressions that was like her father, which had both delighted and frustrated her in equal measure. She had only this one depiction of him, and she did not know how accurate it was.

'Father, what do you know of a . . . curse?'

She imagined the King turning his head to look down on her lovingly. 'Curse?' he would say in a deep, comforting voice. 'There is no such thing, my child.'

But in her heart, Talia knew that was not true. There was something prodding at her. Something that had always been present but unsaid – in the fervent looks of others, in the awkward expressions, in the silences. A curse. It was horrible and terrifying, but it also made sense.

Talia hugged her arms even tighter, her fingernails pressing into her skin as fragments of her life started to click into place with bewildering speed. She could feel tears wetting her cheeks and her legs were trembling. It was like half understanding something you had always known. A chime that rang through her body. It was both familiar and unknown.

'Princess?' a voice called.

Talia jumped.

'Princess? Are you here?'

She turned to see Mistress Rashel peering through the doors she had left ajar, squinting into the gloom. Her curly hair was loose and hanging about her shoulders, and she looked younger and softer.

'There you are, Princess,' she said, catching sight of Talia. 'Everyone is looking for you.'

Talia wiped her sleeve across her face and before she could be reprimanded, she said, 'I need you to tell me everything about the curse.'

Mistress Rashel stared at her.

There was a pause.

'Who told you about the curse, Princess?'

Talia's last little spark of hope that she was mistaken, that her mother's words were just the ravings of sickness, extinguished. 'My mother,' she replied. 'She spoke to me as if . . . as if . . . I do not know. As if she were dreaming, I suppose.'

'I see.'

'So, tell me what you know. I order it.'

There was another pause.

'I thought you might be here, Princess,' said Mistress Rashel finally, her eyes wandering to the portrait behind Talia. 'I have noticed you come here sometimes.'

'Do not change the subject.'

'Have you never wondered what happened in here?'

Talia glanced at the boarded windows and the furniture covered in sheets. 'Dottie said there was a storm . . .'

Mistress Rashel shook her head.

'All right. What happened, then?'

'I think you are old enough to know the truth. Come with me to your chambers and I will explain. It is too cold to stay in here.'

'There is a curse on me?' cried Talia. 'I cannot believe my mother never told me. How could she keep a secret like this? And Dottie and you – you all knew!'

'Princess, it is not an easy thing to explain. No one fully understands what happened.'

Talia sniffed and wiped her face on her sleeve again. 'It is why he hates me, is it not?' she said, nodding at the portrait of her father.

'Princess—'

'It is why we are on this island, is it not? It is why my father took a new wife, why he never comes here and why my mother went mad.'

Mistress Rashel's eyes dropped to the floor and Talia knew she was right. She had suspected that her banishment to Mont Isle had something to do with her mother, but she had been wrong – it was worse than that.

'It is all because of the curse,' said Talia, her voice breaking with tears. 'It is all because of me.'

Sel

Turow, South-west Bavaugh

SEL RAN BETWEEN the scrubby dunes, sand flicking up into her boots. A heavy pack thumped on her back and another dangled from her left hand, dragging behind her. She emerged on to the flat stretch of the beach, turned her face into the icy wind and yelled, 'Briar!'

Scanning left and right, she saw a shining blonde head by the shore, standing beside two horses and the back of Jacken's gangly figure. 'Briar!' she called again. Before she could stop herself, she added, 'Come here!'

The girl turned and immediately began walking towards her. As Briar grew closer, Sel could see the girl's frustrated expression and feel the tang of magic in the air.

'Why are you here?' huffed Briar. 'You said I could stay later at the beach tonight because there aren't lessons tomorrow for Midwinter Day. You *said*.'

Sel squinted as grains of sand caught in the wind were flung across her cheeks. She had not thought about what she would tell Briar. Since she had fled from Sandi in Turow's town square, she had been acting purely upon impulse.

'Briar . . . we need to go now.'

There was a pause. Behind Briar, Jacken appeared with the two horses ambling either side of him.

'We need to go home?' said Briar, her voice tinged with uncertainty.

Sel bit her lip as the wind howled around them and the grey waves crashed on the sand. 'No. We need to go away from Turow.'

Briar frowned. 'You do not mean . . .' she began, trailing off as she met Sel's gaze.

'Briar—'

'No!' Briar cried, shaking her head. 'No, Auntie! You said we used to move about because we were looking for a home, but now we've found one. Turow is our home.'

Sel felt her stomach clench with guilt. She did not want to send them back out on the road again either, but she did not know what else to do.

'Leave?' echoed Jacken.

'Auntie, I'll come back to the schoolhouse later,' said Briar. 'Go away!'

Sel grabbed Briar, dropping the bag she was holding on the sand. Briar stared at it, Dolly Emly's arm reaching out from its mouth.

'I'm sorry,' said Sel. 'I'm so sorry, Briar.' She thought of the nights she had stroked the girl's golden head after she had woken from a bad dream, reassuring her that she was safe, that she was home, that all was well.

'What's happened?' asked Jacken.

'She's taking me away!' wailed Briar, tears streaming from her eyes.

Sel fought to keep her own voice steady. 'Briar, please——'

'But why do you need to go?' asked Jacken.

Both children looked at Sel with wide, questioning eyes and her chest tightened. She thought quickly; she had always known the day would come when she would have to tell Briar something about their past. The girl would not fall for her evasions and excuses for ever.

'Briar, do you remember I told you your mother died after you were born?' she began.

Briar nodded.

'When she died . . . some people tried to take you away from me – some bad people. So we ran and we went from place to place, just as I have said. But now those people have found us and they're coming to take you from me. That's why we must leave.'

'But I always stay in the attic anyway, so no one will find me. I don't want to leave,' cried Briar, stamping her foot.

Even with tears pouring across her face and her skin beaten red by the wind, she still looked peculiarly beautiful. Sel knew she could make Briar leave with her if she wanted to – all she need do was utter the command – but she did not want it to be that way.

After a pause, Jacken said, 'If you go, can I come with you?'

Both Sel and Briar turned to him in surprise.

'We can take these horses,' added Jacken. 'And I'll be really good, I promise. Briar, we should go with your aunt. It'll be like an adventure.'

Sel shook her head, but the children ignored her.

'You can come with us?' Briar asked Jacken.

He nodded.

'I can't—' began Sel, but Briar interrupted her.

'I'll only go if Jacken comes too.'

Sel looked from one to the other, still shaking her head.

'We'll get away faster with the horses,' said Jacken, his eyes pleading. 'And you could take more stuff with you,' he added, glancing at her bag.

'No,' said Sel, but she thought about the books she had left behind, hidden under a loose floorboard in the schoolhouse because she could not bear to burn them. 'I can't take you,' she said, but her eyes flicked to the horses, both sturdy, healthy animals.

'You're not taking me,' said Jacken, pushing out his bony chest. 'I'm leaving. I was gonna leave some time.'

Sel felt herself wavering. She saw a cut that snaked down Jacken's temple, and a fading bruise on his chin. She looked into his fierce, imploring eyes and she recognized what she saw – desperation. It was how she had looked at Florentina when they first met, the day Florentina had caught her trying to lift a gold fleck from her purse in the slums of Fakcil. And suddenly Sel was back there, all those winters ago.

She had fancied herself skilled at pickpocketing in her childhood and she had not thought twice about sidling up to the woman in a black cloak in the market. But then a hand had grasped hold of her wrist and the woman had dragged her down a side street with surprising strength.

Sel had opened her mouth to scream, but no sound would come out.

'I will let you speak if you promise not to cry.'

Sel had regarded the woman suspiciously but, finally, she nodded.

'You chose the wrong pocket to steal from,' the woman said, after muttering something in a language Sel did not understand. 'But I am feeling generous, so follow me and I will buy you a meal.'

'Are you a madam?' Sel asked, her voice returned to her. She had almost been caught in a trick like this before.

The woman's expression softened. 'No,' she replied after a pause. 'You need not worry about that.'

Sel had still been suspicious, but the lure of food was too much to resist. They had gone to a tavern where they sat at a proper table, waited on by a server. The food had been plentiful and delicious and Sel had crammed every morsel she could into her mouth, gulping it down until she felt sick.

'What is your name?' the woman had asked when the meal was finished. She had not eaten much and had been watching Sel closely.

'Selhah.'

'Pretty. A family name?'

'My mam was called Selhah and that's what the madam she worked for called me.'

'You were born in a whorehouse, then?'

Sel had nodded, picked up her plate and started licking at the congealed sauce.

'Do you work there now?'

'It got burnt down and I ran away.'

Sel had put down her plate, wiped her mouth on her sleeve and burped.

Even now, she could remember that moment vividly. Sitting opposite Florentina in the tavern, it had dawned on her that this was a person to be trusted. It was a feeling, an intuition. This person was different from anyone she had met before. This person was safe.

'Do you need someone to work for you?' she had asked suddenly, leaning across the table.

'No—'

'I can work hard.'

'I do not doubt it, Selhah, but I must go now. Take my advice – if you see someone wearing a black cloak like this again, do not try to pick their pocket.'

The woman had walked away, out of the tavern and down the street.

But Sel had followed.

Florentina had not gone far when she stopped in an alleyway and sighed loudly. Then she called over her shoulder, 'If you are going to follow me, Selhah, then you had better make yourself useful and carry my pack. Do not even think of running off with it, because I will do much more than take away your voice if you disobey me.'

Sel had scampered from the shadows, grinning. She gladly shouldered the woman's bag, hoisting it on to her back while also trying to peek inside.

'You will do this for me and I will buy you a meal again tonight in payment,' the woman had said, tucking her long white hair behind her ears. 'Then we will part ways, understand?'

Sel had nodded.

But they never did part ways.

Sel had continued to follow Florentina like a shadow, despite the Master's growing frustration. Even when Florentina left Fakcil, Sel had wandered after her, leaving behind the other street kids and her makeshift home by the river. It was desperation and instinct that propelled her, and she had not given up until, in exasperation, Florentina finally offered her a job as a kitchen girl.

'Now stop skulking behind me and walk by my side!' Florentina had snapped after Sel accepted the position. 'And carry this bag. Make yourself useful until we reach Marshec, then it is straight to the kitchen with you.'

Sel had nodded, relief flooding through her. She would have accepted anything to follow this woman and get away from her old life. She could still remember that feeling – that this was the start of good things, that a miracle had happened. And she had been right. She had worked in Florentina's kitchen for a few moons until the Master caught her nosing through books in the library and decided to teach her to read. That was the day Sel's apprenticeship started and the day the course of her life changed for ever. She had been saved because someone had let her escape.

Now she had the chance to do the same for Jacken. Looking into the begging, defiant face before her, she could almost feel the dirt caked in her palms from the Fakcil slums, could almost smell the hot, fetid scent of the river that snaked through the city, and she could almost taste the creamy sauce from the dish Florentina had bought her at the tavern. She felt an old, familiar twist of grief in her gut, and she nearly gasped from the shock of it.

'You can come with us, Jacken,' she said, hoping she would not regret this.

Briar clasped Jacken's hand in delight, tugging on his arm excitedly, but the boy only nodded in dazed wonder.

Around them, the wind roared, and the waves crashed on to the shore.

'We'll go back to the schoolhouse and pick up more things to load on to the horses,' said Sel. 'Then we'll leave.'

'Thank you,' said Jacken quietly. 'Thank you.'

'We're going on an adventure, Jacken!' Briar cried. 'Just like you said.'

Violanna

The Queen's Chambers, Mont Isle

SHE HAD FRIGHTENED Talia. Shivering and feverish, tossing and turning in rancid, sweaty sheets, Violanna realized what she had done.

Two maids had appeared moments ago to wash and change her, and they had entered the room, whispering to each other. As Violanna lay with eyelids flickering and limbs twitching, she had heard one maid say to the other that the Princess had finally discovered the secret of her past. Princess Talia knew of her curse. And now she was demanding to speak to every servant who had witnessed the Blessing ceremony – she wanted as many details as possible.

As the maids twittered and gossiped together, Violanna's scrambled mind picked through this shocking news. She wondered who had disobeyed her and revealed such a terrible thing. Whoever it was, there must be consequences, and she was just debating what those could be when she remembered with a jolt that there had been a girl in her bedchamber earlier. Not just any girl. It had been her daughter – her other daughter. The one she had sent away, the one she dearly missed and the one she could never stop thinking about. *That* daughter had been standing at her bedside and Violanna had felt such relief, such joy, to see her. Her delight had been so great that she had seized upon the girl, trying to explain herself in panting, wheezy breaths. But it had frightened the child away. Violanna had a hazy memory of the back of a small, braided head, stumbling out of her bedchamber in terror.

But wait. No.

That had been Talia – she recognized that smooth, mousey hair and gangly frame. It had not been her other daughter, the missing one. Violanna felt her joy turn to dread. When she had thought she was speaking to her long-lost child, she had actually been speaking to Talia . . .

She had told Talia about the curse. She had finally revealed the secret.

Violanna groaned, a low, guttural sound.

Yesterday she had similarly mistaken the scullery maid who brought her a bowl of broth for one of her sisters in their youth. 'Gelrahim!' she had exclaimed. 'You must help me speak to Father . . .' The scullery maid had run off whimpering and Violanna had only realized her error later, when she awoke from a fitful doze to remember that she no longer lived in the Diaspass Kingdom – she was now a middle-aged woman residing in the Kingdom of Bavaugh. It had been a painful realization. But this mistake was far worse.

Talia would be furious. And devastated. And scared. Violanna had always known that she must tell Talia about the curse one day – Meredyth was forever badgering her to do so in her letters – but whenever Violanna had come close, she had found herself shrinking back, unable to utter the words. She already felt like a terrible mother. She had sent one of her daughters away with a stranger and she had punished herself by shunning her remaining child. She did not think that she deserved Talia's love and so she had kept her at a distance, though it made her miserable. She had wanted to be the one to tell Talia about the curse herself – some part of her had hoped that it might mend things between them, but she had left it too long and now her opportunity was gone.

The maids cleaning her finished up their tasks and began shuffling around the room, preparing to leave. Violanna wanted to ask them to stay and tell her more about the Princess, but she could not summon the energy even to open her eyes, let alone speak.

One of the maids poured something sweet and hot on to Violanna's cracked lips, which oozed into her mouth and dribbled down her cheeks. She tried to swallow what she could, though it seared her throat. Then she felt a cold flannel wipe her face and, a few moments later, she heard the creak of her bedchamber door closing.

The maids were gone.

Alone again, Violanna's mind sank back into jumbled thoughts. This illness that made her body ache and her stomach burn also muddled her head. Her thoughts were a snarled, elastic tangle of snippets and memories. Sometimes childhood songs and ditties flitted into her mind and circled round and round, the words warping and losing all meaning. Sometimes she relived the awful day of the Royal Blessing and felt the terror of that event as if it were really happening again. And sometimes she was pulled back into the depths of her past, remembering days at the palace in the capital of the Diaspass Kingdom – her old home – with mingled nostalgia and sorrow.

She remembered her eleven sisters, playing and squabbling together in the nursery and the palace courtyards, hugging and pinching each other, crying and laughing together. She remembered dull days in the schoolroom, following the lessons of the Masters who taught the Diaspass royal family basic magic principles and history. She had loathed every moment, except for the classes taken by Florentina Samara the Wise, her kind, favoured teacher. And she remembered long, hot summer afternoons in the palace gardens, feeding the tame palinkies that roamed the grounds and chasing her sisters through the hedge maze.

Then Violanna's thoughts would shift, and the flashes of her past would darken. She tried to pull away from such memories, but she could not control the visions that flared into life.

She saw herself waking at night in her childhood bedroom and creeping down to the schoolroom. There she secretly watched as magic, powerful and dark, crackled in the air and billowed to the ceiling, conjured by a familiar figure who now looked like a stranger. Violanna stood frozen in terror for several long moments, until a vicious *crack* sounded and she ran back to her room, shaking with fear.

Then she saw herself standing before her father, the King – a hard and proud man. She heard herself warning him of another's growing greatness. She was worried and she hoped he would soothe her, but instead seeds of doubt and fury were planted in his heart. He feared that his rule could be challenged by one so powerful, and ordered that all lessons in magic must cease. Anyone found to have disobeyed his command would face a most severe punishment.

Next she saw herself, almost a young woman, writing to Florentina Samara the Wise in the north of Diaspass and appealing to her favoured Master for counsel. Violanna explained her growing fears that dark magic was corrupting someone she loved dearly. She did not know what to do.

And lastly, the most terrible of all, Violanna saw herself hurrying through the Diaspass palace at night, guilty tears wetting her cheeks. Tearing down a corridor, she saw herself stumble to a halt by an open doorway, peering inside at the figure hunched over the floor.

Shaking and dishevelled, the figure raised its head and Violanna looked upon a bloody, beaten face. 'I am sorry!' she heard herself crying, knowing it made no difference. 'Please forgive me.'

But the figure only stared back.

PART FOUR

PART FOUR

THE SOUTH-EAST CORNER of the Kingdom of Bavaugh was strange – everyone knew that. At some point the borders of the kingdom ended and the Wildlands began: a stretch of uncultivated, unknown forests, hills and moorland ending in a great lake that bridged the Central Realm. There was a saying in Bavaugh that went: *He's had a walk through the Wildlands* – meaning the individual in question had lost their mind.

The Kingdom of Bavaugh mostly ignored this border, preferring to look outwards to the surrounding Fringe Islands. King Felipe's great-grandfather, King Chrithlop, famously forgot it altogether, once remarking that Bavaugh was 'the greatest of the Fringe Islands', until someone gently pointed out that Bavaugh was not an island at all.

'Well, it might as well be,' was King Chrithlop's infamous response. 'Everybody knows that the Wildlands do not count.'

Only those with true adventure in their hearts struck out into the Wildlands, attempting to clear and claim the wilderness. Or, as many privately thought, only those who were a little soft in the head. Even the folk from the border towns thought those who ventured further were odd. It was a peculiar kind of spirit that propelled you into that nothingness for no good reason.

Sel

Norrale, South-east Bavaugh

SEL WAITED ON the steps of the chapel, a bouquet of twigs and winter berries growing damp and slippery in her hands despite the chilled air. She had picked them on the walk from their lodgings, gathering the bunch from the hedgerows, and frost still clung to some of the thin branches like a velvet fuzz that glistened in the silvery morning light.

'Are you sure about this?' asked Briar for the fifth time.

Sel nodded. From inside the chapel, she could hear the faint murmur of voices, and behind them were the stirrings of the village: the thud of horses' hooves ambling down the main street, the clack of shutters opening in the shop windows, and the low mumble of residents calling greetings.

What will everyone think when they hear the news? Sel wondered.

It would be scandalous in a village like Norrale, where an escaped cow was the most exciting recent event. But by then she would be gone – settling into life on the Wildlands frontier – and she would not have to face anyone until she returned for supplies. Gaddeous visited the village in winter and summer to trade, and he said she was welcome to join him if she wished; otherwise, they would stay on the farm.

'You know, I can go in right now and tell Jacken you've changed your mind,' said Briar. 'He can distract Gaddeous and we'll run away.'

'We wouldn't need to run; Gaddeous isn't a brute.'

'You barely know him.'

This was true. If Sel tried to conjure his face in her mind, it was hazy. She could see his thick dark beard and his large red hands, pitted and scarred, but she could not remember if his eyes were grey or brown.

It was his hands that she had first noticed when they met. She had been holding a batch of fresh rolls at the counter of the bakery in Norrale, concentrating on haggling with the owner, and she had not realized there was someone standing beside her until a large, calloused hand shot out, grabbed a roll and broke it in half.

'A superior bake,' a deep voice said. 'You should take the lady on. I'll buy three right now.'

The baker made some noises of protest before reluctantly giving in.

'Thank you,' Sel said, turning to the stranger beside her. He was standing in shadow, his tall, broad frame hunched in the cramped space.

'No bother. This is good bread.' He looked at her for a long moment and added, 'I don't think I've ever seen you in Norrale before. What's your name?'

Without thinking, Sel replied truthfully, 'Selhah.' She stood in a shocked daze, her cheeks flushing pink. She had not uttered her true name in a long time and she did not know what had compelled her to give it to this man.

'Good day, Selhah,' he replied, and after paying for the rolls, he turned and left the bakery.

Sel had expected to bump into him again as she settled into life in Norrale. It was not a large village and her arrival with Briar and Jacken had caused a little stir of excitement in a place that rarely experienced newcomers. It was harder to keep to themselves than she had hoped. But she did not see the tall, broad stranger again until the following winter.

'It's you!' she said, catching sight of him in the main street.

'And it's you, Selhah,' he replied in his deep rumble, not seeming at all as surprised to see her. 'The bread at the bakery is much improved. I've just got myself a loaf.'

'What's your name?' she asked, since she still did not know.

'Gaddeous.'

Before Sel could ask another question, Briar came running down the street, holding aloft Sel's forgotten shawl. She was a beautiful, dazzling sight; a slight, golden girl of thirteen winters, so unnervingly delicate and graceful. Immediately Sel ushered Briar back to their lodgings, reminding the girl that she was not supposed to leave in the middle of the day. In all that panic, Gaddeous was forgotten.

The next morning, Sel enquired after him at the bakery.

'Gaddeous?' the man said over his shoulder as he stacked loaves on the shelves. 'He's a frontier man with a farmstead out yonder. One of those.'

A frontier man. A farmstead on the edge of the Borders.

Sel ruminated on this for the rest of the winter. In the evenings, as she read her books beside the fire, she often found herself wondering what Gaddeous was doing at that moment. It was a peculiar, confusing feeling; she had never found herself thinking such things about anyone before and she did not know why she had started now, but she could not seem to stop it. She wondered what it was like to live beside the wilderness. The idea of a wide expanse of unknown, unowned land was strange and exciting. She had seen the Wildlands on various maps and she had read about them in books, but never in great detail. She wondered what had drawn Gaddeous to such a place and she decided she would ask him when she saw him again. *If* she saw him again.

And at the following Summer Solstice celebration, she had found herself searching for him in the crowd. She had guessed he would be there for the market, and she was right. When she spotted him, Gaddeous was standing at the edge of a group, listening to a lute player. Before he even had a chance to greet her, Sel had rushed up to him and said, 'I want to know what it's like living next to the wilderness.'

He regarded her for a long moment before saying, 'Truthfully, it's a hard and lonely life, but it's beautiful and freeing too.'

'If you're lonely, you ought to take a wife.'

Sel did not know why she had said it and immediately she felt her cheeks blush bright pink. She had never imagined herself someone's wife – she had never imagined herself in this life at all – but perhaps it might be beneficial for now. The thought had been forming in the back of her mind all winter as she sat before her books, dreaming of somewhere so remote that surely no one would ever be able to find them. Somewhere without questions that she could not answer. Somewhere without curious eyes, where they could all hide. It would be nice to stop running for a while – and a marriage of convenience was not for ever. It would allow Sel a few winters of respite and when she was done, she would disappear, as she had disappeared many times before.

'I had a wife once,' Gaddeous replied in his deep rumble. 'But she died.'

'Would you like another?'

The laughs and shrieks of the celebration around them faded to nothing.

'I wouldn't turn down some company,' Gaddeous finally replied. 'But it isn't a life for everyone. Perhaps . . . perhaps when I return this coming winter, you could decide if it's a life for you?'

Sel held his gaze as she nodded, then turned and walked away because she was not sure what she should do next. Her hands were trembling and her chest felt tight. She marched over to Briar, who was lingering near the dancing – though she was under strict instructions *not to dance* – and Sel explained that she felt sick and needed to leave. Then she dragged Briar and Jacken back to their lodgings, where she took to her bed, complaining of a headache.

For the rest of the summer and all through the autumn, Sel had thought over the proposition, though she was already sure of her answer. The Winter Solstice arrived, and she watched and waited for Gaddeous to appear. When she finally caught sight of him, walking on the other side of the main street, she felt her throat squeeze as their eyes met.

She nodded.

Then he smiled.

'So I'm to take away Norrale's best baker?' he asked as he approached her. 'I'll not be popular.'

'I also have a niece and a dependent. They must go wherever I go.'

'Then we'll need to build more rooms at my farmhouse.'

'You must meet them first.'

This was to be the deciding factor. Sel led Gaddeous back to her lodgings and invited him inside. Jacken was just leaving, readying himself for a long day working with the farrier, and he greeted their guest with some confusion before rushing out of the door. Briar was slouched before the fire, twirling a lock of her hair, and initially she jumped up in excitement at the rare prospect of a visitor.

'This is Briar,' Sel said, watching Gaddeous closely.

His face remained impassive. 'I'm pleased to meet you, Briar.'

Briar looked at him with a surly expression – as surly an expression as a beautiful face can manage.

Gaddeous nodded back at her, polite and placid.

Any reservations Sel had had before vanished.

'Shall I see you tomorrow morning at the chapel?' Gaddeous asked.

'Tomorrow?'

'I'll be returning to the farm in the afternoon.'

'Then . . . yes,' Sel replied, with a churning sensation in her stomach. 'Tomorrow morning at the chapel.'

Gaddeous tipped his hat, leaving with a smile.

'Tomorrow?' Briar echoed. 'What's happening tomorrow?'

So Sel had told her. Then she had repeated the whole thing when Jacken returned at the end of the day. They could not understand her decision and there had been tears and more than one tantrum from Briar. But despite it all, Sel had not changed her mind. *This is the best decision for everyone*, she had told herself over and over as she packed up their things. *This will keep us all safe*, she had added as she dressed the next morning. And she had repeated it, like a mantra, as she walked to the chapel.

She said it out loud again now: 'This will keep us safe, Briar. This is the best decision for everyone.'

'But we're not in danger!' cried Briar, throwing up her hands.

Sel paused to look at her, and even though she saw the girl every day and knew the placement of each freckle on her body, she caught her breath at the sight. It was like looking into the heart of the fierce summer sun. At fourteen winters, Briar was glaringly beautiful and only growing more so by the day, as the spells around her consolidated and wound tighter and tighter. As time passed, the enmeshed magic was becoming more tangled and erratic, the gentle charms of the Blessing fusing with the dark magic of the curse. Briar's sweetness was souring, while her beauty flourished, and her gracefulness veered from exceptional lightness-of-foot to unexplained stumbling. Briar could not be in the presence of others without raising suspicion – even from the magic-ignorant Bavaughians. She was too strange, too odd. She needed to stay hidden.

'Briar, we're always in danger,' Sel replied.

'From *who*?' insisted Briar, not for the first time. 'Who're these "bad people" you've always said are coming after us?'

As usual, Sel ignored her. 'Our lives will be better with Gaddeous,' she said. 'Your life will be better.'

Briar sighed and shook her head. 'Jacken says you know what you're doing, but I'm not so sure.'

'You must trust me.'

Because I'm doing it for you, to keep you safe, Sel added silently.

She longed to pull Briar to her and tuck the girl's face into the crook of her neck, like she used to when she was small, feeling the soft puffs of breath on her skin, the knot of knees hugging her waist, and the pattering beat of Briar's heart against her shoulder.

Beside them, the door of the chapel opened, and Jacken peered out. He had combed back his dark hair for the occasion and scrubbed the collar of his shirt until it was almost white again.

'The minister's ready,' he said.

Sel drew back her shoulders and shivered. It was as though she was already at the edge of the wilderness; she felt reckless and free.

'Auntie—'

'Please try to trust me, Briar.'

The girl scowled and scuffed her boot against the top step.

'Now let's both smile,' said Sel. 'It's my wedding day.'

Meredyth

Guil, West Bavaugh

MEREDYTH TASTED SALT on her lips before she saw the castle, erupting from the sea in the distance, waves rolling at its walls and gulls spinning around its turrets. She had not visited the island for almost seven winters, but the sight of it brought up a familiar mixture of nausea and elation, like a burning lump at the back of her throat. It was springtime and the rest of Bavaugh was blooming with bright, cheerful colours, but seasons were slow to reach the windswept greyness of Mont Isle. Meredyth retreated into the carriage, snapping the flap of the window shut behind her.

'Are we almost there, Grandmama?' asked Hiberah, who sat opposite her, rubbing his round, dark eyes. 'I am so bored I could die.'

'Do not say such things!' snapped Meredyth. She was not a superstitious woman, but it did not strike her as wise to tempt the Great Creator. 'But yes, we are almost there. I can see it in the distance. Take a look for yourself.'

After much eye rolling and groaning, Hiberah hauled himself up and hung out of the carriage window.

'Is *that* it?' he cried, collapsing back into his seat, his long, lean limbs flapping. 'It looks as dire as everyone says it is.'

'I will have you know there is a lot of history on that island, young man!' hissed Meredyth, although a large part of her was inclined to agree with him. 'An ancient castle built by the early peoples and the birthplace of our own King.'

'A lot of death and misery, by the looks of things. Why must you go there? Why must *I* go there?'

This time it was Meredyth's turn to roll her eyes. Always the same protests from her eldest grandson since they had set out from Lustore days earlier.

'You are accompanying me while I visit because your father thinks I am too old to travel alone. If you have a problem, take it up with him.'

Hiberah stuck out his bottom lip and crossed his arms. 'I am missing the end of the hunting season.'

'So you keep saying.'

'And I am not just accompanying you, am I? Anyone could have done that. Mother says you have plans for me with the Princess.'

Meredyth sucked her teeth. In her opinion, her daughter-in-law was too soft on Hiberah. The boy had a sweep of dark stubble across his chin, and he was old enough to know his duty.

'It will do you no harm to meet her.'

'What is she like?'

'She is a *Princess*.'

'A cursed one,' muttered Hiberah, picking at his nails.

They fell into a silence that lasted until Meredyth felt the carriage judder on to the causeway. She peered out of the window once more to see the stony road stretching ahead of them and the castle walls looming close.

'Sort yourself out, young man,' she barked as she sat down again. 'You appear scruffy and travel-worn.'

In fact, Hiberah looked as classically handsome as always, but it pleased Meredyth to see him anxiously pat at his curly black hair and tug at the creases in his jacket.

Outside, they heard the clop of the horses' hooves on the cobbles as the carriage rolled inside the castle walls and started up the incline towards the front courtyard. Finally, it rocked to a halt and the horses snorted and stamped in relief. Meredyth and Hiberah hauled themselves to their feet and alighted with much groaning and stretching.

'Grandmama, take my arm,' said Hiberah as they set off for the entrance.

'I am not an invalid.'

'You have a cane.'

'The cane is for my hips,' said Meredyth, but she took her grandson's proffered arm. 'They are getting worse.'

Hiberah patted her hand in a disinterested way.

'So the Princess lives here and never leaves?' he asked as they trudged inside.

Behind them, two manservants ferried their luggage from the carriage.

'As far as I am aware, she has never left,' replied Meredyth. She noticed that the entrance floor had been scrubbed and swept recently, which was an improvement on her last visit. *Although everything else could do with a good dust*, she thought, her gaze falling on a clouded mirror opposite.

'Grandmama, do you know if—'

'Hush,' hissed Meredyth, straightening up as the door opposite opened and a girl strode towards them.

Meredyth did not know what she had been expecting, but Princess Talia did not look as she had imagined. The small child she had left after her last visit was now tall and sturdy, with none of Queen Violanna's daintiness. Princess Talia's mousey hair was scooped back into a simple braid – far too childish for a girl of fourteen winters, thought Meredyth, making a mental note to speak to Rashel about that. Talia's gown was neat but simple. Meredyth had ordered the dress herself, cut in the latest, fitted fashion, but she could see from a quick glance that Talia's stays had not been pulled tight enough and the matching embroidered sash that ought to have accompanied the gown was nowhere to be seen.

'Hello, Princess,' said Meredyth, dropping to a curtsey. 'It is a pleasure to see you again.'

The Princess stopped a few paces into the room, her eyes falling on Hiberah. She frowned.

'I hope you do not mind, but my eldest grandson has accompanied me,' added Meredyth. 'Princess, this is Hiberah Lansin, heir to the Lansin estate.'

Hiberah bowed and murmured, 'Hello, Princess.'

With visible reluctance, Princess Talia nodded. 'It is a great joy to see you . . . both.'

'Thank you, Princess. It is a greater joy for me to see you so grown,' said Meredyth. 'Now you are taller than me!'

Princess Talia made a gesture that was half a shrug, her eyes flicking to Hiberah.

'How is your mother, Princess?' asked Meredyth. 'I have been writing to her, but I have not had a response for some time. Is she still bedridden?'

The Princess scratched at her arm then seemed to remember herself and quickly clasped her hands in her skirts. 'More or less,' she replied. 'Mother lost her strength – the little she had – in a fever some winters ago and never made a full recovery.'

Meredyth made a worried *hmm* noise. It was as she had suspected. She would go to Queen Violanna's chambers as soon the luggage was unpacked. Her old friend needed coaxing back to better health.

'Did you receive *my* last letter, Lady Lansin?' asked Talia, planting her hands on her hips. 'I asked you to procure a few study books for me.'

'Yes, Princess,' replied Meredyth slowly. This was on her list of things to tackle while at Mont Isle, but she had not expected to do so yet. 'I could not help but notice that the books all appear to be studies of magic.'

'And?'

'I cannot understand what you would want with such things, Princess?'

The Princess made a *tssk* noise and folded her arms. 'I have read every book I can find in this castle that mentions magic,' she said. 'All I have discovered is that there is so much more for me to learn.'

'But—'

'I must understand this curse upon me, Lady Lansin. Neither you nor anyone else will tell me anything useful, so I am forced to go looking for it myself.'

Meredyth blinked rapidly, feeling unusually flustered. 'Princess, as I have said in our many letters on the subject, I cannot tell you anything because I do not know—'

'I need to find out what happened to me, Lady Lansin. I need to know everything about the curse. Or else how can I do anything about it?'

Meredyth gulped back her surprise. Princess Talia's letters were always blunt and direct, but in person her manner was overwhelmingly forthright.

'Those titles are just the beginning,' Talia continued before Meredyth could respond. 'They are everything I could find referenced in the books I have already read, but I am sure I will need many more as my studies progress. We might have to send off for some titles from the Central Realm, where their magical knowledge is so much more advanced.'

'I see . . .' replied Meredyth faintly. Here was another issue she must urgently discuss with Queen Violanna. Meredyth was about to try to change the topic of conversation, when the Princess abruptly clapped her hands.

Both Meredyth and Hiberah jumped.

'Right, I have some study scheduled now, so I shall leave you,' she said.

'Study?' echoed Meredyth. 'But I thought you practised music in the afternoons, Princess?'

'Oh . . . yes, of course,' said Princess Talia after a moment's hesitation. 'Anyway, goodbye.'

Meredyth was preparing to sink into another curtsey when she realized that the Princess had already gone. She was alone in the hall with her grandson once more.

'So *that* is the Princess,' said Hiberah.

There was a pause.

'She is quite strange and quite . . . plain.'

'She is not!' lied Meredyth. 'You are just used to trussed-up, bejewelled court ladies.'

'She does not look much like a princess. She looks like a . . . like a governess, or a healthy milkmaid.'

'Enough,' snapped Meredyth, giving his shin a prod with her cane.

'And she certainly does not act like a Princess,' Hiberah added. 'Her manner is most odd. Not exactly welcoming.'

Meredyth gave her grandson an even harder poke. 'Go outside and make sure all of the luggage has been taken in,' she said. 'You would do well to remember your own manners.'

Hiberah disappeared, muttering things under his breath that she pretended not to hear.

Meredyth remained in the entrance hall, thinking over her grandson's observations. She tapped her cane on the flagstones, dulled and worn with age, and her brow creased into a frown.

Briar

The Wildlands

BRIAR LEANT FORWARD and rested her chin on the top bar of the fence. There were bluebells at her feet, brushing the edges of her homespun skirt, but these signs of spring did not bring her the usual joy. She kicked at a nearby clump of flowers, swishing her leg back and forth, and flattening them with grim satisfaction.

'How was that?' yelled a voice from the paddock.

Briar looked up to where Jacken was sitting astride a skewbald mare, squinting in her direction.

'Umm . . . it was fine,' she called back.

'Were you even watching?'

'Yes!'

Jacken nudged the mare forward, trotting over to the fence. As always, he sat tall, his seat perfect and natural. Halting, he peered down at Briar with a look of mixed frustration and concern, his head tilted to one side, his dark hair falling over his eyes.

'What?' she said finally.

'You're upset.'

'I'm fine.'

Jacken let the mare's reins loose. 'Conker's coming on well, don't you think?' he said. 'Gaddeous is impressed with what we've done. He said we could take her to Norrale for the summer market and he reckoned she'd get snapped right up. He said we can keep the flecks.'

'Of course we can keep the flecks!' snapped Briar. 'She's *our* horse. We caught and trained her.'

'Yes, but—'

'And *you'll* get to go to Norrale and stay for the Summer Solstice, but I already know Auntie won't let me go.'

Jacken fiddled with a tuft of Conker's dark mane. 'You've got to be careful because of those people—' he began.

'What people? Who are these people Auntie keeps making us run from? Sometimes I think . . . sometimes I think she's made it all up!'

Briar flopped against the fence, gritting her teeth. An unsettled, sceptical feeling had lodged inside her since they had fled Turow almost seven winters ago. It had started small; something about Auntie's tale of Briar's deceased mother and the 'bad people' who wanted to take Briar away did not ring true. The feeling had grown into a deeper-rooted suspicion as the winters passed and they moved from place to place, never settling, and it had intensified since they had arrived in this peculiar, remote place.

Briar hated the feeling and she knew that it made her grumpy and snappy sometimes, but she did not know how to make it go away. Sometimes Briar questioned her aunt about their past but always Auntie gave the same evasive answers. Briar tried to believe them – she *wanted* to believe them – but something did not feel quite right.

A loud snort made Briar look up. Conker was leaning over her, lipping at her braid.

'That's not hay, you cheeky thing,' she muttered, scooping her hair away.

'Did something happen this morning?' asked Jacken, scratching at the stubble around his jaw. 'Did you fight with Sel again?'

'*Sel?* Sel,' snapped Briar. 'Who even knows what her real name is. First it was Arla. When we were working at Copperhill it was Lyillia, and now it's Selhah. I can't keep track.'

Jacken swung himself off Conker's back and slid down into the long grass at the verge. Briar noticed that it was not far for him to land these days. He had been growing at an alarming rate since they had moved to the farmstead – Auntie said she almost thought she had seen him grow a whole inch over breakfast one morning – and now all his clothes were too small, and he kept banging his head on doorways and knocking over pots in the kitchen.

'Don't you miss Copperhill?' Briar added, thinking of the grand estate in the mid-country where they had worked before moving to Norrale. 'You never talk about it.'

'Not really.'

'What about Smoke? You must miss him. You said he was the best horse you'd ever ridden.'

Jacken sighed and ruffled his hair. 'I suppose I do miss Smoke, but he belonged to the Sir of Copperhill and all my training got ruined every time they went out on a hunt. It's better here; we don't have to work for no one and we can catch our own horses.'

Briar shook her head. 'Well, *I* miss Copperhill,' she said.

'You only liked it because the mistress said you were an angel and gave you presents,' Jacken muttered.

'Not true!'

'And you didn't have to do any work.'

'Yes, I did! I had to keep the cottage clean while you and Auntie were out. And I had to do my lessons.'

Jacken shook his head and started to unbuckle Conker's saddle.

'I didn't mind it so much in Norrale either,' Briar carried on. 'Except I hated having to stay inside all day and not see anyone. But at least I could watch people out of the window.'

'Exactly. Here you're free. You can go anywhere you want at any time you want and not have to worry.'

'But there's no one to see or talk to.'

'There's me.'

Briar sighed. 'That's not the same,' she said. 'That's just like talking to myself.'

Jacken slung the saddle over the side of the fence and wiped his hand across his brow. 'You'll get used to it here,' he said.

'You said that when we arrived at Midwinter, and I'm still not used to it.'

Briar scowled and folded her arms as Jacken crouched down then vaulted on to Conker's back.

'I'm going to do some work without the saddle,' he said. 'Then do you want to do some training?'

Briar stared straight ahead, refusing to answer. She stayed like that for some time, pretending not to watch as Jacken cantered Conker in steady figures of eight around the paddock, holding the reins loosely in one hand and steering the mare with his knees. Finally, she grew tired of keeping her silence, and the spring sunshine was making her hot and itchy. She called over that Conker wanted a break and ambled to the shaded side of the paddock, where the rough fence ran along the edge of the forest. There were knotted clusters of snowdrops beneath the trees, and patches of yellow primroses sprouting among the gnarled roots. Briar picked one and twirled it between her fingers, while Jacken unbuckled Conker's reins and let the mare trot off to graze.

'Do you remember the daffodils at Turow outside the schoolhouse?' Briar asked.

'No, I never went there.'

'They were beautiful. There aren't any daffodils here.'

Jacken dragged over the knapsack he had left in the shade and pulled out some bread and cheese wrapped in cloths.

'Paleen had lots of daffodils in her garden too.'

'Who?'

'The minister's wife. I know you remember; I talked about her all the time. You're just pretending you don't,' said Briar, narrowing her eyes.

Jacken broke the bread and cheese in half and handed pieces to her. She nibbled at the corner of the cheese, thinking of the evenings she used to spend with Paleen when they lived in Turow. They would sit together in the parlour at the minister's house, and she would play with her doll on the floor while Paleen worked at her spinning wheel. Briar could still hear the low crackle of the fire and the steady, soothing *clack, clack, clack* of the wheel.

'I wrote to Paleen,' she said after a pause.

'Briar!'

'She's my friend and we left so suddenly; I bet she didn't know what had happened. I miss her.'

'Does Sel know?'

'Of course not, and you'd better not tell her!'

Briar lunged forward and grabbed hold of Jacken's shirt, trying to hold the collar tight like she did when they were younger, but it did not seem as threatening now as it used to. She could tell that Jacken was shocked that she had done something like this and kept it a secret for so long. They normally told each other everything. But lately it felt like Jacken didn't understand her any more. When Briar tried to explain the uncomfortable, suspicious feeling she had about Auntie, Jacken would always interrupt and say that they must trust her aunt.

'All right, I won't tell,' said Jacken, shaking Briar off. 'But you shouldn't have done that.'

'I never said where we were.'

'When did you send it?'

'I sent her the last letter when we were at Norrale.' Then, before Jacken could reply, she added, 'It's fine, we can trust Paleen; she's a good person.'

'How did you even manage to do it?'

'I wrote when Auntie was out and paid to send it myself by selling one of those ribbons the mistress at Copperhill was always giving me,' replied Briar, grinning smugly. Auntie did not exactly say she was dim, but she was always complaining about what she called Briar's 'lack of aptitude', so maybe she would be a little bit impressed if she ever found out.

'You shouldn't send any more letters,' said Jacken, swallowing a mouthful of cheese.

'I can't being stuck here, can I?'

Briar noticed that he had already finished his bread, so she gave him the rest of her crust, which he devoured in two bites.

'We could ask Gaddeous if we can go into the forest tomorrow and try to catch another horse?' said Jacken, gesturing to the tangle of trees and nettles behind them. 'We'll need one if we sell Conker in the summer.'

'Why do we need to ask Gaddeous?'

'He said we should always tell him if we leave the borders of the farmstead. Anything could happen in the wilderness. We don't want to find another griffin.'

On the day they had caught Conker, Briar and Jacken had stumbled across a hulking, sleeping bird in a shadowed clearing. Briar had tried to edge closer for a better look at its huge, folded wings and glinting beak, but Jacken had pulled her away.

'I can do what I want and it's no concern of his,' replied Briar.

Jacken rubbed his neck. 'You know, he's a good man.'

'What makes him so good?'

'The way he treats his animals, the way he tends the farm, the way he is with you.'

'With me?' spluttered Briar. 'What does that mean?'

Jacken shrugged. 'People can be weird around you, but he isn't.'

'Weird? In what way? What are you saying?'

'Nothing,' said Jacken with a sigh. 'But Gad makes your aunt happy and he's kind to us – isn't that enough?'

Briar frowned. She did not like this man that Auntie was so obsessed with. '*No*,' she replied. Then she added, 'I won't stay here for ever, you know. One day I'm going to leave.'

'All right,' said Jacken.

'I'm serious!'

'All right, all right.'

She knew he did not really believe her, but it was true – she meant every word.

Violanna

The Castle, Mont Isle

THE GROUND BENEATH Violanna's feet was crusted with tiny shells and straggly locks of seaweed caught around rocks, like food trapped between teeth. Above her, the sky was pale grey and filled with the swooping, arching shapes of gulls, screeching at one another. The sound jangled her nerves and the salty breeze on her cheeks felt raw. She could hear her heartbeat thumping in her ears and her breath came in short, sharp gulps from her chest.

'Are you all right, Your Majesty?' called Meredyth. She was a few paces ahead, her cane sinking into the waterlogged black sand, the hem of her dress dark and damp.

Violanna licked her dry lips and tried not to squint into the brightness. She could already feel a headache building at the base of her skull. 'I cannot go further,' she replied. 'I cannot risk it.'

'But you are still on the island . . .' Meredyth must have seen

Violanna's expression, because she quickly added, 'Maybe we will just pause here a moment, Your Majesty.'

They stood on the rocks of Mont Isle, the castle walls to one side of them and a sandy expanse stretching into the distance on the other.

'It is good to get some fresh air,' said Meredyth in a forcefully cheerful voice. 'I know you were not so keen on my idea of a walk, but I think it will do you well.'

Violanna sighed. She had become accustomed to spending most of her days in her bedchamber with the shutters closed, and she would not have changed that for anyone but her old friend.

'You should sit,' she said, noticing Meredyth shift from foot to foot with a grimace. 'There is a flat rock here.'

Meredyth looked as if she were about to refuse, but eventually nodded.

They fell into silence, both staring out to the horizon, the sea breeze tugging at their silver-peppered hair and ruffling their skirts.

'It is a strange place here, is it not?' said Meredyth. 'Bleak and beautiful and troubling all at once. Talia said that someone was caught in the tides and killed this last moon? She said it happens a lot.'

'It is dangerous if you are not careful.' After a moment, Violanna added, 'Talia used to play out there when she was little. Sometimes I would see her from my chambers. I wanted to tell her to stop, but she looked so happy it did not seem fair. Then she was caught out by the tide herself one day . . .' The memory of Talia standing dripping wet before her still made Violanna's body tense with fear. 'She has not left the castle walls since.'

Meredyth cleared her throat. 'Do you think that it is wise for her to have stayed cooped up for so long, Your Majesty? I know you cannot leave the island, but Talia could visit the mainland once in a while.'

Violanna reached out a hand and flattened her palm against the castle wall beside her. It was slick and cold like skin, and she could feel dregs of magic still pulsating through its foundations. She had never wielded magic – she did not have an appetite for such things – but she knew its taste, its touch, its smell. Magic still seeped through the core of Mont Isle, waiting.

'She must stay on the island,' said Violanna. 'She must stay close to the magic so that everyone will mistake it for the curse bound to her.'

After a pause, Meredyth asked, 'Do you think we can stop the curse, Your Majesty?'

Violanna wanted to scream back in fear and desperation. How could her friend not realize that the answer to that question consumed her every moment? She managed to reply, 'The switching of the Princesses . . . I think it is the only hope we have.'

'And I suppose you have heard no news of the *other* Princess?'

Violanna winced. 'No. I have heard nothing and I must hear nothing until this is all over. We cannot speak of it to anyone.'

'But Talia is aware of the curse now. She is even trying to learn about magic herself.'

'You must not let her. She must not disrupt anything.'

'Have you met your daughter? I do not think I could stop her doing what she has set her mind to. Perhaps . . . perhaps you should speak to her? Perhaps if she knew that—'

'No!' Violanna hissed. Her eyes fluttered shut and she waited for a wave of nausea to crash through her. 'She cannot know.'

'I do not understand—'

'Of course you do not understand!' snapped Violanna. 'Everything Bavaugh knows of magic could fit into my little finger.' As she held up her hand, she noticed her Olier, and she touched the gold bands on her forefinger and thumb, and rubbed the fine chain strung between them. 'It is why I came to this land in the first place. I thought I could hide.'

'From the sorceress?'

Violanna had said too much. Meredyth was trying to sound calmly curious, as if she had just asked what was planned for lunch, but Violanna could hear the eager probing behind her friend's tone. If only she could explain everything. But it was not safe. It was too soon.

'The curse is in place,' she replied finally, carefully. 'We must not say or do anything to unsettle it. I once hoped I could call on the Diaspass Masters to untangle the spell, but they have abandoned me. We do not hear much of Central Realm news or politics here, but I understand that they are preoccupied with the long and costly warring over Journier and I have started to suspect that . . .' Violanna's voice dropped to a whisper. 'That *she* is involved in the Journier battle somehow.'

'What did you say, Your Majesty?'

Violanna shook her head. 'Nothing. Meredyth, our only hope of success is the misdirection of the spell – the switch.'

'But are you sure you could not tell the Princess *something* about it all? She believes she is going to die.'

Tears smarted in the corners of Violanna's eyes. She remembered lying on the floor of the chapel, a mewing baby in her arms, and opposite her another daughter, beautiful and doomed, held by a stranger. 'Am I a good mother?' she asked suddenly, her gaze locked on the horizon.

After a moment, Meredyth replied, 'You have given up everything for your daughters.'

'But it might not be enough.'

The words of the curse rang through Violanna's mind: *Before seventeen winters have passed, I will return for you. On that day, the spell will end and you will die.*

'The sorceress will want me to suffer as much as possible,' she added. 'I have come to believe she will wait until the last moment to finish the spell.'

'Then there is time yet, Your Majesty.'

Violanna nodded. A gull dived down beside them with a shriek, splashing into a rock pool. Ahead, dark clouds were gathering on the horizon and bad weather looked to be sweeping towards the shore.

'Three more winters,' she whispered.

Sel

The Wildlands

SEL LEFT HER stockings and boots on the bank and waded into the water. The stream rushed around her ankles, numbing her skin with its chill, and she gasped, waiting for the feeling to return to her toes. She had laundry slung across her shoulders and when she had waded further, she tugged free a petticoat and pushed it into the riverbed, weighing it down with rocks.

Next, she submerged a jacket and a bodice, and pulled free a large shirt, smiling to herself as she did so. It was frayed at the collar, there was mud splattered across the front and a tie was missing on one sleeve. Sel brought the shirt quickly to her face and inhaled deeply. It had his smell – earth, sweat and hay. She shivered, remembering how she had pulled the shirt over his head the night before and flung it to the bedroom floor.

Sel had not realized that lovemaking could be tender and sweet. From her childhood in the whorehouse, she had understood it to be impersonal and rough, and later, her own experience had been forced and violent. She had heard others describe it as urgent and passionate, but to her it had always seemed a transaction, a payment or a chore. Things were different with Gaddeous.

She had spent their wedding night curled around Briar as they slept in a wagon, on the way to their new home. After the ceremony at the chapel in Norrale, they had all left for the farmstead, and when night fell, Gaddeous had told them to bed down in the wagon while he kept watch. Sel had wondered if he would expect her to consummate their vows. She had felt apprehensive and a little sick at the thought, all her bravado about the marriage waning as the day ended. But Gaddeous did not mention it, and even when they reached the farmstead, he did not appear to be expecting anything.

At first, it was a relief. In the farmhouse, she slept in the single bedroom with Briar, while Jacken and Gaddeous made up pallets in the kitchen each night. Work started on extending the house to build extra bedrooms, and Sel threw herself into life on the farm. She collapsed most evenings, exhausted after a gruelling day of cooking, cleaning and tending to the animals. She barely had enough energy to look over her books, let alone anything else. But after a while, she began to worry.

One evening, she was clattering around the kitchen by candle-light, making a batch of sweet rolls, when Gaddeous put a large hand on her arm. 'You don't need to do all this,' he said in his deep rumble.

Sel tried to laugh, but her voice sounded strained. 'You thought you were marrying the best baker in Norrale. I'd hate to think we were wed under false pretences.'

'I don't expect anything of you.'

Sel picked at some of the globs of dough stuck between her

fingers. 'You've just finished building one of the extra bedrooms. You're going to a lot of trouble for us.'

'When I first built this house, I thought I'd soon be extending it,' said Gaddeous, the candlelight sending shadows flickering across his face. 'But Yoline died and it seemed like that was the end of that. Then I met you.'

He was close to her; she could feel the warmth of his skin and the tickle of his breath on her cheek.

'I'm happy to do it,' he added. 'I'm happy you're all here.'

His brown eyes seemed sad and soft, and she had the sudden urge to step closer to him and lean against his broad, solid frame.

I must be tired, she told herself.

'Well, I'm glad to hear that,' she said.

Gaddeous looked as though he was about to say something else, but then the kitchen door opened, and Jacken appeared. The boy glanced at them and hesitated. 'I can come back later—' he began and Sel found herself blushing although she did not know why.

'*No*,' she replied, a little too forcefully. 'I'm just finishing these rolls. You should get ready for bed – it's late.'

'And so should you, Selhah,' said Gaddeous. 'Let me wait up for these to bake. Go and get some sleep.'

He reached across and took the tray from her, his hand brushing her own, and she flinched as if she had been burnt.

'All right,' she replied, her voice high. 'Thank you.'

Sel took herself swiftly off to bed, but lying beside Briar that night, she found that she could not sleep. *I do not know what is the matter with me*, she thought. *I hope I am not getting ill*.

Over the next moon, she found that these strange feelings would not go away. When she resumed her magical studies, she was often preoccupied, glancing frequently at the kitchen door, wondering when Gaddeous would return for dinner. She caught herself taking care over the way she pinned her hair and checking her reflection in the pigs' water trough. Strangest of all was the bubbling, giddy feeling that came over her whenever Gaddeous was around, like a pot of boiling water that was about to overflow.

She found herself making excuses to seek him out. On a rainy day, she suddenly paused halfway through milking the cows and announced that she was going to take Gaddeous his hat in case he caught a chill.

'Shouldn't you take Jacken a hat, too?' asked Briar, who was plaiting together pieces of straw near by.

'Of course,' Sel replied quickly. 'They must both have their hats.'

On another occasion, she told Briar she wanted to see some spring flowers, so they walked the long way back from the far barn in order to pass Gaddeous and Jacken at work, mending fencing in a field. Briar moaned the whole way and the bale of hay Sel carried across her shoulders from the barn made her neck ache, but she forgot these troubles when Gaddeous turned to her and smiled.

'You're a mighty strong woman,' he said. 'Where're you taking that hay?'

'It's for the chickens,' replied Sel, feeling herself glow at the compliment.

'You should've said you needed it; I could've brought it back and saved you the trip.'

'It's no bother.'

They had shared a few more pleasantries, while Briar huffed and moaned about wanting lunch, and Sel had reluctantly returned to the farmhouse. But for the rest of that day, she smiled to herself, remembering Gaddeous's expression brighten when he caught sight of her, and the way his brown hair curled around his forehead in damp coils in the heat.

Next, she started to dream about him. She would wake and lie staring at the ceiling, thinking of his hands stroking her cheek, tangled in her hair, touching her. By their first Summer Solstice at the farmstead, the extension to the house was complete, and now Sel had her own bedroom. For the first time since she had left the Diaspass Kingdom, she had a space that was just for her, but somehow she was not satisfied. When Gaddeous presented her with the room, he pointed out a hexagonal pattern carved into the headboard of the bed.

'I was rushing to finish everything, but I wanted to add a bit of decoration,' he said. 'You've a dress with a pattern like that on the skirt so I thought you might like it.'

'I love it,' Sel had replied quietly. 'Thank you.'

At night, she would often run her fingers over the bumps and grooves of the carved headboard, imagining Gaddeous making it. *Did he think of me as he worked?* she wondered. *Does he think of me as often as I think of him?* Sometimes she felt his brown eyes on her, as she was scrubbing a pot in the kitchen or carrying a pail of milk across the yard, but if he longed for her the way she did for him, he never acted on it. He was always attentive, but at a polite distance.

Finally, towards the end of summer, Sel could bear it no longer. She dressed one morning after a night of tossing and turning and decided that she would get Gaddeous alone and confront him. She prepared breakfast as usual, managing to catch him as he was about to leave for the fields.

She placed a hand on his arm and he stopped short with a jump.

'I've yet to see the wilderness,' she said. 'Will you show me today?'

Gaddeous stared back in surprise. 'You just need to go to the edge of the fields—' he began.

'Will *you* show me?'

He nodded slowly, his tanned brow creased. 'If you like,' he said.

Sel's palm tingled where it touched his skin and she pulled her hand away with some difficulty.

'Meet me by the far barn at the end of the day,' he added. 'We can walk up the hill and there's a nice view.'

Sel agreed, then busied herself with clearing the breakfast things, her cheeks hot.

For the rest of the day, she was good for nothing. She could not look at her books or even hold a conversation, much to Briar's annoyance. She kept starting a task then stopping, her fingers fumbling over everything and her mind elsewhere.

'Why do you keep humming?' asked Briar sharply, while they collected eggs from the yard.

'I didn't realize I was.'

'Well, you are, and it's out of tune, so stop. It's frightening the hens.'

Even Briar's relentless surliness could not perturb Sel. She awaited the evening anxiously, watching the summer sun's maddeningly slow descent with mingled excitement and trepidation. When, finally, the light seemed to be fading, Sel wrapped herself in a shawl and stopped before the little mirror above the fire in the kitchen.

She had never bothered too much with her appearance – in her youth it had been a dangerous thing to be pretty, and later, when she began training for her Masterhood, it had been of no consequence at all. She had tried a few beauty charms in her apprenticeship out of curiosity, though the study of enhancement had never interested her much. But just then, she wished she might have been blessed with some natural beauty. She had an annoying scatter of spots along her jawline that never seemed to heal, and her eyes were small and squinty. But she reminded herself that her hair was still dark and thick, and her teeth were straight. That was something.

'You'll have to do as you are,' she muttered at her reflection. Then she turned and forced herself out of the door.

The sky above the yard was a dusky lilac and the air was warm and smelt like baked hay. One of the farm cats had recently spawned kittens and Briar had sloped off earlier to play with them, so Sel easily slipped away without needing to make awkward excuses.

As she hurried down one of the trodden paths through the fields, she pulled the pins from her hair and let it fall down her back. When she saw the barn, her breath caught in her throat. A figure stood at the opening, silhouetted against the stacks of hay by the setting sun. A hot feeling rushed over Sel, and she slowed her pace, wanting the excitement of the moment to last.

'Good evening, Selhah,' said Gaddeous.

She could see that he had washed and changed into a fresh shirt after a day working in the fields. He must have taken the shirt with him that morning in preparation and the thought made her smile.

'Good evening, Gaddeous. I'm looking forward to seeing this view of the wilderness.'

'It's this way.'

He led her down the side of the barn and over a fence, into a steep, wooded area. They began to climb up the slope and, as they walked, Sel commented on how well the animals were looking in the fields. Gaddeous agreed that with her extra help and Jacken's hard graft, the farm was thriving.

'No thanks to Briar,' said Sel carefully, glancing sideways at Gaddeous's face in profile. 'She's not much help at all.'

'She's fine,' he replied with a shrug. 'You know, she taught my youngest dog to turn left and right on command. That dog's been troublesome since he was a pup, but he seems settled now.'

'Well, that's good.'

Sel did not want to dwell on Briar so she asked how the borders of the farm had been formed instead. As they crested the top of the hill, Gaddeous explained the back-breaking work that had gone into clearing the land and building the fences over the seasons.

'Perhaps we'll expand the farm if things keep going well,' he added. 'That's the joy of this place. You can grow as much as you need. It belongs to no one.'

They stopped at a break in the trees, the ground falling away in front of them in tumbling rolls, covered in vegetation. A river wound through the valley, glinting silver in the fading light, and a slight breeze ruffled the leaves of the trees, making them tremble and sway so that it looked like a shudder running down the hillside.

'It's beautiful,' said Sel. 'And strange to think that once the whole of Bavaugh looked like this – once the whole of the Western Realm, probably. Is it completely wild?'

'There are tales of folk who live out there, but I've not come across anyone. Just trees and animals – hogs, horses, wolves and the like. I've seen some lynx too.'

'Dragons?'

'I've not seen them, but I'd imagine there'd be some in there.'

Sel nodded, her gaze skimming across the view, trying to take it all in.

'This is what you wanted to see?' asked Gaddeous tentatively.

'Yes. I've always known about the Wildlands, of course, but I couldn't imagine what it was like.'

Gaddeous shifted beside her and his hand brushed her arm, making her jump. 'Do you like it?' he asked.

'Yes. I do.'

They stood in silence. Then, without agreeing to, they both turned and began making their way back down the slope. The light was fading quickly, and it was dark beneath the canopy of the woodland. Gaddeous tripped over a tree root, almost losing his footing, and Sel stumbled upon a rock and nearly fell on to her knees.

'Would you take my hand?' asked Gaddeous, chuckling. 'We could try to stop each other from falling.'

'That sounds like a good idea.'

Sel felt his large hand fold around her own in the darkness and she almost gasped at the bolt of longing that rushed through her. As they made their way down the rest of the slope and climbed over the fence at the bottom, she flinched at every sensation: the stroke of the breeze on her cheek, the swish of her skirts between her legs and the brush of her hair against her neck. Everything felt tender. When she had to let go of Gaddeous's hand to climb over the fence, she did so reluctantly, worried that there would not be an excuse to hold on to each other again. But as they walked around the barn, back to the main trail, he reached for her and she clasped his hand tightly, the callouses on his fingers rough against her skin.

They stopped outside the barn and turned to one another. Sel looked into Gaddeous's eyes and shivered, though she was not cold. She stepped forward, pressing her body against him, and his fingers clutched at her waist. Lifting her chin, she placed her hands on his broad chest and she felt the steady thud of his heartbeat against her palms and the warm brush of his breath on her lips.

'Is this what you want?' he asked.

Sel found that she could not reply, so she nodded.

She had told herself that she had accepted his proposal for

Briar — to escape prying eyes and keep the girl safe — but that was not wholly true. Sel had felt something when they met that she had not understood at the time. It had been steadily growing as the days passed and now she thought she knew what it was: a connection. A connection growing with trust day after day. Gaddeous was not traditionally handsome, and he was not the first man to have caught her eye, but she had never wanted to be with someone like this before.

'You don't have to—' he began, but Sel reached up and pulled his lips to her own, feeling her body collapse against him in relief.

The kiss started off delicate and sweet. Sel had never kissed someone like that. Then Gaddeous's hands were in her hair, gently pulling her closer, and she could feel the push of his hips against her, suddenly growing harder and more urgent. They tore away from one another, both gasping, and Sel turned her head to see the open entrance of the barn, dimly lit in the growing moonlight. Without speaking, she took Gaddeous's hand and led him inside, where dust motes shimmered in the air, and it smelt of wood and earth. Smiling, she tumbled on to the soft hay and pulled him after her, their hands and lips reaching for each other.

Not once while Gaddeous was tugging her dress from her shoulders or running his hands down her body did Sel think of the other times, when she had been full of terror and fear. In the past, she had sometimes wondered whether she would ever happily lie with someone. To be so close and intimate had felt dangerous, and she could not shake the old memories that clouded her mind. But with Gaddeous, it was different. It was not easy or perfect or simple, but something about it was right. She surprised herself with her urgency to kiss, caress and melt into him, her worries and fears forgotten. It was like a kind of magic — one that could not be studied or learnt in books.

Gaddeous was gentle and careful. When she winced, he stopped and pulled back from her, kissing the corners of her mouth. She reached for him again and he pressed her close, whispering, 'There's no rush; we can come back tomorrow.'

'I'd like that,' Sel replied with a smile, tracing the line of his collarbone with her finger.

And they did come back the next night, and the night after that, and the night after that too, until Sel suggested they meet in Gaddeous's room instead and save themselves the bother of pulling strands of hay from their hair and clothes afterwards.

And so Sel would wait until the farmhouse was quiet before creeping across the kitchen to Gaddeous's door and slipping soundlessly inside. She did not know why she wanted to keep their relationship a secret. It was not that she was embarrassed, but it all felt so exciting and new. She wanted it to be just between the two of them for a little while longer.

She did not think Briar suspected anything. The girl remained consumed by her own misery, moping about the farmstead all day long, waiting for Jacken to finish work. Sel had hoped that Briar would get used to their new life and maybe even grow to enjoy it, but that did not seem to be the case. Whenever she tried to engage Briar in what she was doing, the girl became moody and petulant. Sel thought perhaps it was the entanglement of the magic – that the curse was hurting Briar in some way. But she could not easily ask such a thing without raising unwanted questions, and these days she tried to avoid Briar's prying enquiries as much as possible.

It did not feel so long ago that Sel was bouncing the girl on her hip, Briar's tiny hands clutching at her, giggling as she blew raspberries into Sel's neck. Now she was lucky if Briar would speak to her. There had been times, back then, when Sel had found it too much. Hot hands constantly reaching out, grasping her hair, stroking her cheek, wanting hugs and kisses and love. It had been relentless and overwhelming, but how she would love to return to that now. She had been so caught up in the everyday tasks of life, so preoccupied with keeping them safe, that she had never once stopped to think that the baby she had carried out of the castle would not stay a baby for ever.

Sel grabbed an armful of washing and slung it across her shoulders. *Briar is growing*, she told herself, *and the end of the spell is approaching*.

Talia

The Kitchen Gardens, Mont Isle

TALIA SCANNED THE vegetable patch. It was rudimentary and untidy at best, but it was the only garden on Mont Isle not completely overrun with nettles. At the far corner, she spotted what she was looking for and, with a triumphant 'Ah-ha!' under her breath, she marched down a row of carrots.

Hiberah spun around with a yelp when she prodded him. Then he quickly straightened and brushed down his jacket. He had a funny way of tilting his chin up when he was nervous – one of the many observations Talia had made since he had arrived with Lady Lansin in the spring.

'Princess, do you—' he began, chin lifted.

'Have you met my brothers?'

Hiberah blinked at her.

'Dionathy and Stasthes,' she added. In her mind, they were distant, shadowy children who had the vague look of her father's portrait, and she was always hungry for information. It had struck her this morning that Hiberah might know more. She had only spoken to him alone on a handful of occasions – she mostly tried to keep out of his way. She was too busy for idle chitchat and she found him a bit boring.

'I know who the Princes are. And yes, Princess, I have met them.'

'What are they like?'

'Well, they are Princes. They are good horsemen, like the King, and I believe they are quite adept at archery too . . .'

Talia watched Hiberah as he spoke, wondering if he oiled his dark, curly hair, which glinted in the sunlight. She had overheard two maids giggling about him recently, teasing each other to try to catch his attention, and she was half curious to know if one of them had succeeded. He looked a little like Lady Lansin; they had the same large, deep-set eyes and neat, upturned noses, but Hiberah's features were darker.

'Prince Stasthes is more like the Queen,' Hiberah continued. 'Quiet and thoughtful.'

'Anything else? They must have more about them than that. What do they talk about? What do they do every day?'

Hiberah opened and closed his mouth, before finally saying, 'Those are . . . unusual questions, Princess. But I suppose you have never met them?'

Talia ignored this. 'Do you know anything about magic?' she asked instead. 'I know Bavaugh shuns it in principle, but there must surely be some people who dabble at court?'

Hiberah's dark eyebrows shot up his forehead. 'Magic? I do not know anything about that. No. It is . . . it is really a peculiar interest, Princess.'

'What do you know about the Tolbien threat, then?' she asked, wondering if Hiberah could be any use to her at all. 'I tried to bring it up over dinner last night, but your grandmother stopped me again.'

'Lord Mileaney was executed for treason. He tried to bring the Tolbien army into the kingdom via his coastal estate last season, and had it not been for the storm that waylaid their ships, we might have been in real trouble.'

'I already know that.'

'Then I am not sure there is much more I can tell you,' said Hiberah, fiddling with the pleated fabric at the ends of his sleeves. 'Apparently, we are at war, but I do not see how, because there is no fighting. I should like a proper battle. I would go and kill those Tolbiens. I think we should launch an attack on *them*.' He put his hands on his hips, hooking his thumbs over the edge of the black sash around his narrow waist.

Talia had asked Dottie about the unusual pleats at Hiberah's wrists and the sash he wore around his waist, but the old maid was also none the wiser. She thought perhaps it was a courtly thing. Talia did not think it looked *bad* exactly, but it seemed a bit pointless. What was wrong with straight sleeves and a belt?

'Wars are costly,' she replied. 'Do you know if the Royal Council has requested any peace talks?'

'Why should we do that?' spluttered Hiberah. 'They are the ones attacking us—'

'Because we won the Battle of Karkel during my great-grandfather's reign and took the Karkel Islands off them.'

'But Karkel have independence now. We gave them independence. If we had never intervened, then they would have remained under Tolbien rule.'

'After we mined all of Karkel's copper and precious stones, we graciously allowed them to become part of the Fringe Islands again. How lovely of us.'

Hiberah pursed his lips. 'I have not heard of any peace talks, Princess,' he said. 'I doubt our King would entertain the idea. It is just this new, young Tolbien ruler who thinks he can attack us. But we shall show him.'

'I see,' said Talia, her eyes drifting over his shoulder.

'Would you like to take a turn about the garden with me, Princess?' asked Hiberah, offering her his arm.

'What do you mean?'

'Would you like me to escort you around the garden?'

'But why would we do that?'

Hiberah dropped his arm back to his side. 'That is what people do.'

'Is it? In a vegetable garden?'

When Hiberah did not reply, Talia sighed. 'Oh, I imagine you do lots of walking around gardens with ladies at court? You are very handsome, so I expect you are quite popular.'

Hiberah stared at her. 'Thank you, Princess. I am greatly honoured that you would—'

'But if you wanted to walk somewhere, you would be better off on the battlements. Although it can be a bit windy, even on a nice day like today. Or you should visit the dovecote at the top of the east turret. It is mostly disused – there are just a few gulls nesting there. But it has a good view out to sea.'

Talia nodded at him in what she hoped was an encouraging way. She had noticed that Hiberah spent a lot of time hanging around the castle, looking aimless. Dottie said she ought to try to entertain him, seeing as he was a guest, and the old maid had even suggested that they might become friends. Talia had not had a real friend since Iver all those seasons ago and the thought was mildly appealing, but she considered herself too busy with her studies to be frittering away time. However, having caught Hiberah today trying to amuse himself in the vegetable garden, of all places, she could not help but feel a little sympathetic.

'Shall we walk along the battlements now?' she said. 'I am due to start some reading, but we could do a quick lap. There are seal pups on the rocks over the west side and I once saw merfolk on the rocks on the east side.'

Hiberah looked as though he was about to decline, before thinking better of it. 'I will accompany you if you should wish it, Princess,' he said.

Talia shrugged. 'Perhaps you could tell me about court life while we walk?' she said. 'I should like to know the details.'

'Now, that is something I *can* tell you.'

'And I will tell *you* more history of the Karkel Islands, so you understand why the Tolbiens are attacking us.'

Hiberah looked less keen about that idea, but he nodded. He raised his arm, as if he were going to offer it to her again, but then he clasped his hands behind his back instead.

'Follow me,' said Talia, turning and striding away between the rows of carrots.

Sel

The Wildlands

SEL ROLLED ON to her side and the bedsheets twisted around her bare legs, knotting at her ankles. The guttering flame of a single candle made the yellow light on the walls shudder and glow, and wax dribbled down its holder in rivulets, pooling on the bedside table. Sel giggled softly as Gaddeous moved closer, putting his head against her breasts and kissing her warm, damp skin.

'It must be late now,' she whispered, stroking his brown curls back from his face. 'Are you tired?'

'No, are you?'

'No.'

She had barely slept for the last moon, but Sel rarely felt tired. Summer had turned to autumn in a haze of giddy delight. Her days were full of blushing thoughts of what had occurred in the early hours, as she went about her daily chores, waiting for the night to fall so she could creep across the kitchen to Gaddeous's door again.

'Do you think anyone heard me leave my room?' she asked.

'Probably not,' he replied, his fingertips brushing light circles around her navel. 'But is it so wrong for us to share a bed?'

'When we married, we were not as we are now,' said Sel, propping herself up on her elbow. 'What did you think of me then?' she asked. 'Truthfully.'

'I thought you were the best baker in all the realm.'

Sel tugged on his beard. 'And?' she said, ignoring his protestations.

Gaddeous looked at her for a long moment. 'And I thought you were running away from something.'

There was a pause in which Sel watched the candlelight flicker across the wall. Finally, she swallowed and said, 'You're right.'

'You don't need to tell me if you don't want to.'

Sel had been deliberating over this for some time, even before they had begun sharing a bed. She was growing tired of shrouding her life in secrets and always being cautious. She thought that Gaddeous must suspect something – they were an unusual family, at best – and the fact that he never asked questions or demanded answers somehow made Sel want to share the truth with him more.

'I'm not a native of Bavaugh,' she said carefully. 'The Diaspass Kingdom is my homeland, and I'm only here to protect Briar, who is . . . different. It's hard to explain and I cannot say too much, but she's been wrapped in a spell and bound in magic since infancy.'

'I understand.'

'You do?'

'There's magic all around Briar.'

Sel sat up in surprise. 'You can feel it?' she asked. 'You know the feeling of magic?'

Gaddeous took her hand and laced his fingers through her own. 'Yes. I'm not a native of Bavaugh either.'

Sel raised her eyebrows and gestured for him to carry on.

'I was born on the Karkel Islands and there are some magic-wielders there – nothing on a par with the Diaspass Kingdom or the rest of the Central Realm, mind you, but simple spells. My aunt was apprenticed to a wise woman and she knew some charms and the like. She lived with my mam for a while during her training, so I got to know the feel of magic. Although it was nothing like what's around Briar. I felt it the moment I met her.'

After a shocked pause, Sel leant back on the pillows and murmured, 'I knew there was something different about you.' She thought back to a map of the Fringe Islands that had hung on the wall of the school-house in Turow – a mass of scattered splinters like shattered glass. Karkel was one of the larger groups of islands to the south-west of Bavaugh. 'Why did you leave the Karkel Islands?' she asked.

'Because there was not much there for us back then and we wanted a new life – an adventure.'

'You and Yoline?'

'Yes.'

'What was she like?' asked Sel, fiddling with the edge of the bedsheet.

'She was funny and kind. You would've liked her.'

Digging her fingernails into her palms, Sel asked, 'Do you miss her?'

'Of course. But, you know, often I think I can't really remember her any more. She died some time ago, just a few seasons after we first settled here. She caught a winter fever and it took her. She's buried in the woodland at the back of the house.'

'The rosebush?'

'Yes.'

Gaddeous looked so sad that Sel could only feel compassion. She had come across the rosebush in the woodland behind the farmhouse a few times and always thought it a curious place to plant such a thing. She leant forward and rested her head on Gaddeous's shoulder, breathing in his familiar smell.

'I should've left after Yoline died,' added Gaddeous, 'and returned to what family I might have remaining in Karkel, but I couldn't face the journey. I'm not as strong as you.'

'As strong as me?' said Sel in surprise.

'You've been guarding Briar since her infancy in a land that is not your own. That's a resilience I can't fathom.'

'I didn't have another choice.'

'You could've left her.'

Sel shook her head.

They were quiet for a moment, then Gaddeous said, 'I'm not too proud to realize that you came to the farm to be safe, and I'm glad to be able to give you that at least – but are you happy?'

Sel moved so that she was looking into his brown eyes. 'I feel free,' she said. 'And I've not felt that in a long time.'

'I'm glad. Do you think Jacken is all right? He works so hard.'

'Jacken is happy as long as Briar is near.'

'I had noticed that,' said Gaddeous with a chuckle. 'Do you think he . . . ?'

'Is devoted to her? Yes, certainly. But not in the way that most are. It's not her strange beauty that he loves, but just her, as she is. He's a little older than her, though I don't think he knows his true age, and she's so innocent. Sometimes I think she must realize, but then, in other moments, I'm not so sure.'

'It seems you've thought over it a lot.'

'I spend most of my life thinking about Briar.'

Gaddeous squeezed her fingers. 'Have you ever spoken to Jacken?'

'You mean, have I had a "talk" with him?' said Sel with a giggle. 'Yes, I've tried, but I think he already knows such things.'

During their first moon at the farmstead, Sel had come across Jacken alone in the yard one afternoon. It was unusual to catch him without Briar and Sel had thought it best to make the most of the opportunity to speak to him about something that had been on her mind. Haltingly, with a blush spreading across her cheeks, she had asked if he understood what could happen between lovers. He had confirmed with equal awkwardness that he did. Then Sel had tried to explain that such things must not happen between him and Briar. He had promised that they would not and quickly made an excuse to leave, ending their mortifying conversation.

Sel was relieved to have the task behind her, but she felt a lingering unease. Of course the firstborn Princess of Bavaugh could not court a penniless commoner. Of course not. But then also, why not? Briar was not an ordinary Princess, and who knew what lay in her future. It did not sit well with Sel to interfere like this, though she thought it her duty as a guardian. *Briar is too young for such things*, she told herself, ignoring the fact that at Briar's age, she had already lived for many winters on the streets of Fakcil and knew all too well the relations between lovers.

'And does Jacken know that Briar is different?' asked Gaddeous.

'He must. You can't spend even a moment with her and not realize something is wrong, whether you're familiar with magic or not. We've never spoken of it together, but I think Jacken knows he must be careful.'

'Careful in what way?'

Sel hesitated. 'For instance, you can't give Briar a command because she has no choice but to obey it. I've not told Jacken, but he seems to know it instinctively. That's just one example – there are other things.'

'I didn't realize. I'll be careful too.'

'That's why I keep her close to me,' said Sel with a sigh.

She glanced at the window, where pale-grey light was beginning to creep around the edges of the curtains.

'I was thinking, perhaps Briar would like something to focus on?' said Gaddeous. 'It might make her feel more . . . content.'

'I think I've tried everything. Even the animals don't seem to entertain her,' replied Sel. 'What did you have in mind?'

'I'll look out for something when we next go to town.'

'I'm sure Briar will be furious again when I make her stay on the farm with me,' sighed Sel, rubbing her forehead. 'There's always so much to do. I wish she would help.'

'I'm sorry.'

Sel waved his apology away and yawned. 'I did not say that to complain to you. It is just that these autumn days feel too short.'

'I know it's a hard life,' said Gaddeous, tucking the bedsheet around her. 'And you're not left with much time to study those books you have. I did try to warn you, but I'm also in love with you and so perhaps I did not try hard enough.'

Sel froze. 'You're in love with me?' she whispered.

'Of course.'

She blinked at him.

'You don't need to say it back,' he replied. 'It's enough to have you here.'

'I . . .'

Gaddeous leant forward and kissed her softly on the lips. 'We should both sleep now,' he said. 'It's almost morning.'

Sel nodded and waited as he rolled on to his side and blew out the candle. Then he settled next to her, and she tucked her head under his chin. After a moment, she felt the rhythmic rise and fall of his chest and the low hum of his snores. She tried to close her eyes and fall asleep too, but she could not stop thinking over what he had said: *I'm also in love with you.* She couldn't help but worry that it changed everything.

Meredyth

The Lansin Estate, West Bavaugh

MEREDYTH DID NOT enjoy tracking down the obscure books on magic that Princess Talia had requested. Since leaving Mont Isle at the end of summer, Meredyth had done little else. There were a lot of titles to find, and it inevitably led to her seeking out unsavoury characters, who regarded her with suspicious curiosity. To find these rare dealers of offensive books in the first place, she had to ask around her acquaintances, who received her requests with grimaces of distaste. She knew they thought she was growing ridiculous in her old age and though she wanted to shout that these books were not for her own reading, it was safer not to mention the Princess. Best let them think she was going senile.

I am not even that old, she thought to herself as she held the latest book procured for the Princess. It had just been brought to her chambers with her usual wodge of letters that morning and she knew her son would have tutted over it as he reviewed her correspondence. He thought her constant search for what he called 'dark muck' embarrassing and had almost forbidden her from asking any of his friends for help to secure more. She had said that she could do whatever she wanted in her own home, but he had curtly replied that it was not her home any more. *He* was Lord Lansin now.

It came to something when your own child, whom you had birthed and reared, started ordering you about. *I am not even that old*, Meredyth thought again. *I have many seasons ahead of me under Darel's stewardship*. It was a grim thought. Darel had always been bossy and obstinate and he was not her favourite child. She wished Rolvern had been born the eldest – he was the youngest but the gentlest of her three boys. If he had inherited the estate, he would have left the running of it to her and disappeared off to court, returning only for the holidays. He certainly would not have insisted on treating her like a wayward child to be kept in check. She suspected that Darel worried she might fall prey to some social-climbing charlatan trying to trick her into matrimony, but he need not be concerned on that front. Meredyth had absolutely no desire to be anyone's wife again. Perhaps she should tell him so outright and he would stop opening her letters.

The package in Meredyth's hands had been hurriedly retied and the parchment was bent out of shape. She sighed wearily to herself and tugged off the string. Inside the package was a battered book, its spine loose and creaky, the pages curling at the edges. The title was painted on the cover in peeling letters: *Spell Anatomy: From Formation to Fruition*. She raised her eyebrows and was about to tuck it back into its packaging to send straight on to Mont Isle, when she spotted a folded piece of parchment pressed between the pages, its seal still intact.

She unfolded the parchment to see a few lines scrawled at the bottom.

A note for the collector residing in the Kingdom of Bavaugh, from Gnoxhall Weathernull the Dignified:
   If this book has been purchased in aid of studying the curse placed by Noatina on the Princess of Bavaugh, that is too complex a spell to be found in these pages.
   A number of the conversion theories are also outdated.

Meredyth read over the message again. Then she sat back in her chair.

Noatina.

Reluctantly, she recalled the day of the Blessing. She remembered lying on the stone dais in the Great Hall, pinned to the spot, watching a dark-haired woman approach the cradle that held the Princess. The first Princess.

Noatina.

Meredyth had only ever thought of the sorceress as a dark, malevolent being, but with a name came a person. A woman. And whoever had written this note knew who she was.

Meredyth bit her lip and read the letter again. She wondered if she ought to track down this Gnoxhall Weathernull the Dignified – clearly a Master. She shuddered. If Gnoxhall Weathernull the Dignified knew the name of the sorceress, perhaps there was more he also knew.

A loud knock sounded, then the door of her chambers flew open and Hiberah sauntered in.

'We are all waiting for you at the breakfast table, Grandmama,' he said.

Meredyth quickly folded the parchment and tucked it into her sleeve. 'I was looking over my letters and I lost track of time,' she said, reaching for her cane.

'Anything . . . from the Princess?' asked Hiberah, edging closer and peering at the stack of letters on the table.

Meredyth hid a smile. 'Nothing today,' she replied. 'But if you wanted, you could write to her yourself, you know.'

Hiberah shrugged. 'I am glad to be off that wretched island. It was enough to have spent spring and summer there. Can you imagine what it is like now, in the depths of winter?'

'Lonely, I should think.'

Meredyth shuffled forward a few paces and winced. Her hips were always worse in the morning.

'When are you next visiting Mont Isle?' asked Hiberah, looking out of the window at the cold, misty parkland.

'Perhaps in the summer.' Meredyth felt the edge of the parchment folded into her sleeve scratch at her skin. 'Or maybe sooner,' she added. 'If your father will let me.'

'Late springtime would be good,' said Hiberah, offering her his arm to lean on. 'I would only miss the end of the hunting season then, and if we did not stay too long, I could still spend some of the summer at court.'

'Oh, you are coming with me too, are you?'

Hiberah flushed and shrugged. 'Father will not let you travel alone.'

'Your brother is old enough to accompany me now.'

'No. As the eldest grandson, it is my duty.'

Meredyth smiled to herself. 'How very noble of you,' she said. 'But let us hurry to breakfast before your mother takes all the bacon.'

Briar

The Wildlands

THE FARMHOUSE KITCHEN echoed with a rhythmic *clack, clack, clack*. Outside, the daylight was quickly fading and the black night of Midwinter clouded the windows. Candlelight flickered and shivered up the white walls, casting long shadows across the room. A black-and-white cat named Spot perched on the end of a shelf, pawing at the shadow of the spinning wheel that flashed and spun on the wall. Briar sat on a stool before the fire, her foot pumping the treadle and her fingers rolling and stretching the wool as she fed it into the wheel.

Her back ached from leaning forward all afternoon, and the tips of her fingers were raw from handling the coarse fibres of the fleece, but she would not stop. The clacking beat of the wheel, the repetitive pull and flex of her fingers, and the *tap, tap, tap* of the treadle soothed her. It dragged the loose chaos inside her into order and required her to focus without stopping, ignoring the jumbled, jangling parts of herself that never seemed to settle. She had been spinning every afternoon for days and she would soon run out of wool. The thought made her anxious and she had already asked Gaddeous several times to enquire at the next farm if they had any spare.

'I'll spin it for the Foxtons,' she said, wringing her hands. 'I'll card it, spin it, then give it back. I just want more.'

'All right, I'll ask them,' Gaddeous replied in the voice he used for calming skittish animals. 'Don't fret now.'

But Briar did fret. She needed more wool. If she ran out, she would just have to unwind and pull apart what she had spun and start over again. She knew that was madness, but she did not care. This was the first time she had found something that calmed and controlled the scattered, tumultuous side of herself that lately seemed ready to overcome her. She could not give it up.

She generally started the day fine. She would wake, eat breakfast with everyone, then try to help her aunt with the various, never-ending chores on the farm. They would be collecting eggs or digging the vegetable patch and Briar would start to feel it creeping over her. Something would begin scratching at the back of her mind, then her skin would prickle and itch. Pressure would throb through her head, while everything around her became sharp and distorted, like looking through the bottom of a glass. Her attention would flit from one thing to another, thoughts snapped in half before they had a chance to finish. She would feel nauseous and irritable, and it was almost impossible to focus on anything. She would long for the end of the day when she could be released into sleep. Then the whole thing would start again when she woke.

But the spinning helped. It was like she was pulling together the escaped parts of herself and twisting them back into place. There was something about the repetitive actions, the sounds, and the meditative trance it evoked. In the past, she had tried throwing herself into chores – dusting the house, grooming the animals or chopping wood for the fire – but none of it helped. She knew her aunt thought she was lazy, but Briar could not understand how everyone else managed to keep their minds focused. She had tried to speak to Jacken about it, but every time she asked how he ignored the rattling in his head, he looked confused. Her aunt had suggested on many occasions that Briar use her free time to take up her studies again. But if Briar even looked at a page in a book, the words would disperse into abstract shapes that had no meaning, and flit and waver from side to side so that she could not understand them.

It had not always been like this. When she was younger, she had often felt restless and out of sorts, but those periods of unease had passed in an hour or two and, though they might have made her preoccupied and fidgety, they had not encumbered her like they did now. It was getting steadily worse, too – whatever *it* was – and Briar did not know what to do. Over the last few seasons, she had gradually come to realize that she was not like everyone else. Not just on the outside – she already knew that – but on the inside too.

She saw the way people looked at her and she knew it was not quite normal. It was the same with her singing and dancing, which always made others gasp in awe. She had a natural ability for such things, and she hated having to hide it. When they were living and working at Copperhill, she had only managed one pirouette in the dancing ring at the Summer Solstice celebrations before her aunt had wrenched her away. Even that one pirouette had been enough to catch the eye of everyone present, and Briar had glowed with the attention. She had been approached by every eligible man afterwards, asking for a dance, but her aunt had made her reject them all. Shortly afterwards, they had left Copperhill altogether and set out again on the road.

Briar had tried dancing recently – her aunt said she could dance, sing and fool about as much as she wanted here – but it had not been pleasant. The same with singing. In the past, when she had sung or danced, it was as though something had taken over her body and her feet and lips moved without effort, producing something other-worldly and beautiful. It had always left her with a trembling, buzzing sensation afterwards, but it felt exciting and fun too. Now it just made her sick. Even speaking to animals – that strange gift that had always brought her so much joy – made the pressure and nausea that plagued her each day so much worse. She tried to avoid it when she could. Jacken could not understand her sudden disinterest in helping him train their horses, but she did not try to explain it. Even to him.

She didn't know what she would have done without the spinning wheel. Gaddeous had brought it back from his trip to the winter market, strapped to the side of his wagon, which was packed with supplies to last them until the summer. Briar had stared at it curiously when she had followed her aunt into the yard to greet him on his return.

'I got that for you, Briar,' he had said, following her gaze. 'I thought you might like to have a go?'

She had glared back at him and shrugged, before turning away to pet Patch, the bay shire horse. She could tell that her aunt was itching to kiss Gaddeous and it annoyed her. They still liked to pretend that there was nothing romantic between them and that it was not obvious that they shared a bed.

'I got good flecks for our horses,' Jacken had said, appearing beside her. 'And there was lots of interest. I said I'd be back in the summer with more.'

'That's good,' Briar had replied faintly, rubbing at the back of her neck where an ache was building. 'I'm glad you're here. It feels odd without you.'

Jacken had grinned at her. 'I'm glad to be back too. I got you something.' He had taken a pale-blue velvet ribbon carefully from his pocket. 'I know how much you like ribbons and I saw some of the girls in town wearing them across their foreheads.' Then he had added quietly, 'I got blue because it matches your eyes.'

Patch was butting Briar's arm, trying to tell her that he wanted water, and it was sending shooting pains through her head.

'Thank you,' she had said distractedly. 'It's nice. I need to go inside now.'

She had turned and stumbled away, taking deep breaths to fight down the nausea rising in her throat.

'Briar, will you help bring in the supplies?' Auntie had called, but Briar could not stop.

Without replying, she had hurried into the farmhouse and taken refuge on her bed, waiting until the worst of the sickness had passed and she was left with a dull, throbbing headache.

When she had emerged in the evening, the spinning wheel was set before the fire with a basket of raw wool beside it. Gaddeous and Jacken were out in the yard, looking over the cattle in the barn, and Auntie was fussing with the dinner on the stove.

'Will you be joining us to eat?' she had asked coolly.

Briar had nodded.

Auntie had followed her gaze to the spinning wheel and added, 'I know you don't like it, but Gad was just trying to be nice. Next time, I'll tell him to buy you a new dress instead. I suppose I'll make use of the wheel at some point, although I'll have to learn how it works. I should ask Mrs Foxton to show me.'

Perhaps it was the fact that her aunt did not know how to use it, or maybe it was because it reminded her of Turow and Paleen, but Briar had sat on the stool before the spinning wheel and begun fiddling with the bobbin and wheel. She thought she could vaguely remember watching how Paleen worked the machine. She had taken some of her aunt's yarn from her work basket and threaded it on to the bobbin, being careful to avoid the sharp end of the spindle. Then she had pulled some raw wool from the dense cloud at her feet and experimentally pumped at the treadle, feeding the wool on to the end of the yarn and watching it twist into a thin thread.

She had sat like that for some time, working the wool into the spinning wheel and enjoying the *clack, clack, clack* of the wheel, and the tension of the growing thread in her fingers. After a few moments, Spot had sauntered into the room and rubbed himself against the stool, before settling on the hem of her skirt. His sleepy green eyes watched the wheel spin and his black tail flicked back and forth in time to its steady beat. He was the only animal Briar could tolerate the company of these days. Cats did not talk much.

When she realized Auntie was standing watching her with a strange look on her face, Briar had stopped.

'How do you know how to do that?'

'I used to watch Paleen spin. She was the woman who lived at—'

'I *know* who Paleen is!'

'You never mention her,' Briar had muttered, and then added more loudly, 'I just did what I remembered and worked the rest out.'

'I see. That's . . . good.'

Auntie's expression had not looked like she thought it was good, but Briar had ignored her and carried on. She had teased apart more wool with her fingers, a growing sense of calm coming over her. She had scarcely noticed when Gaddeous and Jacken entered and sat down at the table for dinner.

Eventually, she had torn herself away to eat her meal – after some nagging from her aunt – but as soon as she could, she had returned to her stool before the wheel again. She spun and spun and spun, until her eyelids grew heavy and she was almost falling asleep where she sat.

'That was a successful gift,' she had heard Gaddeous whisper as she shuffled from the kitchen to her bedroom, yawning.

'Yes,' her aunt had answered slowly. 'I suppose so.'

Violanna

The Cloisters, Mont Isle

AT FIRST VIOLANNA thought the figure in the cloisters was just a shadow. Blades of yellowish, wintry light cut through the arches, casting brightness and gloom, and it was not until the shadow moved closer that Violanna realized someone was there. She assumed it was the minister, returning to the chapel after luncheon, but then she caught sight of the rippled edge of a black cloak. She gasped. Then stumbled, her outstretched hands scratching at the rough brick-work, a scream of fear choking her throat. She had always known this day would come, but she had not expected it to occur yet. She thought of Talia, who was finishing luncheon in the parlour, head bent over an open book, chewing. Violanna considered turning and running back to her daughter, calling for the castle guards, though she knew they would be of little use.

'Hello, Your Majesty.'

The Diaspass voice was high and clipped. It was not what

Violanna had been expecting and her surge of fear ebbed. The figure drew closer and pulled back the hood of its cloak, revealing a sheet of grey hair and a thin, angular face.

'Lalious Grele the Mighty?'

The Master dipped her head in a bow.

Violanna snatched her hand to the worn bodice of her gown, waiting for the rushed drum of her heartbeat beneath to ease. It was not what she had feared, but it was still a sickening reminder that danger was coming. The end of the spell lay ahead.

'I did not mean to scare you, Your Majesty,' said Lalious. Then she added, tilting her head to one side, 'Did you think I was someone else?'

'Of course I did!' Violanna managed, the Diaspass language feeling round and awkward in her mouth.

'Has she visited you since the Blessing?'

Violanna shook her head.

'You are sure?'

'Yes, I am sure,' replied Violanna in Bavaughian. 'She said she would return to finish the spell and we both know that she always keeps her word. If she had returned, I would know about it.'

Lalious did not reply. There were a few more lines around the Master's eyes, and her hair had thinned over the seasons, but otherwise she looked just as she always had: wiry and severe.

'Why are you here?' snapped Violanna. 'I have heard nothing from the Diaspass Kingdom or the Masterhood for winters! I have been forgotten by anyone who could help me and now, suddenly, here you are. Why?'

Lalious regarded her with the flinty gaze Violanna remembered from her childhood. She had never enjoyed her lessons with the Masters, who begrudgingly taught the Diaspass royal family when they attended the Royal Assembly, but she had found Lalious, with her strict instruction and painful punishments, particularly grating. She had much preferred Florentina Samara the Wise, who tried to be stern but could not stop the softness of her character seeping into her teaching. Had she lived, Florentina would not have abandoned Violanna after the Blessing. She would have tried to help.

'As I recall it, this is a mess of your own making, Your Majesty,' said Lalious in Bavaughian.

'My own making? I was trying to do the right thing.' Violanna's shoulders sagged. She looked at the muddy, bare quadrangle beside them, and the hushed cloisters. 'What is done is done,' she replied. 'And I am suffering for it. If you have travelled here, then you must know my situation. I am no longer the Queen of Bavaugh. I am a cast-off, waiting on this forsaken island these sixteen winters past for her daughter to die. I cannot sink lower.'

'I am aware of your situation,' replied Lalious. She twitched her black cloak and it flicked at her heels. 'But our attention has been elsewhere; there has been much turmoil in the Central Realm over Journier. Besides . . .' Lalious narrowed her eyes. 'You have stayed on this island with your child and renounced your Queenship. These are strange decisions, all things considered, Your Majesty. It is almost as if there is something you have planned.'

For a moment, Violanna thought she would confess and it would all come tumbling from her mouth. Perhaps it would be a good idea to tell the Masterhood everything. Maybe it would help. But when she tried to summon the strength, she found that she could not do it – the words stayed lodged in her throat. She did not wholly trust them.

'I cannot leave. That is part of the curse,' she replied. 'And if I cannot leave, then neither will my daughter. Anyway, faced with such powerful magic, what can be done?'

Lalious's eyes remained narrowed, but her gaze drifted to the quadrangle beside them and the slice of pale sky above it. 'Yes, it is mighty indeed,' she said. 'The remnants of magic on this island run deep. I felt it as soon as I saw the castle; such dark energy that was drawn together for the spell will never be easily dissipated.'

Violanna glanced down at her fingers and said as lightly as she could manage, 'What you can feel is the spell bound to my daughter.'

'Yes, you are right.'

Violanna bit her lip to stop herself from smiling. If Lalious could mistake the residue of magic on Mont Isle for a spell supposedly bound to the Princess, then surely others would too. In the many winters since the Blessing, Violanna had doubted her plan, but perhaps it was not as foolish as she had sometimes feared. Perhaps it would work.

Violanna lifted her head to see Lalious watching her closely. 'There must be a reason you are here, High Master,' she said. 'It is a long way to travel and if there is warring in the Central Realm, then your time would be better spent there. What is it you want from me?'

Lalious cleared her throat and laced her fingers together. 'Your Majesty, what will you do when Noatina returns to finish the spell?'

Violanna swallowed hard. It had been a long time since she had heard that name.

'I am sure you have something planned,' added Lalious, raising her eyebrows. 'What is it?'

The truth was that Violanna did not know what she would do. When she imagined the confrontation, she saw the sorceress – Noatina – facing Talia and the magic falling flat. Without the right source, the spell would collapse and the magic would scatter. But after that ... Violanna was not sure. She knew the fallen spell would wound Noatina's confidence and she hoped to use that to her advantage. She would scream at Talia to run and she would plant herself in her daughter's place. But she did not know what would happen next.

'I suppose you do not wish to tell me,' continued Lalious when Violanna did not reply. 'Fine. I have come here to propose something to you on behalf of the Masterhood . . . We have decided that when the time comes, we will aid you.'

Violanna blinked in surprise. 'Why?' she asked.

'To stop Noatina would be . . . mutually beneficially to all of us.'

It was Violanna's turn to narrow her eyes. 'I see. Noatina is involved in the turmoil in the Central Realm?' When Lalious did not reply, Violanna added, 'I had begun to suspect as much. So you plan to use my daughter as bait?'

Lalious shrugged. 'The magic has been cast and the spell has been bound. If I were you, I would be thankful for the aid. Perhaps we can stop Noatina before the spell is finished. Maybe we can save your daughter's life.'

Violanna knew that Lalious was right, and she was relieved – more than relieved – to hear that the Diaspass Masterhood would be on her side, but she could not bring herself to show it. 'What do you need from me?' she asked.

'Your cooperation. We believe we have sight of Noatina's movements, but if you sense or hear anything, you must send word.'

'How?'

Lalious raised one hand and flexed her fingers. Her lips uttered the language of magic and the air shivered and snapped.

Violanna felt the charm settle over her; sticky and cloying, as though she had stepped into a spider's web.

'If you suspect anything, say my name and I will hear it.'

Violanna nodded, trying to ignore the ache in her teeth and tingle in her bones.

'I will leave you now, Your Majesty,' said Lalious, stepping away. 'I do not suppose it will be too long before we see each other again.'

Fear swelled through Violanna at the thought.

'Were you seen arriving?' she asked.

'Of course not.'

'Good.'

It was a relief not to have to explain away the presence of a Master to the guards and servants of Mont Isle, but the ease with which Lalious had entered the castle was equally unnerving.

Lalious adjusted the clasp of the black cloak at her neck and made to depart, then she paused. 'Another thing, Your Majesty . . .' she said.

Violanna held herself still. 'Yes?'

'There was a young woman at the Blessing, the apprentice of Florentina Samara the Wise. Do you know what ever became of her?'

Violanna pulled her features into a frown of confusion, ignoring the thump of her heartbeat quickening in her chest. 'I do not remember such a person,' she replied.

'She has been missing since.'

'It was all so long ago.'

Lalious nodded. 'Very well,' she said.

Then the High Master turned and disappeared into the shadows, leaving Violanna doubting everything she had done.

Briar

The Wildlands

BRIAR STOMPED THROUGH the orchard, swinging a bucket in each hand. Pink and white blossom from the apple trees drifted through the air, collecting on her skirts and catching in her golden hair like snowflakes. Last spring, she had gathered some petals and made a watery perfume in the farmhouse kitchen, which she had gifted to Auntie at Midwinter, but this season, she did not want to. Like racing Jacken across the sheep field or teaching the farm dogs tricks, it no longer felt right. All she wanted to do was sit at her wheel and spin, spin, spin, keeping the nausea and headaches at bay. But that morning, Auntie had asked her to fetch water from the well.

'I'd do it myself,' Auntie had said. 'But I feel sick.'

Briar had paused her spinning and glanced up to see that her aunt did look a little grey and weak. 'You're not with child, are you?' she had asked.

Auntie had flinched and grabbed hold of the kitchen table to steady herself. 'What a thing to ask me, Briar—'

'Well, are you?'

Auntie had never explicitly told Briar that she shared a bed with Gaddeous, though she had gradually been more open with her affection for him. Jacken said it was their business and they should be left alone, but Briar didn't like it.

'I'm not with child. It's just an upset stomach.'

'Do you think you'll ever have a baby with Gaddeous?'

Auntie had stared at her aghast.

'Well?'

'I can't . . . I can't bear a child,' Auntie had replied faintly.

A rush of relief had flooded over Briar and she tried to look concerned. 'But you have your cycle?'

Briar's own moon blood had started last season and Auntie had explained the cycle that occurred in a woman's body. 'You are lucky,' she had said at the time with a wry smile. 'My first blood came when I was much younger than sixteen winters, and you have been spared seasons of pain.' But clutching her cramping stomach, Briar had not felt particularly lucky at the time.

'Yes, I have my cycle,' Auntie had said slowly. 'But I cannot carry a baby. I was sterilized in my childhood.' Her free hand had fluttered up to her brow, which was pale and glistening with a sickly sheen.

'What do you mean?' Briar had asked. This was a new, rare snippet of detail from her aunt's shrouded past.

'Where I was born, they did it to me—'

'The "bad people" who are after us?'

'No . . . Yes . . .' As if realizing what she had said, Auntie had rubbed furiously at her eyes and snapped, 'Just go and fetch the water, Briar! I need to rest.'

The air around Briar had grown suddenly hot and dry. A familiar snap had sounded and, before she knew it, Briar had found
herself picking up the empty pails by the stove and hurrying to the
door.

'I'm sorry!' Auntie had called after her. 'I didn't mean to—'

But Briar had not heard the rest because her legs were propelling
her across the yard and towards the orchard. She felt angry and
strange and scared all at once.

Briar climbed over the gate to the next field and jogged down a
slope, clanging the pails together as she went. She had collected
water from the well before, but it was a tedious slog, a chore she
tried to avoid when she could. She snatched at a fellumion flower in
the long grass as she passed, tucking the lilac bloom behind her ear.
She had not seen a fellumion before arriving in the Wildlands and
the pretty, bell-shaped perennial was one of the few things she liked
about the place.

Briar sighed as she approached the stone-lined well. It was a
warm spring morning, and she would have to haul the water from
the well and carry the brimming buckets back to the farmhouse,
her shoulders aching all the way. She had just attached one bucket
to the well rope when she heard a rustle in the grass.

Looking up, she saw a man. She started in shock and almost
dropped the rope in her hands. The man was walking down the
opposite slope, also carrying two empty buckets. He was a little older
than Jacken, with short blond hair and a wide, stocky frame. When
he caught sight of her, he stopped in surprise too.

'You must be one of the Foxton boys,' said Briar after a pause.
'I've seen you all from afar sometimes when you come to help with
the shearing.'

The man seemed almost to shake himself, then he took a few

steps closer. 'You live with Gaddeous?' he said uncertainly. 'You're . . . real?'

Briar laughed, and she saw the man tilt his head at the sound. It had been so long since she had met anyone new that she had forgotten the effect she had on others.

'I don't normally collect the water,' she said. 'But my aunt is sick today.'

Without taking his eyes off her, the man stepped closer. 'I'm Kirkial,' he said.

He had large red hands and small brown eyes. He was staring at her so intently that Briar laughed again, uneasily.

'I'm Briar,' she said.

'I think my mam has mentioned you. You're the one that spins the best yarn she's ever seen.'

Briar nodded, feeling a little flash of pride. Mrs Foxton was a practical woman of very few words, who had visited the farmhouse a handful of times. She had never seemed particularly taken with Briar so it was pleasing to hear she had spoken so highly of her.

'Would you like me to help you draw water from the well?' asked Kirkial.

Briar shrugged, then nodded, wondering if she could convince him to carry the pails back to the farmhouse too. People generally did what she wanted. Especially men.

She stood, fiddling with the thick, golden braid that fell down her back, while Kirkial hauled up their pails of water, his gaze flicking to her all the while, as if expecting her suddenly to disappear. When he had finished, he wiped his face on the sleeve of his shirt and watched her closely while she thanked him.

'Where're you from?' he asked suddenly. 'Where were you born?'

'My aunt says up north,' she replied. 'But we've moved all over the kingdom.'

'Not from the Wildlands?'

Briar gave him a quizzical look and he flushed, his cheeks all the redder against his pale hair.

'My eldest brother says he saw a sprite once in the Wildlands and she was the most beautiful thing he had ever seen. Are you a fae?'

Briar was about to laugh when she remembered that the sound would likely only unnerve the man more.

'No, I'm flesh and blood, see?' she said, holding out her open palm to him. 'And I've never seen any fae in the Wildlands, but I'd like to.'

Kirkial reached forward and gently stroked her hand. It was not an unpleasant feeling and Briar smiled.

'Can I kiss you?' he asked suddenly. 'It's good fortune to kiss a fae.'

Briar dropped her hand in surprise. She had seen plenty of kissing occur at Midsummer celebrations and outside inns and taverns, when folk were merry and drunk, and she had always wondered what it was like.

'All right,' she said, surprising herself. 'But I'm no fae.'

Kirkial grinned. He placed his hands lightly on her waist and pulled her closer to him. Briar could feel his warm breath on her cheeks and suddenly she was not so sure about the kiss. It felt odd and rushed. She was about to say so when Kirkial whispered, 'Kiss me.'

The air around Briar turned suddenly hot and there was a sound like a clap. Before she knew what she was doing, she had leant forward and pressed her lips to his. It was not a horrible feeling, yet it was not what she had thought it would be and she longed to pull away, but her body would not move.

'Briar!' yelled a voice.

Kirkial jumped and Briar was released. She stumbled backwards, feeling dazed and nauseous, wiping her mouth with the back of her hand.

Jacken was striding down the slope towards them.

'I was just talking to your sister,' said Kirkial, hastily grabbing his buckets of water. 'No need to worry.'

'She's not my sister.'

Jacken stopped at the bottom of the slope and glared at them.

'I should be away,' said Kirkial, and he turned and hurried in the opposite direction with a few backwards glances at Briar.

Jacken bent and snatched up the pails of water. Then he turned and strode away without a word.

'Wait!' called Briar, shaking off the dazed feeling that still lingered and made her fingertips sting and her head fuzzy. 'That wasn't . . . that wasn't what you think.'

She ran after him, trying to swallow down the sickness in the back of her throat, but he kept walking as if he had not heard her.

'Stop!' she panted, managing to grasp the back of his shirt and pull at the hem. 'Wait!'

He turned suddenly, water from the buckets sloshing on to the ground. His expression was tense and his dark eyes were narrowed and cold. Briar bumped into him and stumbled back, almost losing her footing in the long grass.

'That wasn't what you think,' she said. 'I didn't want to do it.'

'He forced himself on you?'

'No—'

Jacken grimaced and tried to turn away, but Briar grabbed hold of him.

'I couldn't stop. I'm glad you came—'

'I'm not,' Jacken snapped, wrenching away from her and striding off once more.

Briar opened and closed her mouth, sad and furious all at once. She sprinted ahead of him and turned back so that they were facing one another.

'You can't be angry at *me*,' she hissed, crossing her arms. 'What about the town girl at the Midwinter celebration? The one you kept dancing with?'

Jacken blushed and asked, 'Who told you about that?'

'I heard Auntie and Gaddeous talking.'

'That's different. I didn't kiss nobody.'

Briar felt a rush of relief. She had often wondered what this mysterious town girl looked like and sometimes she found herself watching Jacken closely, trying to guess if he was thinking of her.

'Good,' she said and quickly added, 'I mean, fine. I don't care anyway.'

They scowled at one another. They rarely fought and it felt wrong. She wanted to make it right again and she suddenly wondered if she should kiss Jacken. She thought perhaps it might feel nice and maybe he would like it too. It would help erase the memory of kissing Kirkial, and it was not as though the thought of kissing Jacken had never crossed her mind before. She knew it would change things between them and she had liked it as it was, but maybe now was the right time. Maybe this was the moment.

Briar awkwardly edged forward, but her shin hit one of the pails and made a clanging noise.

'Careful or you'll spill it all!' said Jacken. 'And I won't go and get more. You're the one that's supposed to be doing it. I only came to help.'

'I didn't ask you to help me!' Briar snapped back, feeling foolish.

'And next time I won't!'

Jacken pushed past her and Briar watched this tall figure storm off in the direction of the farmhouse. She sighed and lightly touched her fingertips to her lips, confused and disappointed.

Sel

The Wildlands

SEL FELT THE spell before she heard the dogs barking in the yard. Her eyes snapped open and she sat up in bed, knocking Gaddeous with her elbow. He grunted and rolled over, but did not rise. In a few moments, he was snoring softly once more.

The dogs outside fell silent and Sel felt wisps of magic curling through the air.

Something was wrong.

She held her breath and tried to focus, but she was groggy and dazed with sleep. She slipped out of bed and stumbled down the corridor to Briar's room. Peering through the darkness, she saw a golden-haired head pressed to the pillows and the reassuring rise and fall of Briar's chest. Sel pulled the door to and crept back to the kitchen, wondering if she had been mistaken. She was about to put on her boots to check the yard, when there was a soft knock at the door.

Sel jumped, the sound of her heartbeat crashing in her ears. She considered shouting for help, but then there was another knock. The air in the kitchen shivered and snapped, and the bolts on the front door slid back on their own. It swung open and a figure in a black cloak walked into the room.

Sel grabbed hold of a kitchen knife from the counter and held it aloft. She opened her mouth to scream, when the figure said, 'Selhah Samara the Wise?'

Sel froze.

The figure pushed back the hood of its black cloak and added, 'Can you put the knife down, please?'

Sel blinked at the familiar, thin face before her. 'Lalious Grele the Mighty?' she whispered. She slowly lowered the knife.

Lalious nodded. 'I have finally found you, Selhah.' She glanced around the kitchen and added, 'In strange circumstances.'

Sel stared at the Master. Lalious looked so out of place in the snug familiarity of the farmhouse kitchen. For a moment, Sel wondered if she was still asleep and dreaming. 'You've been looking for me?' she asked.

'Everyone has. On and off.'

Sel let go of the knife and instead grabbed hold of the back of a chair to steady herself. *Everyone had been looking for her?* She was suddenly aware that she was wearing a thin nightgown and her hair had not been washed for days. She rubbed her eyes, trying to throw off her wooziness.

'How have you managed to elude us for so long?' asked Lalious in Diaspass. 'What covering charms have you been using?'

Sel's befuddled mind tried to make sense of what she was seeing and hearing. 'Covering charms?' she said. 'I've used none. I haven't been conjuring. And I'm afraid my Diaspass is a bit rusty.'

Lalious raised her eyebrows.

'And I'm not Selhah Samara the Wise,' Sel carried on in Bavaughian. 'I'm just Selhah.'

'How so?' asked Lalious, speaking in Bavaughian also.

'My Master died before I finished my apprenticeship.'

Sel felt the familiar stab of sorrow and shame. When Florentina died, she should have notified other Masters and held proper burial rites. She should not have set off for the Royal Blessing in the Kingdom of Bavaugh, thinking only of herself.

'You're named as her successor in her testament,' replied Lalious.

'But . . . but I didn't finish my apprenticeship.'

'Florentina must have felt you were ready.'

Sel tightened her grasp on the kitchen chair, her knuckles pale in the dim light. 'I don't understand,' she whispered.

'I have been looking for you for some time,' said Lalious. 'Florentina sent me her testament when she knew that she was ill. She and I were close once and I have been trying to put her affairs in order since I heard of her death. Her house, her possessions, her Masterhood – they are all waiting for you.'

Sel felt her mouth fall open. Then she shook herself and babbled, 'But – but I can't be a Master.' She took a deep breath. 'I . . . I have killed a man.'

There was a beat of silence. 'Just the one?' Lalious replied.

'I used a spell reserved for Masters and I'm not a Master.'

'Selhah, I am also a woman travelling alone through the realm and sometimes we must protect ourselves. Often these things are necessary.'

Sel stared at her.

'I should be furious,' Lalious continued. 'The time I have wasted in trying to find you! But I have a feeling you are not in hiding by choice.'

Sel glanced over her shoulder at the dark opening of the corridor which led to the bedrooms. 'Everyone's sleeping,' she said. 'We should go outside.'

'Not to worry; I will muffle our voices.'

'Don't cast any more spells!' hissed Sel quickly. 'In case . . .'

'In case?'

'It . . . alerts someone. Or unsettles things.'

'It's not my spells you ought to be worried about.'

They watched one another.

'I could feel the magic before I even left the last town,' said Lalious, her eyes glittering with mingled awe and fear. 'It led me here. It is a toxic, potent spell. You are right not to have been conjuring; it would be easy to agitate it. I trust you have not tried to fiddle with the magic?'

Sel shook her head.

'Good. To do so could cause a lot of damage. I would not even attempt it alone myself.'

'The magic led you here?' said Sel hesitantly. If Lalious had found them, perhaps they were not as safe as she had hoped.

'Yes,' said Lalious. 'I tracked you to Dawvin first, where they told me that a long time ago, a young woman had worked at the bakery and lodged near by with her daughter. Her beautiful, angelic daughter, who was wonderful and strange. Then, in Turow, I met a minister's wife who said that a woman had lived at the schoolhouse with her niece. At a mid-country estate called Copperhill, I heard of a family who had stayed a while before disappearing without a trace. Lastly, in Norrale they said that a woman arrived some winters ago with a boy and a girl in her charge, and they went to live in the Wildlands – strange, secluded folk, they said.'

'You really have been tracking me.'

Lalious nodded. 'I do not understand how, but I am guessing that you have the girl? And she is here?'

'Yes,' replied Sel faintly, thinking of Briar's peaceful, sleeping form. 'I have the girl.'

'How is that possible? What happened at Mont Isle after the Blessing?'

Sel took a deep breath and prised her fingers from the back of the chair. 'I have much to tell you,' she said. 'But we must go outside. We can't wake the others. No one else knows.'

Lalious waited while Sel wrapped herself in a shawl and slid her bare feet into her boots. Sel moved slowly, in a numb, dream-like state. She kept glancing at Lalious to make sure she was not imagining it all.

'It is just you, Lalious?' asked Sel suddenly, pausing by the door. 'There's no one else here?'

'I have come alone on behalf of the Masters of the Diaspass Kingdom. When I understand the situation, we will consider what should be done next.'

Despite everything, Sel could not help but feel a little thrilled at the thought of all the Masters discussing her. She stepped outside, followed by Lalious, and closed the door softly behind them.

They stood opposite one another in the yard, the half-moon high in the sky and the spring night air chilled and crisp. Behind her, Sel could hear the swish of straw as Patch shifted in his stable, and, in the corner of the yard, she could see the farm dogs slumped beside their kennels in a deep, magical slumber.

'Is there any news of . . . Noatina?' she asked.

It had been so long since she had said the sorceress's name aloud, though she thought of it often.

'My travels through this kingdom have made it clear that the Bavaughians take very little interest in the affairs of the Central Realm, so I do not know what you have heard,' replied Lalious. 'But two winters ago Noatina aligned herself with Journier and turned them against us.'

Sel sucked in her breath.

'We have been helping them gain independence from the rest of the Central Realm, and this is how they repay us. They want to extend their territory into the Ofarim Hills, past our borders.'

'But that does not make sense. The Ofarim Hills have always been part of the Diaspass Kingdom.'

'Some think Noatina has bewitched the minds of the Journierian leaders, but perhaps greed is powerful enough without magic. Whatever it is, with her help our forces are well matched. There has been much bloodshed.'

Sel shivered and pulled her shawl tighter around her. 'I've heard nothing of this,' she whispered.

'All of our Masters are at the front line. The magical warfare is fierce.'

'But you're not with them?'

'I was until something changed. The force of the attack stopped and Journier are no longer pushing forward. The power of the attack has lessened – it is almost as if Noatina has gone.'

Sel felt the back of her neck prickle. 'Gone?' she echoed.

'Yes, and the battle has not yet been won. It is odd. We can only think of one reason for it.'

Sel heard the roar of her pulse in her ears and she felt her throat turn dry.

'That is why I came to Bavaugh,' Lalious continued. 'I visited Queen Violanna, but I could tell that something was not right. As I said before, I have been trying to find you for some time. You disappeared after the Blessing and, over the winters that followed, I started to suspect that you were connected to what had happened in some way.' Her eyes flicked to the farmhouse, the curtains drawn across the windows and the front door in shadow. 'When I discovered you were travelling with a child, I started to wonder . . . and now I am here, it is clear. I can feel it. I know Queen Violanna's secret. *You* have the cursed Princess.'

Sel nodded, unable to speak.

'And Noatina will return to see out the end of the spell,' added Lalious. 'There is only one person she hates more than the Diaspass King.'

'Queen Violanna,' Sel whispered.

'Yes. Now, I have said enough and it is your turn to speak. Who is the girl on Mont Isle in the place of the Princess? You must tell me everything that happened after the Blessing.'

Briar

The Wildlands

BRIAR SAT DOWN heavily on the edge of her bed. Tight, painful breaths squeezed from her chest and her head spun with dizzying thoughts. The thudding beat of her pulse rang in her ears and her hands trembled; she tried tucking her fingers beneath her legs to keep them still, only to realize that her whole body was shaking, quivering in shock.

Beside her, curled in the folds of a blanket, Spot stirred and stretched. Briar felt the needling of the cat's thoughts scratching at her mind, asking why she was awake in the middle of the night.

Nothing's wrong. Go to sleep, she replied quickly, as a throb of pain shot through her forehead.

Spot did not need to be told twice. He settled in a new position, sleepy eyes closing with a soft purr.

Briar stared at the dark bedroom around her. What she had just seen and heard did not make sense. And yet . . . it felt terribly true.

She had woken moments ago, confused and groggy. There had been a strange warmth and intensity to the air, and she could not explain it, but instantly she had known that something was wrong. Climbing out of bed, she had crept out of her room and down the corridor, still half asleep, wondering if a wolf or a hog from the surrounding Wildlands had ventured on to the farmland again.

But as she drew closer to the kitchen, she had heard a voice she did not recognize and the very air had become taut and prickly. Alarmed, Briar had crouched down into the shadows and inched closer, peering around the corner to see a grey-haired woman wearing a long black cloak, speaking to her aunt. Briar had pinched her arm so hard it left a dark-red mark, but the stranger remained. This was not a dream.

Their voices were quiet, but Briar had heard the woman say, 'You have the girl?'

Auntie had replied, 'Yes, I have the girl.'

Then they had said something about Mont Isle and a blessing. Briar had known that what she was hearing was important and she had wondered if she should leap from the shadows and reveal herself, demanding answers. But before she could do anything, Auntie and the stranger had stepped outside, and the front door had closed behind them.

Briar had remained crouching in the shadows for a while, her head ringing and her senses scrambled. Of course, she had always known she was different, and recently her doubts and questions about her past had only grown. But she had wanted to believe that there was nothing amiss. She had told herself that the strange nausea and oddness that plagued her was just a passing sickness, and the quirks of her character that marked her as different from others were a result of her unusual upbringing or natural gifts. But in the back of her mind, she had suspected Auntie was keeping something from her – there was a reason they moved from place to place in hiding, there was a reason she was so strange.

You have the girl?

Yes, I have the girl.

The girl. *She* must be the girl.

It was significant, although she did not yet understand why.

Forcing herself up from the shadows, Briar had walked on shaky legs back to her room. Now she sat on her bed in the darkness. She replayed what she had heard over and over again until the words blurred, and her head thumped with their echoes: *the girl*, *Mont Isle*, *the Blessing*.

What did it all mean?

Briar did not know how long she sat on her bed, but eventually she heard the soft click of the farmhouse's front door closing. Then muffled footsteps padding down the corridor and passing by to Gaddeous's room.

The girl. Mont Isle. The Blessing.

Auntie was keeping something from her. Auntie had been lying.

Briar had long suspected this, but it still hurt. She grabbed hold of her bedsheet and crushed it into her fists. She considered running out of her bedroom right now and confronting her aunt, but she was not sure that she could trust the answer. Likely all she would get were more excuses and evasions.

Tears rose at the back of Briar's throat, but she swallowed them down. She could not trust Auntie. She could not trust anyone. If she wanted to find out the truth, then she needed to discover it for herself.

Talia

Mont Isle

TALIA STOOD ON the battlements of the castle, breathing in the fresh spring air. She had paused in her morning stroll to stare out at the town of Guil, her mind lost to Novtook symbols. The wind pulled at the curls pinned to her temples, blowing them across her face. Apparently, ringlets were all the rage at court, but Talia just found them annoying. With a huff, she tucked her hair firmly behind her ears and returned to thinking over what she had studied the night before.

As far as she could understand, Novtook symbols were a written form of the language of magic, and their shapes, if correctly read, could be layered into spells. *But* – she reminded herself, as she watched a group of children scamper across the wet sand in the distance – the symbols alone uttered aloud were not enough to conjure. They needed to be applied to wielded magic and drawn into the spell. At least, that was as much as she could deduce from her reading. She always felt like she was bridging huge gaps when she studied magic. The books all assumed a certain base level of understanding that she did not have, and she wished there was someone who could answer her many questions. For example, how did you even pronounce a Novtook symbol? The dashes and curved lines were meant to form a sound, but Talia could not make any sense of it. She thought perhaps she should ask her mother, but she also knew that Mother would only plead ignorance.

A seagull screeched and swooped overhead, diving to the rocks below, and Talia rubbed her eyes. She might have stayed up a little too late last night reading. It was just that if she stumbled upon a word or a principle she could not wholly grasp, it inevitably meant she must refer to another book, then she would get diverted by something else, and before she knew it, it was midnight. Mistress Rashel said she thought Talia was spending too much of her time in the study of magic and it was becoming a detriment to her education. This was worrying. Talia had heard Mistress Rashel tell Lady Lansin and her mother on numerous occasions that she was a gifted student and in different circumstances the governess would recommend a scholarly career. Whether the 'different circumstances' referred to the fact she was a Princess or the fact she was cursed, she was not sure.

But what people did not seem to understand – not Mistress Rashel or Lady Lansin or Mother – was that she *had* to study magic. She could not just wait around idly for the curse to strike. There must be something she could do. She had written to Lady Lansin recently to ask if they could engage a Master to advise them – perhaps one who had been at the Blessing and had witnessed the curse? Surely that was a good idea. But Lady Lansin had replied simply that contacting a Master was not within her power. So Talia had written to

Hiberah, asking if he knew of anyone at court who could find a Diaspass Master. As she had suspected, he did not, but it had been worth trying. Peculiarly, he had written her a rather long response about his season of hunting over the winter and how he hoped to accompany his grandmother to visit Mont Isle again soon. He had even included a poem about a fair, sweet maiden, which Talia had found most confusing. When she showed it to Dottie, the maid had laughed heartily and said perhaps the young man was trying to tell her something.

'Like a coded message?' Talia had replied with a frown.

Dottie had laughed again and said, 'Something like that.'

Talia had read over the poem several times since, trying to understand the hidden meaning. But it was not a particularly good poem and she could not decipher much. In the end, she had cast it aside, since she had more pressing matters on her hands.

Too often, it felt like Talia's attempts to thwart the curse were met with denial or vague excuses from those around her. It was only due to her sheer determination and dogged questioning of long-serving members of the castle serving staff that she had finally pinned down the full wording of the curse a few seasons ago:

Before seventeen winters have passed, I will return for you. On that day, the spell will end and you will die.

Whenever Talia recited the words of the curse, she shuddered. To know that the curse lived in her – ready and waiting to strike – filled her with terror. Unlike everyone else, she could not dismiss it as foolish nonsense or pretend it did not exist.

If only I could speak to a Master, she thought. *A Master could tell me more.*

Talia was just wondering if there might be some way of writing to Mother's family (though it would have to be done without her mother's knowledge), when something caught her eye. She leant over the edge of the wall, squinting into the morning sunshine, and she saw that she had not been mistaken – there was a horse and rider galloping towards the island.

The tide had not completely drawn out and the causeway was still covered in a shallow wash of sea that splashed and foamed at the horse's hooves. Talia shaded her eyes and leant as far forward as she dared, trying to make out the face of the rider. It did not look like one of the townsmen of Guil who brought supplies to the island. There were no packs strapped to the saddle, and the horse, even from a distance, looked a fine animal.

Talia glanced to her left and saw one of the guards standing watch further along the wall spot the approaching rider too. He straightened up in surprise, pulling his pipe from his mouth, and shouted down to the men at the gatehouse.

The horse and rider were closer now and Talia noticed the sweat-drenched sides of the animal as the rider bent forward over its neck, urging it on faster.

Something was wrong.

Unease crept up on her and she spun around, hurrying along the battlements, her feet stumbling on the uneven flagstones. As she raced down the spiral stairs of the nearest turret, she suddenly realized the rider had been dressed in red and green. The royal livery.

Rushing past an open window, Talia heard the clatter of galloping hooves in the courtyard outside and raised voices. She broke into a run, sprinting down a corridor in the direction of the entrance hall, her breath catching in her chest. As she flew down the stairs opposite the double doors, Dottie appeared from a side passage, wiping her hands on her apron.

'What in the realm is—' she began, before the doors were thrown open and the rider staggered inside.

Talia reached the bottom step of the staircase and stopped, grabbing hold of the banister to steady herself.

'The Princess!' cried the rider. 'I must speak to the Princess!'

'I . . . I am here,' said Talia, her fingers gripping the carved wood of the banister. 'I am she.'

The rider lurched forward and fell to his knees before her on the dusty floor. Talia looked down at his dark hair soaked with sweat, the mud covering his boots and the emblem of a leaping stag on the creased sleeves of his tunic. Panic rushed over her, and she froze, unable to speak.

'I have ridden without stopping from Lustore to deliver a message from the King,' panted the rider, his body swaying with exhaustion. 'A great tragedy has struck the kingdom, and Bavaugh will soon descend into mourning.'

From the corner of her eye, Talia saw Dottie press her hands to her mouth with a gasp.

'The Princes have been murdered at the hands of a Tolbien spy and the Queen is critically wounded,' continued the rider, taking a letter from a pocket at his breast and offering it to her.

Talia took it, her hands beginning to tremble.

'Long live Princess Talia,' added the rider, 'heir to Bavaugh.'

PART FIVE

PART FIVE

ONCE UPON A time there was a Princess who was fair and sweet. She lived in a palace with blue gables and spent her days suffering through boring lessons in the schoolroom and making mischief with her eleven sisters.

There was one particular game she loved to play – and one particular sister she loved above all the others. The two of them would stand at opposite ends of their bedchamber, facing one another like a perfect mirror. When the Princess raised her right arm, her Princess reflection would raise her left, and when the Princess tapped her heels together, her Princess reflection would do the same. They would carry on like this until they could not contain their giggles and exploded into hysterics on the floor.

One day, the Princess was sitting by her bedroom window, brushing her long dark hair, when the door behind her flew open.

'You *told*,' screeched a voice, and a girl flew into the room and grabbed hold of her. 'You said you would not tell, but you did! How *could* you?'

The Princess dropped her hairbrush and tried to wriggle free, but the girl held her tightly, nails pinching into her skin.

'You are hurting me!' she gasped.

The girl released her. 'The King said I cannot see a Master again. He is going to have my books taken away!'

'Please don't be angry,' replied the Princess.

She thought of the night a moon ago, when she had followed the girl down to the schoolroom. She had watched the girl conjure and wrangle fierce, dark energy alone, fear and dismay gathering in her chest. The girl had looked mighty and almost cruel – not like herself at all.

'I did it for you,' added the Princess. 'What you are doing is dangerous—'

'Liar!'

'It's true. Anyway, you do not need to study magic; you cannot become a Master.'

The girl glared back at her. 'I will not give it up.'

'But—'

'The Masters will keep my secret; they can see my gifts.'

The Princess folded her arms. 'Not all of them. Florentina Samara the Wise thinks you are not careful enough. She agrees with me; the magic is changing you. You can't control it.'

The girl scowled. She stepped close to the Princess, the tips of their noses almost touching and their dark eyes boring into one another.

'I am warning you,' said the girl softly. 'Do not stand in my way.'

Several winters later, the Princess, now a young woman, stood in the palace library. Panting and sobbing, she looked upon the crumpled figure in the middle of the room.

'I am sorry!' she cried. 'Please, forgive me!'

The figure lifted its head; a young woman, beaten and bloody. She stared back at the Princess and her gaze was fierce, a thorned thicket of hate around her heart.

'I did not mean for this to happen,' said the Princess. 'When I spoke to the King, I did not think that he would order this.'

The library was dark, lit only by the moonlight that pooled through the windows and shifted across the bookshelves.

'When I heard, I came straight away,' added the Princess. 'But I was too late.'

The young woman's breathing was shallow and raspy and her left arm hung strangely from her shoulder. 'You got what you wanted.' The twist of her lips betrayed the pain it brought her to speak.

'I never wanted this!' cried the Princess, hot tears of anguish spilling down her cheeks. 'I just wanted you to stop – you were told to stop, but you did not listen. You never listen.'

The young woman spat and bloody spittle sprayed across the carpet. Her dress was torn and stained, and her knotted hair was flat against her head with sweat. Dark-purple blotches were gathering around her eyes and her nails were ripped and jagged from where she had tried to fight back.

'I am sorry!' cried the Princess again. 'But you are not yourself any more – you are letting it change you.'

She ran forward, but the young woman bared her teeth.

'Get away from me! If I am so terrible and dangerous, you had better stay away!'

The Princess stopped and broke into more sobs, her head in her hands.

'I am banished from my homeland,' the young woman gasped. 'But that will not stop me. I will never allow something like this to happen again, I will never be weak.' She lowered her voice. 'And you had better believe that I will remember what you did. I will always remember, Violanna.'

Briar

On the road

THE NIGHT BRIAR ran away, she was full of reckless courage. It had been two days since she had overheard the conversation between Auntie and the black-cloaked stranger in the farmhouse kitchen, and in that time Briar had been tentatively planning her escape. She had also been waiting, wondering if her aunt might seek her out and explain everything, apologizing for the lies. Briar had half hoped that she would not have to go through with her plan. But Auntie had carried on as normal since the incident, acting as if everything was well. So Briar's resolve had hardened.

Lying in bed the night of her departure, Briar waited until the farmhouse fell quiet and she was sure everyone was asleep. Then she gave Spot a final nuzzle, slipped from her room and padded to the kitchen. There she filled a satchel with leftovers from dinner, before creeping outside to the stables, her stomach bubbling with nerves.

It was all so easy, almost terrifyingly so.

Briar was coaxing the young mare, Dusty, from a stall, when she saw a flicker of a shadow in the doorway of the barn.

'What're you doing?'

Briar jumped, almost dropping the saddle slung over her arm. She spun around to see Jacken and she fell against Dusty's dapple-grey neck in relief. 'It's only you!' she breathed, and then added, 'You didn't wake anyone, did you?'

'No. Tell me what you're doing.'

Briar pursed her lips. 'Leaving,' she replied. Saying it aloud suddenly made it feel very real and fear crept into her chest. She turned away and hoisted the saddle over Dusty's back.

'But—'

'If you try to stop me, I'll hate you for ever.'

'I don't understand,' hissed Jacken, moving closer. 'What's happened?'

Briar busied herself with buckling Dusty's bridle and said, 'It's too much to explain now, but there's somewhere I must go.'

'What're you talking about? You can't just leave.'

Jacken touched her arm and she flinched.

'You haven't thought this through,' he added.

Briar jutted out her chin and said, 'All I know is I can't stay here another moment.'

Jacken paused. Then he turned and grabbed another saddle from a hook on the wall.

'What're *you* doing?' she asked.

'Coming with you.'

Relief washed over Briar, but she shrugged. 'You don't need to,' she replied. 'I can go alone.'

Jacken disappeared into the next stall and Briar could hear him murmuring to the mare, Star, as he saddled her. He led Star out a moment later and it was then that Briar realized he was fully dressed and he had even come out with his jacket and boots.

'How did you know—' she began, but Jacken shushed her.

'I have the flecks that we've saved from selling horses,' he said, patting his pocket. 'You haven't taken anything that belongs to Gad or Sel, have you?'

'No, but—'

'Good. Star and Dusty are our horses, since we caught and trained them, so I reckon it's all right for us to take them, but you should know that I don't like this, Briar. It's wrong.'

'I didn't ask you to come with me!' snapped Briar, hoping that he still would.

'Why didn't you?'

Moonlight leaked around the barn door and shone on Jacken's short dark hair. Briar could still feel the spot where he had touched her arm; tingly and hot.

'I . . . I don't know,' she said. 'I thought you'd try to stop me, I suppose.'

Things had not been right between them lately. They had been sullen and cold with one another since the kissing incident.

'How did you know I was going to leave tonight?' asked Briar.

'You've been strange all day. Something was wrong.'

Dusty snorted and, outside, one of the dogs in the yard whined.

'We need to go now,' hissed Briar. 'Before anyone wakes. I'll explain it all later.'

'This isn't right,' Jacken muttered, but he followed her as they led the horses out of the back of the barn and through the fields.

Once they reached the far orchard, they mounted and set off in the direction of Norrale, urging the horses into a brisk trot.

Briar waited until they were safely on their way, following a track that led to the border towns, before she told Jacken what she had overheard in the farmhouse kitchen. As they rode side by side, she recounted the whole thing, the moon high above them. When she finished, he remained quiet and stared down at Star's bobbing skewbald neck.

'Don't you think you should've just asked your aunt about it?' he said finally.

'No! She's been lying to me, Jacken – to both of us. If I asked her, she would just tell me more lies!'

'But when we get to this place – this *Mont Isle* – what're you going to do there?'

Jacken had touched on the very thing that panicked her and Briar twitched in the saddle. 'I don't know,' she said. 'I'll work it out later.'

After a pause, Jacken added, 'There must be a reason Selhah hasn't told you everything. It might have been better to—'

'I'm angry with her!' Briar snapped, nudging Dusty into a canter to end the conversation. Then she called over her shoulder, 'I'm too angry to hear what she says.'

They rode all that night, and pushed on again the next day. And the next, and the next. They did not stop in any of the border towns in case they were recognized and they avoided the main roads when they could. As time trickled by and the reality of what she had done finally hit Briar, she felt her initial recklessness ebbing, replaced by doubt and worry. Every day she expected to see her aunt appear on the road behind them, ready to drag them back to the farm. She was sure Auntie would be chasing her, full of guilt and remorse. Sometimes Briar felt a little disappointed when she looked back and there was no one there.

She's probably not even my aunt, Briar reminded herself in those moments. *She's probably nothing to me at all.*

Briar's whole life had been swept away in an instant, and what was left was clouded and scattered. Clearly Auntie was not who Briar thought she was, and maybe *she* was not who she thought she was either. The more Briar thought about it, the more confused she felt. Only the momentum of the journey kept her going.

Neither Briar nor Jacken was unaccustomed to life on the road and there was something reassuring about the steady, repetitive days of travel. They passed through hamlets and villages, and skirted the edges of towns. They followed paths they had trodden before and reminisced about times gone by, journeying from place to place, their meagre possessions crammed into saddlebags. Careful enquiries at the beginning of their journey had informed them that Mont Isle was a small island off the west coast of Bavaugh, and they were travelling up and across the kingdom towards it as quickly as they could.

'It sounds like a strange place,' Jacken had muttered on more than one occasion. 'Are you sure it's right?'

'Yes.'

'But there's nothing but the old castle there and the cursed Princess—'

'That's what I heard, Jacken, so that's where we're going!'

And Briar refused to be questioned further on the matter. She knew nothing except that whatever lay in her past, it had something to do with Mont Isle, and that was where she must go to discover the truth.

Almost halfway through their journey, as they were travelling across the rural belly of Bavaugh, they stumbled upon a town in uproar. They had intended to stop and buy or trade for a meal, but as they approached the town centre, they saw an empty bakery with the door battered down and windows smashed. Glass, fragments of wood and mud were piled in the street gutters and, further along the road, a tavern stood blackened by smoke.

Briar and Jacken glanced at one another and quickly turned the horses down a side street, heading away from the centre of town, back towards the main road.

'We'll stop in the next town,' said Jacken and they both tried to ignore the gnawing rumble of their bellies.

At first, when they reached the next town, Briar thought the black clothes everywhere were a peculiar custom of the region they were passing through – like the brown timber that corseted all the buildings – but then she noticed that the travellers passing through were dressed in black as well. It was not until she overheard a conversation later that afternoon between two women chatting beside a market stall that she understood.

'The Princes are dead!' she hissed at Jacken when he returned a few moments later, holding a loaf of bread. 'And the Queen is injured – they think she might die too!'

Briar had been waiting in a side street with their horses, staying away from the main hubbub of the town.

'Everyone's in mourning,' she added. 'That's why they're all wearing black.'

Jacken nodded. 'I was about to tell you the same. I just heard it in the bakery.'

'What does it mean?'

Jacken shrugged.

'Are we . . . are we at war?' Briar asked, echoing what she had overheard.

Jacken did not reply, but he looked worried.

'Did they say anything else at the bakery?'

'They said there have been riots – that's why that place we passed was all smashed up.'

Briar puffed out her cheeks. She knew very little about the Bavaughian royals except the bare facts that everyone picked up, but this news was shocking all the same. She thought she should probably feel sad about the Princes, but she mostly just felt uneasy. She hoped they would not come across any riots on their journey.

'We need to dress in black too so we're less noticeable,' she said.

'We don't have the flecks to spare.'

Briar glanced over her shoulder at the stream of people bustling through the market. 'I saw a stall selling wool; I could offer to spin for them—'

'It's too dangerous.'

Briar did not question this, just as she did not question it when he handed her a shawl to tie over her head like an elderly lady as they passed through towns and villages. The few times that they had stopped for Jacken to labour half a day at a farm for flecks, Briar had kept away with the horses, waiting in an empty field with the hood of her cloak up despite the warm weather. They both knew that she attracted unwanted attention.

'Let's carry on,' said Jacken. 'I'm sure I can pick up some work later and we can buy black clothes then.'

Briar sighed, but she nodded and took Dusty's reins.

They wove down back streets, making their way through the town and returning to the main road.

'What's wrong?' asked Jacken when they were mounted and riding side by side again.

'Nothing,' replied Briar, but she pressed her temple where it felt like a tight band was squeezing her head.

Dusty was trying to speak to her – something about not liking the way the sun cast shivering shadows through the trees – and it was making Briar feel sick. She attempted to ignore the mare, but still her forehead throbbed and bile rose at the back of her throat. She closed her eyes and imagined she was seated at her spinning wheel in the kitchen of the farmstead, her foot pumping the treadle and the wool stretching and twisting in her fingers.

'Do you want to stop a moment and rest?' asked Jacken.

Briar shook her head. 'No,' she replied between clenched teeth. 'We're still eight days' ride from Mont Isle. We must not stop.'

Meredyth

The Great Hall, Mont Isle

MEREDYTH TOOK A deep breath and stepped into the Great Hall. She had not set foot in that room since the Blessing and she shivered, trying to push back the unwanted memories that crowded her mind: the blackness, the screams and the sorceress, bending over the cradle with a cruel, determined look.

'Princess?' Meredyth called into the darkness. 'Princess? It is me.'

She had tried to send a servant to Princess Talia, but none would go. They said that, since the tragedy, the Princess spent her days standing before the portrait of the King and everyone was under strict instructions to leave her alone.

'Princess?' Meredyth called again. 'Princess Talia?'

As her eyes adjusted to the dimness, Meredyth saw a tall figure on the opposite side of the room. Chinks of daylight shone through the boarded windows and created a jagged pattern on the tiled floor that flickered and glowed. Meredyth did not allow herself to look towards the dais where she could too easily remember lying, pinned and unable to move. It was a memory that often surfaced late at night, when it was dark and she was alone in her bed.

'Long live Princess Talia,' she said, walking towards the figure, her cane tapping, 'heir to Bavaugh.'

There was no reply. If the Princess was surprised by her unannounced arrival, she did not show it.

Meredyth curtsied then looked up at the portrait of the King. It had been painted in his youth, when they had been in love. In it, he was standing with his legs apart, his hand resting on the jewelled handle of a sword, and he looked handsome, strong and arrogant – nothing like the broken, grief-stricken old man she had left at the palace in Lustore.

'I offer you my deepest condolences, Princess.'

'Why?' replied Princess Talia, her voice thin and choked. 'I never met them. They were my brothers, but they were strangers to me.'

Meredyth reached forward and placed a hand on the Princess's shoulder.

'I cannot imagine how you feel, Princess,' she said. 'It is a great tragedy that has changed everything. Prince Dionathy and Prince Stasthes rest with the Great Creator now—'

'I will never know them!' cried the Princess suddenly, her voice bouncing off the walls. 'And to have died like that – their throats slit as they slept. It is horrifying.'

Meredyth shivered, unwanted imaginings flitting through her mind. Those poor boys. Poor Queen Hana, made an invalid by her wounds and doomed to live, knowing what had happened to her sons.

'I have come from the King with guards sent to protect you,' said

Meredyth, pushing such thoughts from her mind. 'I was told when I arrived that no one has been allowed on the island since the news.'

'I am not worried for myself,' replied the Princess with a shrug, then she looked over her shoulder and added, 'My father sent the guards for me?'

'He did.'

Princess Talia's eyes were bloodshot, her face red and puffy. 'How is he?' she asked.

Meredyth hesitated, thinking of the hunched, sagging figure she had last seen standing outside the palace as the ceremonial weeping and wailing began. 'He is distraught,' she said. 'It has shocked everyone, and there has been uproar and riots across the kingdom since. The King has a hard task ahead of him. He must raise the spirits of the nation and decide how to retaliate. But right now, he has been caught up in the burial rites. At least that has given everyone something to focus on.'

'I wish I could have gone.'

Meredyth patted the Princess's back, her palm brushing the smooth black taffeta of the mourning dress.

'I only saw the start of it before I set off,' she said. 'I wanted to come to you right away, as soon as I heard the news, but it would not have been appropriate.'

'I understand.'

'Hiberah is here, too, and he would like to see you when you are ready. I know you are still grieving, Princess, but we have much that we must do before everyone arrives.'

The Princess turned to her in surprise. 'What do you mean?'

'You are heir to the throne now. You must realize that?'

Princess Talia dropped her chin to her chest. 'Yes . . . I mean, I suppose I do know it,' she whispered. 'I just . . . I have not thought about it much. I have not thought about anything much recently. But I suppose my father will be coming here, to Mont Isle? Finally.'

Meredyth's eyes wandered to the portrait before them. 'Your father may not be what you are expecting,' she said. 'He is a changed man.'

But the Princess did not seem to be listening; instead, she was glancing around the Great Hall, as if seeing it with fresh eyes.

'Is the King travelling alone?' she asked.

'He certainly will not be travelling alone. For the first time since . . . well, for many winters, Mont Isle will be full of courtiers again. I have come to see you, of course, but I have also come to prepare the castle for everyone's arrival.'

Princess Talia's eyes widened and she let out a bark of laughter. 'I always wanted him to visit me, but I would never have wished for circumstances like these. What will he think of me?'

'He will think that he has a strong, clever daughter,' said Meredyth, hoping it would be true. 'He is lucky.'

She glanced at the ridiculous curls pinned to Princess Talia's forehead and inwardly sighed. They were the latest fashion at court, but on the Princess they just looked wrong. Preparing her for the King's arrival would almost be more challenging than readying the castle.

'No Tolbien assassin came for me,' said Princess Talia. 'I am the cursed Princess that everyone forgot.'

Meredyth could not deny that it was true. 'But not any more,' she replied. 'This tragedy, terrible and horrifying though it is, has returned your birthright to you. You are Princess Talia, sole heir to the Bavaughian throne.'

Meredyth saw panic flash across the Princess's face.

'I am cursed!' she spluttered, spinning away. 'I am no good to Bavaugh.'

Meredyth rested her hand on Princess Talia's shoulder once more and gently turned her back. 'I have always promised you that you need not fear the curse and I pray that you will believe it is true,' she said. 'I will not let you come to harm – *we* will not let you come to harm. I and the Bavaughians who now serve you.'

Talia did not look wholly convinced, but she stayed quiet.

'You are the true Princess of Bavaugh,' Meredyth continued. 'You are all we have left.'

Sel

On the road

SEL HAD NEVER liked horses. She thought them big, skittish creatures and she would rather walk than ride, even if it doubled the length of a journey. Sitting high up in the saddle made her nervous. The tossing and shaking of a horse's head made her nervous. Their big hooves and swishing tails made her nervous. She had never understood why Jacken and Briar spent so much time catching, training and fussing over horses; she was just glad that none of those chores had ever fallen to her.

Gaddeous knew her equine aversion, of course, so when she announced that she would set out after Briar and Jacken immediately on Patch, their huge, clumpy shire, he hesitated.

'Are you sure, Selhah?' he asked, following her outside into the yard. 'They'll be a night's ride ahead of you now and they'll be moving fast.'

Sel knew he was gently implying that she would be a slow,

unsteady chaser, and he was right. She had woken that morning as dawn broke, slid from beneath Gaddeous's warm limbs and padded to the kitchen to boil the water for tea. There was something about the silence and the clear freshness in the air that had bothered her. Then, as she'd stood by the stove, she had noticed Spot perched on the table, licking his paws and flicking his tail. She had frowned. The little black cat always slept at Briar's feet. With a growing sense of unease, Sel had lurched, still half asleep, down the corridor to Briar's bedroom. When she pulled back the door, she had seen that the bed was empty. A quick glance into Jacken's room had confirmed that his bed was empty too. Sel had run back to the kitchen, crying out for Gaddeous, knowing that it was too late. Briar and Jacken had gone.

'I could ride after them?' Gaddeous suggested.

Sel shook her head as she hurried to the barn. 'It has to be me,' she said. 'Briar won't come back with you and . . . there're other complications.'

She grabbed a large saddle off a hook on the wall and hauled it over to Patch's stall. The gelding sniffed at her with some surprise and stamped his great, white-feathered feet. Sel attempted to flop the saddle over his back, but the horse was too tall and she groaned in frustration.

'Here,' said Gaddeous, grabbing a stool. 'And watch how I buckle it all. I'm not sure I've ever seen you tack up a horse.'

Sel stepped back gratefully and wrung her hands, peering over his shoulder. 'A woman – someone I knew long ago – came to the farm to speak to me two nights ago,' she said to the back of his head. 'I'm sorry I didn't tell you before. I'd hoped we could carry on as we were, but I think . . . I think Briar overheard something. She must have.'

Gaddeous finished bridling Patch and moved aside. He seemed

to accept without concern the fact that she had hosted an unknown visitor. 'Do you know where Briar is headed?' he asked.

Sel put her face in her hands. She took a deep breath and straightened up. 'I think so,' she said. 'And it's not good.'

'No?'

'She's in great danger, Gad.'

'You'd better be away, then,' he said, leading Patch out of the barn and into the yard. 'At least Jacken is with her.'

'Yes, that's something.'

Gaddeous held Patch's head while Sel climbed up the mounting block. 'How will I do this on my own?' she said, gingerly fitting her boot into the stirrup. 'He's so big.'

'You'll manage. You can use a tree stump or a fence or anything, really.'

Sel swung herself on to Patch's back and wriggled into the seat, relieved to find that he was broad and sturdy. 'I've taken some flecks—' she began.

'Good. You must take many.'

Sel leant down and touched his bearded cheek. 'I'm sorry,' she said. 'I've not even properly explained it all.'

'You don't need to.'

Gaddeous stepped on to the mounting block and reached up, pressing his lips to her own. 'I'm glad you have Patch,' he said. 'He's a well-mannered old fellow, who will treat you kindly. I know you're more than capable of looking after yourself, but please be careful.'

'I will.'

'And I know that you might not return,' said Gaddeous, his dark eyes suddenly shiny. 'You're not obliged to. You had another life before you took Briar as your ward and I'm guessing your stewardship is coming to an end. You should know that I love you and you're always welcome here if that's what you want.'

Sel's breath caught in her throat and she felt tears prickling her eyes. She had been so consumed with panic that she had not realized what was happening. She was leaving, and who knew what lay ahead. Perhaps Gaddeous was right. Maybe she would not be coming back.

'I don't . . .' she began. 'I can't know what will happen—'

Gaddeous stopped her with a wave of his hand. 'You don't need to explain it to me,' he said. 'You must be away now. Briar and Jacken need you.' He stepped on to the mounting block once more, and wrapped his arm around her waist, almost pulling her from the saddle. He kissed her again, his lips tender and hot.

'Goodbye, Gad,' said Sel, her voice trembling. There was so much more she wanted to say, but she did not know how and she did not have the time to spare. 'Goodbye,' she repeated instead.

She squeezed Patch's sides with her heels and the gelding ambled into a trot, his dinner plate-sized hooves clopping on the hard ground. Sel concentrated on staying balanced in the saddle and did not let herself glance over her shoulder. She knew Gaddeous would be standing at the gate, watching her leave; a lonely figure in the shadow of the wooden farmhouse, the last of the white blossom from the nearby orchard fluttering around his head, and the hens – *her* hens that she had named and doted on – pecking the ground by his feet. Instead, Sel turned Patch in the direction of the border towns and urged the gelding into a canter, gritting her teeth at the thought of the journey ahead.

As predicted, their progress was slow. Sel would push Patch too fast one moment and pull him back to a plod the next, when her nerves got the better of her. Eventually, they settled on a mutually agreed steady jog that carried them along the roads and through the towns and villages at a relatively even pace. And as the days passed, Sel grew more thankful for Patch, the gentle, giant horse, who was patient with her anxious yanks on the reins and picked his own way through crowded market squares. She even became quite fond of him. He was her only companion on what was a fretful, lonely journey.

When she had first set out on the road, Sel had held on to some distant hope that she might catch up with Jacken and Briar soon, but, as Gaddeous had guessed, they were too far ahead. Occasionally, passing through a hamlet or crossing a river, she would feel a faint trace of magic and she would know that Briar had travelled this path. The thought buoyed her, and she would urge Patch on a little faster, but the magic residue would soon fade and there would still be no sign of a slight, golden figure on the road ahead. Then Sel's spirits would plummet, and she would sit slumped in the saddle for the rest of the day.

It worried Sel that if she could feel hints of Briar's magic, then others would be able to sense it also. She found herself praying to the Great Creator that Briar and Jacken would not be set upon by thieves or worse. Since Briar was a baby, she had not been far from Sel's side and now Sel felt her absence keenly. At first, she thought it was the lack of magic that had left a raw ache – she had spent so long living with the intense force of the intricate spells wound around Briar that the sudden lack of it was sure to disturb her – but late at night, when she sheltered at an inn or bedded down in a hay barn, she knew it was Briar that she missed. The girl. Her daughter who was not her daughter.

Sel spent a great deal of the journey replaying as much of her conversation with Lalious as she could remember, trying to work out what Briar might have overheard. Sometimes she wished Briar had confronted them. Perhaps then she would not have run off like this. But that was wishful thinking. Even if Briar had asked her outright what was going on, Sel did not know what she would have said. Not really. Even now, if she did manage to catch up to Briar and Jacken, Sel was not sure how she would explain it all.

Towards the end of their conversation, she and Lalious had agreed that it was best Briar knew as little as possible. It was safer for her to stay on the farmstead, far away from Mont Isle and the oncoming summit of the spell. Then maybe – just maybe – Noatina might fall for the trap, and she would try to kill the wrong princess.

'Queen Violanna came up with this scheme herself?' Lalious had asked as they stood in the yard, after Sel had explained everything. 'I knew she was hiding something. And that is why she kept the second Princess on that island all this time. It is a clever trick, I will give her that.'

'I could be mistaken, but back then it seemed . . . that she knew she was carrying another child,' Sel replied. 'She knew she would have two babies, born apart.' Sel's eyes darted from one shadow to another in the yard. They were at the edge of the Wilderness, far away from civilization, but she still felt anxious voicing what she had kept secret for so long.

'I will send word to the Masterhood and ask some members to join me in Bavaugh,' said Lalious. 'If our assumptions are correct, Noatina will strike soon.'

'You're going to attack her?'

'It is an opportunity we cannot miss.'

'And the Princess?' Sel asked. 'The other one on the island. Will she be safe?'

Lalious looked as if the thought had not occurred to her before.

'As long as Noatina does not realize she has the wrong girl, there should not be a problem. We will act the moment we get the chance this time; we will be prepared.'

'But—'

'Noatina is difficult to predict, but we have been studying her approach and combat for some time now. The best thing you can do is stay away.'

And the lives of the Princesses are of no consequence, thought Sel. But she nodded in agreement and Lalious took her leave.

Afterwards, Sel had managed to convince herself that this was the best outcome for Briar. She was far away from Mont Isle and Noatina. They just needed to carry on as they were. If all went well, Briar could stay at the farmstead and remain none the wiser until the spell was broken. Or perhaps Briar would never have to know who she truly was at all. This was a wish Sel entertained in the deepest part of herself, barely even acknowledging it was there. If Briar never discovered her birthright, Sel could keep her for ever. They could stay in the wilderness instead and never be found. The Queen could not claim Briar back if she could not find her.

But none of that mattered any more. Briar had overheard something and now she was gone, heading right into the heart of the danger. The thought made Sel's stomach churn until she was sick and dizzy. Occasionally she wondered if she should try sending out some kind of a retrieving spell to bring Briar back against her will, but she had never attempted such a thing before and there was so much magic knotted around the girl that it would doubtless go wrong. It was not a risk she could take.

Instead, she pushed on, urging Patch through forests and across moorland. Sometimes they passed through towns and villages she recognized from past travels, but Sel did not stop. She remained vigilant, looking out for two familiar figures on horseback, and feeling for magic. As the days slid by, she moved steadily closer to the west coast, heading in the direction of Mont Isle, her fear and dread rising. Sel told herself that she must find Briar before the girl reached the castle, or else . . . or else she did not know what might happen.

Violanna

The Queen's Chambers, Mont Isle

VIOLANNA STOOD IN the middle of her room, a piece of parchment scrunched between her fingers. Neat, looping Diaspass writing could just be seen at its edges.

A knock at the door made her jump and one of the castle maids appeared.

'Lady Lansin would like to see you, Your Majesty.'

Violanna nodded.

The maid disappeared and, a moment later, Violanna heard the tap of a cane on the stone floor as Meredyth entered. As usual, she was impeccably dressed in a smart, tight black gown with a pleated skirt.

'Good morning, Your Majesty. Long live Queen Violanna of Bavaugh.'

Violanna felt her stomach flip. 'There is no need for that,' she said. 'I am still not the Queen while Hana lives.'

'But you are mother to the heir of the kingdom, Your Majesty. It is the proper way I should address you.'

'Talia is the heir now, but Queen Hana might yet bear more children.'

Meredyth shook her head. 'No, Your Majesty,' she replied quietly. 'She will not.'

Violanna crushed the parchment in her hands tighter and asked, 'What is it that you need, Lady Lansin? Why are you here?'

Meredyth shuffled further into the room. Whatever she was planning to say was clearly important.

'I apologize that I have not sought out time alone with you since I arrived,' she began. 'I have been busy preparing the castle and assisting the Princess. She does not quite . . . look as the heir to the throne should. I have been doing my best to . . . *enhance* her.'

Violanna nodded. 'How is Talia?' she asked. She had not seen much of her daughter since news of the royal tragedy had reached Mont Isle. Talia ate meals alone in her chambers and did not walk about the castle or take her lessons any more. Violanna had tried seeking her out many times, knowing how her daughter must be struggling, but Talia had responded with cool indifference. Violanna had not been an attentive mother over the winters, and she could not blame her daughter for rejecting her attempts to play the part now, but the snub still hurt.

'I think the Princess is scared,' replied Meredyth. 'The whole future of the kingdom rests on her shoulders and her father – a man she has never met – is coming to officially appoint her as heir to the throne.'

'He is definitely coming?'

'Of course . . .' replied Meredyth with a frown. 'He has already set out from Lustore and he is bringing most of the court with him. They will be here in a few days. You know this, Your Majesty.'

Violanna turned away and paced back and forth. 'This was not supposed to happen,' she muttered. 'We were meant to be forgotten. We were meant to be safe.'

'The murder of the Princes must be a great inconvenience.'

Violanna winced. 'I did not mean it like that,' she said. 'Those children . . . it is horrifying.'

'I do not mean to be difficult with you, Your Majesty,' said Meredyth. 'But the King and the court are on their way. They are coming to watch the Appointment of the new heir to the throne – your daughter. You will not be able to hide from them. You must face this.'

Violanna rubbed at her head as she turned about the room like a cornered animal. 'I tried so hard to stop it. I gave up everything.'

'I know, Your Majesty.'

'Talia was never meant to ascend the throne!'

'We cannot change what has happened.'

When Violanna did not reply, Meredyth cleared her throat and added, 'I came to speak to you this morning because there is something else we must discuss. I have been so caught up with everything that I have neglected to talk to you properly, but this cannot wait any longer . . .' She took a deep breath and continued, 'I know about Noatina.'

Violanna stopped short and her body stilled.

The sound of waves crashing against the rocks outside the castle walls drifted through the open window and mingled with the bang and clatter of workers repairing the windows in the Great Hall.

'What do you know?'

'I know the sorceress has a name and I have come to understand that she must be a person. We Bavaughians are ignorant of magic and I suppose, like everyone else, I thought her to be an evil being, but that is not exactly true, is it? She is a person. A woman. Like you and I.'

Violanna was silent for a moment as she glanced down at the letter balled in her hand. 'I have a message here from one of my sisters,' she said. 'You always used to ask me about my many sisters, but I never wanted to speak of them. It was all too painful. This letter is from Fayia, married to a Diaspass Duke – a handsome man we all made eyes at when we were young – and she has nine children and a large estate outside the capital.'

Meredyth sighed. 'Your Majesty, do not change the subject—'

'She has written to tell me that she believes the sorceress is coming. It is what the Diaspass Assembly are saying and it is what I heard from an old acquaintance this past winter. But I do not need to be told, because I know it to be true; I feel it in my bones. She will strike soon – seventeen winters have almost passed and she will not have forgotten.'

'But *who* is she?' cried Meredyth, banging her cane on the dusty rug with a thud. 'Who is this woman?'

'Noatina is a sorceress.'

'And?'

Violanna took a deep breath. She had always known she would one day explain it all and now that time had come.

'In her girlhood, Noatina trained as a Master,' she began. 'Though she was forbidden to do so by the King of the Diaspass Kingdom. Royalty cannot join the Masterhood, but Noatina was a rare, gifted student. Magic can be learnt, but some have a natural propensity for it and she was almost unique – all the Masters said so. They tried to teach her secretly, but she was betrayed by . . . someone close to her.

When the King found out she had disobeyed him, she was punished severely for it, but she did not give up. Instead, she became a lone wielder of magic. A sorceress.'

Through her window, Violanna could see the extra hired hands scrubbing and sweeping the courtyard below. She tried to focus on them so her mind would not wander back to her childhood and the palace with the blue gables.

'Noatina hates the Diaspass Kingdom,' she added. 'When the King finally cast her out, it was harsh and violent. Before she disappeared, she vowed she would seek revenge.'

'And you?' Meredyth prompted. 'Why does she hate you?'

Violanna sighed and turned away from the window. 'Because I was her betrayer,' she replied. 'I was young; I did not really know what I was doing. I could see that the magic was changing Noatina and it terrified me. I just wanted her to stop, to be herself again. I should have realized that the King's reaction would be fierce. He has always been ruthless and cruel, and he couldn't bear the thought of his own daughter becoming more powerful than him.'

Violanna could see that Meredyth was struggling to follow her – there was a deep furrow of confusion in her friend's brow. But the words were tumbling out of Violanna's mouth and her hands were shaking with the relief of finally speaking what she had hidden for so long.

'The Masters blamed me for what happened. I should not have involved the King – of course, I can see that now, but back then I felt I had to do something. Magic can corrupt. I knew Noatina best of all and I could see what was happening.'

Violanna dropped the crumpled parchment in her hands and grabbed hold of the back of a chair to steady herself.

'So this sorceress,' began Meredyth after a pause, staring at Violanna with wide, shocked eyes. 'She is your . . .'

'She is my kin.'

'Your sister?'

'Yes, the third daughter of the King of the Diaspass Kingdom. The wicked one. The one they tried to forget,' replied Violanna. 'Noatina is my double. My sister. My twin.'

Briar

Guil, West Bavaugh

IT WAS A warm day, but Briar kept the hood of her cloak pulled over her head. She was tired and sore and not even the thought that they had almost reached their destination could lift her spirits. They had arrived that morning in Guil, which looked much the same as any fishing town, and Briar had felt surprisingly deflated. On the coastal path into Guil, she had seen Mont Isle in the distance – that strange, walled island in the sea with a castle sprouting from its centre, stretching up to the sky. She had spent so long imagining it that the reality was somehow disappointing; there was no spark of recognition or moment of clarity. The sight of Mont Isle made her feel itchy and tense, but that was all. On the road, Briar had been full of purpose, assuring herself that the answers to her questions lay ahead. But now the journey was almost over and she feared that she was no closer to the truth.

A droplet of sweat trickled across Briar's scalp. It was uncomfortably hot in the busy streets of Guil and she was wearing a shawl wrapped around her head under her cloak. She longed to take it off, but she knew it was not safe. She attracted attention, even in her muddy, travel-worn state. Jacken had already suggested they go to the shore later and find a quiet spot to paddle in the sea, like they used to in Turow. Briar was looking forward to it. She wanted to throw off her cloak and dunk her head into the cool water. She longed to smile and laugh again – it seemed that all they had done since they set out on the road was stay alert, discuss the journey and worry.

The streets of Guil were swarming with people as they made their way to the central square and there was a high-spirited, excited tang in the air that confused Briar. It seemed like rather a small fishing town to have this many residents and she wondered if there was a market or festival about to be held.

'Perhaps we could pay a fisherman to row us over to the island?' she suggested, chewing on her lip as they trudged through a cramped alleyway.

'But the castle guards will just send us away,' Jacken replied, dragging the tired horses after them. 'Briar . . . are you sure this is right?'

'Yes!' she snapped back, ignoring a prod of doubt. 'We're so close, Jacken.'

He sighed. 'You go and find a fishing boat to give us passage. I'll try and get an inn to stable the horses.'

'All right. I'll meet you by the shore.'

They parted and were quickly swallowed into the bustling, packed streets.

As she made her way to Guil's shoreline, Briar noticed a throng of chattering people gathering around her, all heading in the same direction. Over the heads of the crowd, she could see the grey band of the churning sea as they descended together to the beach, then there was the castle on the island, like a jagged finger rising from the waves.

As she stared at the castle, something stirred in Briar. It was a sharp, intense feeling that made her body tremble. The air around her seemed to shudder and ring, and suddenly it was almost as if the castle were staring back at her, seeing her, and beckoning her onwards.

This was what she had been waiting for.

This felt right. This was where she was meant to be. Something was pulling her towards the castle with an overwhelming urgency. She just needed to work out how to get there.

'Any spinners?' yelled out a voice.

Briar turned to see a man standing on a rowing boat that had been pulled up the beach. 'We need spinners and carpenters and scrubbers,' he cried.

There was a crowd gathered around the man, and as more people flooded to the shore, they joined the mass, muttering and giggling to one another.

Briar edged closer, trying not to catch anyone's eye, but she was soon swept up in the group and shoved forward by those joining behind.

'Whatcha paying?' called a voice from the crowd.

The man smoothed down his moustache and said, 'We're paying the normal rate, but you'll be granted a spot in the Great Hall to watch the Appointment and you can't put a price on that.'

There were general murmurings from the jostling hordes. A

man raised his hand and shouted, 'I'll do it; I'm handy with a hammer.'

A moment later, a woman raised her hand and said, 'Count me in too. I can scrub a floor. Done plenty in my time.'

The man on the rowing boat nodded and beckoned his volunteers over. Then he yelled, 'Anyone else?'

'I'd rather watch the parade afterwards with a mug of cider, myself,' said an old woman standing next to Briar. 'I didn't walk all morning from Sowuell to scrub a floor, even if it is in a castle.'

There were mutterings of agreement from those around her and some of the crowd began peeling off and heading back towards the town.

'Do we have any spinners?' bellowed the man on the rowing boat. 'We need threads to repair the curtains.'

No hands were raised.

'Come on, folks,' added the man. 'This is your only chance. History is about to be made! And you'll see all the fine Lords and Ladies of court up close.'

Briar looked from the castle in the sea to the man standing on the boat, and before she knew what she was doing, she had raised her hand. 'I can spin,' she called, her heart thudding in her chest. 'I'll do it.'

Her voice was clear and sweet, and it turned the heads of everyone who heard it. Pulling her cloak around her, Briar hurried through the bodies to the front of the crowd.

'You're young,' said the man with the moustache, trying to peer under the hood of her cloak. 'We need competent spinners.' He turned back to the thinning crowd and scanned around for another offer.

'I'll spin the finest thread you've ever seen.'

The man glanced at her, shrugging. 'All right,' he said. 'You'll have to do.' Then he jumped down from the boat and called out, 'Come on, help us push this back into the sea.'

The volunteers and a few stragglers from the crowd began dragging the rowing boat down the beach.

'Wait!' said Briar, hurrying to keep up, the pebbles clashing and clattering under her boots. 'We're leaving now? I need to tell someone where I'm going.'

The man with the moustache frowned. 'There's no time,' he snapped. 'We can't even wait for the tide to go out. The King's arriving today!'

Briar stopped at the shoreline in surprise. 'The King?' she echoed. 'He's coming *here*?'

The man with the moustache gave her a funny look. 'Yes, His Majesty set out days earlier than planned,' he replied. When she still appeared confused, he added, 'For the Appointment? Are you a halfwit, girl?'

'I only heard he was so close this morning,' piped up the woman who had offered to scrub floors. 'I rushed right here because I thought I might see him at the parade, but I never imagined I'd get the chance to watch the Appointment! We're lucky.' She grinned at Briar and strode through the waves to the boat, which was bobbing on the water.

Briar hesitated. She looked over her shoulder, down the pebbly beach, as if Jacken might suddenly appear through the milling groups of people.

'We need to go, girl,' said the man with the moustache. 'You're either coming or you're not.'

Briar bit her lip, glancing ahead of them across the rolling grey waves of the sea to the island. Her gaze fixed on the castle and something inside her settled like a bolt sliding into place. She needed to get to Mont Isle; it was where she was meant to be.

'I'm coming,' she said, and she waded through the water and climbed into the boat.

Talia

The Princess's Chambers, Mont Isle

TALIA DID NOT recognize the girl in the mirror. She tended to avoid gazing at her reflection if she could help it. She was no great beauty and she did not like to stand and pick out her flaws – not when there were so many other things she could be doing. She knew what she looked like: the high forehead, the blue-grey eyes, the rounded face and tall, sturdy frame. But the girl staring back at her in the mirror, with maids fussing at her hair and dress, looked different.

Yesterday Lady Lansin had appeared in her chambers, accompanied by a woman with red-painted lips who called herself a 'Dresser'. The woman wore an elaborate gown and heavy perfume and, even in her sorry, anxious state, Talia found herself intrigued.

'We have come to make some . . . minor adjustments,' Meredyth had said, ushering Talia to a chair.

'Adjustments?' she echoed, sitting down.

Talia felt the assessing eyes of the Dresser sweep over her. 'I can make the hair lighter and put some colour in her cheeks,' the woman said. 'Perhaps a little bit of plucking around the eyebrows. Is that what you want?'

Meredyth nodded and added quietly, 'This is to remain between us. It must go no further.'

The Dresser began rummaging through a large carpet bag.

'You are going to dye my hair?' cried Talia.

'Oh, lots of people do it at court, Princess,' said Meredyth quickly. 'It will just make it a bit brighter. We want you to look your best for the Appointment.'

'But what does it matter—'

'Sit still and it will be done before you know it.'

Too bewildered to protest, Talia had sat and let the Dresser work on her: brushing, plucking and pinching. She had emerged some time later looking quite different. Dottie said she thought the light shade was very becoming, but to Talia it was wrong. She had not minded her hair as it was before, or her eyebrows, which were now thinned and arched. She could not deny that her appearance had been improved in a conventional sense – although she was still not sure anyone would describe her as beautiful – but she would rather have stayed as she was.

Dottie said she was getting uppity about nothing. 'You want to look nice for your big day, don't you?' she tutted. 'No one has ever seen you before. It's important to make a good impression.'

But Talia would rather have looked like herself. She was nervous enough as it was, without staring in the mirror at a stranger. Not to mention all these people fussing around her, dabbing at her cheeks, smoothing her hair, tightening her stays. Most of them were the new staff, hurriedly hired by Meredyth to prepare for the Appointment, and Talia did not know them. They gave her long, awed looks and fluttered around her with devout focus.

'That is enough!' she found herself snapping, when their hovering presence became too much to bear. 'Leave me!'

They all shrank back, curtseying earnestly and hurrying from her chambers.

'Not you, Dottie.'

The maid gave her a haughty look, but obediently hung back.

When they were alone, Talia said, 'Dottie, how do I really look? Be honest.'

The maid's lined red face softened and she uncrossed her arms. 'Nice,' she said.

'Like a Princess?'

'Like the heir to the throne.'

Talia turned back to the mirror and sighed. A string of diamonds were wound around her throat, interspersed with sapphires – 'To bring out the blue in your eyes,' Lady Lansin had said – and her wrists clattered with jewelled bracelets. Her gown was tight and pale blue with a full, trailing skirt trimmed in lace and encrusted with beads; apparently, a fleet of seamstresses had worked on it throughout the night. There were flowers woven into her fairer hair and – Talia frowned and leant closer – were those . . . *berries*?

There was a soft knock at the door and Mistress Rashel appeared.

'Long live Princess Talia, heir to Bavaugh,' she said, curtseying. Then she straightened and blinked at Talia. 'Princess, you look wonderful. I scarcely recognize you.'

Talia tried not to grimace. 'Is all well?' she asked.

'We have just had news that the King is soon to arrive in Guil. The royal party have slowed their progress to avoid waiting for the tides on the beach. There is a great crowd of people already there in preparation for the Appointment parade later.'

Talia felt a stab of panic and wished she could sit down, but her gown was too tight. 'I thought they were not due until this evening!' she squeaked.

'They are moving swiftly.'

'The workers will still be sewing the curtains as you walk into the Great Hall, at this rate,' snorted Dottie. 'I even heard we ran out of thread!'

'The important thing is that you are ready, Princess,' said Mistress Rashel. 'And do not fear, the castle is looking magnificent. The place is quite changed. It looks as it once did.'

'When you weren't around,' muttered Dottie.

Talia walked to the bedroom window, the heavy, beaded skirts of her dress dragging behind her, and peered out at the gardens below, which were cleared of their tangled mess and speckled with servants raking and planting.

Lady Lansin had explained what would happen at the Appointment. They had even spent yesterday morning in the Great Hall walking through what Talia would do and where she would stand, while men had hammered at the window frames and sealed the cracks in the floor. Last night Talia had lain in bed, staring at the canopy above, going over and over it all again in her head. But no matter how many times she reminded herself to stand *there* and kneel *here*, she still trembled at the thought. Not to mention the parade on the mainland that would follow the ceremony. She shuddered.

'Princess?' said Mistress Rashel. 'Are you well?'

Talia turned back to the room, her heart thumping in her chest. 'Truthfully, I do not know what scares me more,' she blurted out. 'Becoming heir to the throne or the thought of meeting my father.'

Mistress Rashel and Dottie exchanged a look.

'Yours is the most brilliant mind I have ever taught,' said Mistress Rashel after a pause. 'Bavaugh is fortunate to have such a person as heir to the throne. Never doubt it.'

Talia stared at her in surprise. She did not think she had ever received praise like that from her governess.

'And your father might be the King, but he is also a man,' said Dottie. 'A man who abandoned his daughter and is now returning to claim her again. He might well be nervous too.' Then she added quietly, 'Forgive my impertinence, but it is true.'

Talia swallowed and bent her head, tears welling in her eyes.

'There now,' murmured Dottie, moving closer. 'You'll mess up your dress.'

'But the curse!' hissed Talia, trying to force back the sobs rising in her throat. 'Lady Lansin says I need not fear it, but I do.'

'There are guards all over the castle, Princess,' said Mistress Rashel in her matter-of-fact tone. 'No one can get to you. Besides, a curse? It was all so long ago.'

'A spell does not work that way—' Talia began, but Mistress Rashel continued.

'The Tolbiens are the real threat. Princess, you are wise – you always have been – and your father could do with your counsel. The nation's hearts are broken, but you will bring them back together again. I know you will.'

Talia tried to believe it, but her uneasiness would not budge. That morning, in the early hours, she had pulled out her notebooks, filled with jottings from her studies of magic, and pored over them again. She had not touched them since the day the messenger had galloped up the causeway with news of the tragedy. She was not sure what she was looking for, exactly. Perhaps a detail that would reassure her that she need not fear the curse, as everyone said. But she found the systems and theories as confusing and impenetrable as before, and she was left more anxious and frustrated.

'Heir or no heir, it don't matter much to me,' muttered Dottie, taking hold of Talia's hands. 'But I couldn't bear to see a hair on your head harmed.' The maid's pale eyes grew watery and her voice wavered a little as she added, 'You should listen to your Mistress – she's right in this. You have guards who will watch over you from now on, day and night. You're the safest you've ever been. Besides, anyone who wanted to harm you would have to get through me first.'

Talia smiled. 'I do not like their chances,' she replied.

Dottie winked and pulled a handkerchief from the pocket of her apron. When Talia tried to take it, she tutted and said, 'No, let me do it. You'll only mess yourself up.'

Talia stood as the maid dabbed carefully at the corners of her eyes, trying not to smudge the powder and rouge. When she had finished, Talia cleared her throat and took as deep a breath as her stays would allow.

'I suppose it is time for me to become the heir to the kingdom,' she said.

Dottie and Mistress Rashel both smiled. 'Long live Princess Talia,' they said together, 'heir to Bavaugh.'

Sel

Guil, West Bavaugh

SEL'S FIRST SIGHT of the castle gave her a jolt. She had been so focused on tracking Briar and reaching Mont Isle that she had not considered how it would feel to see it again after all this time. Cresting a hill as she rode along the coastal path, she spotted it in the distance, waves beating its tan walls in bursts of white foam, and she remembered the day of the Blessing: the screams, the black smoke, the fear and the perfect baby she had cradled awkwardly in her arms, promising to take her far away. Promising to keep her safe.

In the first few winters of Briar's life, Sel had often fantasized about returning to the castle. She would hand the Princess over, all responsibility sliding from her shoulders. Then she would receive her reward, reclaim her black cloak and escape this dreary kingdom without a backwards glance. But somewhere along the way, that dream had faded. Now the thought of handing Briar back no longer gave her relief. Instead, she wanted to bundle Briar up tight and pretend the girl was that little baby again – tranquil, pure and belonging to no one else.

Pushing memories of Briar's early winters from her mind, Sel hurried along the coastal path, her jaw clenched and the wind whipping at her cheeks. As she neared Guil, she noticed the roads growing busier. Eventually she was forced to slow Patch to a plod behind families piled into carts and wagons full of chattering passengers. Tutting to herself in frustration, she overheard a conversation between two women ambling side by side near by. They were excitedly discussing the Appointment taking place later that day and wondering when the King would arrive.

The King? thought Sel. *The Appointment . . . ?*

Something was wrong. Her worry turned to hot, sick panic.

She tried to urge Patch to move faster, but the flow of travellers was too great. She was stuck in the throng, moving steadily along the roads, her fear and dread growing greater with each step.

By the time they reached the main street of Guil, Sel had dismounted and was weaving through the crowds, dragging Patch behind her. Ignoring the shouts and protests of those she pushed past, she fought her way to the beach, where the tide was beginning to recede. Sel frantically scanned the shoreline, but she knew instinctively that Briar was not among the hordes. She could not sense her presence.

Guards stood on the shore, turning away the revellers who ventured too close, and clearing a path for the King.

With horror rushing through her, Sel looked towards Mont Isle and felt the skin on the back of her neck prickle. The magic emanating from the island was thick and fresh, the distinct, bitter smell of it carried to the mainland by the wind. Briar must have found a way into the castle.

'Make way for the King!' bellowed the guards, waving their swords, and Sel pulled Patch back from them.

'You can't stand at the front of the line with a horse,' slurred a man to Sel's right who stank of mead. 'You're taking the place of five people!'

There were grunts and shouts of agreement from those around her and Sel reluctantly drew away into the crowds until she found herself at the back with the stragglers. There were many heads in front of her and she could barely see anything.

I must get to that castle, she thought, her panic curdling in her stomach. *I must get to Briar before it's too late.*

Sel felt someone grab her shoulder.

She yelped in alarm and bunched her right hand into a fist, ready to strike as hard as she could, but a familiar voice cried, 'Sel! Selhah, it's me!'

She spun around to see Jacken behind her, looking worn and thin.

'I thought I spotted Patch in the crowds,' he added, slapping the neck of the big horse in delight. 'I hoped it was you.'

Sel wanted to throw her arms around him with joy and shake him in anger at the same time. She had been worried for Jacken since leaving the Wildlands too, but in a different way. Tears of relief filled her eyes, but she snapped, 'Where's Briar?'

'I don't know,' replied Jacken, the happiness upon seeing her fading from his expression. 'She came to the beach this morning to find a crossing to the island and didn't return. I'm trying to find her, but there are too many people.'

Suddenly trumpets sounded and the crowd around them rushed forward, clapping and cheering.

'We need to get to the island!' Sel yelled over the roar. 'Briar's there and she's in great danger.'

'But the guards aren't letting anyone through. How would Briar have got there?'

'She's on the island, Jacken. Trust me.'

He hesitated, his gaze searching her face, eventually nodding.

The drumming of cantering hooves signalled the arrival of the King and his large party of courtiers. Sel turned and pulled Patch away, further down the beach.

'There's someone who wants to hurt Briar,' she called over her shoulder. 'I've been trying to keep Briar away from here for her own safety.'

'Someone on the island?' asked Jacken, following her.

'If they're not there yet, they will be soon. All of this is too tempting.' Sel gestured to the crowds behind them. 'They've been waiting for the right moment and this is it.'

'Who?'

'I'll explain, but first we must find a way on to the island without alerting the guards. We'll have to move along the coast and circle around to approach it from the back while the tide is out,' said Sel, scanning the horizon. She added under her breath, 'We don't have a moment to spare.'

Violanna

The Queen's Chambers, Mont Isle

VIOLANNA LOOKED DOWN at the crown held out towards her. Plump sapphires were set along its base and diamonds braided in gold arches formed its peak. It was a dazzling thing to behold, but it did not belong to her.

'No,' she said.

The maid who held it blinked in surprise. Her hands were shaking and she looked as though she would quite like to be freed from the burden of carrying such a thing.

'I will not wear it,' Violanna added. 'Send it back to the King.'

The maid let out a little yip of fear at the thought of delivering such a message. She was spared from responding further by a knock at the door.

Meredyth entered, leaning on her cane and squinting her dark eyes against the afternoon sunshine that spilt through the windows. She paused a few paces into the room, the hem of her extravagant, beaded gown rippling, and dipped into a curtsey. 'Long live Queen Violanna of Bavaugh.' She rose and added, 'I came to tell you that the King and royal party are almost ready, Your Majesty. But I see you have received the crown.' Her gaze slid from the dithering maid to Violanna and back again.

'I will not wear a crown; I am not a Queen.'

Meredyth looked concerned but not surprised. 'Your Majesty—'

'This was Queen Aruelle's crown. I did not wear it when I was Queen of Bavaugh and I will not wear it now. The *real* Queen of Bavaugh, Queen Hana, remains in Lustore, recovering from her injuries. Send this crown to her.'

'But—'

'No.'

In the smooth, measured manner she had always possessed, Meredyth took the crown from the hands of the grateful maid and placed it back in the velvet-lined box on the side table. Then she carried the box to one of the guards by the door and muttered a few words at him. After a moment, the guards and the servants swept from the room, pulling the doors shut behind them.

When they were alone, Violanna sighed and scratched at her temples. Her hair had been wound back tightly and pinned high upon her head. It had been so long since she had dressed for company like this and she felt itchy and awkward.

'Did you sleep last night, Your Majesty?'

'No.'

Violanna felt Meredyth watching her. Over the last few days, if her friend had not been with Talia, encouraging and coaching the Princess through what lay ahead, then she had spent her time in Violanna's chambers, trying to soothe and comfort. Since Violanna had finally spoken of Noatina, she had found that she could not

335

stop, and she had recounted her sister's many childhood antics to Meredyth. Late one night, she had admitted, 'I have never loved someone like I loved her. It is a twisted, difficult thing.' Meredyth had nodded back as if she understood, but Violanna knew she could not. Meredyth had had a younger sister who had died in their childhood, but that was not the same. A twin was something different.

'Have there been any letters for me?' Violanna asked. 'I thought I might have heard from the Diaspass Masterhood. I am sure they know by now about Princess Talia's succession to the throne.'

'There have been no letters, Your Majesty.'

Violanna moved to the open window and breathed in the salty freshness of the breeze. The tide was out, and beyond the castle walls she could see the flat tan expanse of the waterlogged beach cut against the blue-grey sky.

'Has the King sent word to you since he arrived, Your Majesty?'

Violanna looked over her shoulder in surprise. 'Felipe? The royal party only crossed the causeway at midday and I imagine they have been busy readying themselves for the Appointment. Besides, what should he have to say to me?'

'You are not nervous to see him?'

'He is the least of my worries.'

'But might the King consider the refusal of the crown a snub, Your Majesty? Perhaps he sent it as a sort of peace offering?'

Violanna snorted. 'With two broken wives behind him, Felipe deserves the snub.'

'You might find him quite changed, Your Majesty,' said Meredyth lightly, fiddling with some of the beads that cascaded in loops from the waist of her gown. 'The tragedy of the Princes has left him distraught. And Princess Talia's new status also leaves you in . . . an opportunistic position. Perhaps you might rethink the crown?'

'Meredyth, I am not interested,' snapped Violanna, waving her hand. *I am not like you*, she stopped herself from adding.

An ache was building between Violanna's shoulders and she stretched her arms behind her back.

'How is Talia?' she asked, changing the subject. 'I tried to visit her chambers this morning, but the maids were fixing her hair and she turned me away.'

Violanna lowered her chin to hide the sadness that flashed across her face. She had hoped to take her daughter aside and tell Talia how proud she was, but the Princess had ordered her off without so much as a glance.

'The Princess is dressed and ready, Your Majesty,' replied Meredyth. 'Everything is in place for the Appointment ceremony.'

Violanna pinched the skin on her brow and scratched at her head again.

'Be careful, Your Majesty. Your hair looks so lovely and you will undo it if you keep rubbing.'

'They must have used something different to set my braids,' replied Violanna. 'My head is sore . . .'

Suddenly she paused, her hand hovering by her face.

'Your Majesty?'

The ache between Violanna's shoulders contracted again and her temples throbbed. She turned abruptly and hurried to the window, gripping the frame with pale, thin fingers. Her eyes scanned the horizon and she saw only the flat dark of the sand and the blanched slice of the sky. But she did not need to *see* it, because she could *feel* it.

'I thought it was the Appointment that was making me feel so strange,' she hissed. 'I did not realize . . .'

'Your Majesty, what is it?' asked Meredyth, drawing closer.

'I have been waiting for news from the Diaspass Masterhood. Lalious said that they would know when Noatina was coming.'

'You mean—'

'She is coming. I can feel it.'

Violanna saw her panic reflected in Meredyth's gaze. She turned back to the window. 'Lalious Grele the Mighty,' she hissed into the wind, summoning the charm that had been laid upon her by the High Master. She felt the magic bubble up and simmer, the heat of it rushing over her like a hot flush. A sharp smell filled the air and she saw Meredyth wince.

'What just happened, Your Majesty?'

'I called on the Masterhood for aid,' Violanna replied. 'I just pray that it is not too late.'

Briar

The Anteroom, Mont Isle

IT FELT SO good to spin again. The *clack, clack, clack* of the wheel. The rhythmic beat of her foot on the treadle. The roughness of the flax in her fingers, twisting together into a single thread. She had missed the steady focus of a task like this. After so long on the road, strained and tense, it was simple and comforting. Soothing and familiar. She was pulling together the straggly parts of herself that felt wild and uncontrollable, and binding them back in place.

'That's fine work,' said a young woman who sat at another spinning wheel beside her. 'You've a gift for it.'

There were four wheels crammed into the anteroom, clacking in unison. They spun continuous lines of thread, while seamstresses flitted about, hurriedly sewing great piles of heavy curtains.

'Where did you learn to spin?' asked the woman.

Briar had not raised her head since sitting down before her wheel and she blinked in surprise. The woman was a little older than herself, with a wide, freckled face and small, calloused hands.

'I taught myself.'

'That's mighty impressive. Your thread is as good as my mam's – maybe better – and she was a fine spinner. She was the one that taught me.'

Briar glanced at the woman's wheel. Her thread was neat but thick. Not particularly remarkable.

'I'm Corie,' added the woman when Briar did not reply. 'I grew up in Guil, looking at the castle from the mainland. I heard they were searching for spinners to get everything ready for the King today and I just had to come. It's so grand.'

Briar let her eyes wander around the anteroom, taking in the deep-green walls hung with tapestries, and the glinting, painted ceiling. As soon as she had arrived on the island, an attendant had whisked her away and hurried her through winding, dark passages. Figures had squeezed past them, backwards and forwards, carrying barrels of mead, dishes of food and buckets of water. Everyone was frantic and hurried. The attendant had finally led her to this small room off the Great Hall, where three women were already spinning and the thread was running low. Briar had been put straight to work and she had been glad to lose herself to the task. The castle made her feel odd.

'Have you ever seen such riches?' gushed Corie. 'It's magnificent! And we're so lucky to get to watch the Appointment. I can't wait.'

Briar nodded, though she did not share in the excitement. She had travelled to the island expecting to find answers to her past, and this royal ceremony was getting in the way. In her hurry she had left Jacken on the mainland without an explanation, and he would likely be searching for her right now. She was annoyed at herself.

And disappointed. And *something else*. The castle had beckoned her towards it and now that she was here, she felt an unsettling mixture of things. It was a faint, shadowy sensation, almost as if she were waiting for something.

A door at the back of the anteroom opened and an attendant burst in, crying, 'The King has arrived! He is readying himself for the Appointment this very moment!'

There were gasps from everyone in the room.

'Stop your work and take those curtains through to the Great Hall to be hung,' barked the attendant, waving his arms.

'But this edge isn't finished—' began a seamstress.

'There's no time!' he bellowed. 'All of you stop what you're doing.'

Briar noticed Corie drop the thread in her hands and brush down her skirts.

'Leave everything as it is,' continued the attendant. 'And make sure the doors to the Great Hall are shut. Then take your places in the servants' gallery, or if there's no room, stay at the back of the hall.'

Without waiting for a response, he disappeared.

The seamstresses immediately gathered up the curtains they had been sewing, scooping lengths of thick, velvet-lined fabric into their arms. Together they heaved them into the Great Hall, gasping and twittering to each other. As the double doors swung open, Briar caught a glimpse of servants rushing back and forth across a huge, grand room – far larger and grander than anything she had ever seen – lighting braziers and wafting incense. As the doors clicked shut, she was hit with a rich wave of herbs and spices. For the first time, she felt a prickle of awe.

'I can't wait to see all the Ladies with their dresses,' said Corie, clapping her hands and smiling at Briar.

Their eyes met and something in Corie's expression faltered.

'Your eyes are so blue!' she said suddenly. 'Like a newborn babe.'

Briar ducked her chin. She had tried to keep her cloak clutched tightly at her throat and the shawl bound low over her head, but, lost in her spinning, she had let both slip.

'It must be the light in here.'

Briar could feel Corie's gaze moving across her face.

'You're mighty pretty, you know,' she breathed. She raised one hand as if to touch Briar then dropped it back to her side.

From the other side of the doors to the Great Hall, they could hear a low rumble of chatter growing louder.

'The Royal Court will be entering any moment,' squeaked Corie. 'We should hurry if we want to get a good spot.'

Briar released the thread in her hands and rose from the stool. She adjusted the shawl around her head so that it fell low over her brow and followed Corie.

Together they slipped through the double doors into the busy splendour of the Great Hall.

Meredyth

IT WAS A long time since Meredyth had been Chief Lady-in-Waiting and duty-bound to stand as one of the royal party. She had forgotten what it was like to face a crowd, their heads turned to you, their gaze heavy on your person. She had not thought she would be up here for the Appointment, on the dais in the Great Hall, but she was pleased. After being looked upon as old and unimportant for so long, she had not hesitated when called to take a position beside the Queen. She had missed all the grandeur and pomp of court life and she was enjoying herself, despite the fraught circumstances.

Beside her, the Queen was tense and rigid. Queen Violanna had insisted that she did not want a throne set out for her on the dais, and instead she stood a few steps behind the King's throne with Meredyth at her side. Upon entering, as they took this position, Meredyth had noticed the King incline his head and glance at his

343

former Queen. His eyes scanned up and down her figure, but if Violanna noticed, she did not look back at him. Her gaze remained fixed ahead, her expression blank, and after a moment, the King had turned away.

The trumpets that had marked the entrance of the royal parade fell quiet. Meredyth glanced around, noticing the freshly painted ceiling, the new, lavish curtains and the glinting, polished frames of the portraits and paintings hung on the walls. Under her careful management, the Great Hall had been restored to its original splendour.

'Welcome, one and all,' boomed a voice.

Meredyth watched as Lord Rosford stepped forward, addressing the crowd.

'Long live King Felipe,' he cried, 'King of Bavaugh.'

'Long live King Felipe,' chorused the crowd, their voices roaring and echoing around the Great Hall, 'King of Bavaugh.'

'It is the King's pleasure to welcome you to this Appointment,' continued Lord Rosford, 'a prestigious moment in the history of our kingdom . . .'

As he spoke, Meredyth's gaze skittered across the crowd. She could not see any black cloaks among the sea of people, but perhaps the Masters would just suddenly appear, peculiar, alarming beings that they were. The Queen had called on them before leaving her chambers for the Appointment, but Meredyth did not know how long it would take for the Masters to answer. She hoped it would be soon. 'Should we request to postpone the Appointment, Your Majesty?' Meredyth had asked her before they left for the Great Hall, though she did not know if such a thing would be possible. 'No,' the Queen had answered. 'We always knew this day was coming and now it is time to face it.'

Meredyth's gaze snagged on a few familiar Lords and Ladies in the crowd who rarely visited court. One smiled at her and she tried to return the gesture, but her mouth felt stiff. A strange feeling was settling over her. From the corner of her eye, she could see Queen Violanna's chest rising and falling above her gown in tight, hurried breaths. And there was a bitter tang to the air. Meredyth tried to ignore it and focus on Lord Rosford, who was finishing his introduction with a bow.

After another blast from the trumpets, King Felipe hauled himself up from his throne. He moved to the front of the dais, his gait slow and unsteady. Meredyth was relieved that he looked better than when she had seen him last. His face was still waxen and puffy, and his shoulders still rounded and stooped, but his eyes had returned to their blue-grey brightness. He was dressed in his ceremonial robes, but his shirt and breeches were black and undecorated.

'It is with great sorrow that we are gathered here following a tragedy that shocked the hearts of this nation,' he said, his voice rougher and thinner than it had once been. 'We remember the lives of Prince Stasthes and Prince Dionathy, brutally taken by our enemy. May they rest with the Great Creator. They will never be forgotten.'

The crowd bent their heads in agreement and there were murmurs of, 'Praise the Great Creator,' that echoed around the hall.

'Our enemy may think that they have defeated us,' continued the King, his face contorting with pain. 'But we will not be beaten. Together, we will forge ahead and look to the future. Today we appoint an heir to the Kingdom of Bavaugh and begin a new chapter in the history of our great kingdom.'

The trumpets sounded again and Meredyth thought of the Princess waiting in the passageway – the Princess who had never entered

345

a room of more than a handful of people before today. No doubt she would be nervous. So many Bavaughians were eager to see her – the forgotten, cursed Princess, who would now be their future Queen.

The doors at the back of the Great Hall opened and Princess Talia appeared, flanked on all sides by guards. She stood tall, her chin raised and her hands held in front of her. Only her small, pinched lips betrayed her nerves. As she moved across the Great Hall, she looked dazzling and strong. Meredyth heard a sigh of awe from the crowd, who parted to watch her pass.

The people of Bavaugh may think they are settling for second best, she thought, *but they do not know Princess Talia*.

The Princess strode to the front of the dais without faltering. She stopped before the King as the trumpets fell quiet and raised her eyes to his. Meredyth saw King Felipe flinch – perhaps surprised to see his own blue-grey gaze staring back at him – and father and daughter faced one another for the first time.

Lord Rosford cleared his throat and the King startled, as if coming back to himself.

'Princess Talia,' he began. 'I call you to your duty as heir to the Kingdom of Bavaugh. I, King Felipe, who ascended the throne after King Douguthur and Queen Aruelle . . .'

As King Felipe continued, Meredyth glanced around the Great Hall again. All eyes were on the Appointment and she tried to ignore the pain prickling her brow. It was a dull ache with a familiarity that filled her with dread.

At the front of the dais, King Felipe paused in his speech. An attendant stepped forward bearing a velvet cushion upon which sat a tiara, its band dusted with diamonds and strings of pearls and sapphires looping across its length.

The Princess trembled slightly at the sight of it.

'Princess Talia,' said the King, his hand hovering over the tiara, 'as is your birthright, you have been called to the position of heir to the Kingdom of Bavaugh. Do you accept?'

Meredyth saw the Princess gulp for breath, but when she spoke, her voice rang out loud and clear. 'I do.'

The King lifted the crown from the cushion and placed it on her head, the strings of pearls and sapphires glinting in the Princess's newly bright hair.

Across the dais, Lord Rosford caught Meredyth's eye and held it. He looked nervous too and Meredyth felt her own concern expanding. The sickening reek in the air and the pain she could feel at her temples was all too familiar. She bit back a cry of alarm.

'As the King of Bavaugh,' said King Felipe. 'I appoint you—'

The King froze mid-sentence as the air in the hall suddenly seemed to crack and break.

Meredyth tried to run, but her body had become heavy and still. She could not move, not even to turn her head.

All around the Great Hall, Meredyth saw others becoming fixed and still, and beside her she heard Queen Violanna gasp as, from the depths of the crowd, a figure appeared.

Violanna

The Great Hall, Mont Isle

VIOLANNA STARED AT the woman walking steadily towards the dais. Noatina. The other half of herself. The one she had loved above all others before dark magic came between them.

Noatina was not large, but she seemed vast and the air around her curled and swelled unnaturally. Time had slackened Violanna's own skin, made her hair brittle and her features soft, but Noatina was unblemished. Her dark eyes remained bright, her lips thin and wide. If she had not looked so terrible, she might have been beautiful.

'Hello, Violanna,' she said, and her voice was both soft and loud.

Violanna's ears were filled with the roar of her own heartbeat and she found she could not reply. It was strange to see her twin sister again – this unnatural being, both familiar and grotesque, whom she had feared for so long. The sunlight streaming through the windows shifted across Noatina's face and for a moment she looked like the girl Violanna had known in her childhood. She had sudden visions of them splashing together in the Diaspass Palace fountain or feeding the tame palinkies that roamed the gardens. But then the shadows stirred and Noatina's features changed. She became someone else: a stranger, corrupted with dark magic; a sorceress who wished her harm.

'It has almost been seventeen winters,' said Noatina, stepping on to the dais. 'I hope you did not think I had forgotten.' She wore a long grey cloak, her dark hair was loose down her back and her brown eyes held Violanna's gaze with an abnormal intensity. 'I have been waiting for the right time.'

'What . . . what is happening?' Talia stuttered.

The sound of her daughter's voice startled Violanna. She lurched towards Talia, but before she reached her, Noatina raised a hand in warning.

'Do not worry, Princess,' replied Noatina, moving closer. 'Everyone can see and hear us. It was like this before at the Blessing, but, of course, you were just a baby then.' She paused and inclined her head. 'You do not seem to have much Diaspass blood in you, Princess,' she added. 'You do not look how I had imagined.'

'W-Who are you?'

Noatina's jaw clenched. 'Your mother did not tell you?'

'Please, Noatina,' Violanna whispered. 'Please do not do this.'

'I do not want to hear your pleas!' came the snapped reply. 'I told you that you would regret what you did to me, Violanna. I hope you have lived in fear. I hope it has been torture.'

Violanna put her head in her hands and fell to her knees, dragging a sob from her chest. If her sister wanted remorse, then she could provide it sincerely. 'I have suffered,' she said. 'I never doubted you would return. I never doubted your power, Noatina. On the contrary, it scared me.' Between her fingers, Violanna saw her sister watching her, listening. 'Since the awful day of the Blessing, I have lived in fear of your return.'

Noatina smiled. 'You tried to escape to this little kingdom,' she replied. 'But I was always watching you, Violanna. I saw your hurried marriage to a selfish, cruel King and I heard of your barrenness. When you finally managed to birth a child, I knew that my time had come. I wanted you to suffer as I have suffered. I wanted you to regret what you did.'

'Then you have got what you wanted!' Violanna gasped. 'I have always regretted what happened to you. Now, please, I beg, stop this.'

Violanna held Noatina's gaze, sinking into the depths of her sister's brown eyes, searching for someone she had once known. But all she could see was pain and hatred.

'I begged *you* to keep my secrets, do you remember?' said Noatina. 'And instead you betrayed me.'

Violanna knew it was true. From the day she left the Diaspass Kingdom, she had known her sister would come after her. She had fooled herself into believing that she could escape, but part of her had always been waiting for Noatina's return. She had been shocked to see her at the Blessing, over sixteen winters ago, but it had not surprised her.

'You, who knew me best, betrayed me,' Noatina continued. 'I was beaten and cast out. Do you know what those guards did to me? Do you know the struggle it has been since – what I have had to do to survive? You sentenced me to live a cursed life, so it was only right that I should do the same to you.'

'I am sorry,' Violanna whispered. 'I was young and foolish. Please, take my life instead.'

'No. You cannot stop this, Violanna. I will make sure you regret what you did to me for ever.' Noatina turned to Talia and flicked back her cloak, raising her hands ready to conjure. 'Princess, the time has come,' she said and her voice echoed around the Great Hall. 'I am here to end the spell bound to you in infancy. I am here to take your life.'

Briar

The Great Hall, Mont Isle

BRIAR'S GAZE BOUNCED from one guard to the next around the Great Hall. Why were they just standing there? Why were they not doing something? She had been watching the scene unfold on the dais and it was clear to her that the Princess was in danger, yet no one was moving.

She turned to say this to Corie, but the words faded on her lips. The spinner was standing with her arms half raised, as if about to clap, and her eyes were fixed and unblinking.

'Corie?' Briar whispered.

Like the guards, Corie did not move.

Briar glanced at the person on her other side – a servant-woman who had been muttering relentlessly throughout the ceremony. She was also unmoving, frozen with her face turned to the front of the Great Hall.

Briar gasped. She forced herself to look at the other faces in the crowd around her.

They were all terrifyingly still.

Only the three women at the front of the Great Hall seemed unaffected: the Princess, the Queen and this strange figure called Noatina.

Magic. Briar knew very little about that exotic, suspicious force, except what she had occasionally glimpsed in her aunt's old books, but the air in the Great Hall felt so charged and bizarre that she did not think it could be anything else. It had to be some kind of enchantment, and, for whatever reason, she was unaffected.

Is this why I'm here? The thought struck Briar with unsettling clarity. But if she was involved in some way, she could not easily see how.

The three women on the dais were speaking to each other in low, tight voices and Briar could not hear exactly what they were saying. Despite instinct telling her it would be safer to stay away, something else – something she could not quite explain – compelled her to move closer.

Briar edged forward. First a little, then a bit more. She began weaving through the statues of guests, trying not to notice their disturbing, frozen expressions, keeping her gaze ahead.

As she moved closer to the front of the Great Hall, she began to catch more snatches of what the women were saying. Briar was almost at the front of the crowd when she saw Noatina raise her hands.

'Princess, the time has come,' Noatina said. 'I am here to end the spell bound to you in infancy. I am here to take your life.'

The Queen cried out in protest and the Princess cowered.

Noatina moved her hands in a gesture Briar did not understand and spoke words in a language that was muffled and strange.

The air around the Princess shook and shadows rose from the ground, engulfing her like flames. Heat blazed through the room, the walls rang with taut power and pressure howled at the windows and doors.

Briar felt the swell of the spell and something within her shuddered in relief.

On the dais, the Princess wilted. Her arms turned limp, her legs buckled and her body started to crumple.

The shadows spun around the Princess, tearing at her blue gown and yellow hair, pulling her to the floor.

Briar could not stop watching. She moved closer still, weaving through the last of the guests and stepping on to the dais as darkness consumed the Princess. For a moment, it looked as though she would vanish, overcome with shadows that would burn her to nothing, but, suddenly, the ground shivered.

The Princess threw back her head and gasped.

Around her the shadows fell away, disintegrating to nothing.

The Princess staggered to her feet. Then she drew in several spluttering breaths, as though emerging from deep water.

The Queen ran to her daughter, pulling the Princess into her arms and holding her tightly. 'You are safe, Talia!' she cried. 'It is over and you are safe.'

Noatina stared at them, her brow furrowed in disbelief. 'No,' she muttered. 'I do not understand . . .'

The Queen wheeled around and tugged the Princess behind her. She squared her shoulders at Noatina and took a deep breath, as if about to shout.

Then she caught sight of Briar.

The Queen's arms dropped to her sides and her mouth fell open. Briar stood still, confused and unsure.

Following her sister's gaze, Noatina turned and saw Briar too. The sorceress's brow furrowed further, then a glimmer of understanding flashed in her eyes. She muttered a low, guttural sound, flexing her fingers.

A warm flurry rushed over Briar, tacky and clinging. The cloak she wore slid from her shoulders along with the scarf wrapped around her head. Her golden hair tumbled down her back, her face and figure exposed.

Noatina's mouth stretched into a smile. 'Oh, sister,' she said. 'I see what you have done.'

Sel

Guil, West Bavaugh

THE WET SAND slurped at Patch's hooves as the horse picked his way through the rocks. Sel stared ahead of her at the back of Mont Isle, her gaze focused, alert for any signs of danger.

'We're almost through this rocky part,' said Jacken, who was riding pillion behind her. 'Then we can get a good run up to the castle.'

'And we'll just need to pray that none of the guards see us,' she replied.

Patch flicked his ears at their voices, but he kept his head down and his lumbering gait steady.

'So Briar is a . . . a Princess?' asked Jacken, after a pause.

Sel could not see his expression, but she could hear the mingled shock and dismay in his voice. She had explained everything as quickly as she could in a breathless jumble of facts as they had hurried across the shore of the mainland, hunting for somewhere to cross to the island.

'Yes, she's the firstborn Princess,' said Sel, trying to ignore the lump it brought to the back of her throat. 'The true heir.'

'So the curse—'

'A curse is just a spell with malevolent intent. And yes, the spell is bound to her. That's why she's so . . . well, that's why she's the way she is.'

Jacken made a *hmm* noise.

'You've always known she was different. I know you have.'

Sel felt him shift his seat. He was used to riding without a saddle and he was keeping her balanced in front of him, his arms either side of her, holding the reins. She had often seen him ride like this with Briar and the two of them had always looked comfortable and secure, but she felt nothing of the sort. At any moment, she thought, she was going to tumble off Patch's back and on to the rocks below.

'I suppose I thought she came from the Central Realm like you,' said Jacken, his voice deep and brusque. 'With all those books you read, I thought it must be something to do with magic, but nothing . . . nothing like this. Briar knew there was some secret you weren't telling her, but even she couldn't have imagined the truth. A *Princess*.'

Sel heard him exhale sharply.

'I was trying to protect her,' she said.

'I know. I can see that.'

Patch navigated them through the last stretch of rocky ground, tossing his head as he trotted on to the wet, sleek sand. Sel grabbed a handful of his coarse mane and held on tight.

'And I suppose the Queen must be Briar's mother?'

Sel felt her heart lurch. 'Yes,' she managed to choke out.

'And I guess Briar has a sister too? The other Princess. And a father. The King. She has a whole family!'

Sel swallowed hard. 'It doesn't change anything,' she said unconvincingly.

'It changes everything.'

Sel looked to the island ahead of them. She could see the Bavaughian flags rippling from the battlements and she guessed that if there were any guards patrolling the rear side of the island, they would be able to spot Patch now.

'A *Princess*,' muttered Jacken. 'She'll love that. A *Princess*.'

Sel opened her mouth to reply, then closed it again. She shivered.

Patch side-stepped, his nostrils flaring.

'*What was that?*' she whispered, the hairs on her arms rising. She had let herself become distracted and missed something – a noise, a smell and a tightening of the air. She stared at the approaching island until her eyes watered, trying to detect a change.

'I didn't hear anything,' said Jacken.

Suddenly there was a noise like the sound of bones snapping and the sea breeze fell away to nothing.

Patch threw back his head and snorted, his eyes rolling.

'I heard that!' said Jacken, trying to steady the horse. 'What was it?'

'It was *her*,' hissed Sel, panic seizing her body. 'I knew she was coming. I knew this would happen.'

'Her?' asked Jacken, trying to gather up the reins as Patch stamped and tossed his head again. 'The sorceress?'

Before Sel could reply, the air was split with a deep roar. A sharp gust of humid wind rushed around them with such force that it was hard to breathe, and the ground shook.

Patch whinnied in terror and bucked, almost throwing them from his back.

'The sea!' Sel cried. 'Look!'

They both turned their faces to the horizon, where an unnatural, high wall of water was crashing rapidly towards them.

'Hold on!' yelled Jacken, wrenching Patch's head in the direction of the island and digging his heels into the horse's sides.

Patch lurched into a gallop and they thundered across the sand. Sel buried her hands in his mane, her body crouched low over his neck, and her teeth gritted in fear. The wind whipped at her hair and she could feel droplets of water pelting her cheeks. Jacken was shouting over the gale, urging Patch on faster, and she could hear the crash and splash of rising water around the horse's hooves. Squinting over her shoulder, Sel gasped to see grey waves rolling closer, their crests frothy with white foam as they reared up. She could feel the magic in the air, a heavy, searing presence.

'Almost!' Jacken yelled over the rumble booming around them.

Out of the corner of her eye, Sel saw a flash of grey as the sea rose high above them. She winced, waiting for the water to crash over her and sweep them away, but instead she felt Patch leap. His front hooves hit the rocks of the island with a jolt and he scrambled for purchase. Sel was knocked from his back and almost plunged into the water, but Jacken grabbed her arm and dragged her along as they clambered up the rocks. Behind them, the sea hurtled across the sand, swallowing everything into its churning body.

'Are you all right?' yelled Jacken, finally releasing her when they reached the castle walls.

Sel coughed and spluttered, but nodded. She had one wet boot and a bruised hip, but she was otherwise unharmed.

'You're safe now,' cried Jacken, slapping the horse's neck. 'You're safe.'

Patch snorted, his sides heaving and his eyes rolling with fright.

'We need to hurry,' gasped Sel. 'We must get to Briar before Noatina does.'

Jacken nodded, squinting against the fierce whip of the wind.

They moved as swiftly as possible across the rocks that crowded the bottom of the castle walls, making their way around the island.

Sel could feel the weight of the magic hanging in the air, turning it thick and sticky. This was a deep, dense magic that had layered over time. She did not think she had ever felt anything quite like it before. She sent up a desperate prayer to the Great Creator that Noatina had not found Briar yet.

When they reached the gates of the castle, they came upon guards standing still, their bodies fixed in position, their faces frozen.

Jacken turned to Sel in horror and she tried not to look as alarmed as she felt.

'Magic,' she explained weakly.

Around them, the sea was flinging great waves against the rocks, crashing and roaring as if in the midst of a storm. Sel was struggling to stand up against the battering wind and Patch was stamping and rearing in fear, while Jacken clung to his reins.

A flash of colour in the distance caught Sel's eye – an iridescent spark against the grey sky. She squinted across the rough waters to see a huddle of black-cloaked figures on the mainland shore.

'It's the Masters!' she called to Jacken. 'They're trying to part the sea and cross over. But these are not ordinary waters; the sea has been summoned. It may take them some time.'

'What should we do?'

'You wait here for them; I've got to keep going.'

Before Jacken could reply, Sel turned and ran through the gates. She passed the statue-like guards and sprinted up the steep, cobbled streets.

When she dived into the body of the castle, she expected the booming tumult of the sea to dwindle, but if anything it sounded louder, as if the waves were crashing through the walls. Sel ran across courtyards and down passages that were eerily familiar, but she did not stop to take her bearings. She could feel the pull of the magic, like running towards a burning blaze. Servants and more guards were frozen mid-step in corridors and doorways, and she averted her eyes as she rushed past. She kept running, panting and sick, thinking only of Briar. Her Briar.

When she saw a set of double doors ahead of her that must lead to the Great Hall, Sel forced herself to stop. Her boots skidded on a thick rug. She did not know what lay upon the other side and if she was going to be any use at all, she must be careful.

Imagining all manner of awful things, Sel gently pushed one of the doors ajar and peered through the crack. Inside, she could see a mass of people standing silent and still. Like the guards and servants in the castle, they were unmoving. Sel pushed the door open further and slipped into the Great Hall. The magic in the room was thick and choking, and she guessed that Noatina must be here. She peered over the heads of the crowd, her gaze bouncing left and right until she caught sight of the shadowy figure on the dais.

Noatina.

The sorceress who had been something of a myth until she appeared in this very room, almost seventeen winters ago. Sel had been told tales of her greatness by Florentina, who had taught all the Diaspass Princesses in their youth and could vouch for the sorceress's unique talent. But Noatina had vanished after her banishment and she had not been seen again until the fateful day of Briar's Blessing, when she had returned to seek her revenge. The day that Sel's life had changed irrevocably.

'You have tried to trick me,' Noatina was saying. 'And it is a good trick. I underestimated you, Violanna, but I understand now.'

Standing before Noatina on the steps of the dais was Briar. Sel choked back a cry of fear.

'Two girls,' continued Noatina. 'They are like you and me. One born first, the other following. How pleased you must have been when you birthed another. You must have thought it was such good fortune.'

Sel did not wait to hear any more – she ran.

Weaving through the crowd, she raced towards the dais, knowing what must be coming next.

'Princess, did you even know you had a sister?' Noatina asked a young woman who was standing on the dais dishevelled and shivering, the crown on her head slightly askew. 'I suspect not. When I listened for news from this kingdom, I only heard of one cursed Princess. What a shock this must be. Do you see now that your mother is a liar?'

The Princess looked from the Queen to Briar and back again, dazed.

'Violanna, you tried to trick me,' Noatina continued. 'But you cannot stop this.' Without waiting for a response, she turned upon the cowering Briar. 'It is a pity,' she added quietly, almost to herself. 'I think you are the most beautiful thing I have ever seen.'

Noatina raised one hand and Sel felt magic being drawn through the air, energy gathering together, collecting into the spell. Noatina opened her mouth to speak the language of magic and Sel tore through the front of the crowd and threw herself upon the steps of the dais, her hands stretched out.

'No!' she screamed.

The air rippled and the ground shook as Sel pulled the magic towards her, bending it off course with every shred of strength she could muster.

The spell struck her with such force that the breath was knocked from her chest. She had never wielded anything as powerful as this before and it raged savagely. The magic engulfed her, burning agony coursing through her limbs and biting into every part of her.

A strangled howl escaped her lips. It had been so long since she had held magic; it was magnificent and terrible. It longed to escape from her, but she hung on, clinging to tendrils of energy that crackled and snapped. She did not think she could stop it – it was too great, too raw, too slippery. But she was ready to die trying.

Briar

The Great Hall, Mont Isle

DARKNESS CLOGGED THE air, growing thicker as wind rushed through the Great Hall like a storm. Shadows swirled, reaching for Briar, but something was holding them back.

Auntie knelt on the steps of the dais. She had appeared out of the crowd and was screaming, her face upturned to the ceiling. The darkness surged around her, biting at her skin and clawing at her clothes as her body convulsed.

'Auntie!' Briar cried, but her voice was lost in the wind.

She could see nothing but Auntie at the centre of the spiralling shadows, her skin turning grey and her body sagging in defeat.

Briar's teeth chattered. She was shaking with shock, fear and something else – the part of herself that she did not understand, that was always shifting. It craved the shadows, urging her to disappear into the dark oblivion.

She wanted to run to Auntie's aid, but she could not risk getting closer to the darkness. She knew that given the chance, it would consume her. But she must do *something*; her aunt's screams were growing faint. Briar felt as though she was being dragged in different directions, her very self torn apart. She shrank away, retching, and almost toppled down the steps of the dais.

Then she remembered the spinning wheels.

She turned and plunged into the crowd, feeling her way through the statues of guests.

Instinctively Briar knew that she must spin. The shadows wanted *her* and she needed a way of controlling them, a way of getting them off Auntie. They were terrible and yet familiar. She recognized them as the same erratic, hostile part of herself that she could only control when seated at her spinning wheel.

The wind lashed at Briar as she ran and stray shadows scratched her skin, but she did not stop. When she reached the doors to the anteroom, she clutched at the handles and pushed.

The doors burst open with a crack like thunder and shadows surged inside.

In the murky gloom, Briar saw the outline of a spinning wheel.

She lunged at it, feeling the chaos around her try to trip and stop her. She dragged herself on to the stool and stamped desperately on the treadle. Distantly, over the crashing of the wind and the echo of Auntie's screams, she heard the familiar, soothing *clack, clack, clack*.

Closing her eyes, she began to spin.

Round and round the wheel went.

Briar focused on the rhythm of it, forcing herself to forget the darkness and the shadows and the Great Hall. Her fingers teased and stretched. She imagined herself in Paleen's parlour in Turow, playing with her doll on the rug, listening to the minister's wife spin at her wheel. She saw herself racing Jacken across the beach in

Turow, their horses' hooves splashing in the salty waters. She thought of drifting off to sleep, watching Auntie study by firelight as the wood crackled. And she pictured herself in the Wildlands farmhouse kitchen, spinning into a dark winter's evening with Spot curled at her feet.

With a jolt, Briar realized there was something burning and crackling in her fingers.

She opened her eyes to see the shadows flexing and fusing in her hands as she fed them into the wheel. She was drawing them from the air around her somehow and spinning them into a single thread. For a split second she faltered, and the power surged back towards the hall. She forced herself to continue, her fingers grabbing, wrangling and twisting intuitively.

The darkness in the Great Hall was ebbing, sucked into the anteroom and forced on to her wheel. She could hear her aunt's distant cries turning to coughs and splutters.

The shadows were coming to Briar faster now, so fast that she could barely keep up. Her hands pulled, teased and stretched until they ached, the skin on her fingers blistering and splitting. She fought to keep her foot pumping the treadle at a regular pace, but it was moving with a force of its own. The *clack, clack, clack* of the wheel ran faster and faster until it was spiralling out of her control.

Briar tumbled off her stool, landing flat on the floor, as the air around the spinning wheel began to hiss. Fissures glowed across the body of the wheel and the spokes splintered and snapped. Dark energy coursed through it and the humming howl of the wheel became a deafening roar.

Briar threw her arms over her face as the spinning wheel exploded, the force of it blasting through the open doors and scattering jagged shards of wood across the Great Hall.

Violanna

The Great Hall, Mont Isle

VIOLANNA'S SKIN BURNT. She had been knocked off her feet and she lay sprawled on the dais, her cheek pressed to the thick embroidered carpet. She blinked and peered at the fingers of her right hand clenched in front of her, expecting to see them red and blistered, but they appeared unharmed. All around her was magic, raw and unbound, set free from the spell.

Lifting her head, Violanna saw Talia lying near by, staring dazedly at the ceiling. Her crown sat lopsided on her brow and a cut slashed across her left cheek where she had been caught by a stray splinter.

My daughter, thought Violanna, *my brave, strong daughter*.

Then she turned her head the other way and looked out across the crowd still frozen in the Great Hall.

My other daughter, she thought. *She is here. Somewhere. I saw her.*

Ignoring the searing pain of her skin, Violanna pressed her palms to the floor and pushed herself to her knees. Her ears were ringing and there was a bitter taste in her mouth. She could see black, wispy shadows flitting through the air, but they were remnants of a spell that had been dispersed.

Violanna had lived in fear of this moment for so long that she felt an eerie sense of peace. It had happened and it was over. They had survived.

A few paces from her, Noatina was also scrambling to her feet. Her twin's waxen, enchanted face was bewildered. Noatina looked around the Great Hall at the fading shadows and shook her head. 'You!' she cried suddenly, pointing at a woman sprawled across the steps of the dais. 'Who *are* you?'

The woman raised her head and Violanna swallowed a gasp. It had been so long, but she knew this woman. It was Selhah. The apprentice of Florentina Samara the Wise, the girl who had run from the castle the day of the Blessing, carrying the first Princess away. The girl Violanna had thought of so often over the seasons, praying that both she and the child were safe. She was older – there were silver threads in her hair and lines creased into her forehead – but her broad, open face was still the same.

'What have you done?' added Noatina, a tremor in her voice revealing her distress. 'How did you do this?'

Selhah's breathing was laboured; she could barely lift her head. She looked back at Noatina with blurry, unfocused eyes.

'Who are you?' Noatina repeated.

But the woman did not seem to be listening. Instead, she murmured, 'Briar?'

On her other side, Violanna noticed Talia stirring. She was struggling to her feet, groggy and shaking. Beads of blood from the cut on her cheek trickled across her chin and her eyes were red and streaming.

Noatina caught sight of her too and moved towards Talia, arms raised. 'You will still die . . .' she hissed between clenched teeth.

'No!' screamed Violanna, and before she knew what she was doing, she had grabbed hold of a piece of wood that had fallen beside her.

It was the spindle of a spinning wheel, and its sharp, pointed end still smouldered with the remains of the magic. Violanna lurched forward, her fingers clasped tightly around it even though the wood scalded her skin. She raised the spindle high and, with every last ounce of strength she had, sank it into her sister's neck.

Noatina spun around in surprise. Shadows erupted instantly from the wound and her skin blackened around it. The darkness seeped down her collarbone and disappeared beneath her cloak.

Violanna stumbled back, her own hand burning.

What have I done? she thought, watching as inky tendrils climbed up her sister's chin and bloomed across her cheeks.

Blood oozed and Violanna watched, horrified, as her twin gagged and clutched at her throat. Noatina's lips tried to form the words of a spell, but shadows were clawing at her face. She crumpled and fell to her knees, coughing and choking.

Behind her, the side doors of the Great Hall were thrown open. Figures in black cloaks rushed into the room and through the crowd, their hands already raised, ready to conjure.

But Noatina had collapsed on to her front, her body writhing, screams of fear and anger gurgling from her mouth. Her limbs twisted and snapped and her spine curled and cracked as her entire body was engulfed in flickering shadows.

Then, finally, she was still.

PART SIX

WHEN THE SEA swept in, pouring over the shore of Guil with peculiar speed, the revellers on the beach knew that something was wrong. A crowd collected on the sand, mugs of cider and mead in hands, their heads a little hazy from the drinking and merriment that had already taken place. With unease, they peered across the choppy waves – Mont Isle seemed oddly distant and still.

The townsfolk of Guil started muttering that they had witnessed something like this before. Whispers of *the curse, the curse, the curse* began to circulate. The guards who were blocking passage to the island exchanged glances and paced back and forth at the edge of the heaving waves. Children dropped their games and ran to their mothers. The fishermen who lived in the cottages that clung to the surrounding cliffs shook their heads. They told anyone who would listen that the tide should not be in. This was unnatural. This was magic.

When the black-cloaked figures appeared without warning and sliced through the crowd, gathering at the shore, the people of Bavaugh drew back and even the guards edged away, retreating up the beach. They watched from a distance as the foreigners clustered together before the rolling waves, gesturing wildly at one another and shouting in a language no one could understand.

A spark flared, rippling through the air and crackling like fire. It was followed by another, then another. They blazed towards the sea, striking the surging waves then fading to embers.

The onlookers watched in horrified fascination as the spells cast fell to nothing. The atmosphere on the beach grew heavy and hot; the crowd began to feel nausea rising in their throats.

Someone yelled and pointed as a swell of darkness burst from the castle. It billowed into the sky like rolling clouds before descending on the turrets and walls. There were gasps and screams from the Bavaughians. The guards drew their swords, helpless in the face of this unknown enemy.

The black-cloaked figures frantically cast more spells as the darkness thickened, shrouding the island from view. Panic set in, and the Bavaughians began jostling and shouting, some wanting to run for the town, others wanting to stay and watch the spectacle. Then a sound like the ripping of a seam rang through the air and everyone – even the black-cloaked figures – paused. Across the sea, the smoke around Mont Isle started to thin. Within a few moments, only a smudge of darkness remained.

All was still.

One of the black-cloaked figures stepped forward, striding over to the crowd. She pushed back her hood to reveal a sheet of long grey hair and bright, glittering eyes. Before anyone could stop her, she raised her hands and uttered a sound.

The air along the beach quivered. The crowd did not see the sea slowly roll back from the shore. They did not see the black-cloaked figures hurry across the sand and vanish behind the castle walls, or the last threads of darkness that curled around the castle battlements fade into the horizon.

Next thing they knew, they were shaking themselves awake, blinking and stretching. Each thought they had nodded off for a moment in the heat. They rubbed their eyes in surprise to see a spectacle coming towards them. Marching down the causeway were the beginnings of the Appointment parade, trumpets blaring, horses high-stepping and streamers swaying.

A few of the Bavaughians frowned and scratched their heads, the wisps of a memory niggling their minds, but such things were soon forgotten in the excitement that bubbled through the crowd.

'The Princess is coming!' they cried. 'Our Princess is coming! Long live Princess Talia, heir to Bavaugh.'

Meredyth

The Castle, Mont Isle

MEREDYTH PAUSED UNDER a tree in the western courtyard. It was a surprisingly warm morning and she had not stopped to rest since waking at first light. Standing in the dappled shade, she watched as servants criss-crossed the courtyard in front of her, carrying trunks and folded linens, their brows beaded with sweat. Underneath the ripe tang of salt in the air hung a buttery aroma – freshly baked goods cooling on racks, waiting to be packed for the imminent journey. In the distance, against the backdrop of the receding slop and suck of the waves, she could hear the thud of horses' hooves stamping impatiently in the stables as they were groomed and saddled in preparation for departure.

Meredyth leant on her cane and, underneath her pale green skirts, she stretched out first one leg then the other. In the days since the Appointment, she had found that her joints would often seize up without warning. Princess Talia said it was likely strands of magic still lingering in her limbs after standing unmoving for so long. The thought of that horrifying spell – or any kind of magic – still inhabiting her body made Meredyth queasy; she preferred to blame old age. It was some comfort to know that she was not alone. Only yesterday at dinner, during a lull between courses, she had noticed the King gripping his wrist as he rotated his hand, his face etched into a frown of pain.

At least she knew the reason for her aches. The Masters had unfrozen Meredyth first and, at Talia and Violanna's request, she had kept her memory of the event. At the time, shaking and sick, Meredyth had said, 'Princess, when everyone else wakes, you must reassure them that all is well.' And seeing that Princess Talia was about to protest, she had added, 'Act quickly – your mother is injured and needs to return to her chambers.'

Princess Talia had looked from the limp figure of Queen Violanna to the many faces of the guests, about to be released from their stillness. Finally, she had nodded.

Taking up position on the royal dais, Princess Talia had waited until the guests began to stir. They had woken suddenly with temples throbbing, uttering shouts of shock and dismay to see the ruined Great Hall. Before they could ask too many questions, the Princess had announced in a high, clear voice that though her curse had struck, all attacks had been thwarted. It was not exactly a lie. 'And the curse is over now. It is finished,' she had declared. The Great Hall had burst into applause and shouts of delight.

No one had noticed the black-cloaked figures slipping away and disappearing from this kingdom as swiftly as they had arrived.

Though Meredyth had kept her memories, she sometimes wondered if, given the choice, she might have asked for blissful ignorance. In the days since the Appointment, she had often glanced down to see her hands trembling, thoughts of smoke-like blackness and clawing shadows overtaking her mind. She was pleased to be leaving Mont Isle today. She longed to put some distance between herself and the island, and she sensed that she was not alone. The courtiers in the King's party were uncharacteristically quiet and subdued. There were no games, no gambling and no liaisons. Perhaps, though they did not remember exactly what had occurred at the Appointment, they knew something was not quite right. Meredyth might have imagined it, but when the King had announced last night that they would be departing for Lustore, she had thought she heard sighs of relief.

Forcing herself to leave the shade of the tree, Meredyth walked to the other side of the courtyard. She followed a passageway through the castle and arrived at the Princess's chambers, nodding to the guards standing watch. Gone were the days when she could rap on the door with her cane and march inside. The curse might be over, but there were still many who would wish to hurt the Princess, and Bavaugh could not lose another heir.

After she had been checked and approved, Meredyth entered the chambers. Inside, she found the Princess packing books into a chest. A few servants dithered at some distance.

'Long live Princess Talia, heir to Bavaugh,' said Meredyth, curtseying. 'Someone else should be doing that, Princess.'

'My books need to be handled with care! I will not have them all bent and scuffed.'

Meredyth raised her eyebrows.

'I am sorry, Lady Lansin,' Talia sighed. 'This all feels . . . strange.'

The sunlight from the open window cast a shaft of light over the Princess's face, making the scar on her cheek glint silver. In the chaos after the Appointment, Meredyth had heard one of the Masters ask the Princess if she would like to have the scar smoothed over. 'No,' had been the reply. 'Leave me as I am.'

Meredyth shuffled across the room and rested her cane against the table. Taking one of the books from the pile, she carefully wrapped it in a scrap of fabric and placed it in the chest.

'You do not need—'

'I would like to help, Princess. You can trust me – I am very careful.'

'I do trust you.'

They worked silently beside one another, listening to the squeal of gulls outside.

'I think you will like Lustore,' said Meredyth when they had finished.

The Princess grimaced. 'I imagine the capital is loud and dirty,' she said, sliding a bolt across the chest. 'That is what Mistress Rashel says.'

'Yes, but it is exciting too. You must not forget that.'

'I will be too busy to pay it much heed. My father wants to launch an attack on the Tolbiens and I need to dissuade him. The Tolbiens are trying to provoke us because our defences are too strong. We would be wise to resist despite their atrocities.'

Meredyth tried to hide her surprise. Had anyone else suggested this, she would have scoffed at it, but Princess Talia was not just anyone. 'The King is renowned for being . . . shall we say . . . stubborn,' she replied.

'I know.'

'You have many brilliant ideas, Princess, but you will need to tread lightly around the King and the Royal Council.'

'Which is why I would like you to be one of my advisors.'

Meredyth blinked. She felt a little flicker of hopeful excitement, but she replied levelly, 'I do not understand what you mean.'

'I intend to be a worthy Princess and a great Queen. I will need good counsel because I want to rule. Properly. You know I did not grow up at court, so I will need your wisdom.'

'I could not possibly—'

'You do not really have a choice, Lady Lansin. I can think of no one better to advise me.'

'Advise you? Advise you as what?'

'My Chief Lady-in-Waiting.'

Meredyth opened her mouth to protest that she was far too old. The young ladies at court would be furious to discover she had taken such a coveted position. Everyone would think it was ridiculous. But then a little voice in her head said, *Why not?* She could do it and she would do it better than anyone else. Chief Lady-in-Waiting, again. It was thrilling.

'Thank you, Princess,' she replied finally with a curtsey. 'That is a great honour.'

'Perhaps you will not thank me when we get to Lustore. I have many things I should like to change about Bavaugh and I plan to begin right away.'

'I do not doubt it, Princess.'

'I imagine the next few winters will not be easy for us. Especially with that advisor who whispers things in my father's ear.'

'Lord Rosford?'

'He does not like me.'

Meredyth pursed her lips. 'Perhaps it is time for Lord Rosford to retire to his country estate. I am sure together that is something we can arrange.'

They smiled at one another.

Meredyth motioned for one of the servants to take away the chest of books and the Princess wandered over to the open window. She rested her hands on the sill and sighed. 'I will miss the sea,' she murmured. 'The King speaks of this island like it is a prison, but he is wrong. It is my home.'

'You will come back, Princess.'

The light breeze from the window tugged at the loose strands of hair around Princess Talia's face. 'It will be so odd to leave, Lady Lansin.'

'It is a new beginning.'

The Princess nodded and, taking a deep breath, she pushed herself away from the window. 'The tide is out,' she said. 'We will need to depart soon. I must say goodbye to my mother. And Briar.'

Meredyth saw something flicker across the Princess's face. It had not escaped her notice that Princess Talia became different whenever Briar was near. Uncharacteristically quiet and brooding, all her usual outspokenness mellowed with something almost like resentment. Meredyth wondered if perhaps a little distance from this long-lost sister might be a good thing. She had not spent much time with Briar herself, but she found the girl unsettling. Too beautiful and odd.

'I will see you in the courtyard when we depart, Lady Lansin,' said the Princess. 'Thank you for your help.'

Meredyth curtsied, leaning over her cane, and waited until Princess Talia had stridden from the room. When she was alone, Meredyth rose again. She took a pouch from the pocket of her jacket and held it in her hands. It shifted and clinked.

She sighed.

She had one last task to complete before she could finally leave this bleak, strange island behind.

Sel

The Dovecote, Mont Isle

WIND CUT THROUGH the crumbling stone walls, sending flurries of pale feathers whirling from the pigeonholes above. Gulls flapped and scratched in the few occupied nests and a rickety ladder led to the grimy trough overhead, its rungs glazed with the grit of salt and sand.

As she stepped around the edges of the dovecote, Sel's boots crunched on the white, encrusted bird excrement layered upon the floor. She wrinkled her nose. This place was ideally deserted, but it was not exactly pleasant. Through the cracks and breaks in the wall, she could glimpse a flat, dark expanse where the sea had faded into the distance, leaving rocks and seaweed behind.

Sel paced the circular edge of the room once more, feeling the beady gaze of the gulls above watching her. She was about to turn and pace back again when she heard the scuffle of footsteps. A shadow fell across the entrance and a slight figure appeared.

'There you are, Briar,' she said, a hitch in her voice.

If Briar noticed her strange tone, she did not show it. 'So many stairs!' she puffed. 'Why're there so many stairs?'

'Because it's a tower.'

Briar folded her arms. 'I don't see why we couldn't meet in my room; no one's there during the day.'

'We can't risk it.'

Briar tossed a lock of blonde hair over her shoulder. It was a rich, buttery hue, but it was no longer the astonishing gold it had once been. Like the rest of Briar, it had settled into a peculiar beauty after the spell had been broken. More unusual than unnatural.

'Fine,' said Briar. 'Why did you need to see me so urgently?'

Sel opened her mouth to answer, but found herself stalling instead. 'How's the Queen? Is she feeling more comfortable?'

The magic that had ravaged Queen Violanna's body when she had wielded the spindle could not be undone, and 'comfortable' was about the best that could be hoped for. Sel suspected the Queen knew this too, though neither of them had acknowledged it the few times they had spoken since the Appointment. Sel also suffered tremors and sudden bouts of burning pain since handling the magic in the Great Hall, but her winters of studying magic and practice as a Master's apprentice had built up immunity. She was recuperating slowly from the ordeal, but at least she would recover.

'The Queen seems much the same,' said Briar with a half-shrug. 'I have sat by her bed for the last few days and given her sips of water. She sleeps a lot.'

'Good. That's a kind thing to do for . . . your mother.' Sel swallowed, her throat tight. 'And you, Briar?' she added quickly. 'Are you feeling well?'

She watched closely as Briar's gaze wandered to a gap in the wall showing the bright, blustery sky outside.

'Yes,' she replied slowly. 'I feel . . . all right.'

Potent magic no longer radiated from Briar. She was still unusually graceful and still favoured by animals, even if Sel suspected that Briar could not exactly speak to them like she used to – the stable dogs sought her out each night for petting and gulls would sidle up to her in the courtyards to peer into her large blue eyes. But she was different. In Sel's mind, Briar would always be Briar, but she could not deny that the girl was changed.

'You're certain to feel strange as you adjust to everything, but it's a good thing,' said Sel, not for the first time, her tone forcibly bright. 'It's all over and now you're free. You're safe. It's a good thing.'

As usual, Briar made a non-committal noise, her head turned away. In the days since the Appointment, Sel had tried over and over to explain everything. She had made her voice hoarse attempting to recount the tale of Briar's birth and the spell bound to her – why Sel had hidden her and raised Briar as her niece. But the more she explained, the more she felt Briar slipping away. Sel told herself that the girl just needed time. Of course she was bound to feel bewildered by it all, and perhaps angry and hurt. It was complicated to understand, but she would accept it all eventually. She had to.

'And the magic will never fully leave,' Sel added. 'It was powerful and dark. I know I've said that before, but it's important for you to remember that you'll always—'

'Why do you have a pack?' Briar interrupted.

Sel paused. She fiddled with the straps of the pack hung over her shoulder and took a deep breath. 'Briar, I'm leaving.'

'You're *leaving*?'

Briar's raised voice echoed around the stone walls of the dovecote. Above them, a startled gull flew from its nest, squawking and flapping.

'I must go.'

'Why?'

Briar's blue eyes were wide and bright with tears. Her expression, always so clear and readable to Sel, became a mixture of panic and fury.

'You need time with the Queen,' replied Sel. 'And I'm . . . getting in the way.'

Yesterday Sel had returned to the room she shared with the kitchen girls to find a black cloak folded neatly on her cramped bed. It was Florentina's cloak; the black cloak of a Master. She had held it in her hands, weighing the coarse heaviness of it, feeling relieved and elated. She had not allowed herself long to enjoy the moment before quickly hiding the cloak. The sight of it would surely raise suspicions from the other servants, who were already curious about her presence in the castle – a woman who had appeared after the Appointment and did not seem to have a duty. The royal household staff thought she was an island servant and the island servants assumed the reverse, but Sel did not know how long that confusion could hold. There was no note accompanying the cloak, but Sel understood the message: *It is time for you to leave.*

'Briar, I must go,' she repeated.

'No.'

'Briar—'

'No!'

Sel grabbed hold of Briar's arms and wrenched her close. Sel's pack thumped to the floor and Briar pulled back, but she was locked in the embrace. After a wail of frustration, she collapsed against Sel's chest, sobbing.

'I can't believe you're leaving me here!'

Sel wrapped her arms around the girl's dainty shoulders and held her tightly. 'You need to be with the Qu—your mother. You must get to know her.'

Sel did not add, *before she is gone*.

'But I'm all wrong in this place. No one knows what to do with me.'

Sel winced. It was true. After Noatina's death, as the Masters were dispersing the remnants of dark magic in the Great Hall and removing the memory of the event from the minds of the guests, Sel had hurried away to the chapel with Briar. There they had sheltered, listening to the sounds of the guests awoken from their stillness in the Great Hall and the trumpeting of the Princess's Appointment parade. Still reeling from what had happened, Sel had not thought to question why Briar was hiding and not in place as the rightful, firstborn heir, and no one else seemed bothered by such thoughts either. After the parade had set off, Lady Lansin had appeared in the chapel and swiftly concocted a tale in which Briar was a companion she had hired for the Queen; the orphan of a merchant left in her care. 'No one will suspect anything,' she had said firmly. 'It can remain as it should be.'

But, Sel wondered, was this really how things should be?

Briar had not spoken about the arrangement. With so much changed, it was unlikely she had considered it yet, but Sel felt the affront on her behalf. She had tentatively raised the issue with Queen Violanna in their last audience, taking the opportunity when Briar had left the room to wonder aloud when the secret Princess might be made known to the Kingdom of Bavaugh. The Queen had gazed back at her, confused and weak. 'My lost daughter has returned to me and I want to keep her near. Nothing else matters,' she had replied. 'You are not a mother, so you would not understand.' Sel had managed to stop herself from retorting that this lost daughter had a name and it was Briar. Briar, the firstborn

Princess of Bavaugh. And she, Sel, was as much a mother to Briar as anyone.

But though she did not say it, Sel wondered if the Queen suspected her views on the matter; Sel had not been invited for another audience.

'Please take me with you, Auntie,' said Briar, soaking Sel's jacket with her tears. 'Please!'

Sel's heart wavered. She had promised herself that she would not meddle – she was not Briar's kin, no matter how much she loved her. But she could feel a prickle of temptation. She cupped Briar's beautiful, tear-stained cheeks in her hands. 'It's important that you stay here for now,' she said. 'But when your time here's done, if you wish it, you can come back to me. Wherever I am, there will always be a place for you.'

Briar squeezed her eyes shut, more tears trickling across her cheeks.

'Wherever I am, there will be a place for you. I promise, Briar.'

Finally, the girl sniffed and slowly nodded.

Sel bent and retrieved her pack from the floor. 'I love you, Briar,' she said, swallowing back her own tears.

Briar mumbled something that sounded like it could have been, 'I love you too.' Then she turned away and faced the crumbling stone walls, her shoulders shaking with silent sobs.

With great difficulty, Sel stepped towards the arched doorway, telling herself that she was doing the right thing and that her heart was not breaking.

This is not for ever, she promised. *But this is how it must be now.*

She paused on the threshold and allowed herself one more look at the shining head. She did not just see a young woman but a tiny infant, a gurgling baby and a smiling little girl too. They were all Briar. Her Briar. And they always would be.

Turning, Sel planted one foot on the stone tread of the tower stairs, then another and another. She began to move swiftly, her palms skimming the cobwebbed stone walls for balance as her boots slipped on the narrow, worn steps. She hurried on, faster and faster, knowing that if she slowed or stopped, she would not be able to leave at all.

With her pack bumping against her shoulder, she rushed from the bottom of the tower, across the eastern courtyard. A flock of court ladies were milling around beside one of the fountains, flanked by attendants, and Sel shot past them, diving into a shadowed passageway. Outside the castle walls, the crossing to the mainland was clear and Sel knew she must leave the island before the sea returned. She must leave right now before she changed her mind.

The end of the passageway shone ahead of her, bright and sunny, and Sel raced towards it. She did not notice the shadow alongside one wall, until it reared up and blocked her path.

She skidded to a halt with a yelp. She was about to raise her hands, ready to conjure or strike out, when she saw that it was Lady Lansin.

'Ah, I have been looking for you,' said Lady Lansin, leaning on her cane. 'A maid told me she saw you heading this way.'

Sel shifted the pack on her shoulder. 'I really must go—' she began.

'I have a gift for you from Queen Violanna.'

Before Sel could respond, Lady Lansin thrust a soft, leather pouch into her hands.

'What—'

'The Queen says it is what you are owed.'

Sel felt the contents shift and mould in her fingers and she heard the clink of gold flecks.

'Now you can be on your way,' added Lady Lansin.

Sel had not realized she was crying, but suddenly she tasted the salt on her lips from her tears. There had once been a time when she had looked forward to this reward, dreaming of how she would use it to bolster her studies and start a new life, but things were different now. No amount of flecks could make up for the winters she had spent with Briar, living in fear, and nothing could compensate for the pain she felt at having to leave the girl behind.

Sel thrust the pouch back at Lady Lansin, taking the noble-woman by surprise. It dropped to the stone floor with a ring.

'Tell the Queen I do not want this!' she hissed.

Then she pushed past Lady Lansin and ran.

Violanna

The Queen's Chambers, Mont Isle

THE DOOR CREAKED and Violanna looked up with a start. She half raised herself from her pillows, ignoring the shoots of pain that twisted through her body, and her fingers clutched at her nightgown.

'Don't worry, it's just the Princess,' said Briar, who was sitting on a stool beside the bed. 'And she's alone.'

When Violanna saw the tall figure of her daughter in the doorway, she relaxed back with a sigh. Servants were always appearing to change the dressing on her hand. The hand that was now burnt black. She had told the physician that it would never heal, but he had ignored her and prescribed a useless poultice. Whenever the servants came to change the bandages, Briar had to pick up a book and pretend to read aloud. Meredyth had told everyone that Briar was a companion she had hired to entertain the Queen, but Violanna sometimes noticed the maids staring doubtfully.

'Hello, Mother,' said Talia, tentatively approaching. She was wearing a burgundy riding habit with black trim, her face set into a sombre expression. 'We are to leave soon,' she added, stopping at a few paces' distance.

The riding habit suited Talia's statuesque frame and Violanna thought how grown up her daughter looked. She had a sudden memory of watching from her bedchamber window as Talia climbed and jumped around the island's rocks during her girlhood, her skirts tucked into her bloomers, her lanky limbs flailing and her mousey hair twirling about her head in the wind. Now she seemed poised – still awkward and not exactly pretty, but stately. She looked like someone important.

'You're going to Lustore?' asked Briar.

'Yes.'

'I've never been to the capital.'

'And you will join me there in the winter as one of my Ladies-in-Waiting,' said Talia. Then she added a little uncertainly, 'That will be nice.'

Violanna glanced from one daughter to the other. Since the Appointment, they had sat at her bedside together once a day in a pretence of sisterly affection, but she saw the glances they shot in each other's direction, and she noticed their tight expressions when the other spoke. In the many winters since their infancy, it had never occurred to Violanna to wonder what it would be like when they were all reunited. It had seemed an outcome too precarious to hope for, but now Violanna wished she had spared it some thought. Everything had happened so fast in the aftermath of the Appointment.

'I will return to Mont Isle, Mother,' said Talia. 'Although I am not exactly sure when.'

Violanna smiled. It hurt for her to talk, so she saved her words. The magic that had thundered through her body when she picked up the spindle had ravaged her, and she lived in perpetual pain. She knew it was unusual for someone who had never wielded magic to have survived such a thing at all. She knew she did not have much longer.

Pain struck her shoulder, and she couldn't stop herself from wincing.

'Do you need your pillows fluffing, Mother?' asked Talia, rushing over. 'You look like you have slipped down.'

Violanna shook her head and tried to settle her expression back into a benign smile.

'Don't worry, she's fine.'

Talia glanced at Briar with a frown and looked as though she were about to snap back a reply before she caught herself.

She is learning, thought Violanna.

Briar must have sensed Talia's disapproval because she quickly added, 'You're fine, aren't you, *Mother*?'

Violanna nodded again and flapped the fingers of her left hand, as if to bat away their concern.

Mother. The word always sounded a little choked coming from Briar's mouth. Violanna tried not to notice. She had spent so many winters imagining this girl – her first daughter – that she often found it bewildering to be in her presence. She knew Briar in the way every mother knows her child, but she also did not know her. Briar was dazzling and odd. And that name – Briar. So provincial and a little foolish. Perhaps it was the magic that made Briar seem different, or perhaps it was their long separation, but Violanna often found herself staring at this stranger beside her bed, wondering if she was really the baby she had sent away to safety all that time ago, or someone else. She could tell that Briar felt it too; it was evident in her awkward, self-conscious chattering, in her painful politeness and the unconvincing way she said *Mother*.

'I ought to take my leave now,' said Talia. 'Everyone will be waiting. Meredyth says I need to ride at the front of the procession, and no one can mount their horse until we – I – do. It is all rather silly.'

Violanna tilted her head in acknowledgement. She could imagine Felipe standing impatiently in the courtyard, smacking his whip against his boot just as he used to do when waiting for her during their marriage. Talia was careful not to refer directly to the King in her mother's presence. Although Violanna did not know why – their estrangement was no secret. Felipe had not visited her chambers since the Appointment and she doubted he would appear before the royal party departed the island. It did not really matter to her; she had nothing to say to him.

'I will write,' insisted Talia, and Violanna thought she sounded more like she was trying to convince herself. 'Lady Lansin says she has organized care for you, Mother. Proper care.' Her eyes flicked to Briar, then she took a deep breath and said, 'I will . . . miss you.'

Violanna wanted to believe that it was true. She smiled at her daughter, forcing back tears. She knew how difficult it must be for Talia to leave Mont Isle and she did not want to upset her further.

'Goodbye, Mother.'

Talia leant over the bed and pressed her lips to her mother's cheek. Violanna breathed in her daughter's clean, warm smell and longed to wrap her arms around her, but before she could even attempt to move, Talia was pulling away again, and turning to Briar.

'Goodbye, sister.'

Violanna watched as her daughters faced one another. She knew it ought to be a glorious and wonderful sight to a mother, but it made her uneasy. They did not look like kin. Talia was a whole head and shoulders taller than her sister, and her frame was stronger and broader. Briar's fair curls were a little like Talia's dyed-blonde hair, and her small, neat nose was similar in shape, but there was not really much resemblance between them.

Not like Noatina and me, thought Violanna. She remembered their childhood game of mirroring one another, trying to hold back delighted giggles. Violanna preferred to remember her sister like that – it was the memory she conjured in her mind when plagued by visions of Noatina in the Great Hall, choking on shadows, blood pouring from her throat. Violanna did not regret what she had done, but she was glad that she was suffering for it.

'It has been . . . good to get to know you,' said Talia.

Violanna clenched her teeth, thinking that perhaps Talia had not quite learnt how to mask her true feelings. But if she sensed her sister's reluctance, Briar did not show it. She stepped forward and embraced Talia.

'I didn't know I had any close family, let alone a sister. I wish you all the best, Talia. You will be a mighty Princess.'

Talia blushed and looked as though she did not know what to say, then she blurted, 'Rightfully it should be you.'

Briar stilled then shook her head, but her gaze lingered on a sapphire ring on Talia's finger.

There was redness around Briar's eyes, as though the girl had been crying, and Violanna thought that perhaps the departure of her long-lost sister was affecting Briar more than she let on. Not for the first time, Violanna wondered if her daughters should be going to the capital together. If it were up to her, they would both stay on Mont Isle for whatever time she had left. But the Kingdom of Bavaugh needed its heir and Violanna could not face parting with them both so soon. She wanted to at least keep Briar near, since they had been separated for so long.

'I really should be going now,' said Talia, striding briskly to the door. 'Goodbye.'

Violanna pushed herself forward, ignoring the burn of agony that rushed through her body. 'I love you,' she croaked, but Talia was already gone.

There was a pause.

'I'm sure she heard that,' said Briar. 'Anyway, perhaps you would like a rest now? You look a little weary.'

Violanna obediently sank back into her pillows and closed her eyes. She had little energy these days and she was indeed weary. Selhah had tried to cast a spell to ease some of Violanna's discomfort, but there was too much damage. Still, she had appreciated the effort. This morning, Violanna had sent Meredyth in search of Selhah with a pouch of gold flecks. She had already instructed the return of Selhah's black cloak and she had almost forgotten the other promise of a reward. She was grateful to Selhah. The Master had faithfully raised her first daughter in safety and rightfully returned Briar to her mother.

As Violanna drifted into sleep, sliding away from the aches and pains of her body, she was vaguely aware of Briar shuffling from the room and the creak of the closing door. From the open window, she could hear horses' hooves on cobblestones, the trundle of wagon wheels and the shouts of farewell from the servants. As she lay in bed alone, Violanna imagined Talia, riding beside the King, fringed with guards. She saw her daughter crossing the causeway, following the coastal path along the cliffs and disappearing into the future.

Violanna's daughters were alive and well. That was enough. That must be enough.

Briar

The Castle, Mont Isle

AS BRIAR WANDERED across the courtyard, she saw a groom hurrying in the opposite direction, a saddle slung over his arm. Instinctively, she pulled away, hiding her face in shadow, but as they passed one another, she remembered that she did not need to do that any more. She turned back, letting the pale sunlight fall on her cheeks and glimmer through her hair. She glanced at the retreating figure of the groom, wondering if he might pause to look at her too. But he did not.

Walking in the direction of the stables, Briar began humming a catchy ditty she had overheard in the kitchens. She could sing, dance and speak as much as she liked now, without fear of attracting too much attention. One of the young courtiers had said that her voice was 'sweet' as she stood next to him at a seventh-day service in the chapel, hoping to coax her into an evening stroll around the battlements and perhaps a kiss and a fondle. He had probably been surprised to see her look so crestfallen. *Sweet*. Her singing no longer had the power to strike awe into the hearts of its listeners. Now it was a light, tuneful sound. It was merely 'sweet'.

As she ducked inside the first stable block, Briar breathed in the reassuring smell of hay and horses. Most of the stalls were now empty and waiting to be cleaned, but a black nose hung over a half-door at one end and Briar smiled. Catching sight of her approaching, Star snorted a greeting, and Briar was so busy scratching the mare's chin that at first she did not realize there was someone else in the stall too.

'You're not going to watch the Royal Court leave?' asked Jacken. His neck shone with sweat where the ties of his shirt were undone, and his black hair was damp on his forehead, falling into his eyes. Briar's fingers itched to brush it aside.

'No.'

Briar picked up a curry comb and began gently teasing out the knots in Star's mane.

'Star doesn't like this castle,' she said after a pause. 'She wants to run about in fields.'

'I thought you couldn't—'

'I still know when an animal isn't happy!'

Jacken shrugged. 'How is the Queen?' he asked instead. 'Everyone says she is very sick.'

'I suppose she is, but it's hard to tell. She doesn't say much.' Briar paused and bit her lip before adding lightly, 'I'm not actually sure she likes me.'

'What do you mean?'

'She's so . . . cold.'

Briar thought of all the times the Queen had flinched when she tried to clasp her hand. Briar could feel Jacken's eyes studying her face, so she busied herself with combing Star's mane again.

'What about the Princess?' he asked. 'You never mention her.'

Briar forced down the strange feeling that always hit when she thought of Talia. They were so different, yet she could not help but notice that her sister chewed on her thumbnail when she was thinking and jutted out her chin if she wanted to get her own way. Briar recognized these gestures as affectations of her own, right down to the pattern of movement their fingers would make when twirling the ends of their hair. It was unnerving.

'Princess Talia's . . . the same,' replied Briar carefully. 'I'm not sure she likes me that much either.'

Yesterday Briar had suggested paddling in the sea to cool down and she had not been prepared for the vehement reaction from her sister. *'You must never swim around the island!'* Talia had barked. 'The tides are too dangerous.' When Briar had tried to laugh off her mistake, Talia had continued to glare at her and even the Queen had looked a little disapproving. It was one of many times when Briar seemed to have said the wrong thing.

'The Princess and the Queen must like you,' said Jacken. 'Everyone likes you.'

Briar knew this was not true – at least, not any more – but she wanted to believe it. It was hard to guess what the Queen and the Princess really thought about anything. Even each other. Briar had found their farewell just now peculiar. It had been stiff and stilted and nothing like the way she had clung to Auntie when they had parted earlier that morning. Even the memory of that farewell brought tears to her eyes and a lump of sorrow to her chest.

'Jacken, there's something I should tell you,' she said. 'I met Auntie this morning and she's . . .'

'Gone,' finished Jacken.

Briar wheeled around on him. 'You knew?'

'She came to the stables first thing this morning.'

Briar pursed her lips. 'Then I don't need to explain anything,' she snapped. 'You already know. Good.'

Briar turned her attention back to grooming Star and tried to push all thoughts of Auntie from her mind. She veered from sorrow that her aunt was gone to anger that the person she had trusted most in the realm had lied to her all her life. It did not matter that it had been for her own good – to save her, even. It changed things.

Auntie had tried to explain it all to Briar more than once. Her words were like links that connected a chain winding throughout Briar's past, pulling everything into place. It made sense of all that Briar had never understood about herself. She knew that it should make her feel good, but actually it just made her feel odd.

'I'm not who I thought I was,' Briar had said when the tale was finished the first time.

'You're still the same to me,' Auntie had replied.

But Briar could not shake the feeling that she was different now. She was a Princess and yet also not a Princess. She had a mother but she also did not have a mother. She was Briar but she was also someone else.

'Are you all right?' asked Jacken, after a pause.

Briar nodded, then shrugged.

'What is it?'

'Auntie's gone and I just don't know when I'll see her again . . .'

'It's all right,' replied Jacken softly. 'I understand.'

Before she knew what she was doing, Briar had moved closer to him, falling against his chest. She felt his arms fold around her and she pressed her face into his damp shirt, breathing in his smell of sweat and horses. She could hear the thump of his heartbeat against her ear and his hands were gently stroking her shoulders and smoothing her hair.

'Do I seem different?' she asked, pulling back to look at him. 'Am I different now?'

She felt his gaze move across her face. 'No,' he said. 'Not to me.'

His hands had slid down her back to her waist and if she moved a little closer and tilted back her head, their lips would touch. She had thought of this moment often and she wanted to kiss him, she did *want* to, but she found herself turning away.

Jacken did not react, though she felt his disappointment clouding the air. She longed to say, 'Not here. Not now. Not yet.' But then a little voice also said, *Maybe never*.

'I've been thinking,' she said, clearing her throat. 'I'd like to go to Turow.'

Jacken frowned. 'What do you mean? I thought you were going to Lustore in the winter to be a Lady-in-Waiting to Princess Talia?'

Briar folded her arms. 'That's what everyone else has decided, but it doesn't mean I have to do it. After all, I'm the *real* Princess. Rightfully, it should be me in Talia's place.'

'But—'

'I want to see Paleen again. She was so kind to me when I was little and I never felt right about leaving her. I only wrote to her that one time. I think . . . I owe her a lot.'

Briar trailed off, remembering sitting at the spinning wheel in the Great Hall, wrangling the magic that wanted to destroy her. She did not know how she had done it – Auntie had tried to explain about magical principles, gesture language and the transfer of energy – but Briar had not understood much of it. What she did know was that she would never have learnt to spin if she had not had such fond memories of sitting with Paleen in her parlour, watching the minister's wife at her wheel.

'I didn't think I'd ever go back to Turow,' muttered Jacken.

Briar glanced at him in surprise. She often forgot that they had not always lived side by side, all their thoughts, feelings and memories intertwined.

'Please can we go? I'd so like to see Paleen. Please, Jacken?'

Jacken's gaze was cool, but then his shoulders dropped in defeat. 'I suppose.'

Briar smiled and thought of the minister's house with its heavy, battered furniture and warm, inviting atmosphere. She hoped it had not changed. Perhaps it might finally bring her back to herself. She knew she ought to feel relieved that she was free of the curse and overjoyed that she was reunited with her real family, but she felt neither. Instead, there was a seed of bitterness lodged in her chest. The curse had stripped away everything that made Briar different. It was supposed to be a good thing, and though it was a relief not to experience the throbbing headaches and itchy agitation to which she had become accustomed, there were things she missed too. Without them, she did not know who she was.

Yesterday, on her way back from luncheon, she had seen the King crossing the western courtyard and she had said to herself, *That must be my father*. She had stopped and watched, expressionless and numb. He was tall and fair and she wondered if perhaps she looked a little like him – more like him than her dark-haired, dark-eyed mother, anyway. But then he had turned down a corridor and disappeared, followed by his guards, and she realized that she had not glimpsed anything familiar in his face. He was a stranger. When she had returned to the Queen's chambers and tried to mention the King to Talia, her sister's expression had soured. 'Oh, him?' she had replied. 'He cares nothing for me. For us.'

King Felipe did not know that he had two daughters and everyone had decided it must stay that way. No one had asked Briar what she wanted. It had all been agreed in a hurry after the events of the Appointment. And even though she had been told that *she* was the true-born heir to the Kingdom of Bavaugh, in the same breath they said that it must be a secret. She must remain Briar. The orphan. While her sister acted like fine clothes, shimmering jewels and everyone bowing when you entered the room was some great hardship, Briar had to pretend to be a companion, then a Lady-in-Waiting, and she must be grateful.

Her life had changed so drastically that it was all she could do to go along with everything. But when she started pulling apart the threads, it did not seem very fair.

'What're you thinking?' asked Jacken, making her jump.

Briar gave Star a final pat then slipped out of the stall. The Queen would wake from her nap soon.

'I wasn't thinking of anything,' she replied. 'I'm just looking forward to going to Turow. I'm looking forward to the day we leave.'

Talia

Guil, West Bavaugh

TALIA SAT TALL in the saddle, ignoring the sweat trickling between her shoulder blades. She was not a particularly skilled rider and, conscious of the many eyes on her, she was trying her best to hold her posture in the way Meredyth had instructed, which apparently 'befitted a Princess', but which also made her achy and uncomfortable. A long afternoon of riding stretched worryingly ahead and she might have wailed in frustration at the thought, but her mind was fixated on something else: she had just left Mont Isle.

It was almost impossible for her to fathom. Mont Isle had been her home for sixteen winters and now she was leaving without knowing when she might return. She knew it was a good thing – everyone kept telling her so. But it did not make it any less strange. Her new home was to be a palace, in the depths of the capital city. She would no longer awake to the sound of keening gulls or smell the constant salty richness of the sea. Everything would be different.

Talia wondered if she would miss Mont Isle more than she would miss her mother. But no, that was not true. As soon as the thought appeared in her head, she chased it off. She *would* miss her mother, in a way. Things between them had changed for the better. Talia had grown up fearing that her mother did not love her, but on the day of the Appointment, she had seen that she had been wrong. The Queen had saved her, and Talia could still remember the feel of her mother's embrace as they knelt together in the Great Hall, watching the sorceress die. She could feel the strength and warmth of her mother's arms around her. A memory both precious and horrifying. But a single event – even one so momentous – could not undo the damage of many winters. Talia could not shake the feeling that her mother was still the distant, detached figure she had always been.

Then there was Briar. The stranger who was her sister. More than that: her twin. A part of herself that she had never known existed. Talia ought to have felt overjoyed and delighted at the discovery – after all, she had always longed to meet her half-brothers when they lived – but she felt neither delighted nor overjoyed. Rather, she felt uncertain. Briar was dazzling, graceful and serene, even without the amplification of the spell. It was difficult for Talia not to look at her sister and think that Briar must be the daughter her mother had always wanted. Sometimes, when all three of them sat together in the Queen's chambers, Talia would secretly watch her mother with Briar and wonder if she loved her more.

Briar was beautiful and she was also the firstborn. She was the *real* Princess. It had taken all of Lady Lansin's persuasive powers to convince Talia not to renounce the crown. In their many private debates about it since the Appointment, Lady Lansin always kept the same argument: 'We cannot reveal the truth to the kingdom – there would be anarchy!' she would cry. 'Besides, you will make a great Queen. A better Queen.' And Talia knew that Lady Lansin was right. As daunting as the thought of leaving Mont Isle and moving to Lustore was, Talia wanted it. She had truly meant it when she said that she intended to be a great Queen. Briar might make a better Princess – pretty, sweet and charming – but she could not rule the kingdom. A short time in her sister's company had assured Talia of that fact and she liked to remind herself of it often. If Briar were in her position, she would inevitably marry someone and *he* would reign. Talia had already decided that she would not allow matrimony to get in the way of her Queenship.

'I shall never marry,' she had told Meredyth last night, while they were walking to the Queen's chambers before dinner.

Meredyth laughed.

'I am serious, Lady Lansin.'

'Perhaps. But you are very young, Princess. You might change your mind.'

'I doubt it.'

'Then you will disappoint poor Hiberah.'

Talia frowned. 'Hiberah? What does he have to do with anything?'

'He is in love with you, Princess.'

Talia was so shocked she stopped still and the guards behind her almost crashed into her back.

'But he says I look like a milkmaid!' she cried.

'People fall in love with milkmaids.'

She stared at Meredyth incredulously. 'It is because I am heir to the throne now, correct?' she said finally.

'Perhaps. But I think you have a certain charm all your own, Princess. Anyway, even though he is my grandson, I would advise against the match. Hiberah would not make a good ruler.'

Talia gave herself a little shake. She had got used to Hiberah the way you grow fond of a comfortable pair of shoes, but that was the sum of it.

'I am not in love with anybody,' she said simply. 'And I shall be too focused on matters of state to concern myself with such things.'

'How very noble, Princess,' replied Meredyth, but she was doing that thing with her mouth that meant she was trying not to smile.

Talia had wanted to insist that this was not a whim but an oath – she *would not* fall in love with anyone – but she was late for dinner already and there was no time to dawdle.

But just now, thoughts of future matrimony did not hold her attention for long. Ahead, she could see the coastal path bending away from the cliffs and moving inland. Soon Mont Isle would be out of sight and the prospect turned her stomach. Sensing her anxiousness, her horse ducked its head and caught its front hoof on a rock, lurching forward.

'Watch the path here,' said the King, who was riding just ahead of her. 'It is narrow and steep. Be careful.'

Talia nodded and tried to focus again on her riding. She often had to remind herself that her father's concern was for the heir of Bavaugh, not his daughter. It was easy to confuse the two and delude herself into believing that he cared for her. But he did not. Not really.

They had had ample opportunity to spend time together over the past few days, but the King had mostly kept to his rooms. Talia supposed he was still grieving – he certainly seemed a sad, distracted figure – but she felt it was more than that. On the few occasions they had spoken alone, she seemed to baffle him. She did not hunt, she did not dance, she did not sing, and she did not spout witty, pleasant conversation. When she had tried to begin a discussion about her thoughts on the recent rise in taxes, alarm had flashed across the King's face. He had snapped that she need not concern herself with such matters. Unperturbed, Talia was already planning to broach the subject again as soon as they reached Lustore and settled into the palace. She would *make* him listen.

Talia had spent so much of her childhood fantasizing about her father, and imagining a nurturing, charismatic figure, that she sometimes had to remind herself that the man was actually in front of her. Felipe was her father, and if he was disappointed when they met, then he was not the only one. Lady Lansin had warned her that the King might not be what she was expecting, but a tiny part of Talia had still hoped Felipe would sweep her into his arms, make a plausible excuse for the fact he had never visited, and demand she tell him everything about herself. Instead, the nicest thing he had said to her was, 'You look a little like my mother,' which she had guessed must be a compliment from the tone of his voice. Perhaps a small part of her still hoped she might win him over. There was time yet.

The bend in the coastal path was almost upon them and, ahead, the King was turning his bay stallion, retreating into the scrub covering the cliff. In just a few moments, Talia would follow and Mont Isle would be out of sight. She swivelled her head towards it and gulped down a mouthful of salty air. She wanted to commit this last view of the island to memory.

The tide was still out and the dark, wet sand gleamed like polished stone under the bright sun, broken by stretches of silt, pebbles and pools that folded into the horizon. Amid the flat, textured land rose the island, boiling up from the ground in a froth of rocks, tan walls and turrets. She had never seen it from this distance before. It sat tall and isolated in the distance, as it always had and always would, waiting to be surrounded by the churning grey waves of the sea. It had witnessed her first breath, sheltered her as she grew, and now it watched her leave.

I will see you again, she silently promised.

Sel

The Wildlands

SEL BREATHED DEEPLY, tipping back her head and letting the fading sunlight warm her cheeks. She had forgotten how clean and fresh it was here. During the many days she had spent travelling through the Bavaughian countryside since leaving Mont Isle, she had not seen another region in the kingdom with a landscape so majestic, and she had not smelt air so pure. It was a surprising relief.

As they wound along a track that was growing more and more familiar, she noticed Patch prick his ears and pick up his feet. She let the reins slip through her fingers and allowed him to choose his own way, while she undid her hair and tried to work her fingers through the toughest knots. She had lost her comb somewhere on the journey and she had spent the last few nights sleeping in woodland, so she knew she must look a sight. There was a spell she could cast to help her with the worst of it, but she could not remember exactly how it went. It was the sort of simple charm she would have easily muttered during her apprenticeship, to free mud from her skirts or freshen her skin, but it was lost in the depths of her memory. She dropped her hands back to her sides with a sigh.

Ahead, she spotted a plume of smoke rising over the tops of the trees. The farmhouse.

She felt a flicker of excitement and panic. It was almost supper-time and the meal would be cooking on the stove in the kitchen. The thought both warmed and worried her, and she tried to ignore the little voice that said she was not supposed to be here. Instead, she should be on a ship bound for the Diaspass Kingdom, heading finally to her homeland. But when she had set off from Mont Isle, almost a moon ago, she had found herself veering south-east, following a different path. She had thought often about turning back and she had lost count of the number of times she had told herself that she was being foolish, but, somehow, she had kept going. Now, here she was.

A sudden rush of nerves swept over Sel. Goosebumps prickled up her arms and she shivered. Perhaps she ought to think this over a little more? She was just reaching forward to gather up Patch's reins and pull him to a halt, when she heard footsteps.

She looked up to see a figure emerging from the trees, a shovel slung over one shoulder. The figure caught sight of her and stopped.

Patch whinnied, then lurched into a jog, almost throwing Sel from the saddle. She grabbed hold of a handful of the gelding's mane and clung on until the horse jerked to a halt in front of his master, snorting and whickering in greeting.

'Hello, Gad,' said Sel after a pause. She looked down at the famil-iar, lined, dark eyes that were staring back at her. 'I've come to return Patch to you,' she added quickly. 'He's an excellent horse. The best. I couldn't bear to sell him.'

Gaddeous blinked.

'I found Briar and Jacken in the end,' she added, feeling a familiar sting of loss that always hit when she thought of Briar. 'They're safe now.'

When Gaddeous still had not replied, Sel fiddled with the reins in her hands and continued, 'I also came back because I wanted to see you.'

'You did?' said Gaddeous finally.

'I did.'

Sel leant forward to dismount, but before her feet had touched the ground, she felt Gaddeous's arms around her waist, pulling her close.

He dropped his shovel and it clanged on the hard earth as he took her hands in his own. 'I thought I'd imagined you,' he said. 'It wouldn't have been the first time that I've been mistaken.'

'I didn't know if I should come here,' she said. 'But I couldn't stop myself.'

'I didn't expect you to come back . . . I mean, you didn't have to.'

'I know.'

Their foreheads touched and Sel shut her eyes, savouring the feeling of having him close to her again. She knew that she had missed him, but she had not realized how much until that moment.

'I'm glad Briar and Jacken are safe. All is well now?' he asked.

Though news of the Princess's Appointment and the lifting of the curse was being proclaimed throughout the towns and villages of Bavaugh, such things took far longer to reach the Wildlands.

'All is well,' she said, pushing thoughts of shadows and black magic from her mind. She would explain it all to Gaddeous one day, but not yet.

'I've missed you,' he whispered, and Sel felt the brush of his breath on her lips. 'I've missed you every moment.'

'I've missed you, too.'

Sel lifted her chin and their lips met, soft and warm. She ran her fingers through his coarse hair and felt the scratch of his beard on her cheeks. She lost herself in the kiss and it was some time before she noticed Patch behind her, nosing at her shoulder. She stepped back, but still held on to Gad's arms, reluctant to let go.

'I'm here, but I can't stay,' she said, hearing her voice tremble. 'I must go back to the Diaspass Kingdom. My homeland. My Master left me an inheritance and I . . . I owe it to myself to go. I'm a Master now too.'

Gaddeous nodded.

'But I wanted to ask if perhaps . . . you'd consider coming with me?' she continued, watching his face closely.

'Come with you?'

'Yes. I realize what I'm asking; I don't expect—'

'I'll come with you.'

Sel felt a smile breaking her lips.

'I'll do whatever I can to stay close to you.'

'But the farm—' she began.

'The eldest Foxton will marry soon and I'd imagine the family will want to keep them close. It'd be easier for them to buy somewhere than start all over from scratch.'

'We might be able to come back,' said Sel. 'But I've got responsibilities to my kingdom and my order.'

Gaddeous ran his thumb across her bottom lip. 'We'll rent it to the Foxtons, then,' he said. 'But I can promise that for as long as you let me, I'll stay by your side.'

Around them, the long grass swayed in the gentle breeze and the evening light was cool and pale.

'I love you, Gad,' whispered Sel.

'I love you too. But you know that.'

They kissed again and when they parted, Sel laced her fingers through his.

'Let's go inside,' said Gaddeous. 'You must be tired after your travels, and I have supper on the stove.'

Sel looped her arm through Patch's reins and Gad picked up his shovel. Then they turned in the direction of the farmhouse, walking side by side in the fading, golden light.

Acknowledgements

3 pp to come

About the Author

Georgia Leighton is a senior marketing manager in publishing. Before working in publishing, she completed an MA in Creative Writing at Royal Holloway, University of London, receiving a distinction.

Georgia lives in London with her husband and daughter. Her debut adult novel, *Spellbound*, is a reimagining of the classic fairy tale of Sleeping Beauty.